STOP!

YOU MAY BE READING THE WRONG WAY.

In keeping with the original Japanese comic format, this book reads from right to left—so action, sound effects and word balloons are completely reversed to preserve the orientation of the original artwork.

D0917841

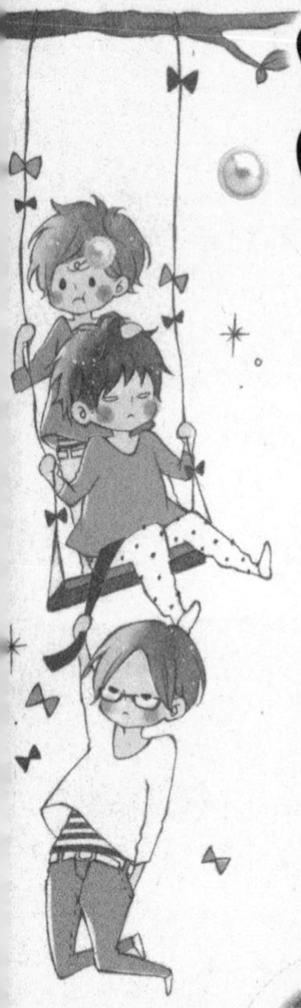

Honey So Sweet

Story and Art by Amu Meguro

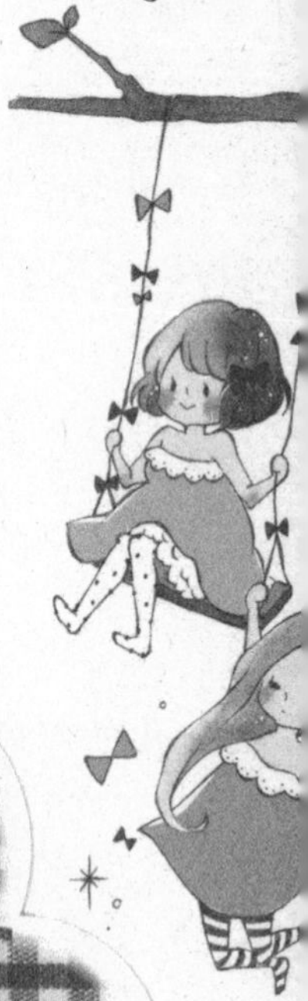

Little did Nao Kogure realize back in middle school that when she left an umbrella and a box of bandages in the rain for injured delinquent Taiga Onise that she would meet him again in high school. Nao wants nothing to do with the gruff and frightening Taiga, but he suddenly presents her with a huge bouquet of flowers and asks her to date him—with marriage in mind! Is Taiga really so scary, or is he a sweetheart in disguise?

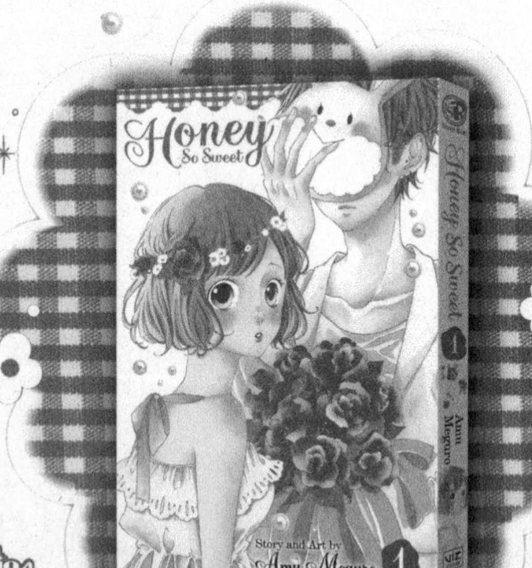
Honey So Sweet
Honey So Sweet 1
Amu Meguro
Story and Art by
Amu Meguro 1

Shojo Beat

RATED T FOR TEEN
ratings.viz.com

VIZ MEDIA
viz.com

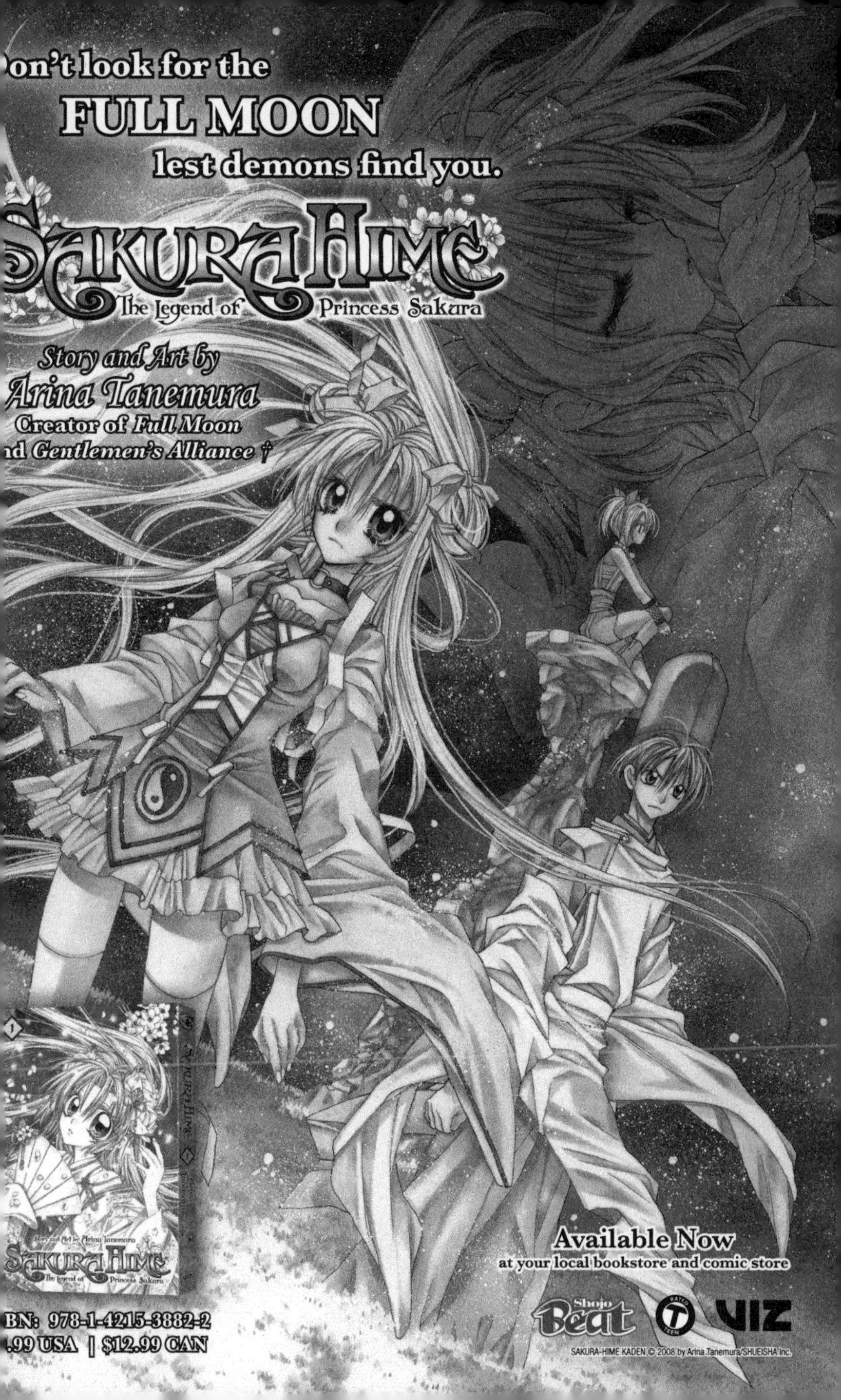
on't look for the
FULL MOON
lest demons find you.
SAKURA HIME
The Legend of Princess Sakura
Story and Art by
Arina Tanemura
Creator of Full Moon
nd Gentlemen's Alliance †
Available Now
at your local bookstore and comic store
BN: 978-1-4215-3882-2
.99 USA | $12.99 CAN
Shojo Beat
RATED T TEEN
VIZ
SAKURA-HIME KADEN © 2008 by Arina Tanemura/SHUEISHA Inc.

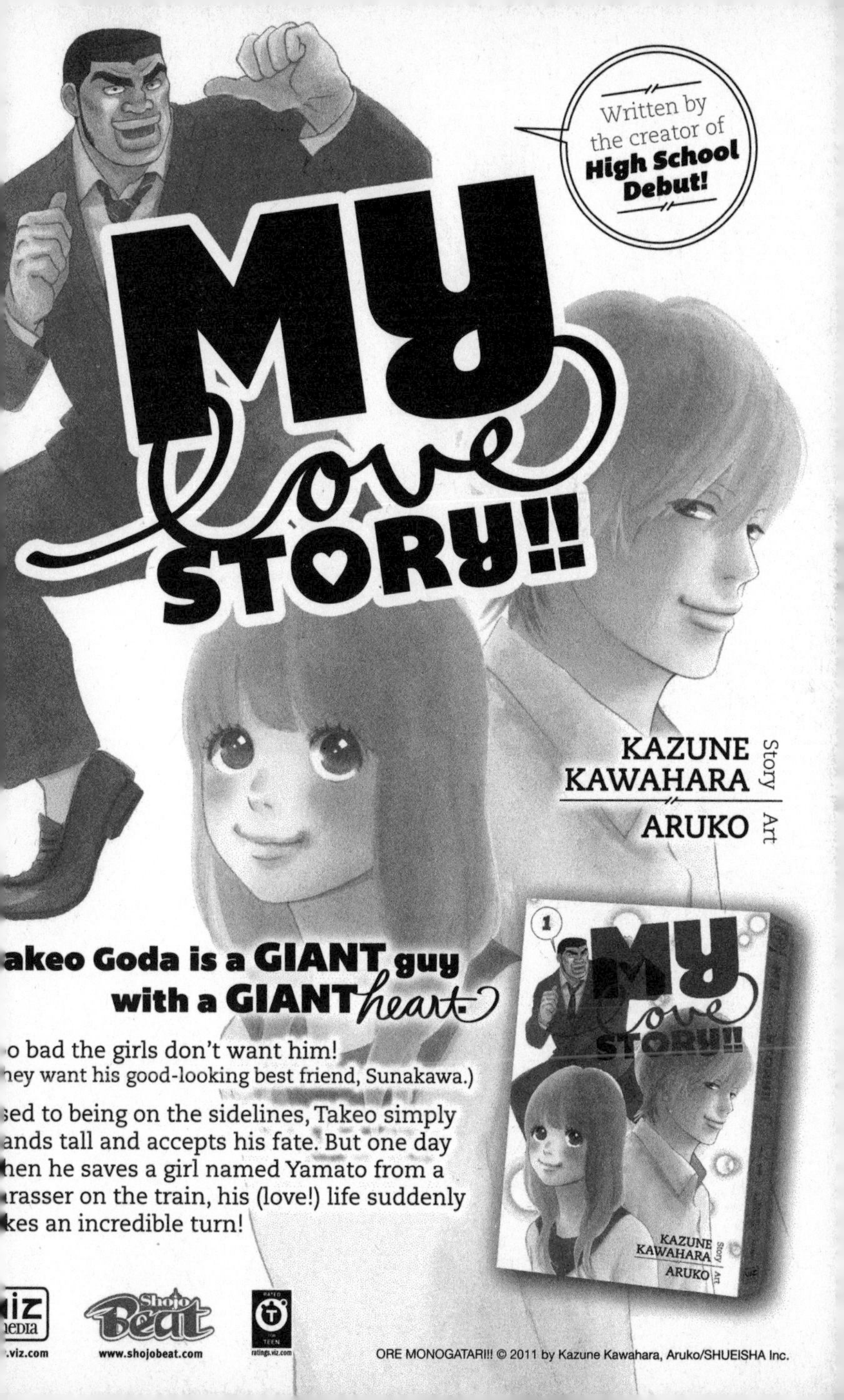
Written by the creator of High School Debut!
MY love STORY!!
KAZUNE KAWAHARA Story
ARUKO Art
akeo Goda is a GIANT guy with a GIANT heart
o bad the girls don't want him!
hey want his good-looking best friend, Sunakawa.)
sed to being on the sidelines, Takeo simply
ands tall and accepts his fate. But one day
hen he saves a girl named Yamato from a
rasser on the train, his (love!) life suddenly
kes an incredible turn!
1
MY love STORY!!
KAZUNE KAWAHARA Story
ARUKO Art
iz
edia
.viz.com
Shojo Beat
www.shojobeat.com
RATED T FOR TEEN
ratings.viz.com
ORE MONOGATARI!! © 2011 by Kazune Kawahara, Aruko/SHUEISHA Inc.

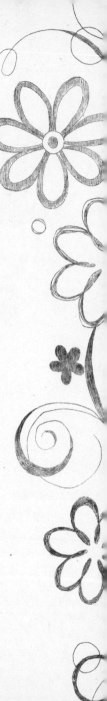

Ao Haru Ride

VOLUME 6
SHOJO BEAT EDITION

STORY AND ART BY IO SAKISAKA

TRANSLATION Emi Louie-Nishikawa
TOUCH-UP ART + LETTERING Inori Fukuda Trant
DESIGN Natalie Chen
EDITOR Nancy Thistlethwaite

First published in Japan in 2011 by SHUEISHA Inc., Tokyo.
English translation rights arranged by SHUEISHA Inc.

Printed in the U.S.A.

Published by VIZ Media, LLC
P.O. Box 77010
San Francisco, CA 94107

10 9 8 7 6 5 4 3 2 1
First printing, August 2019

ratings.viz.com RATED T TEEN

PARENTAL ADVISORY
AO HARU RIDE is rated T for Teen and
is recommended for ages 13 and up.
This volume contains the jealousy of youth.

VIZ MEDIA
viz.com

Shojo Beat
shojobeat.com

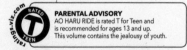

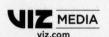

Ao Haru Ride

The scent of air after rain...
In the light around us, I felt your heartbeat.

6

IO SAKISAKA

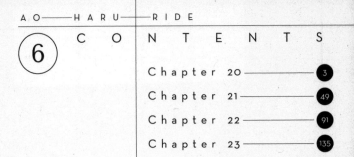

6 C O N T E N T S

S T O R Y   T H U S   F A R

In junior high, Futaba Yoshioka was quiet and disliked all boys—except for Tanaka, her first love. Their romance was cut short when he suddenly transferred schools, leaving behind an unresolved misunderstanding. As a tomboy in high school, Futaba is reunited with a completely changed Tanaka, who goes by the name of Kou Mabuchi.

Futaba is looking forward to going to a festival with Kou, but something comes up that makes him cancel. She barely hears from him for the rest of the summer and waits impatiently for school to resume, but when she sees Kou, she senses there's something different about him.

Kou has been preoccupied with an old classmate from Nagasaki who keeps calling him. Now back at school, the class reps are getting ready for the upcoming school festival. Futaba and Kou are close again after a long afternoon spent prepping until he stops to answer his phone. What Futaba overhears makes her uneasy. On the day of the school festival, Kou's old classmate appears!

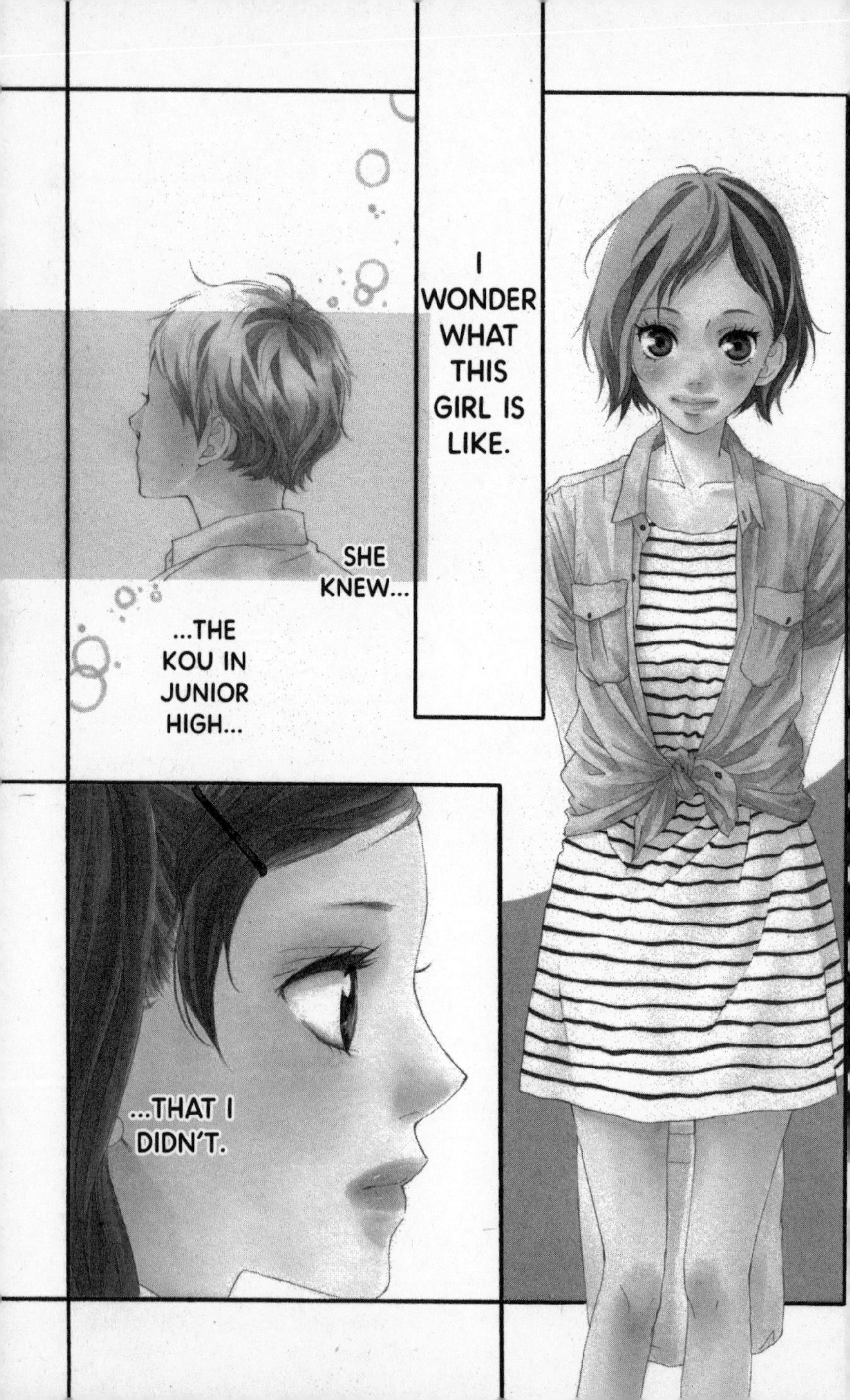
I WONDER WHAT THIS GIRL IS LIKE.
SHE KNEW...
...THE KOU IN JUNIOR HIGH...
...THAT I DIDN'T.

Ao Haru Ride

The scent of air after rain...
In the light around us, I felt your heartbeat.

CHAPTER 20

IO SAKISAKA

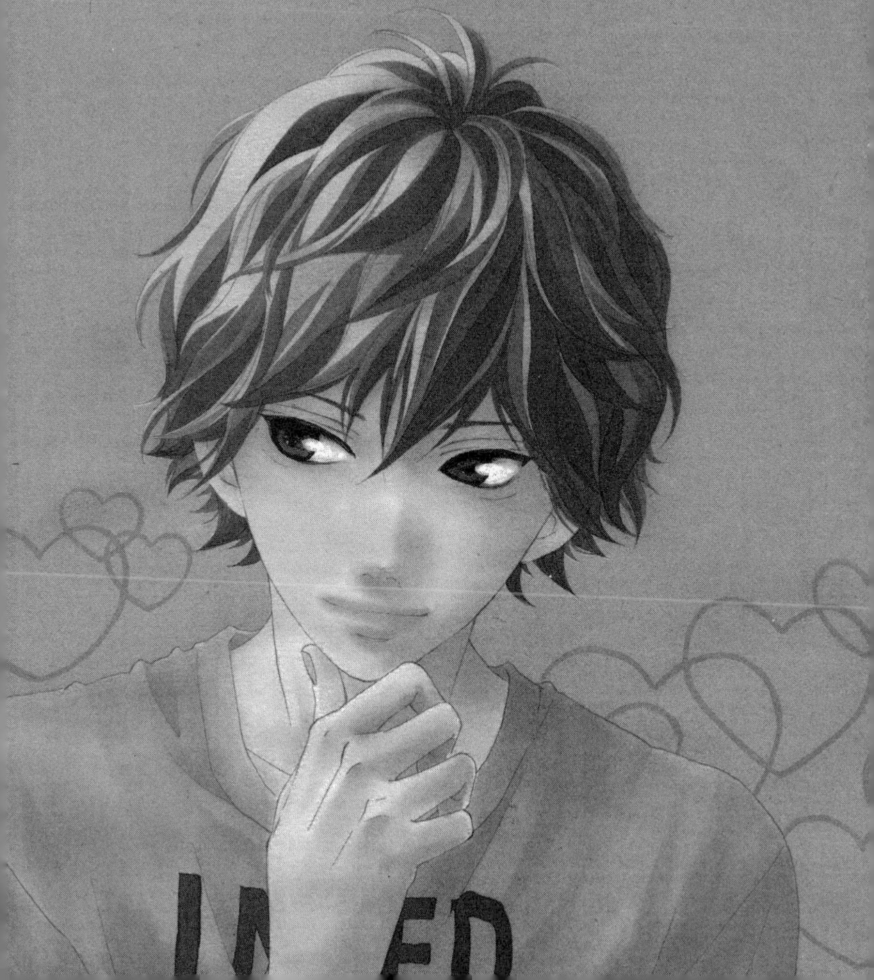

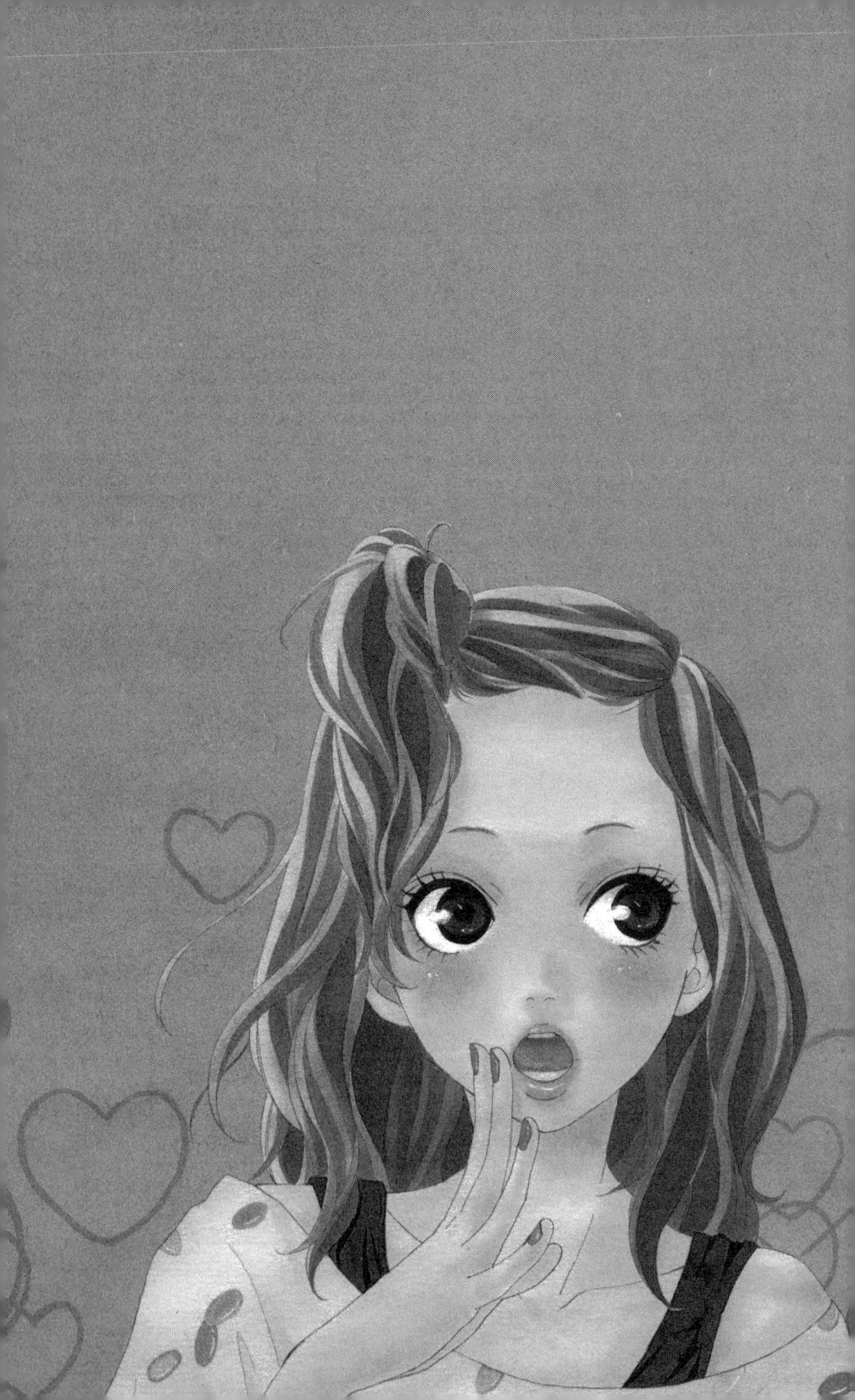

GREETINGS

Hi! I'm Io Sakisaka. Thank you for picking up a copy of *Ao Haru Ride* volume 6!

There are times when I need to look at my old drawings while working, and when I see how awful I drew back then I want to faint. Of course I thought I was doing a good job at the time, and I put everything that I had into drawing them, but man, they are really painful to look at. This happens with older series, more recent work, and even with *Ao Haru Ride* volume 1. While I find it depressing, it's also reassuring because it means I have the ability to improve. You can always get better, you know! Sometimes I don't feel motivated to put in my best effort, so it's a good reminder that it's important.
When I draw, I'm excited and hopeful that my current work will give me reassurance a year from now.

With that, here's *Ao Haru Ride* volume 6. I poured everything I had into it. I hope you'll read through to the end!

    Io Sakisaka

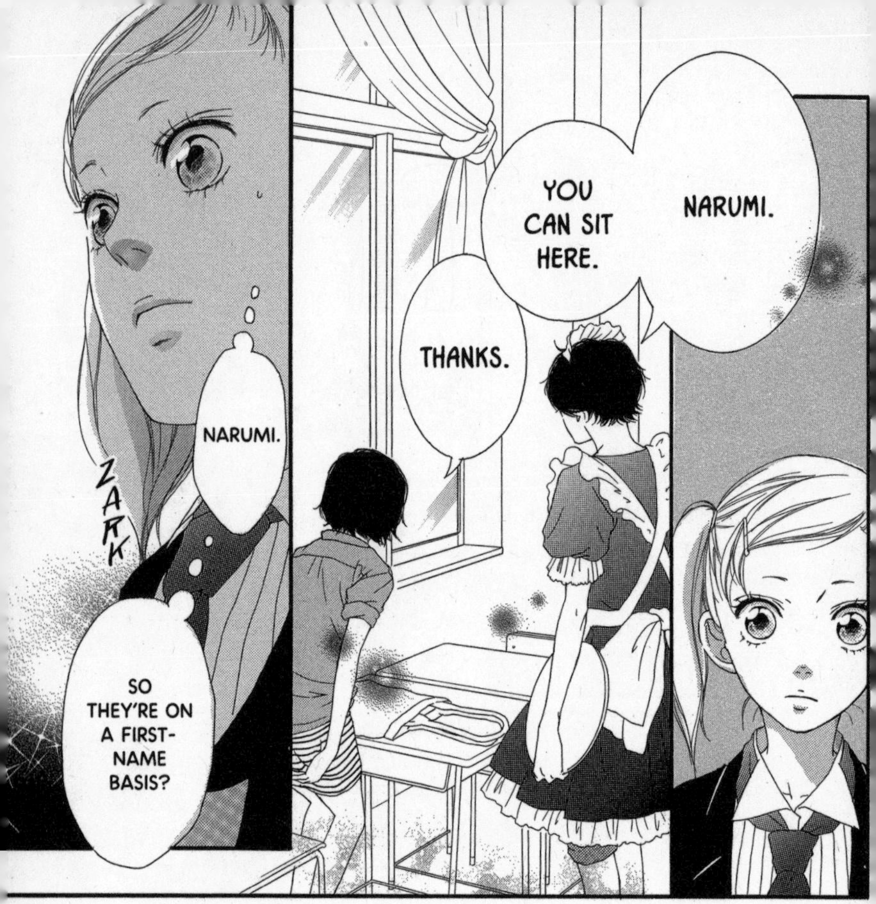
NARUMI.
YOU CAN SIT HERE.
THANKS.
NARUMI.
ZARK
SO THEY'RE ON A FIRST-NAME BASIS?

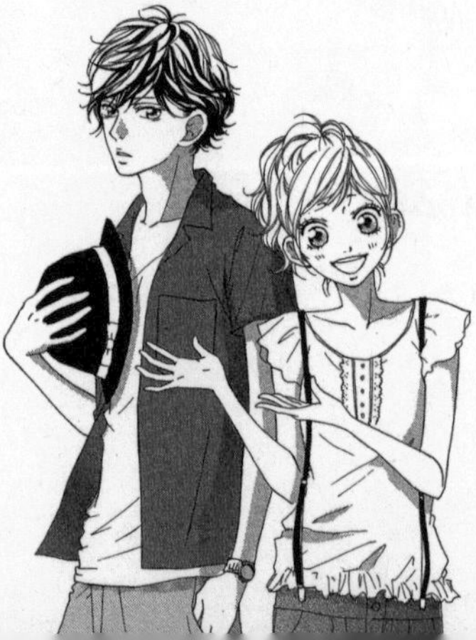

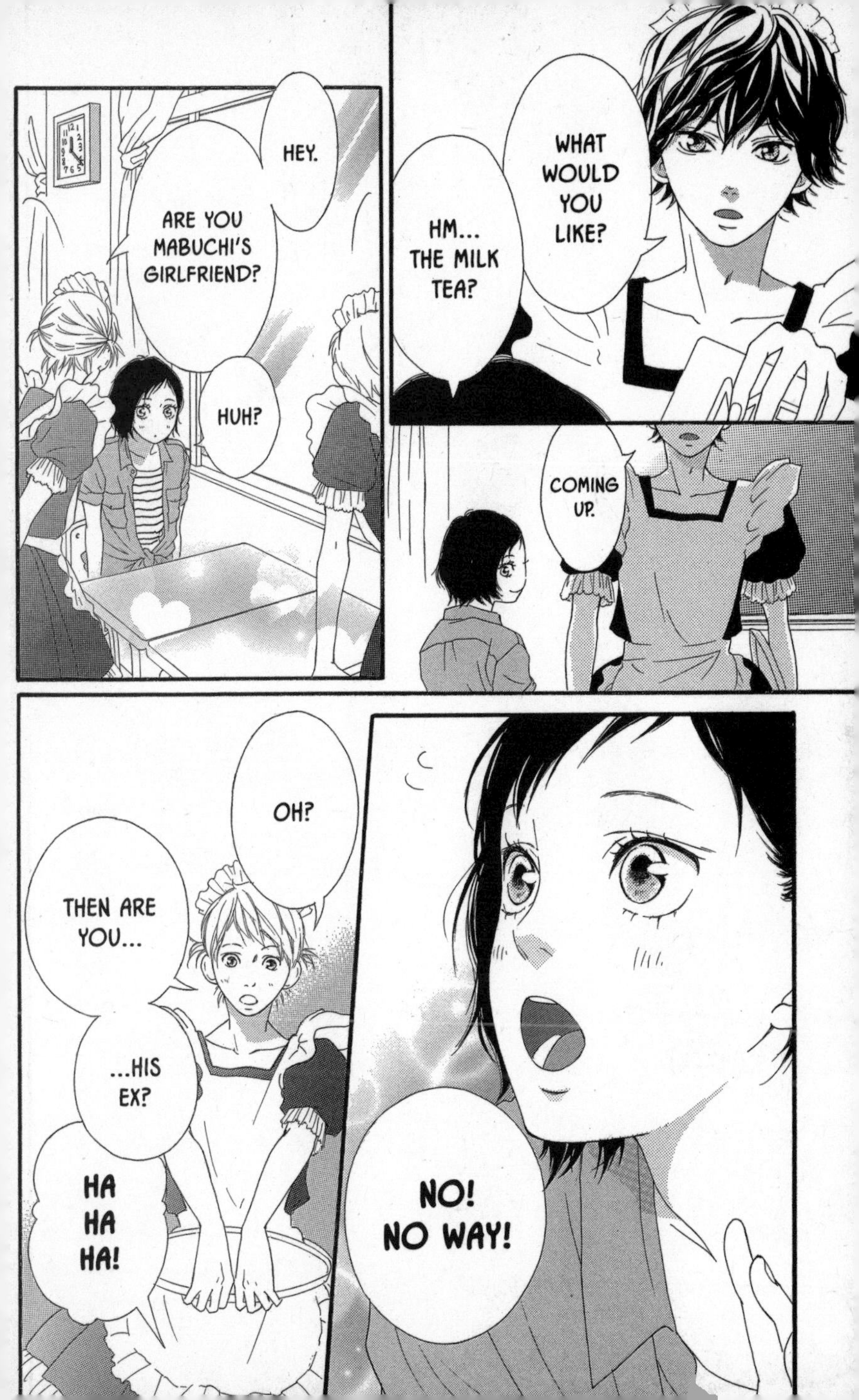
WHAT WOULD YOU LIKE?
HM... THE MILK TEA?
COMING UP.
HEY.
ARE YOU MABUCHI'S GIRLFRIEND?
HUH?
NO! NO WAY!
OH?
THEN ARE YOU...
...HIS EX?
HA HA HA!

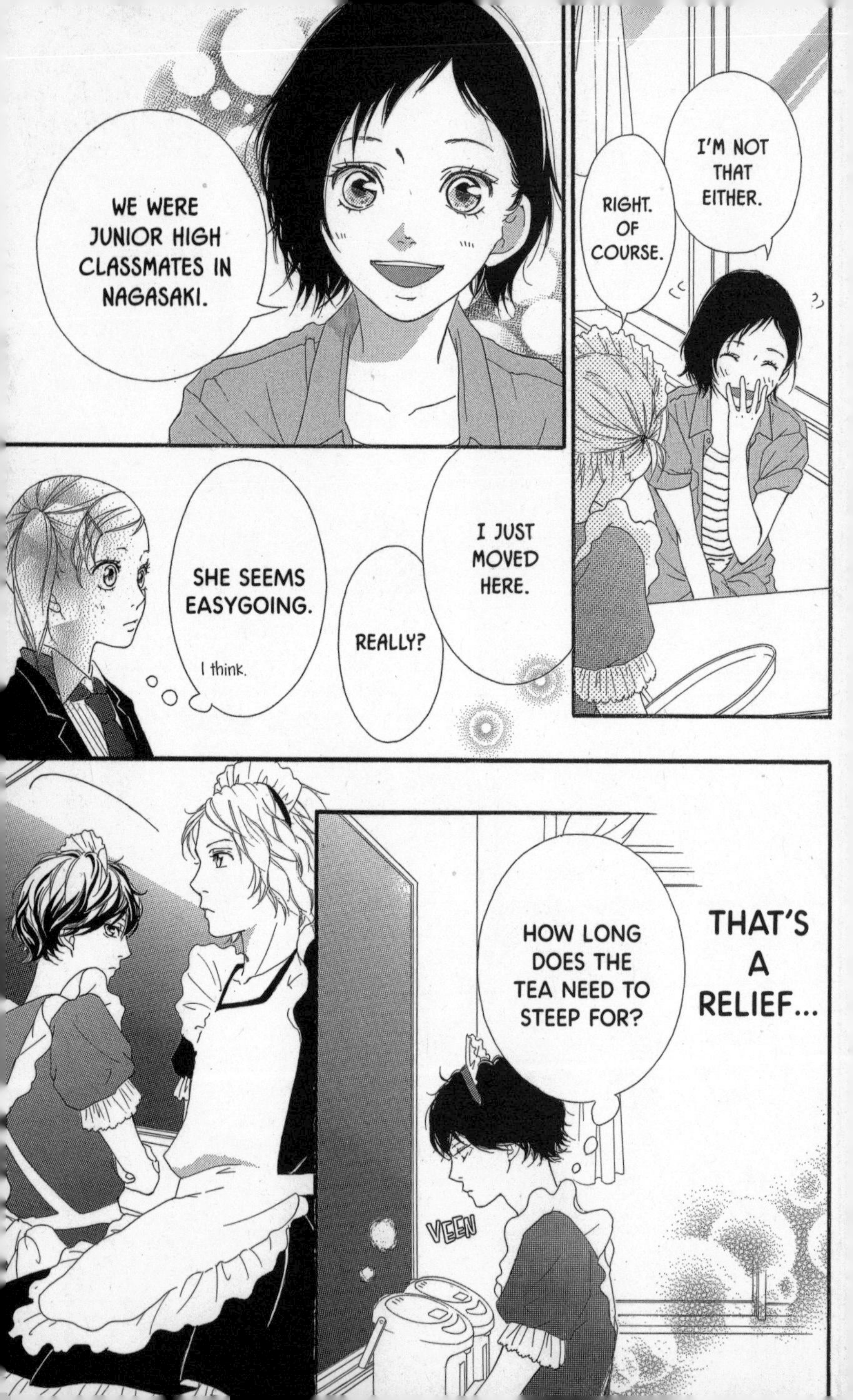
I'M NOT THAT EITHER.
RIGHT. OF COURSE.
WE WERE JUNIOR HIGH CLASSMATES IN NAGASAKI.
I JUST MOVED HERE.
REALLY?
SHE SEEMS EASYGOING.
I think.
THAT'S A RELIEF...
HOW LONG DOES THE TEA NEED TO STEEP FOR?
VEEN

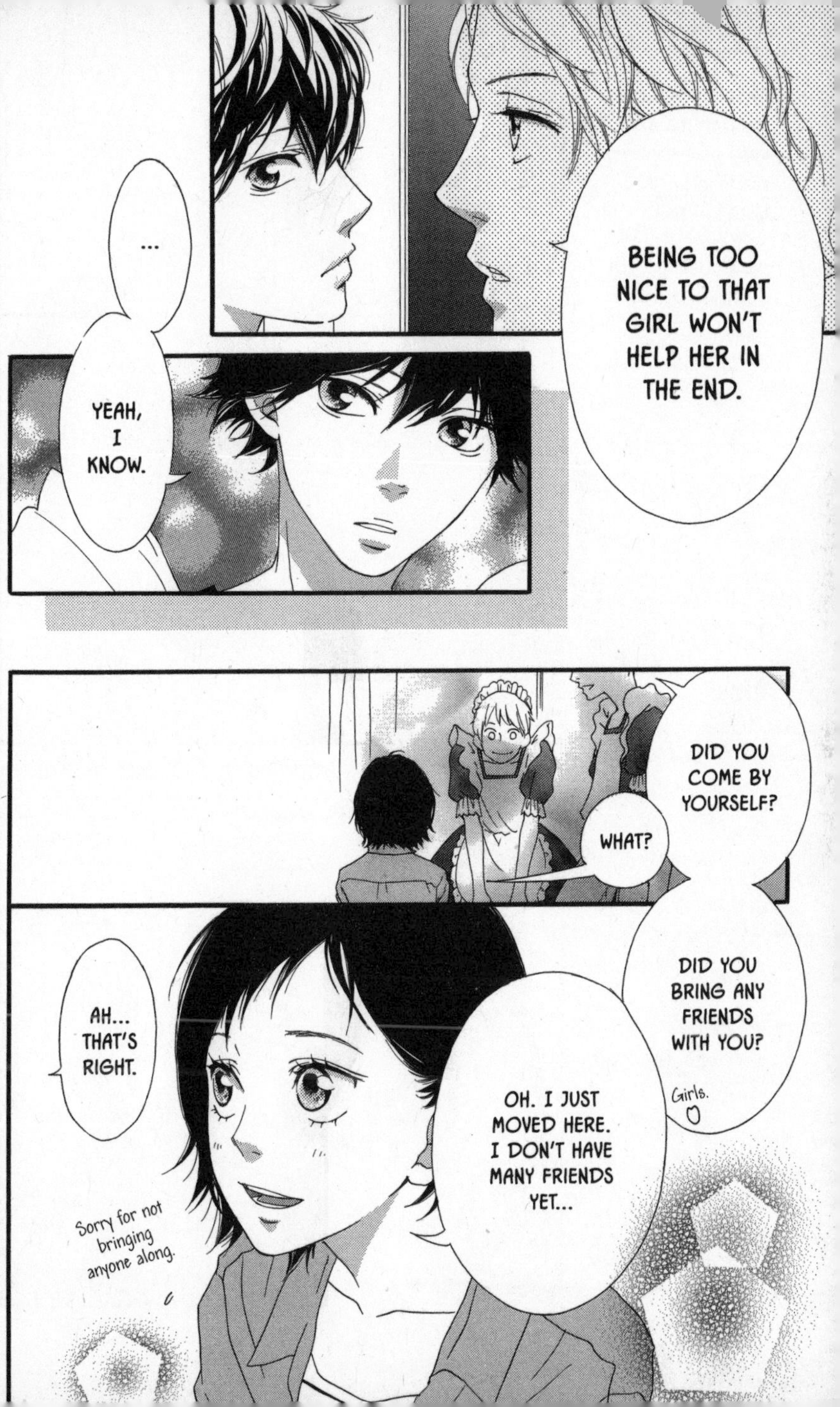
BEING TOO NICE TO THAT GIRL WON'T HELP HER IN THE END.
...
YEAH, I KNOW.
DID YOU COME BY YOURSELF?
WHAT?
DID YOU BRING ANY FRIENDS WITH YOU?
Girls.
OH. I JUST MOVED HERE. I DON'T HAVE MANY FRIENDS YET...
AH... THAT'S RIGHT.
Sorry for not bringing anyone along.

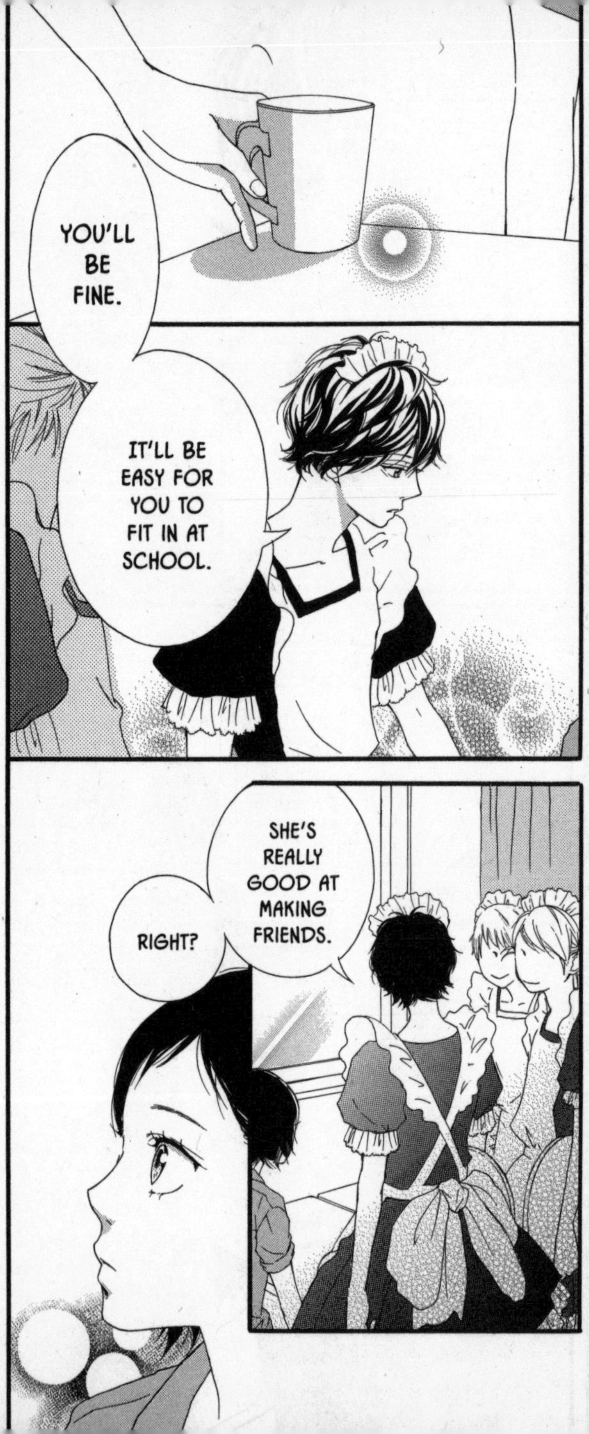
YOU'LL BE FINE.
IT'LL BE EASY FOR YOU TO FIT IN AT SCHOOL.
SHE'S REALLY GOOD AT MAKING FRIENDS.
RIGHT?

When I'm out and see teens having a good time, my body reacts instinctively. I can't help but smile and watch them enjoying their youth. I sense a special something about them. I think I must envy them. But you know what? I say you don't have to be a teen to enjoy youth! I don't care how old I am! I mean, I can't write a story about youth if I'm not living it myself! Anyone got a problem with that?! And what's the definition of "youth" anyway? Well, I looked it up in the dictionary, and—Hey!

Youth [noun]
1. The period between childhood and adult age.

I'm speechless. I'm so speechless that I have to leave the rest of this sidebar blank.

...WEEP WEEP WEEP

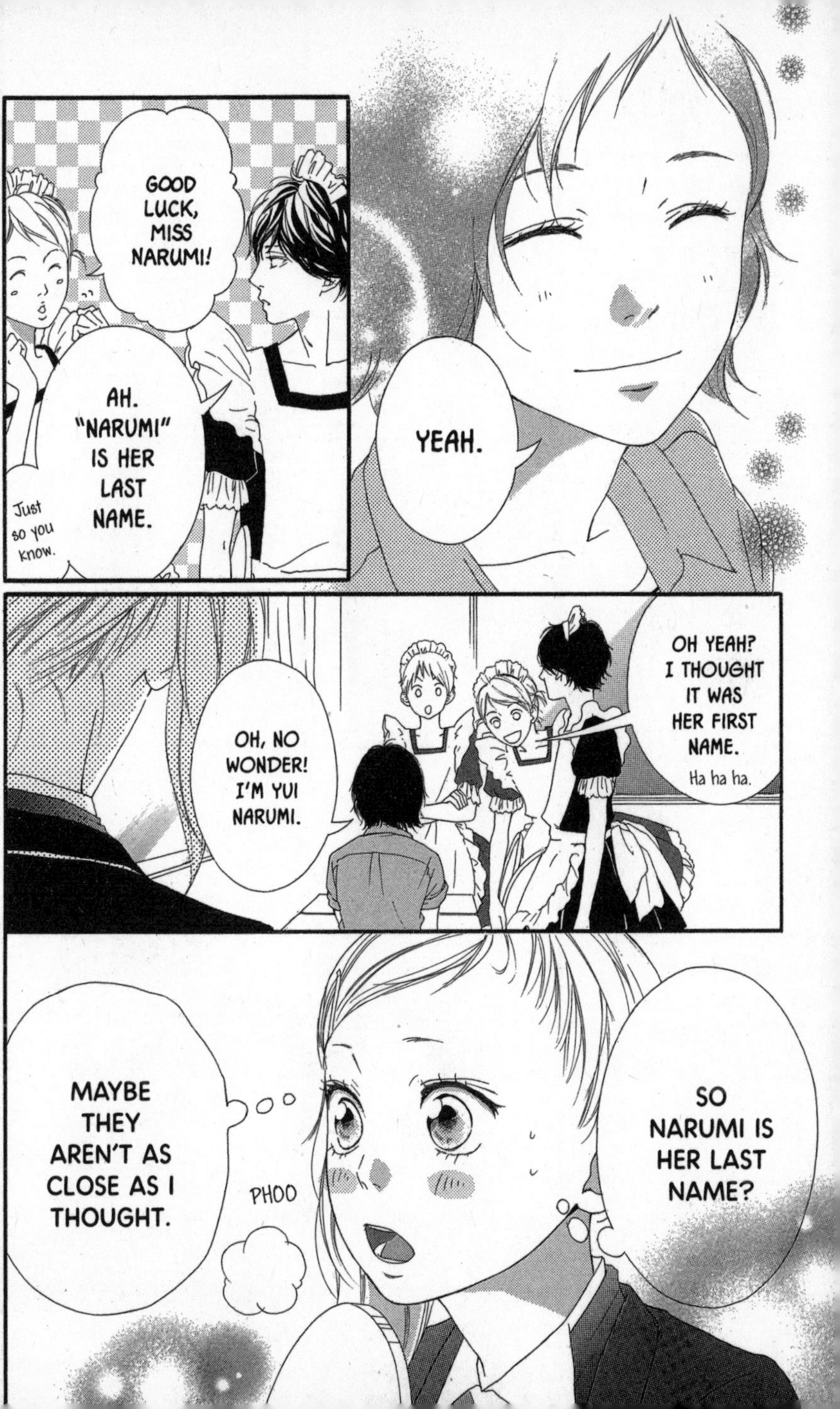
YEAH.
GOOD LUCK, MISS NARUMI!
AH. "NARUMI" IS HER LAST NAME.
Just so you know.
OH YEAH? I THOUGHT IT WAS HER FIRST NAME.
Ha ha ha.
OH, NO WONDER! I'M YUI NARUMI.
SO NARUMI IS HER LAST NAME?
PHOO
MAYBE THEY AREN'T AS CLOSE AS I THOUGHT.

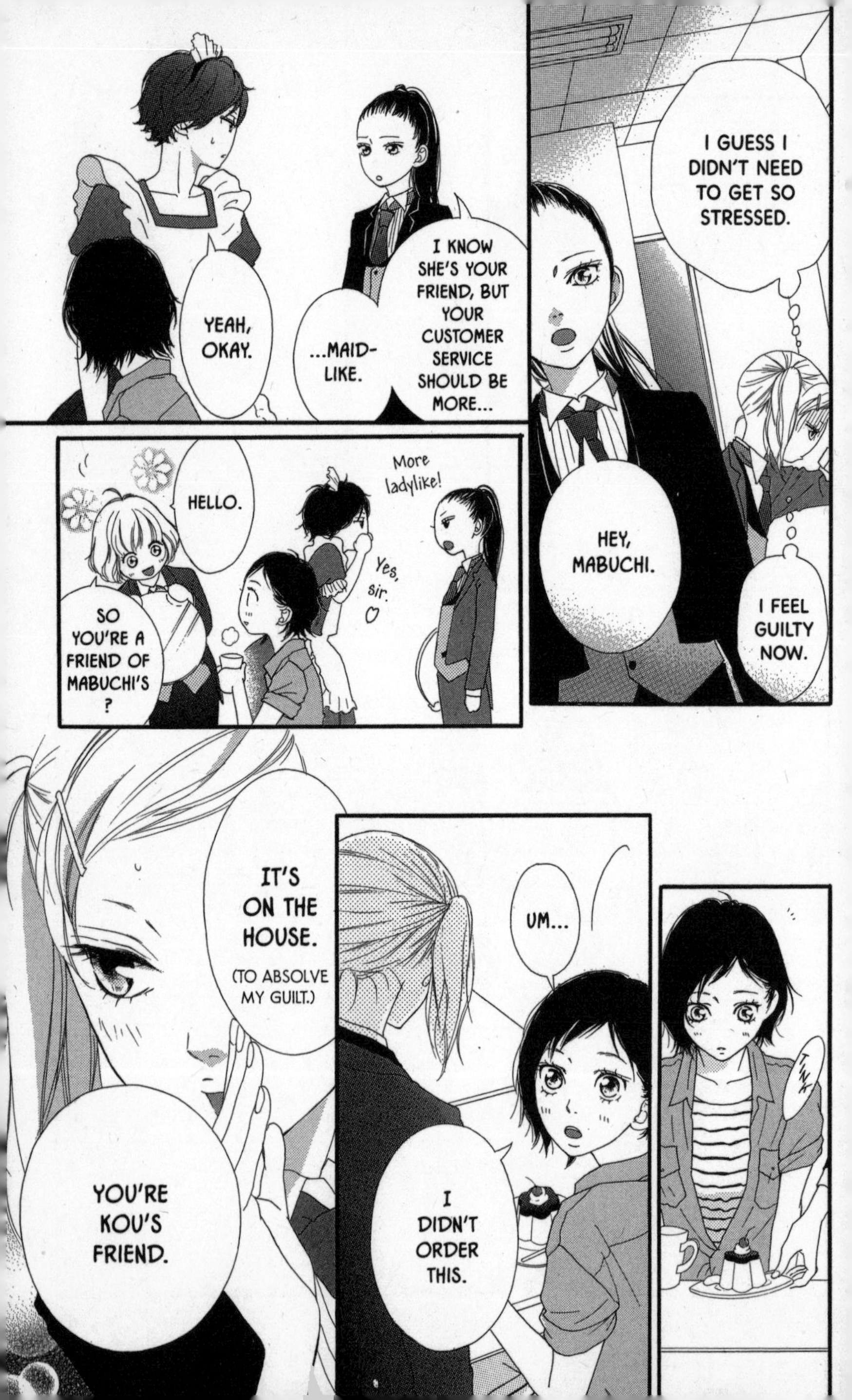
I GUESS I DIDN'T NEED TO GET SO STRESSED.
I FEEL GUILTY NOW.
HEY, MABUCHI.
I KNOW SHE'S YOUR FRIEND, BUT YOUR CUSTOMER SERVICE SHOULD BE MORE...
...MAID-LIKE.
YEAH, OKAY.
More ladylike!
Yes, sir.
HELLO.
SO YOU'RE A FRIEND OF MABUCHI'S?
TINK
UM...
I DIDN'T ORDER THIS.
IT'S ON THE HOUSE.
(TO ABSOLVE MY GUILT.)
YOU'RE KOU'S FRIEND.

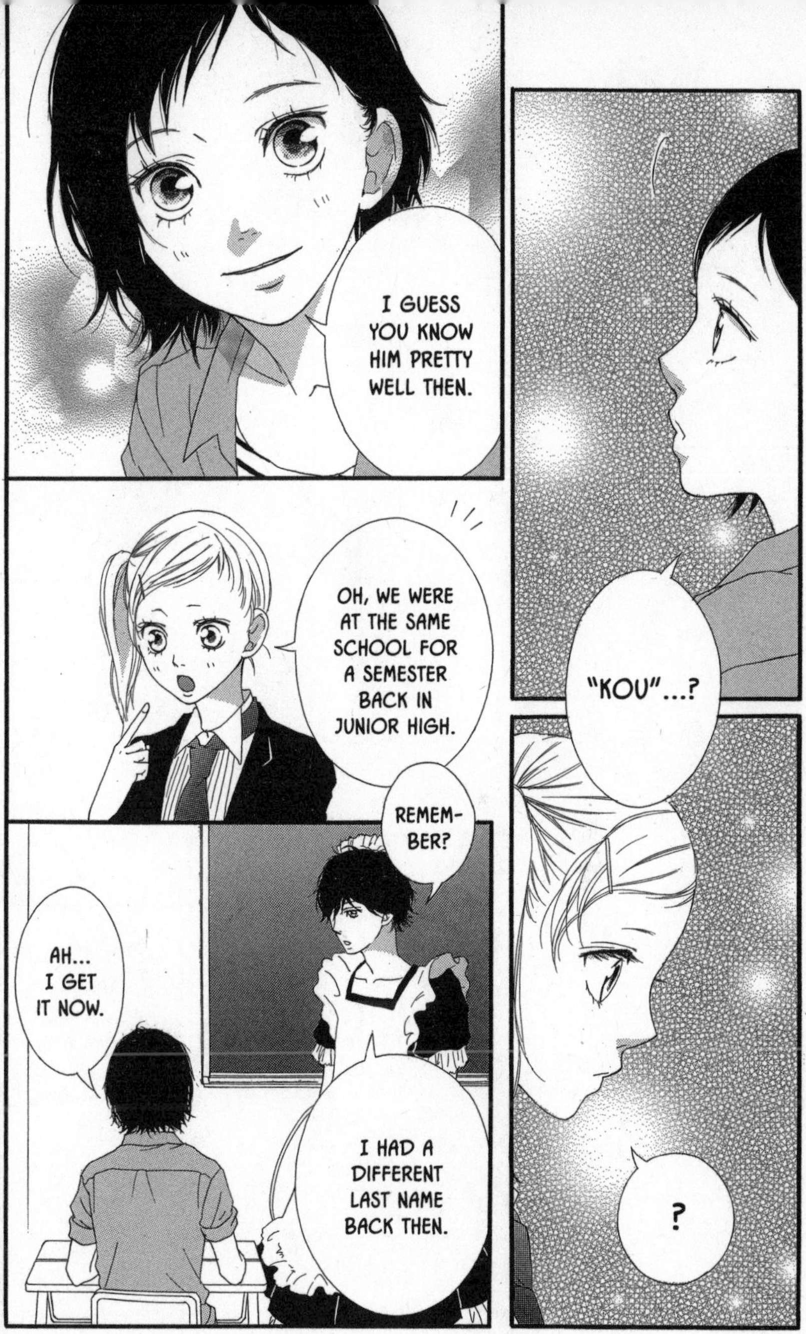
"KOU"...?
?
I GUESS YOU KNOW HIM PRETTY WELL THEN.
OH, WE WERE AT THE SAME SCHOOL FOR A SEMESTER BACK IN JUNIOR HIGH.
REMEMBER?
AH... I GET IT NOW.
I HAD A DIFFERENT LAST NAME BACK THEN.

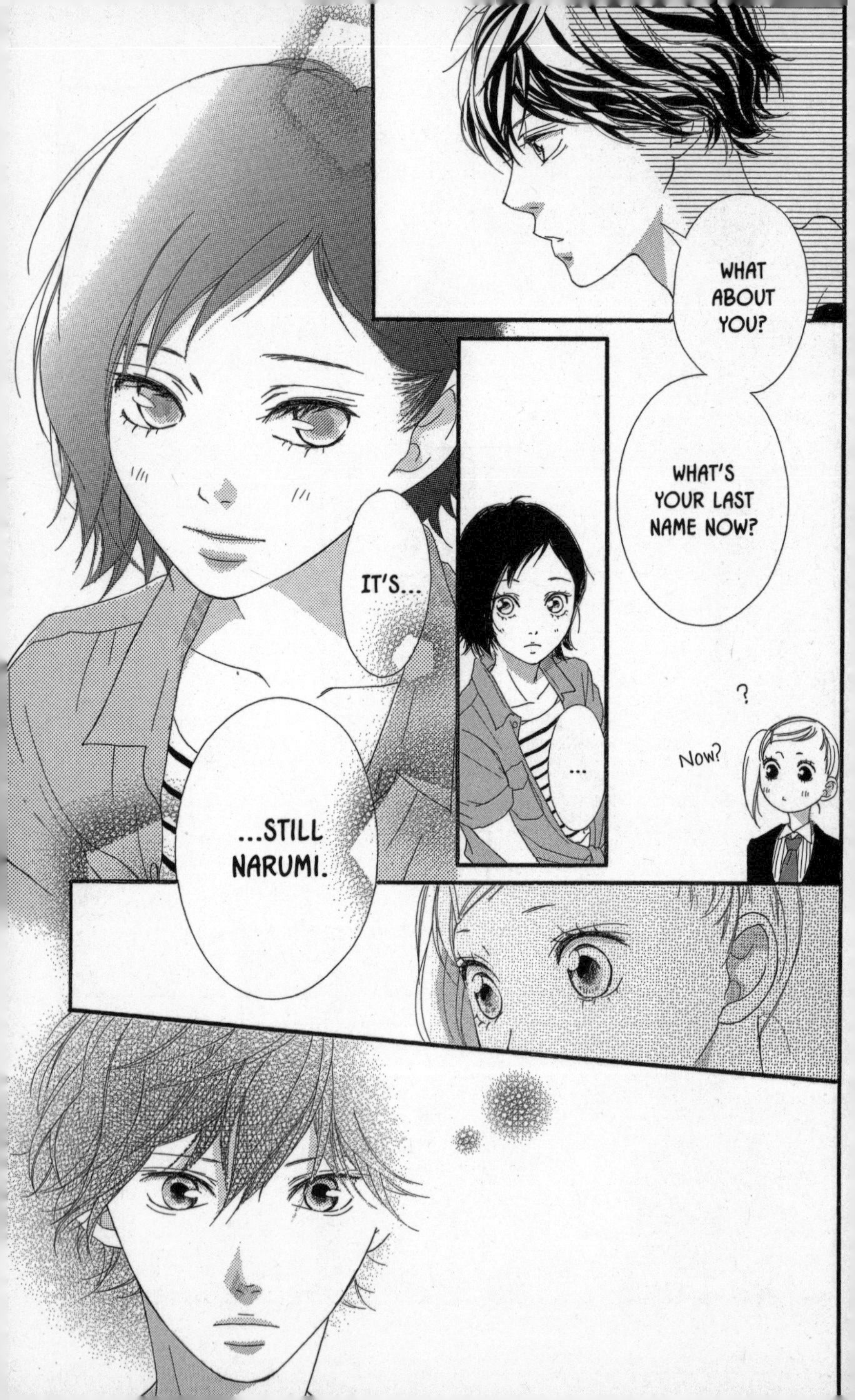
WHAT ABOUT YOU?
WHAT'S YOUR LAST NAME NOW?
?
Now?
...
IT'S...
...STILL NARUMI.

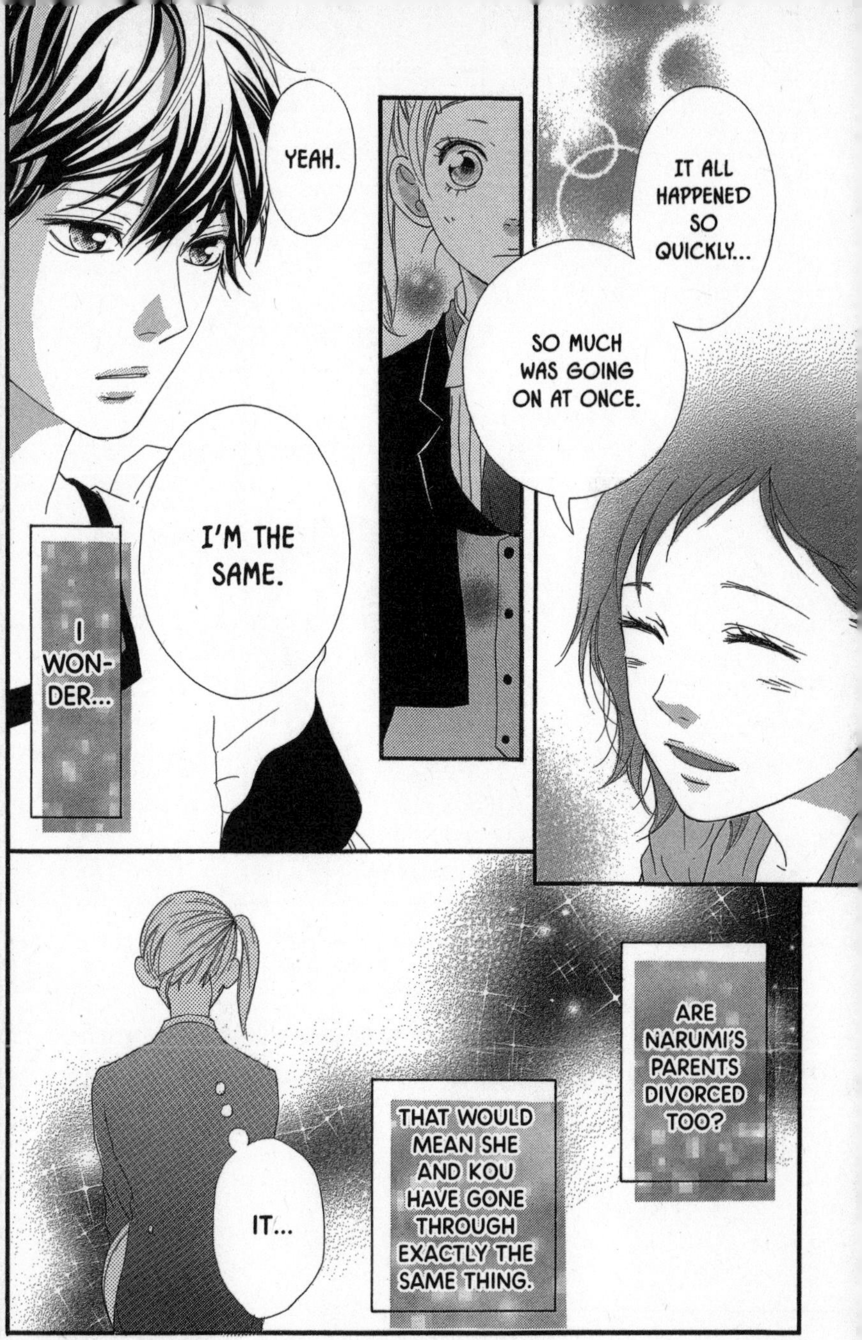
IT ALL HAPPENED SO QUICKLY...
SO MUCH WAS GOING ON AT ONCE.
YEAH.
I'M THE SAME.
I WONDER...
ARE NARUMI'S PARENTS DIVORCED TOO?
THAT WOULD MEAN SHE AND KOU HAVE GONE THROUGH EXACTLY THE SAME THING.
IT...

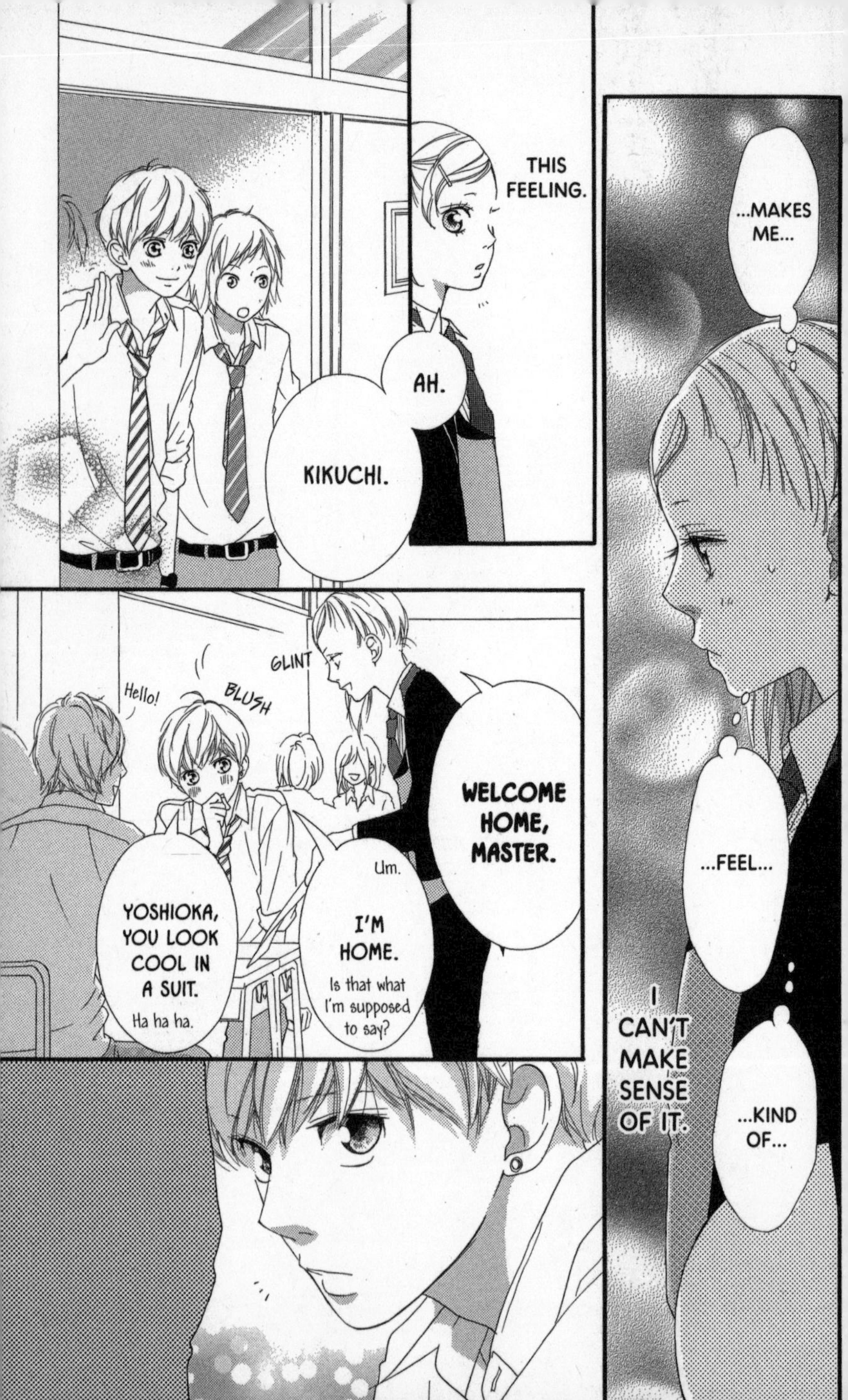
...MAKES ME...
...FEEL...
...KIND OF...
I CAN'T MAKE SENSE OF IT.
THIS FEELING.
AH.
KIKUCHI.
GLINT
WELCOME HOME, MASTER.
BLUSH
Hello!
Um.
I'M HOME.
Is that what I'm supposed to say?
YOSHIOKA, YOU LOOK COOL IN A SUIT.
Ha ha ha.

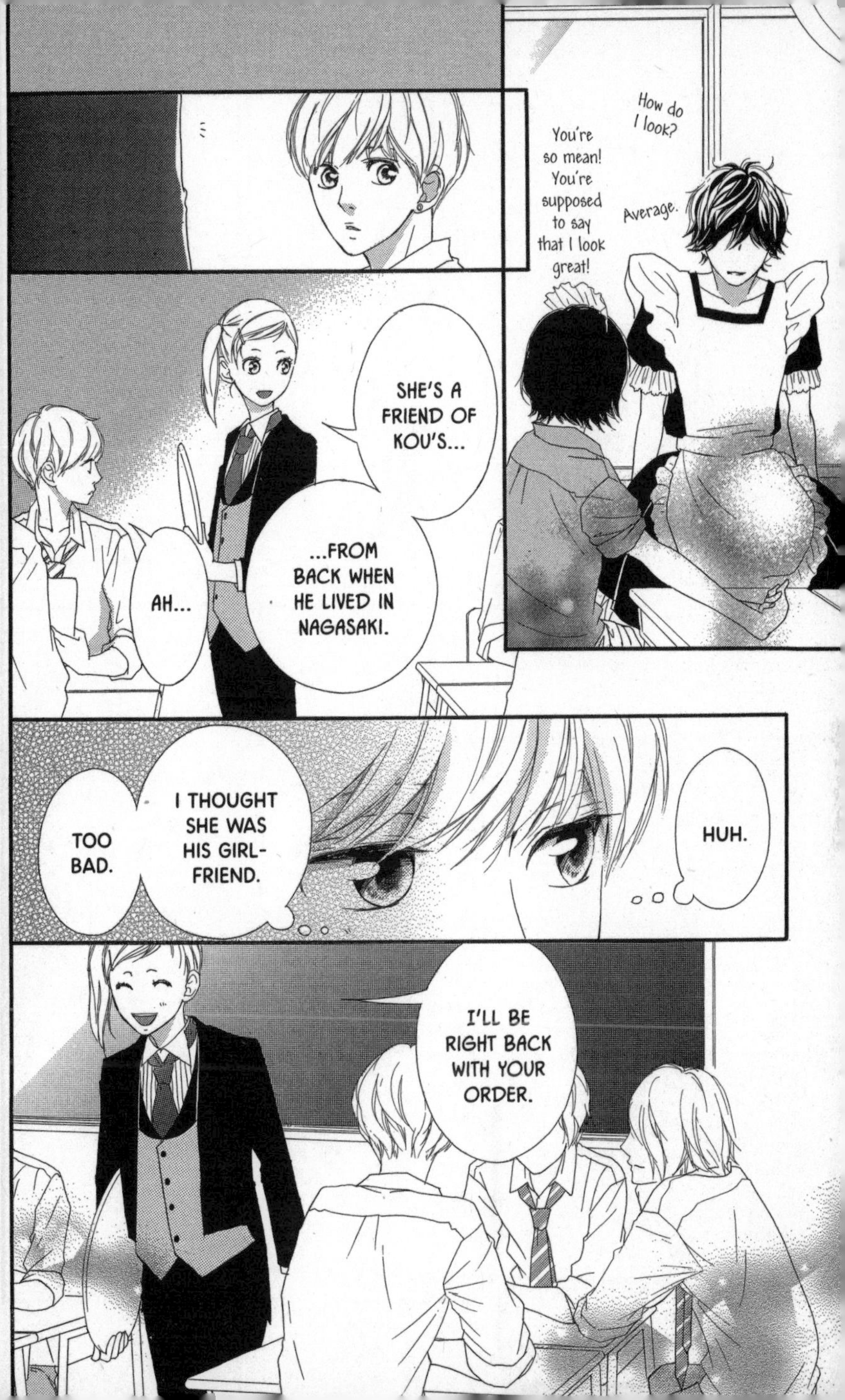
How do I look?
Average.
You're so mean! You're supposed to say that I look great!
SHE'S A FRIEND OF KOU'S...
...FROM BACK WHEN HE LIVED IN NAGASAKI.
AH...
HUH.
I THOUGHT SHE WAS HIS GIRL-FRIEND.
TOO BAD.
I'LL BE RIGHT BACK WITH YOUR ORDER.

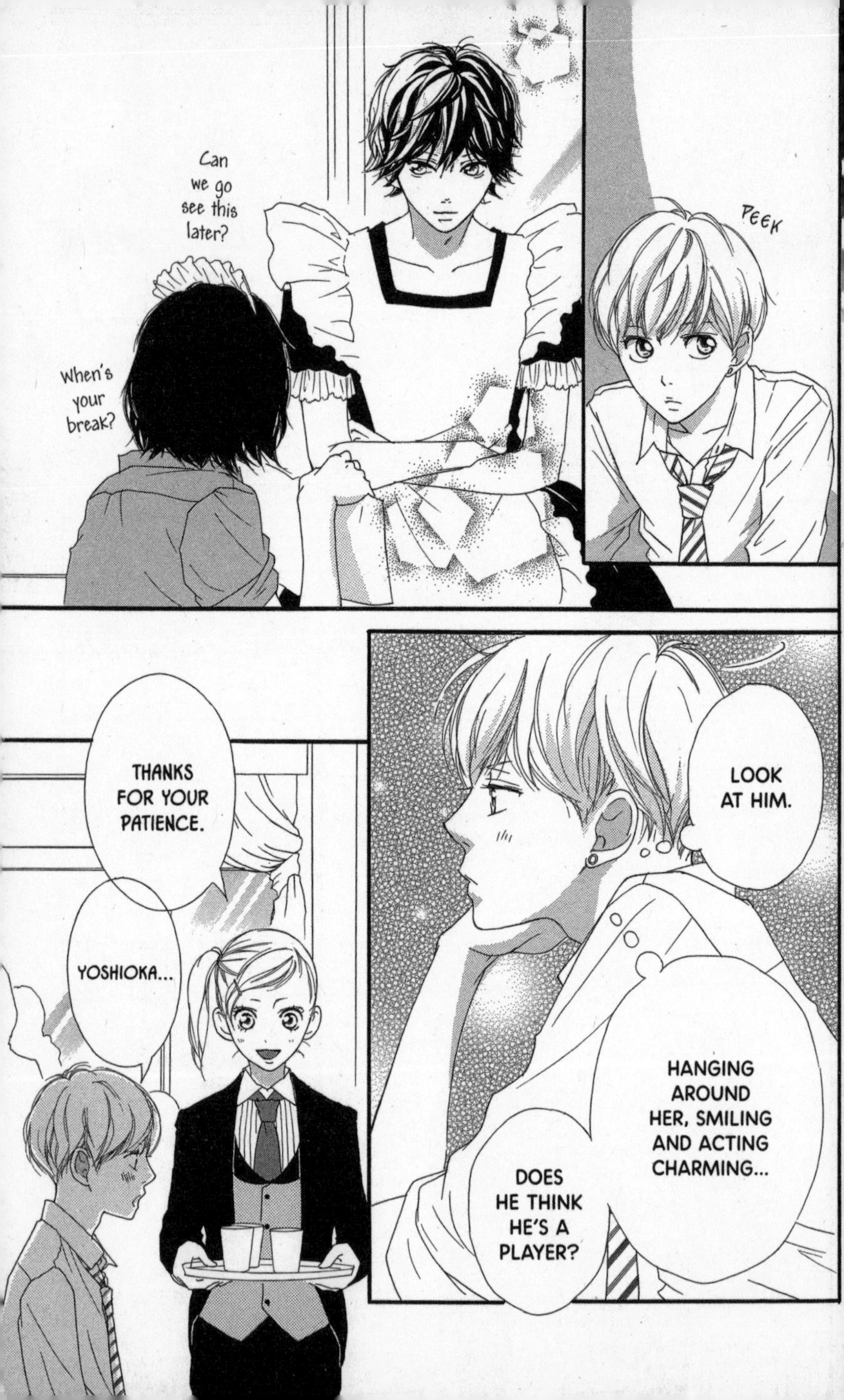
PEEK
Can we go see this later?
When's your break?
LOOK AT HIM.
HANGING AROUND HER, SMILING AND ACTING CHARMING...
DOES HE THINK HE'S A PLAYER?
THANKS FOR YOUR PATIENCE.
YOSHIOKA...

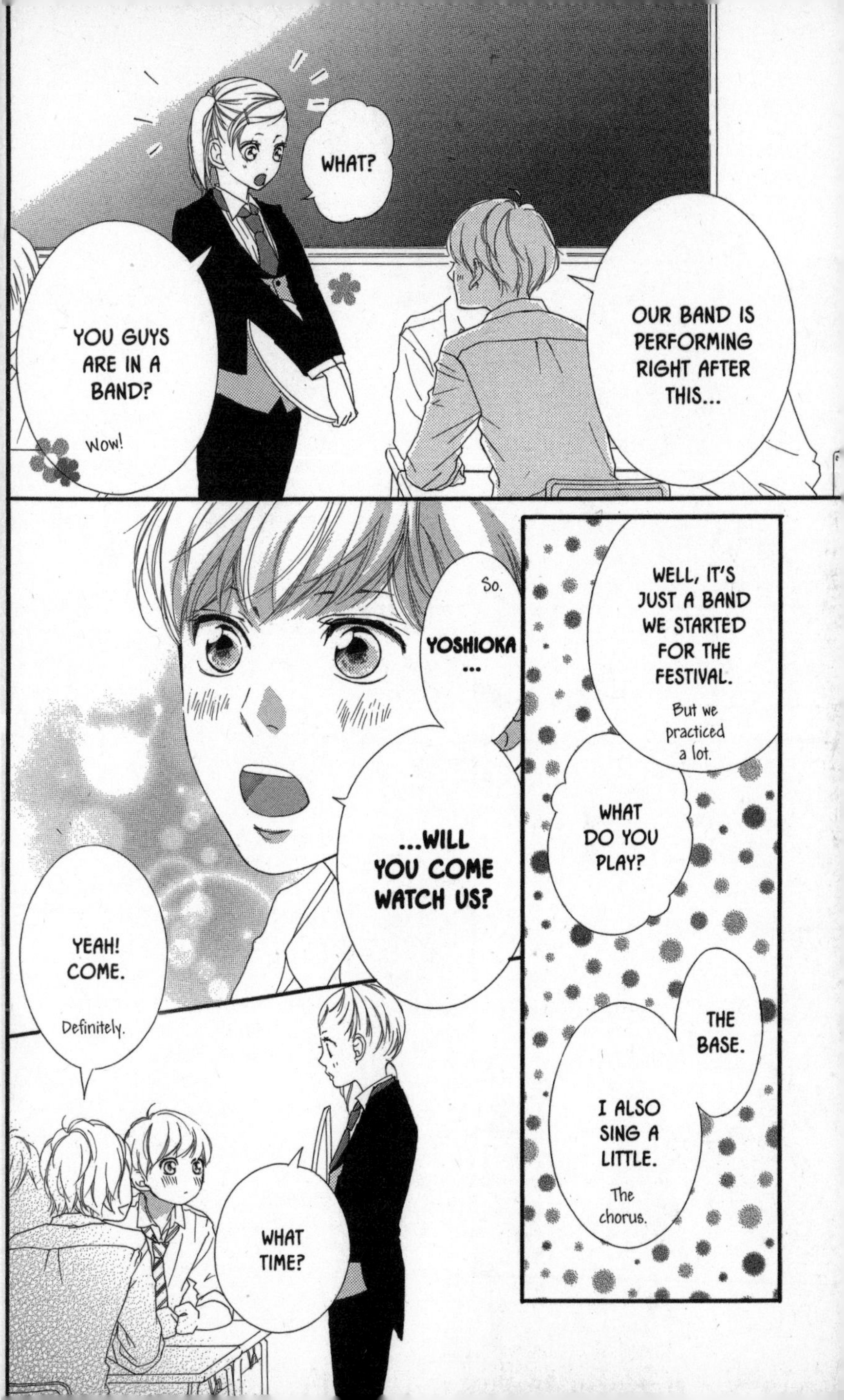

OUR BAND IS PERFORMING RIGHT AFTER THIS...
WHAT?
YOU GUYS ARE IN A BAND?
Wow!
WELL, IT'S JUST A BAND WE STARTED FOR THE FESTIVAL.
But we practiced a lot.
WHAT DO YOU PLAY?
THE BASE.
I ALSO SING A LITTLE.
The chorus.
So.
YOSHIOKA...
...WILL YOU COME WATCH US?
YEAH! COME.
Definitely.
WHAT TIME?

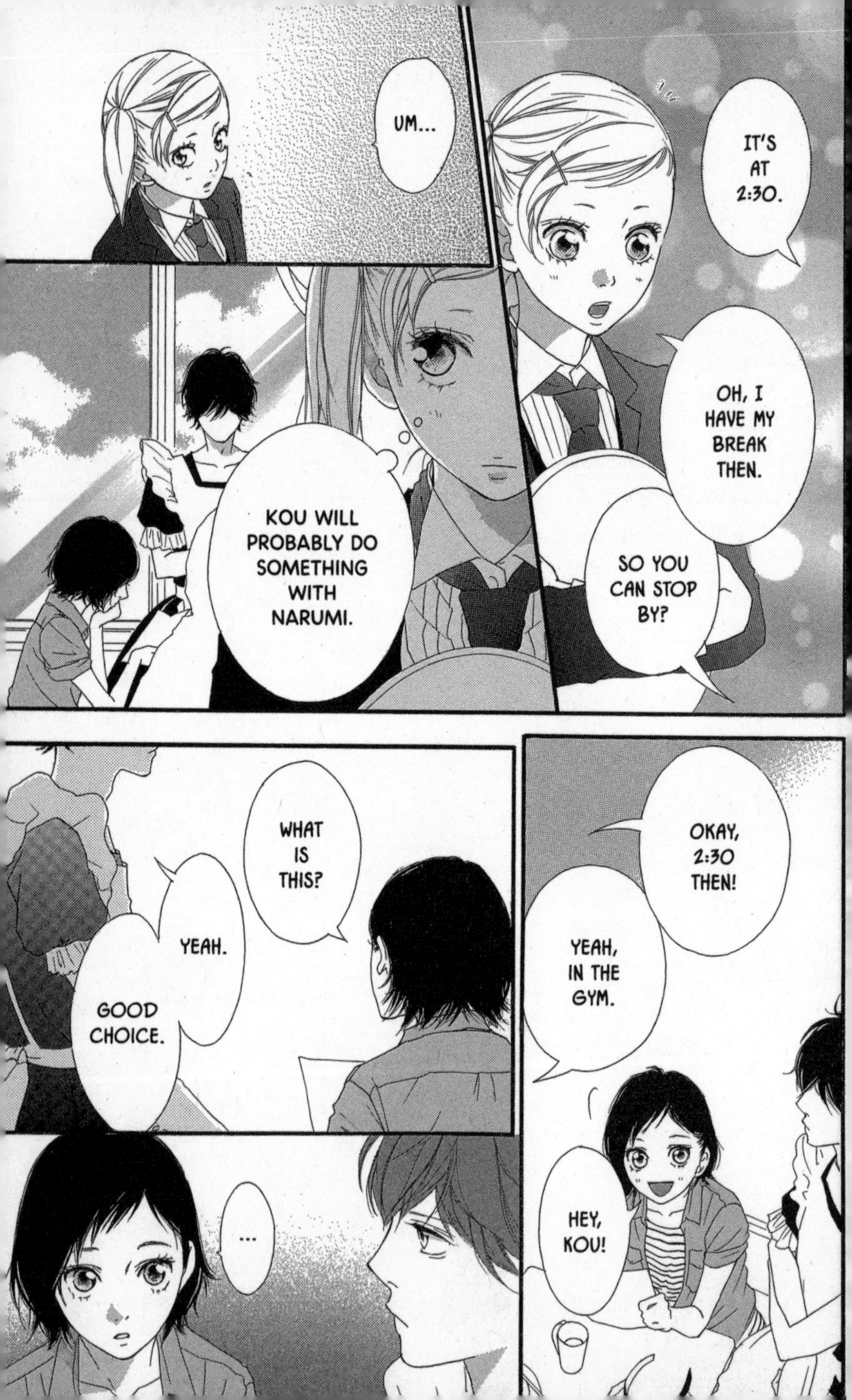
IT'S AT 2:30.
OH, I HAVE MY BREAK THEN.
SO YOU CAN STOP BY?
UM...
KOU WILL PROBABLY DO SOMETHING WITH NARUMI.
OKAY, 2:30 THEN!
YEAH, IN THE GYM.
HEY, KOU!
WHAT IS THIS?
YEAH.
GOOD CHOICE.
...

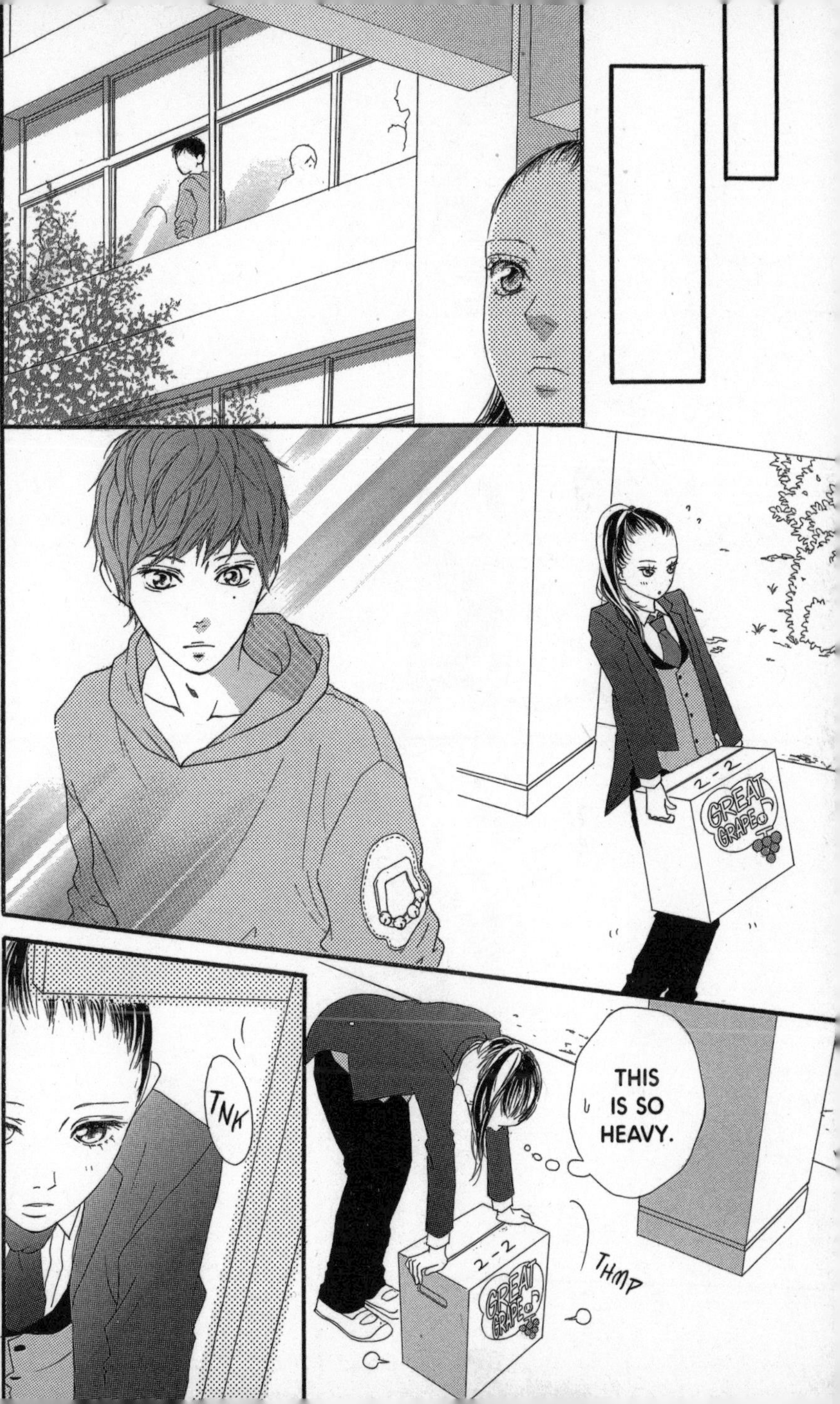
TNK
THIS IS SO HEAVY.
THMP

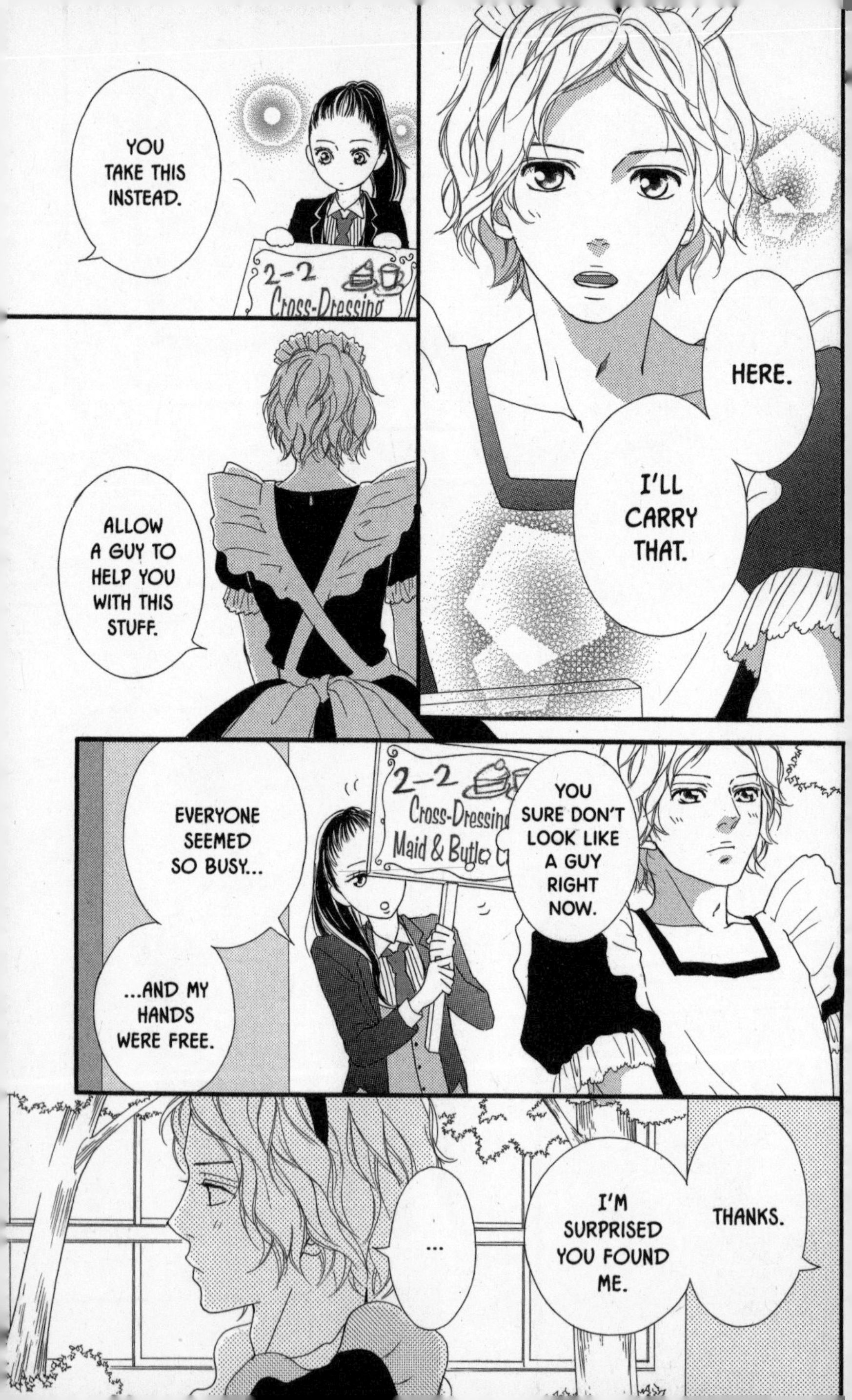
HERE.
I'LL CARRY THAT.
YOU TAKE THIS INSTEAD.
ALLOW A GUY TO HELP YOU WITH THIS STUFF.
YOU SURE DON'T LOOK LIKE A GUY RIGHT NOW.
EVERYONE SEEMED SO BUSY...
...AND MY HANDS WERE FREE.
THANKS.
I'M SURPRISED YOU FOUND ME.
...

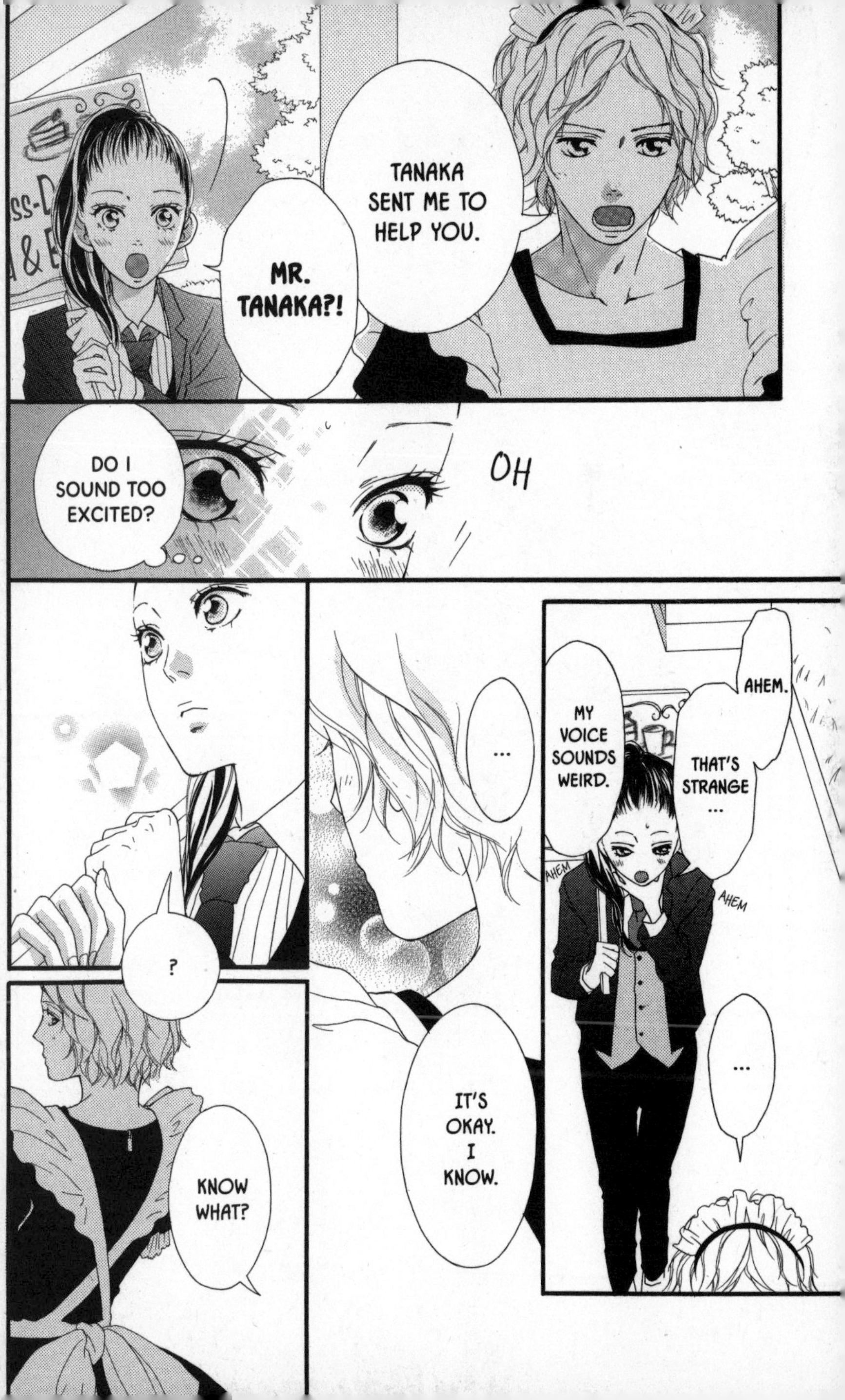
TANAKA SENT ME TO HELP YOU.
MR. TANAKA?!
OH
DO I SOUND TOO EXCITED?
AHEM.
THAT'S STRANGE ...
MY VOICE SOUNDS WEIRD.
AHEM
AHEM
...
...
IT'S OKAY. I KNOW.
?
KNOW WHAT?

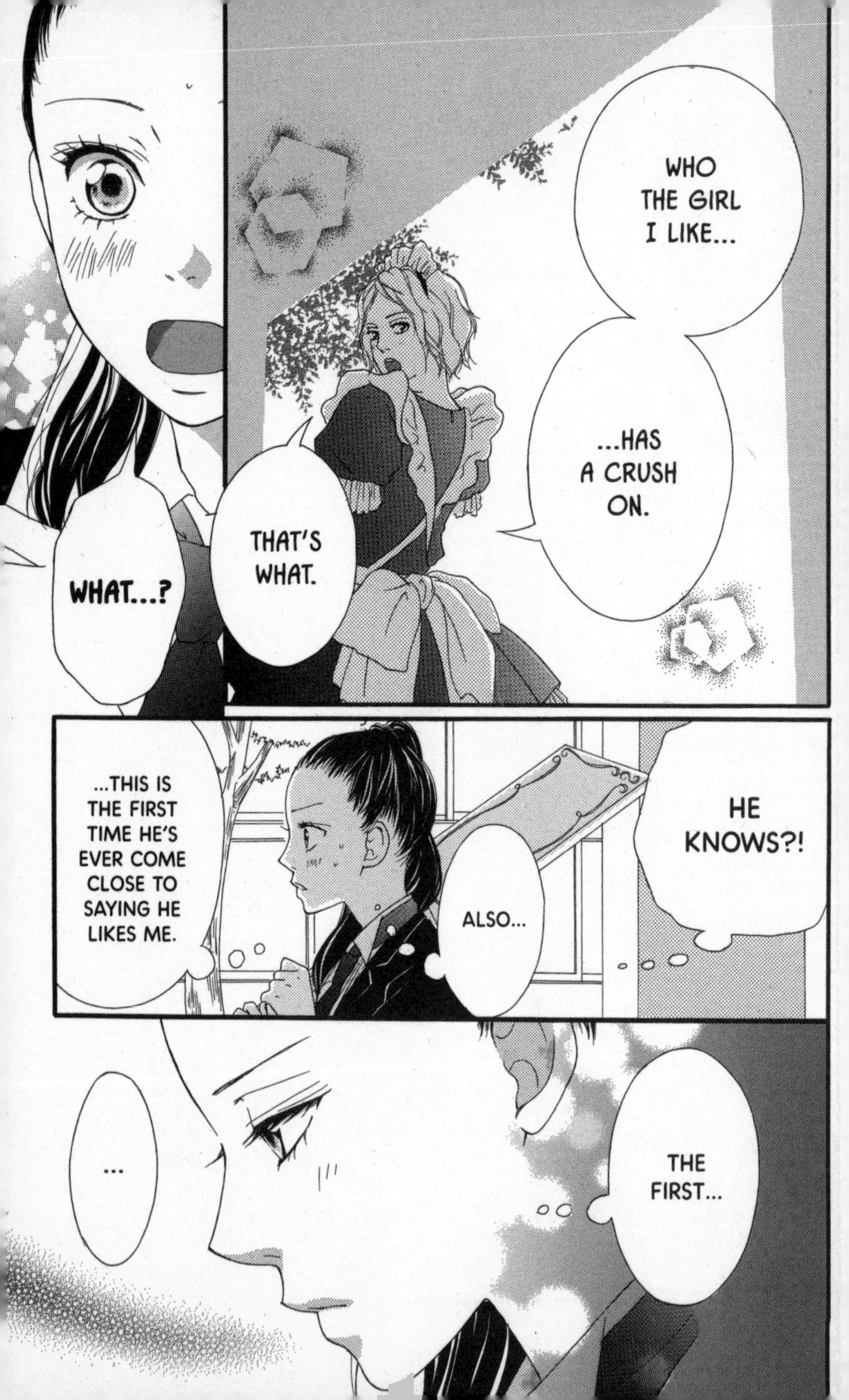
WHO THE GIRL I LIKE...
...HAS A CRUSH ON.
THAT'S WHAT.
WHAT...?
HE KNOWS?!
ALSO...
...THIS IS THE FIRST TIME HE'S EVER COME CLOSE TO SAYING HE LIKES ME.
THE FIRST...
...

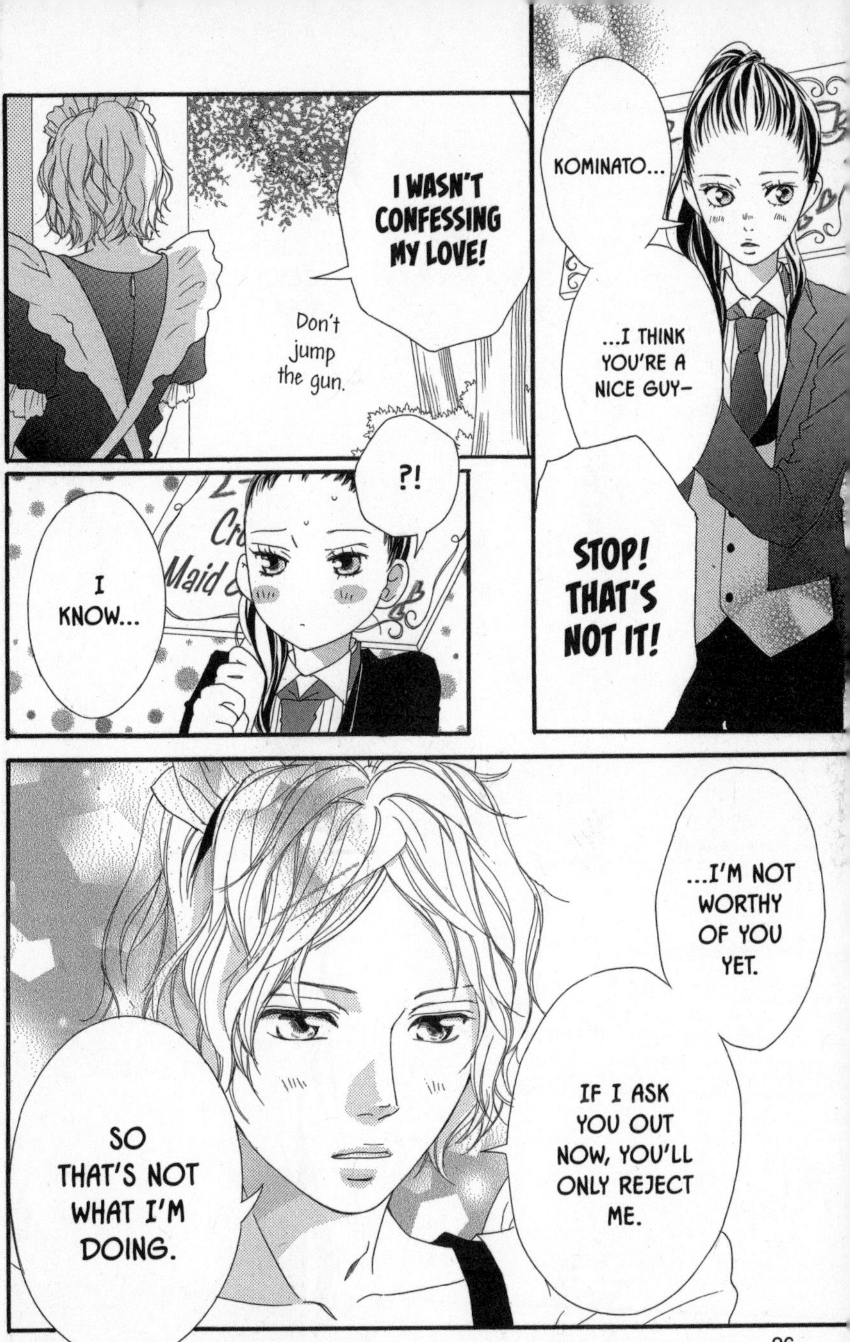
KOMINATO...
...I THINK YOU'RE A NICE GUY—
STOP! THAT'S NOT IT!
I WASN'T CONFESSING MY LOVE!
Don't jump the gun.
?!
I KNOW...
...I'M NOT WORTHY OF YOU YET.
IF I ASK YOU OUT NOW, YOU'LL ONLY REJECT ME.
SO THAT'S NOT WHAT I'M DOING.
Maid

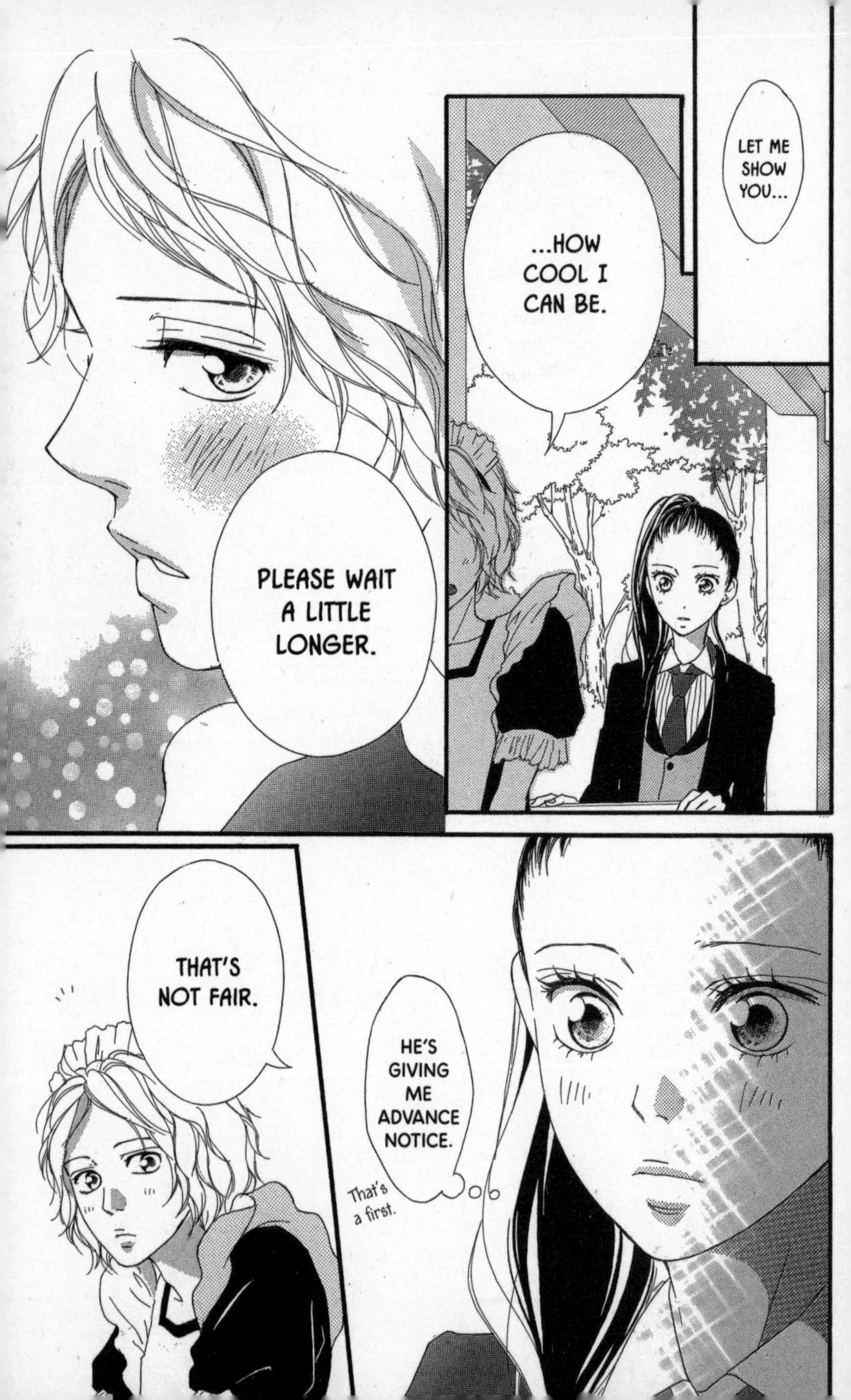
LET ME SHOW YOU...
...HOW COOL I CAN BE.
PLEASE WAIT A LITTLE LONGER.
HE'S GIVING ME ADVANCE NOTICE.
That's a first.
THAT'S NOT FAIR.

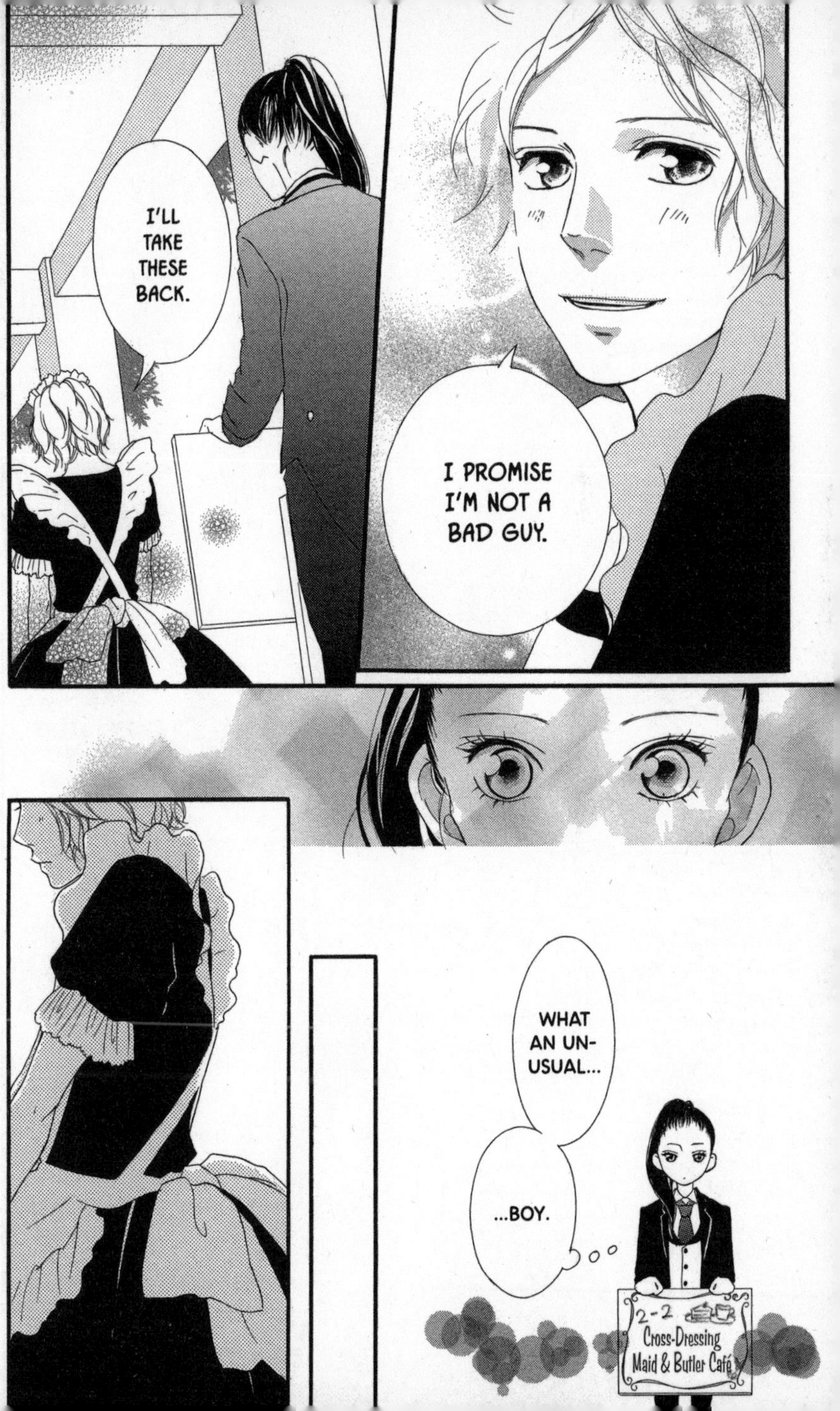
I PROMISE I'M NOT A BAD GUY.
I'LL TAKE THESE BACK.
WHAT AN UN-USUAL...
...BOY.
2-2 Cross-Dressing Maid & Butler Café

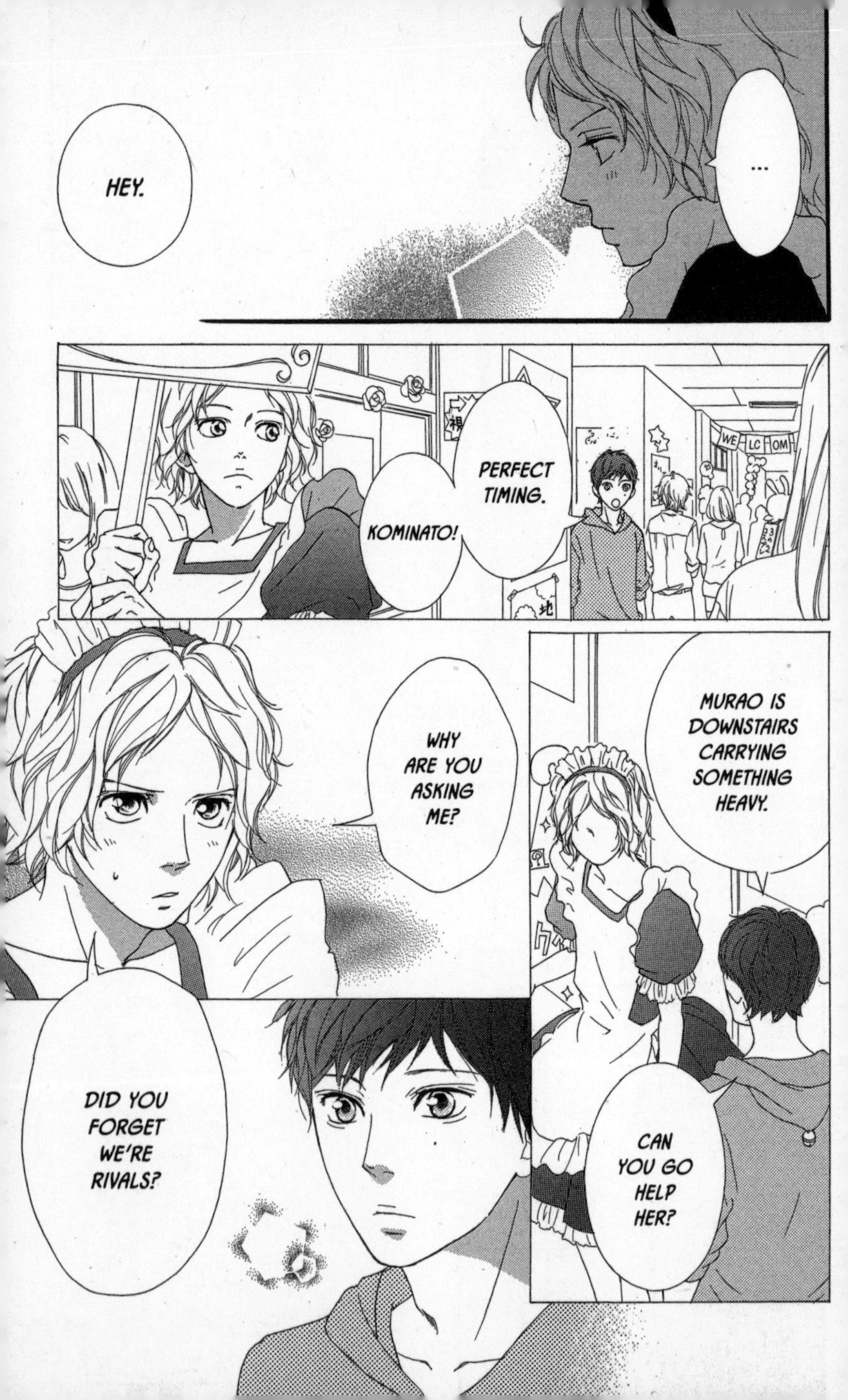
...
HEY.
PERFECT TIMING.
KOMINATO!
MURAO IS DOWNSTAIRS CARRYING SOMETHING HEAVY.
CAN YOU GO HELP HER?
WHY ARE YOU ASKING ME?
DID YOU FORGET WE'RE RIVALS?

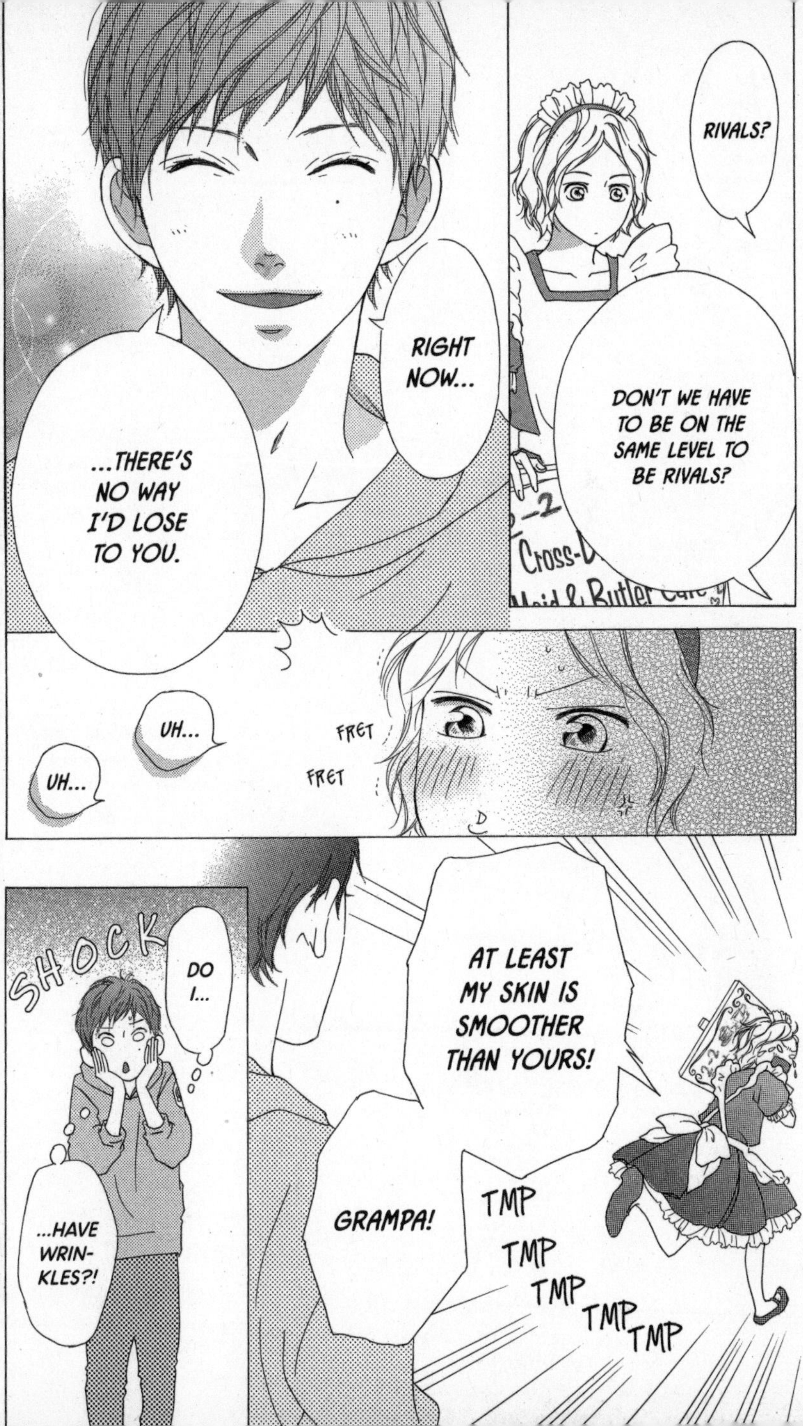
RIVALS?
DON'T WE HAVE TO BE ON THE SAME LEVEL TO BE RIVALS?
RIGHT NOW...
...THERE'S NO WAY I'D LOSE TO YOU.
FRET
FRET
UH...
UH...
AT LEAST MY SKIN IS SMOOTHER THAN YOURS!
GRAMPA!
TMP
TMP
TMP
TMP
TMP
SHOCK
DO I...
...HAVE WRIN-KLES?!

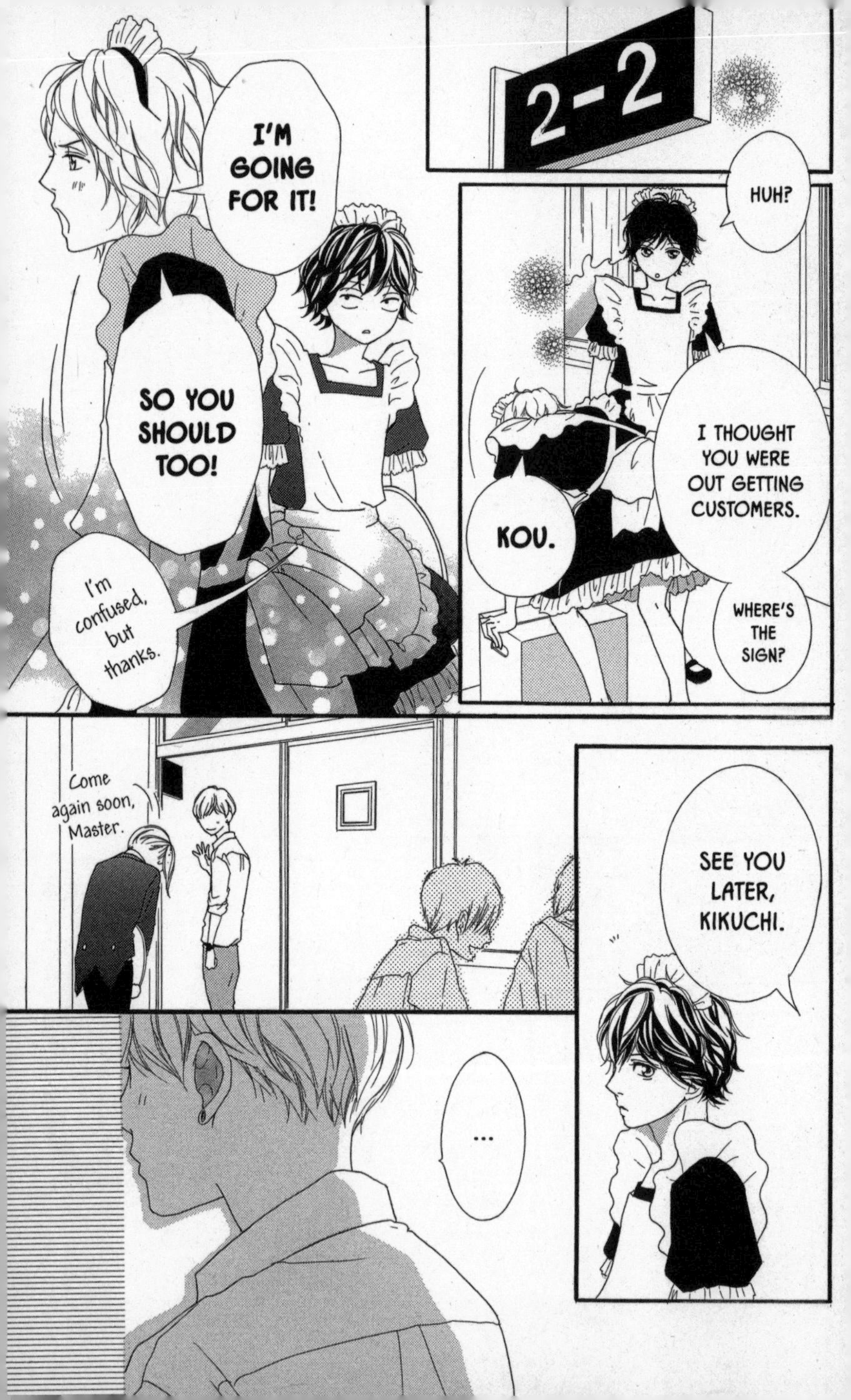
2-2
HUH?
I THOUGHT YOU WERE OUT GETTING CUSTOMERS.
KOU.
WHERE'S THE SIGN?
I'M GOING FOR IT!
SO YOU SHOULD TOO!
I'm confused, but thanks.
SEE YOU LATER, KIKUCHI.
Come again soon, Master.
...

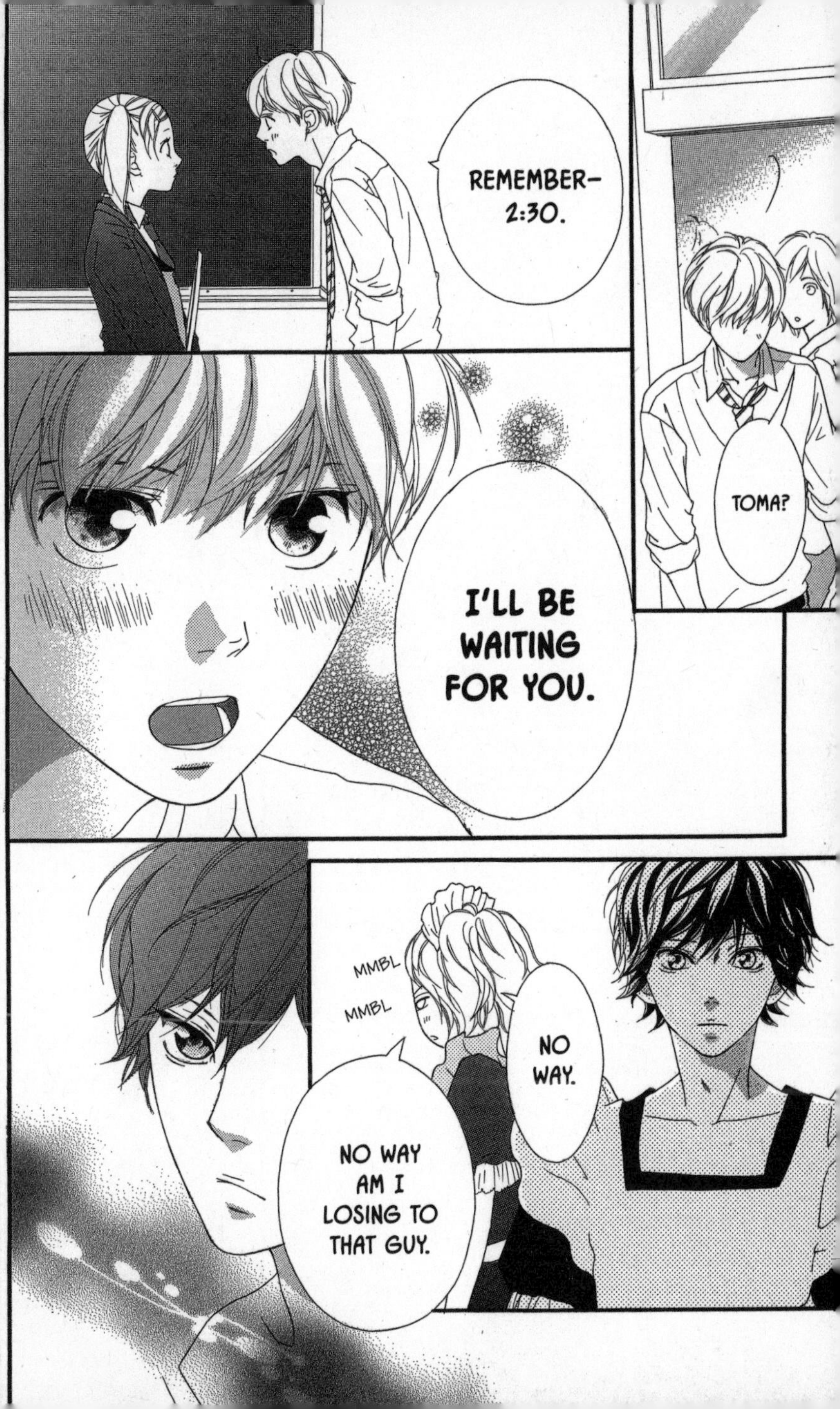
TOMA?
REMEMBER—2:30.
I'LL BE WAITING FOR YOU.
NO WAY.
MMBL MMBL
NO WAY AM I LOSING TO THAT GUY.

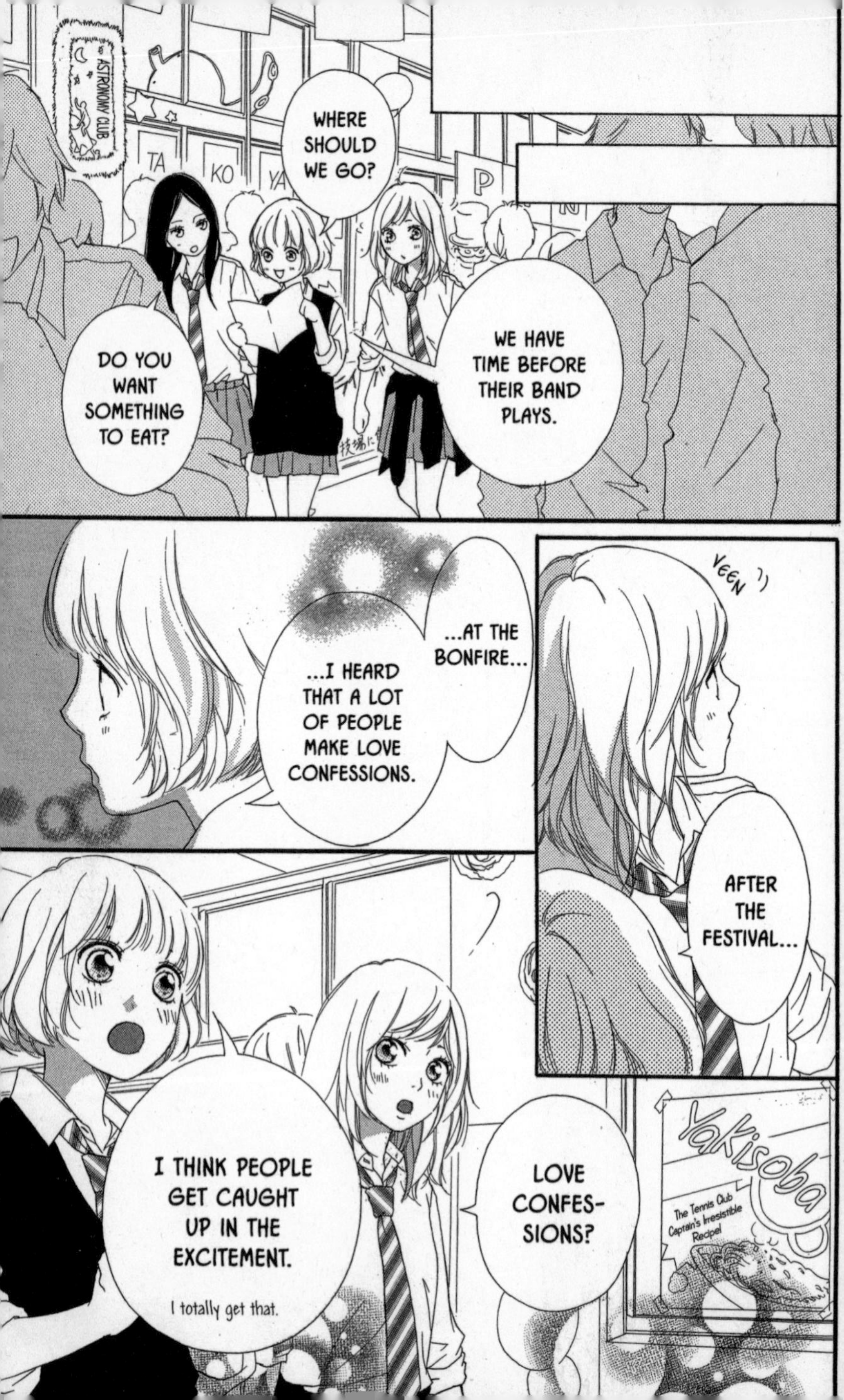
ASTRONOMY CLUB
TA KO YA
WHERE SHOULD WE GO?
WE HAVE TIME BEFORE THEIR BAND PLAYS.
DO YOU WANT SOMETHING TO EAT?
VEEN
AFTER THE FESTIVAL...
...AT THE BONFIRE...
...I HEARD THAT A LOT OF PEOPLE MAKE LOVE CONFESSIONS.
Yakisoba
The Tennis Club Captain's Irresistible Recipe!
LOVE CONFES-SIONS?
I THINK PEOPLE GET CAUGHT UP IN THE EXCITEMENT.
I totally get that.

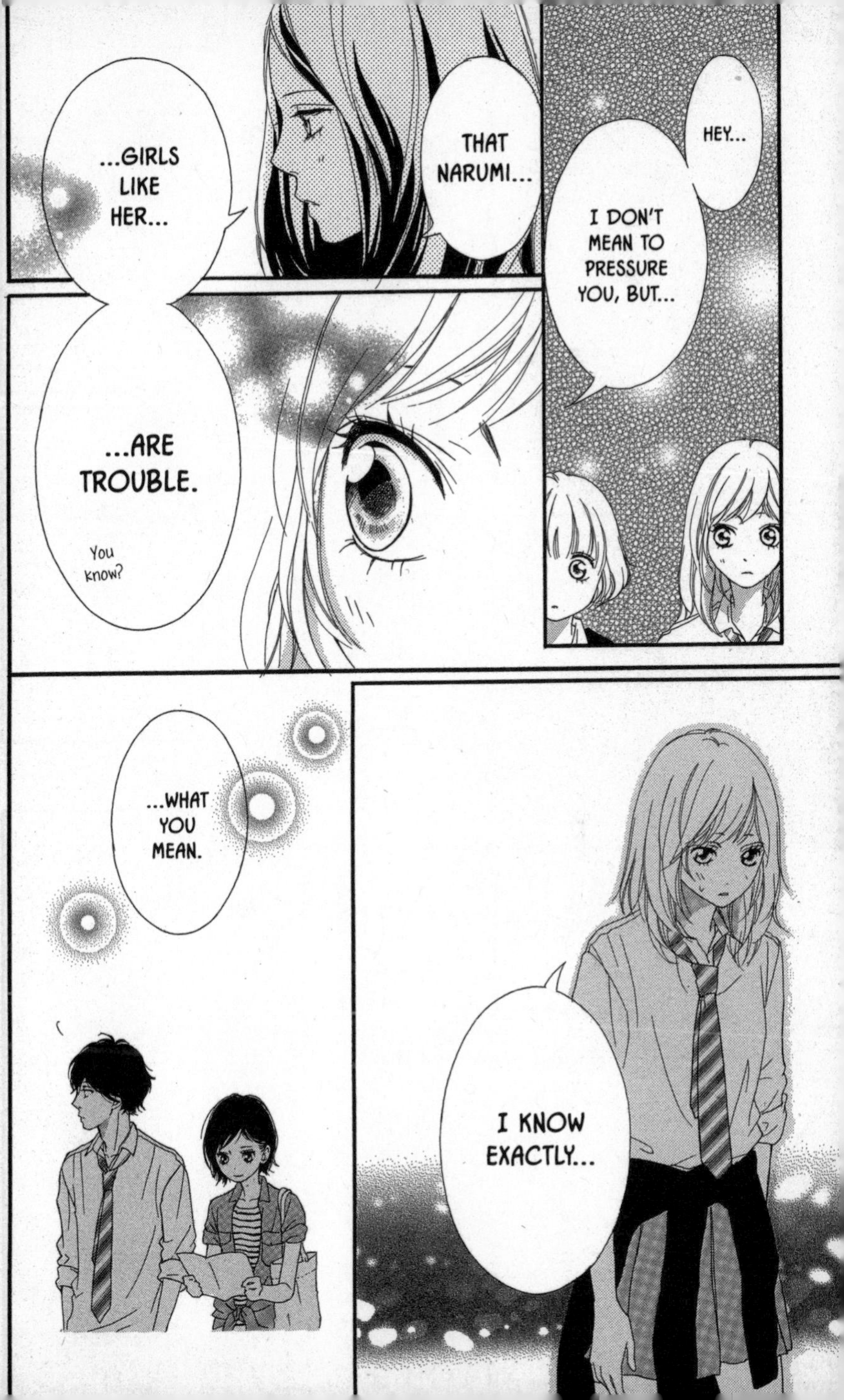
HEY...
I DON'T MEAN TO PRESSURE YOU, BUT...
THAT NARUMI...
...GIRLS LIKE HER...
...ARE TROUBLE.
You know?
I KNOW EXACTLY...
...WHAT YOU MEAN.

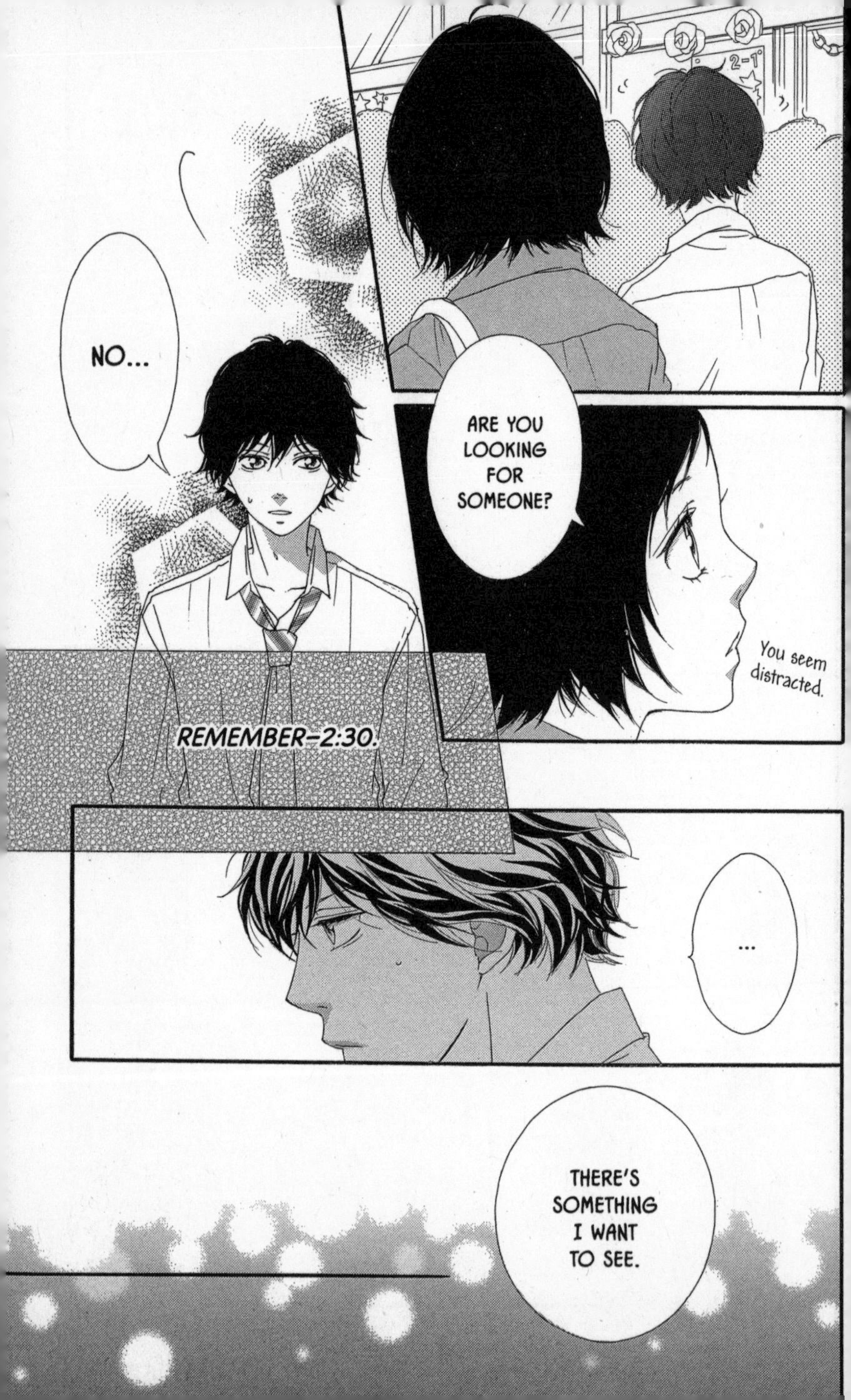
You seem distracted.
ARE YOU LOOKING FOR SOMEONE?
NO...
REMEMBER—2:30.
...
THERE'S SOMETHING I WANT TO SEE.

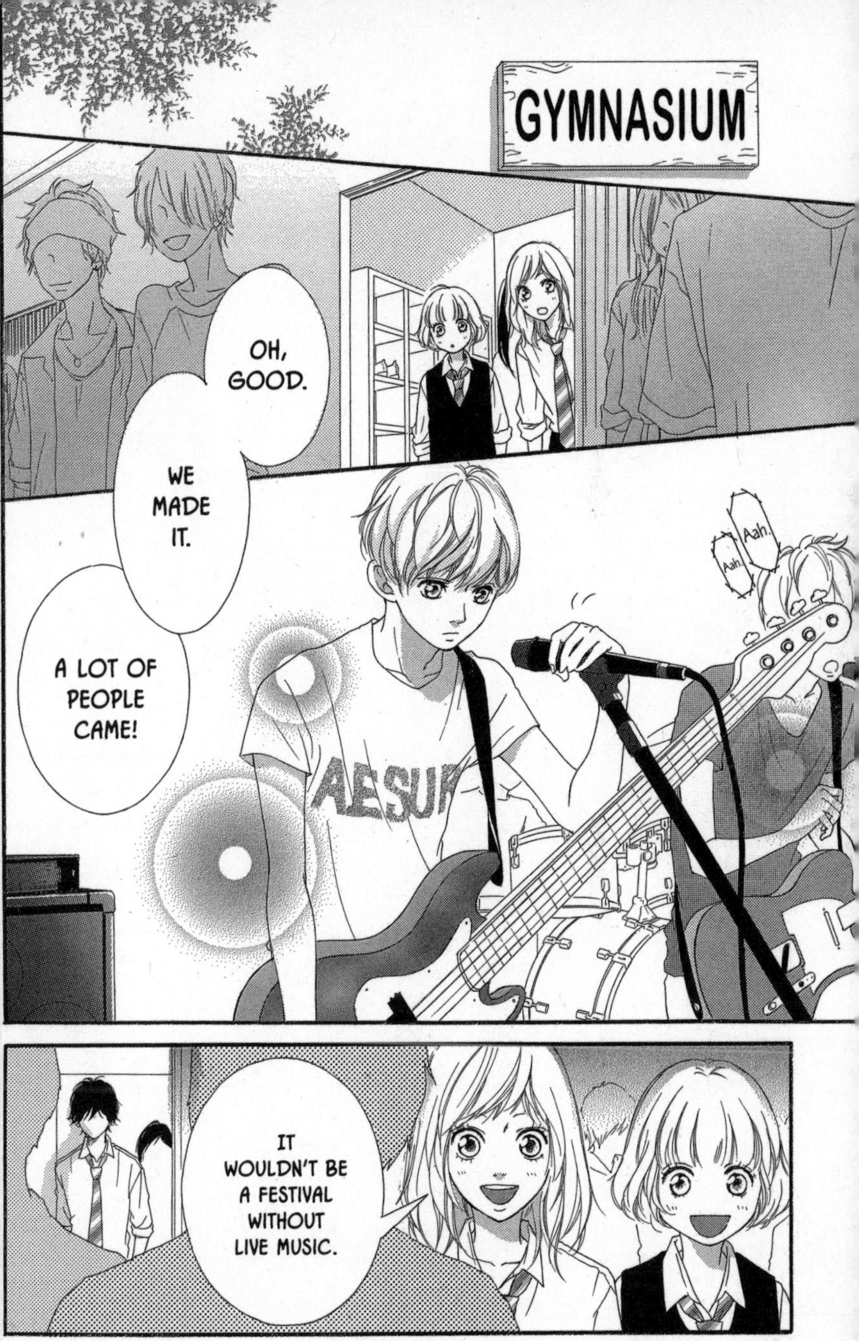
GYMNASIUM
OH, GOOD.
WE MADE IT.
A LOT OF PEOPLE CAME!
Aah.
Aah.
IT WOULDN'T BE A FESTIVAL WITHOUT LIVE MUSIC.

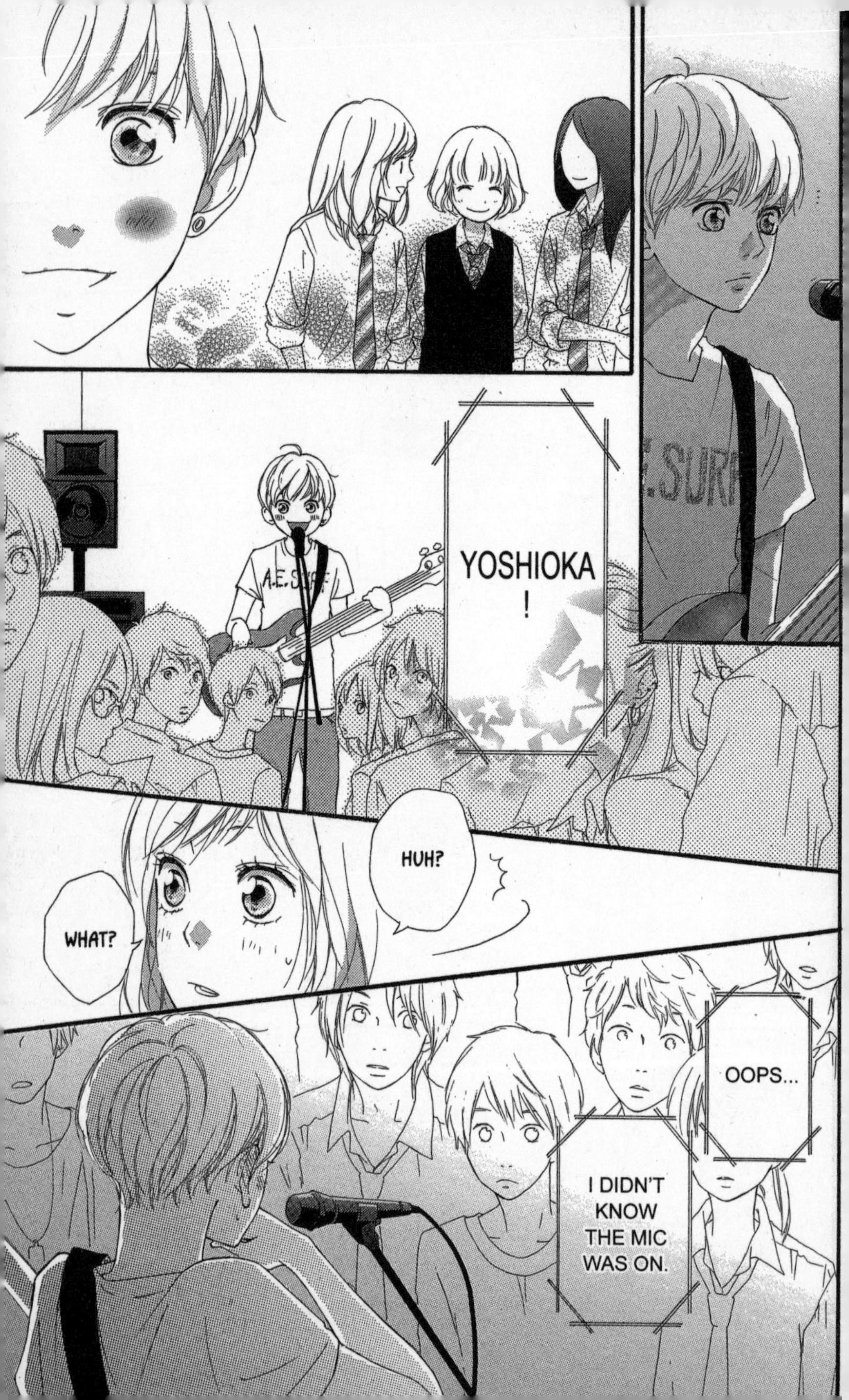
YOSHIOKA!
HUH?
WHAT?
OOPS...
I DIDN'T KNOW THE MIC WAS ON.

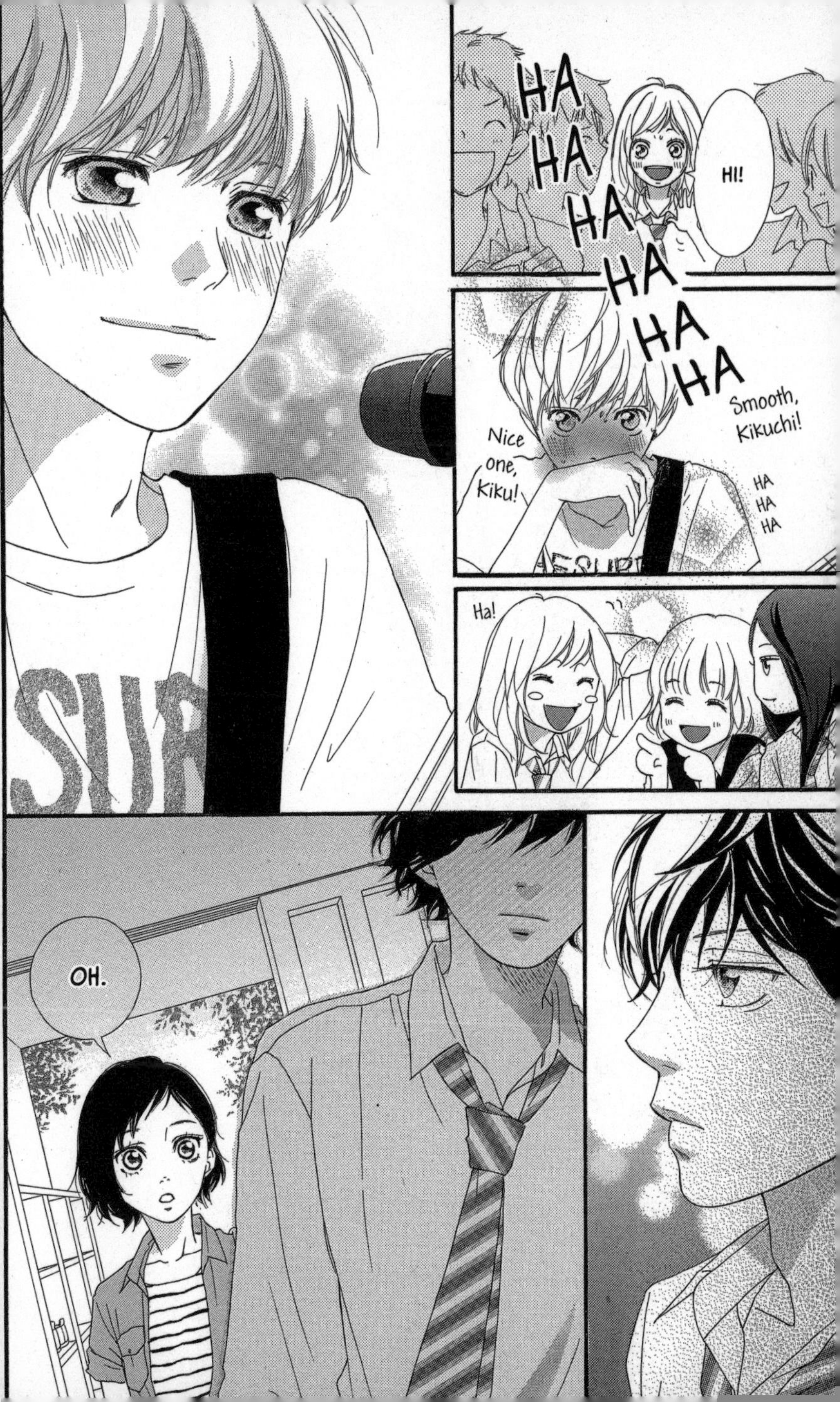
HI!
HA HA HA HA HA HA HA
Smooth, Kikuchi!
HA HA HA
Nice one, Kiku!
Ha!
OH.

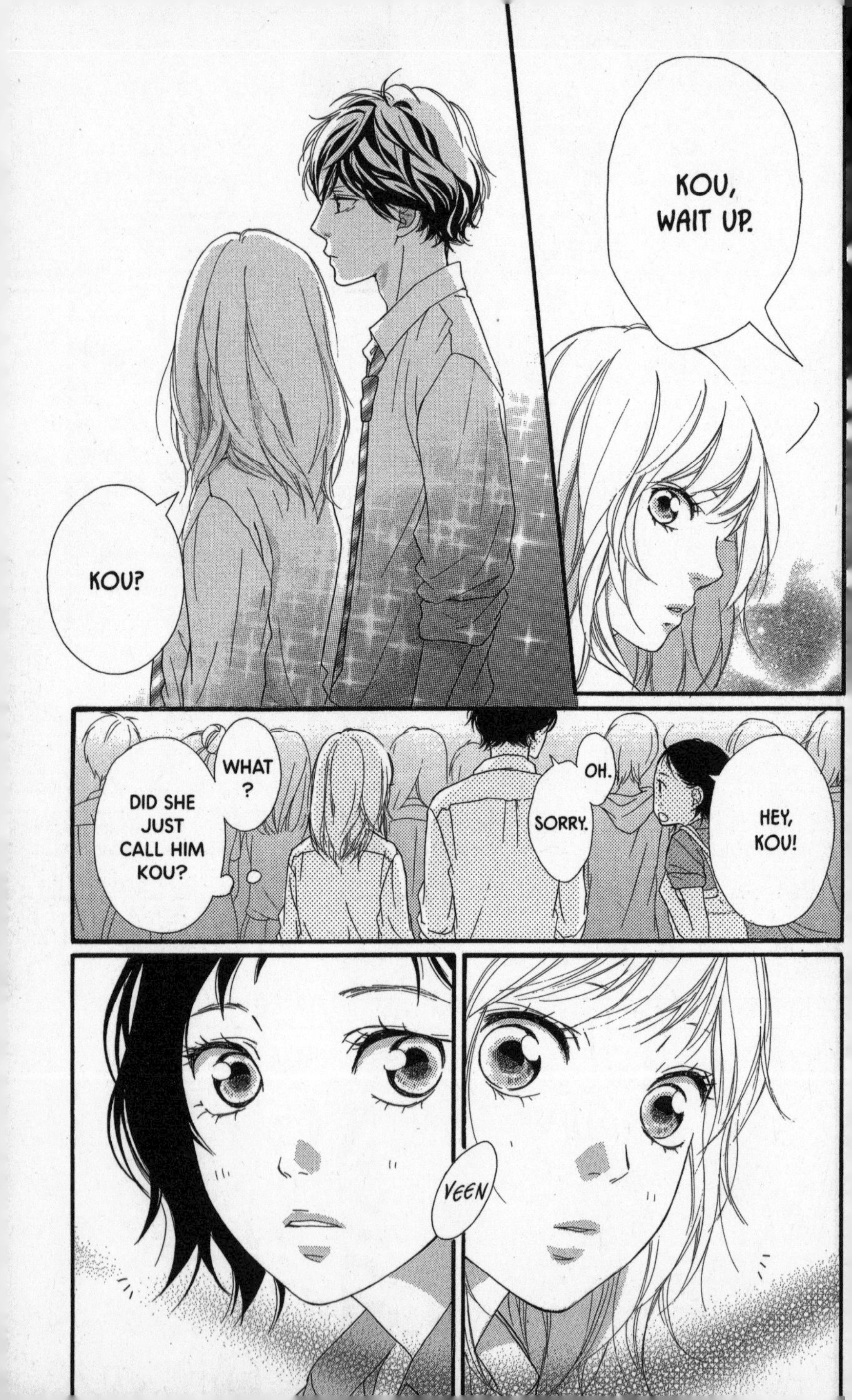
KOU, WAIT UP.
KOU?
HEY, KOU!
OH.
SORRY.
WHAT?
DID SHE JUST CALL HIM KOU?
VEEN

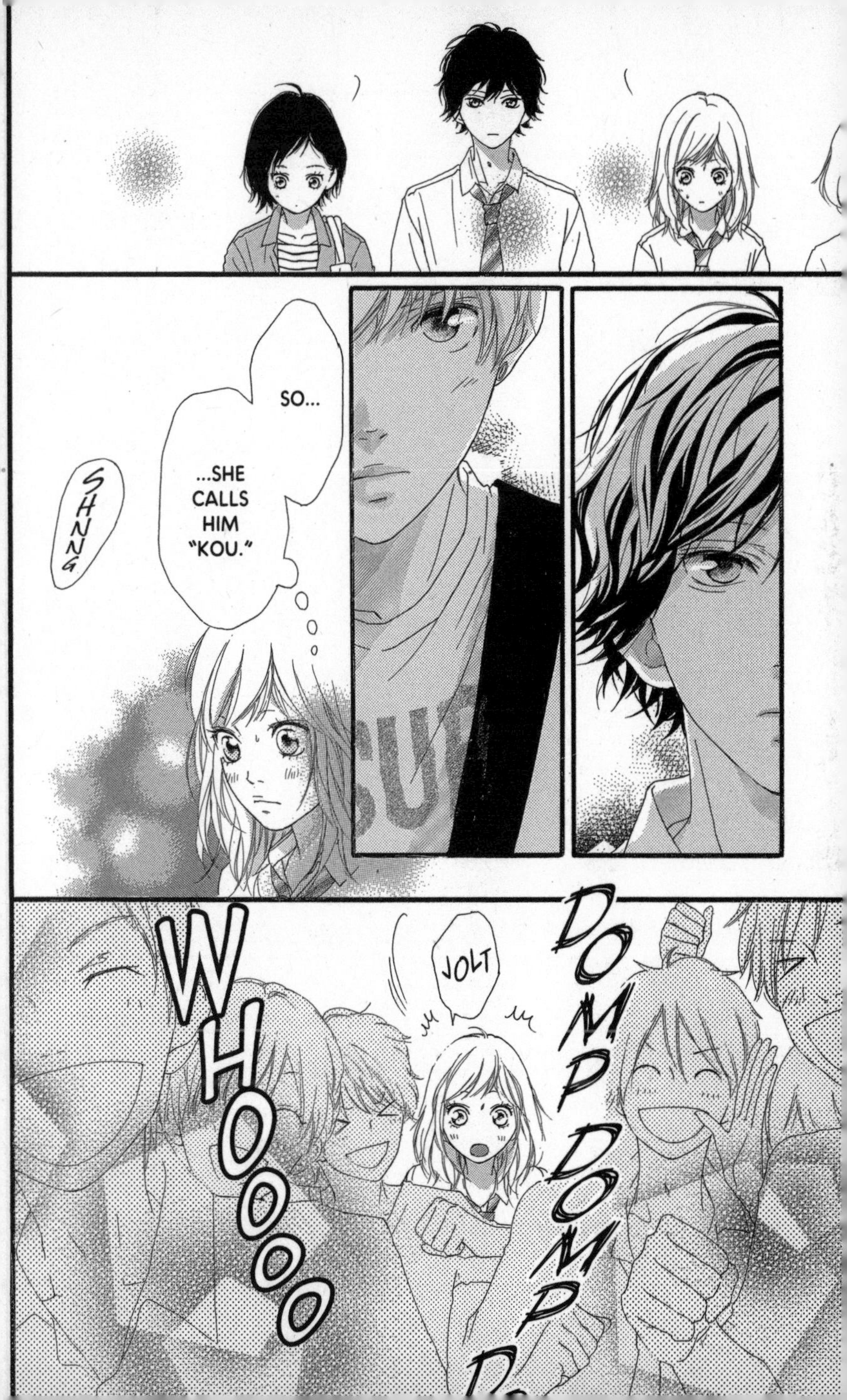
SO...
...SHE CALLS HIM "KOU."
SHNNG
JOLT
WHOOOO
DOMP DOMP DOMP

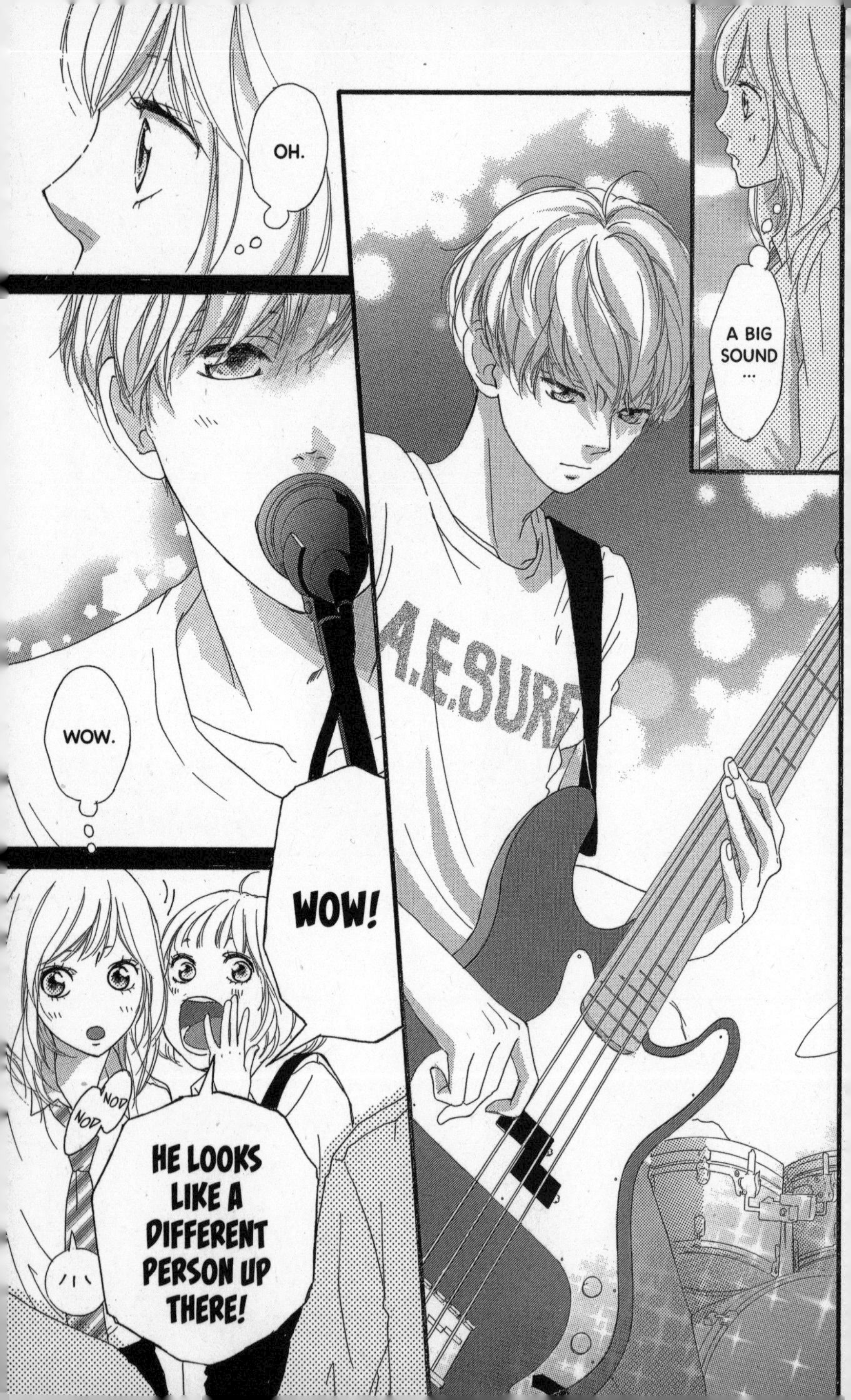
A BIG SOUND ...
OH.
WOW.
WOW!
NOD NOD
HE LOOKS LIKE A DIFFERENT PERSON UP THERE!

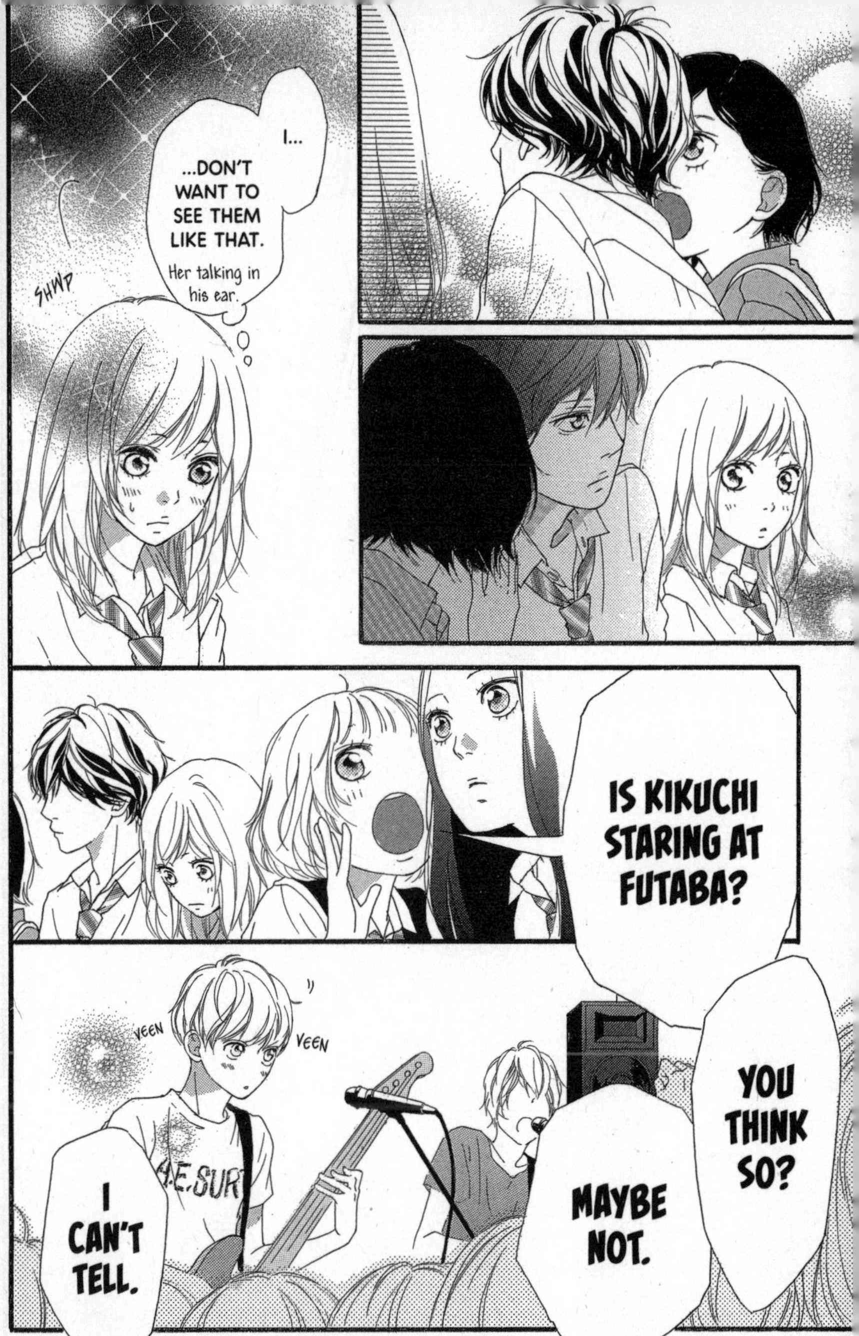
I...
...DON'T WANT TO SEE THEM LIKE THAT.
Her talking in his ear.
SHWP
IS KIKUCHI STARING AT FUTABA?
YOU THINK SO?
MAYBE NOT.
VEEN
VEEN
I CAN'T TELL.

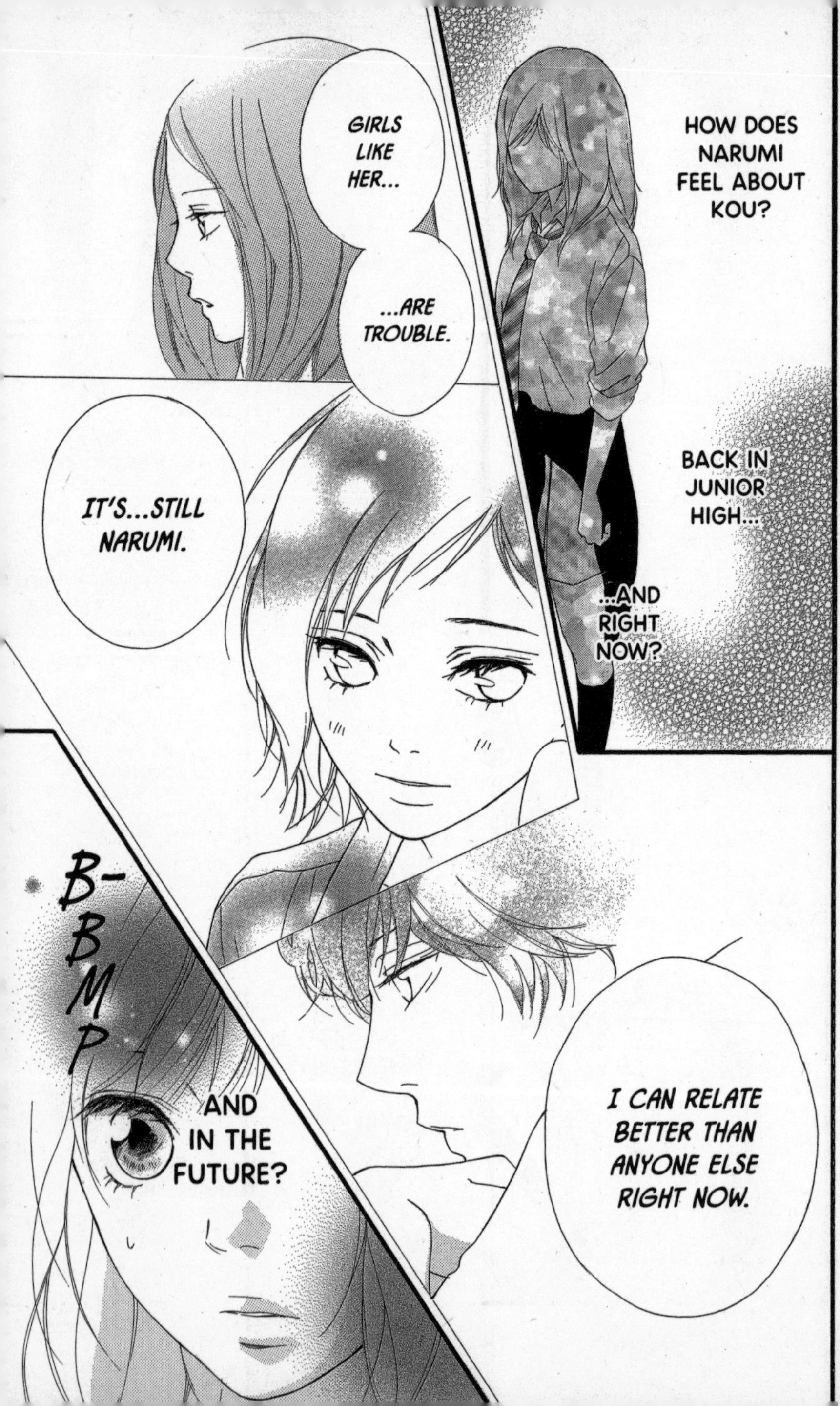
HOW DOES NARUMI FEEL ABOUT KOU?
BACK IN JUNIOR HIGH...
...AND RIGHT NOW?
GIRLS LIKE HER...
...ARE TROUBLE.
IT'S...STILL NARUMI.
I CAN RELATE BETTER THAN ANYONE ELSE RIGHT NOW.
B-BMP
AND IN THE FUTURE?

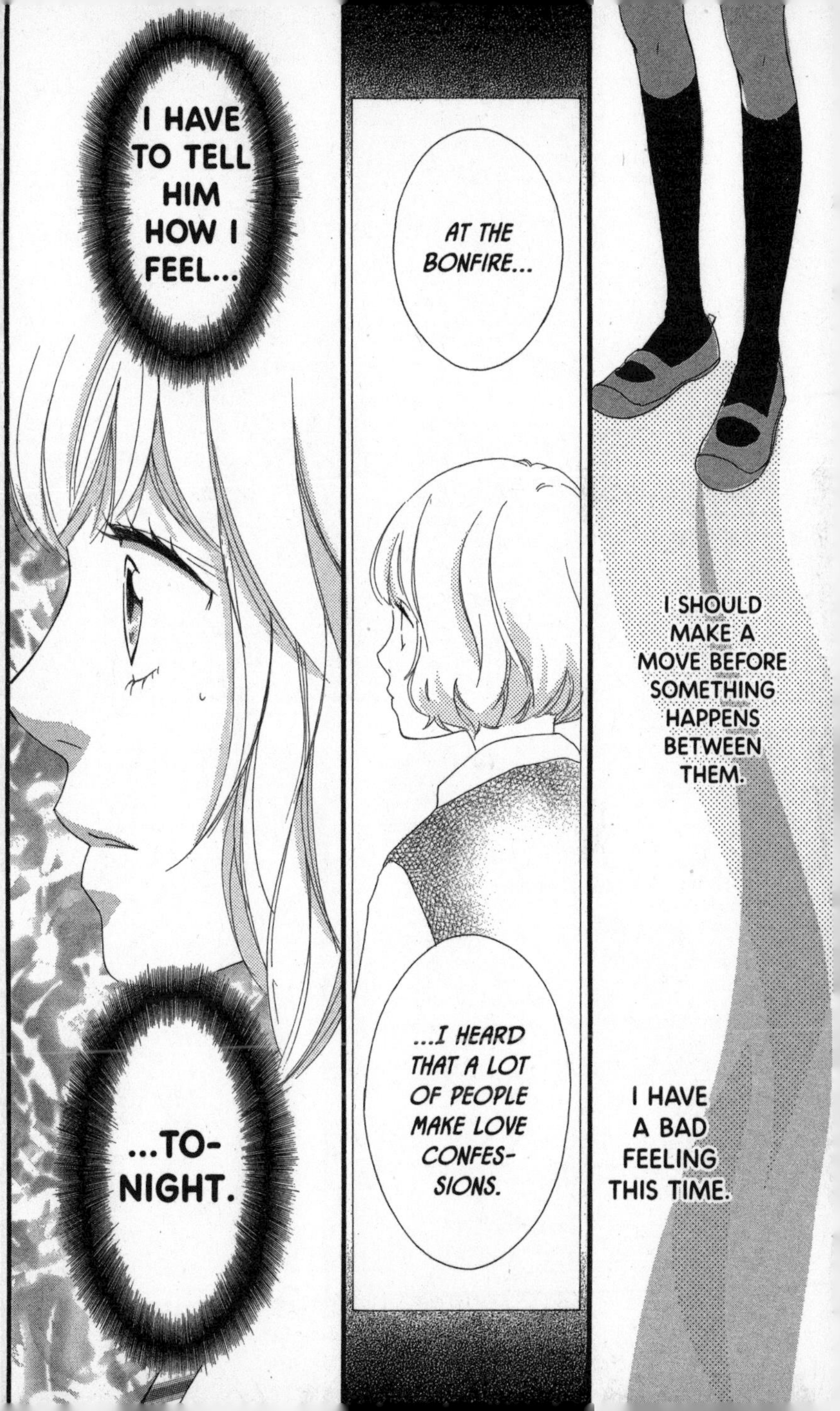
I SHOULD MAKE A MOVE BEFORE SOMETHING HAPPENS BETWEEN THEM.
I HAVE A BAD FEELING THIS TIME.
AT THE BONFIRE...
...I HEARD THAT A LOT OF PEOPLE MAKE LOVE CONFES-SIONS.
I HAVE TO TELL HIM HOW I FEEL...
...TO-NIGHT.

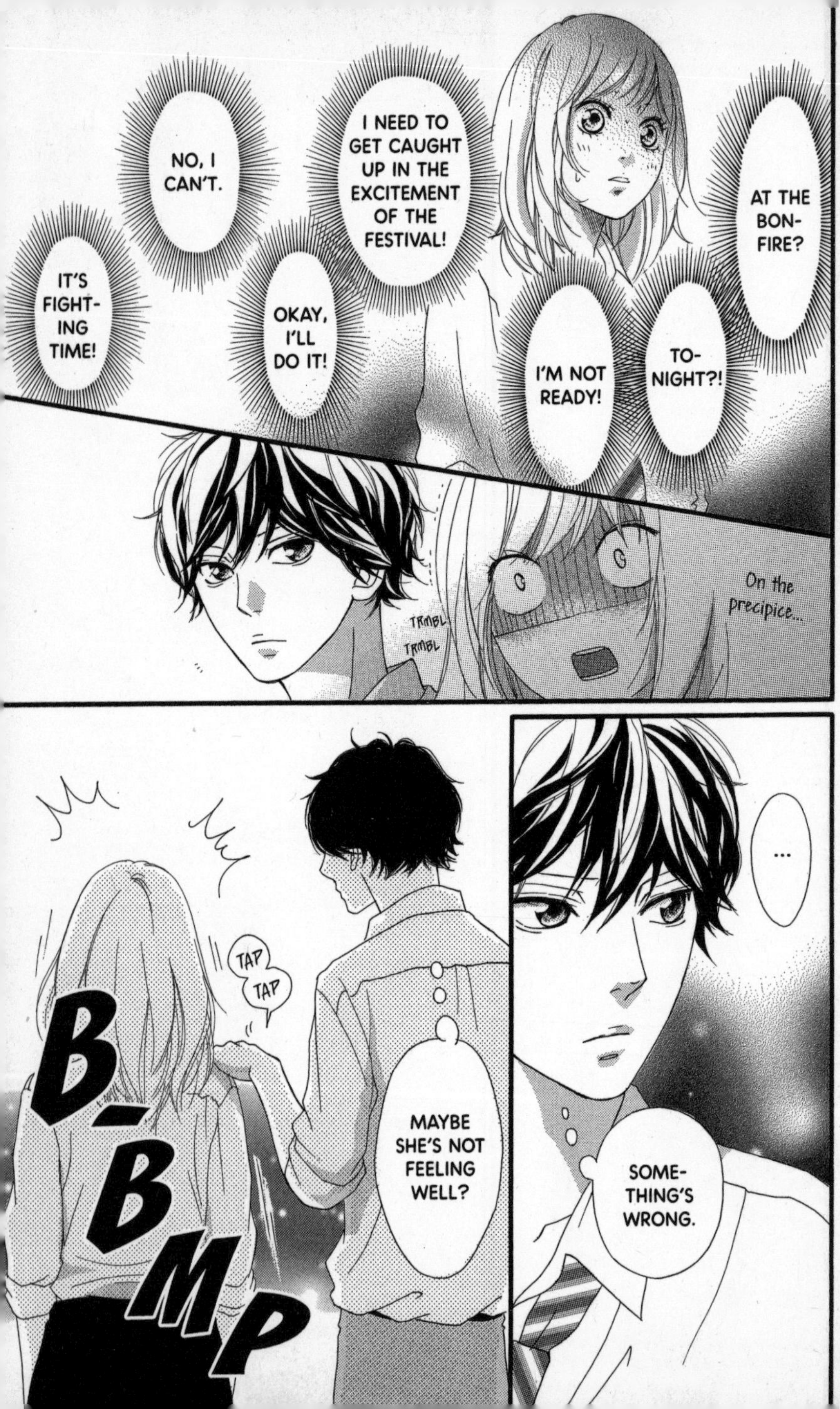
AT THE BON-FIRE?
TO-NIGHT?!
I'M NOT READY!
I NEED TO GET CAUGHT UP IN THE EXCITEMENT OF THE FESTIVAL!
OKAY, I'LL DO IT!
NO, I CAN'T.
IT'S FIGHT-ING TIME!
On the precipice...
TRMBL TRMBL
...
SOME-THING'S WRONG.
MAYBE SHE'S NOT FEELING WELL?
TAP TAP
B-BMP

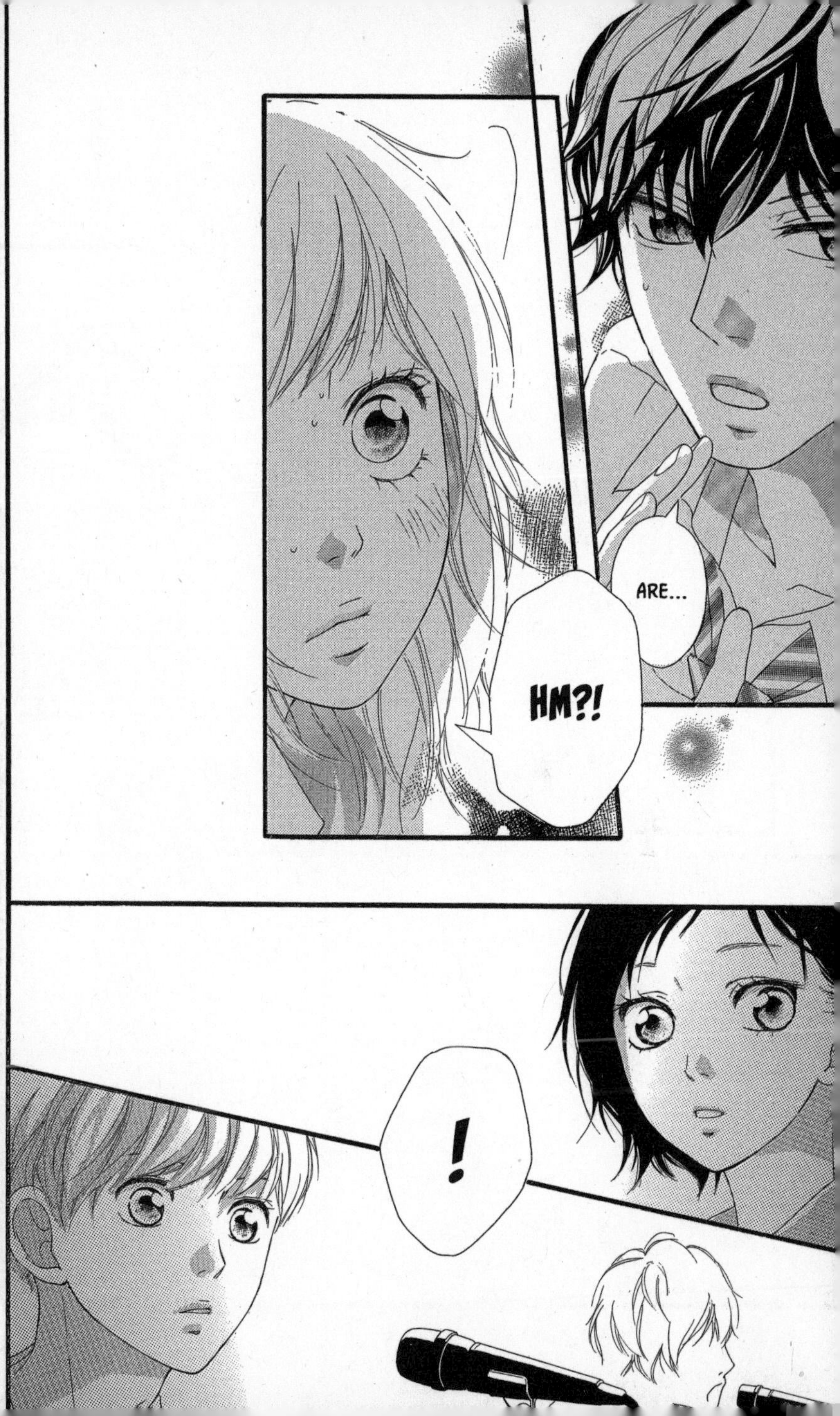
ARE...
HM?!
!

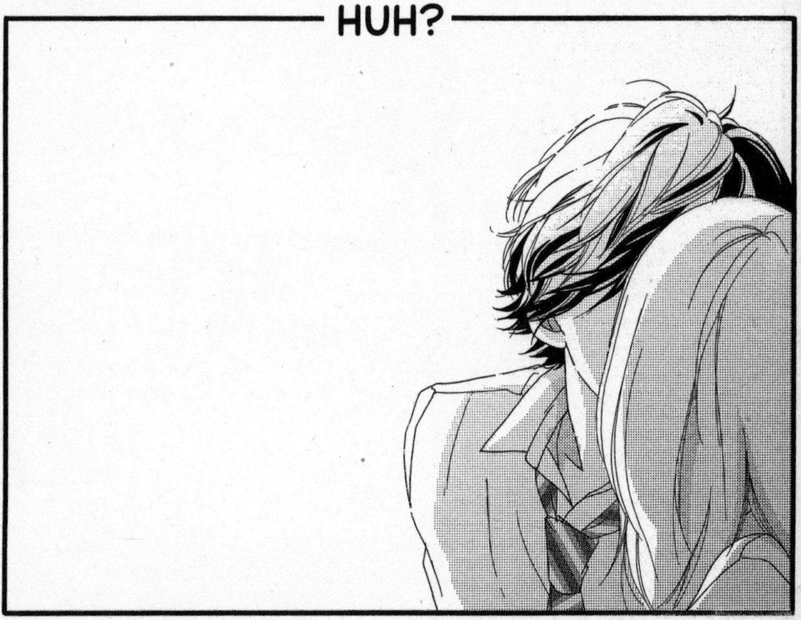
HUH?
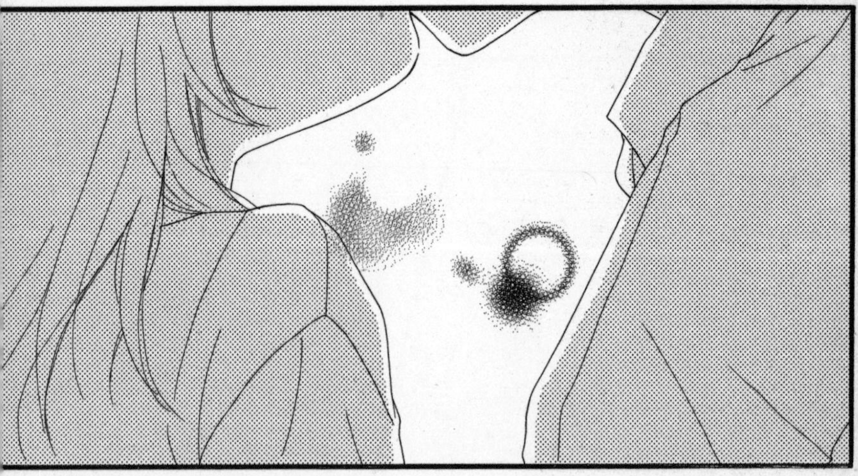

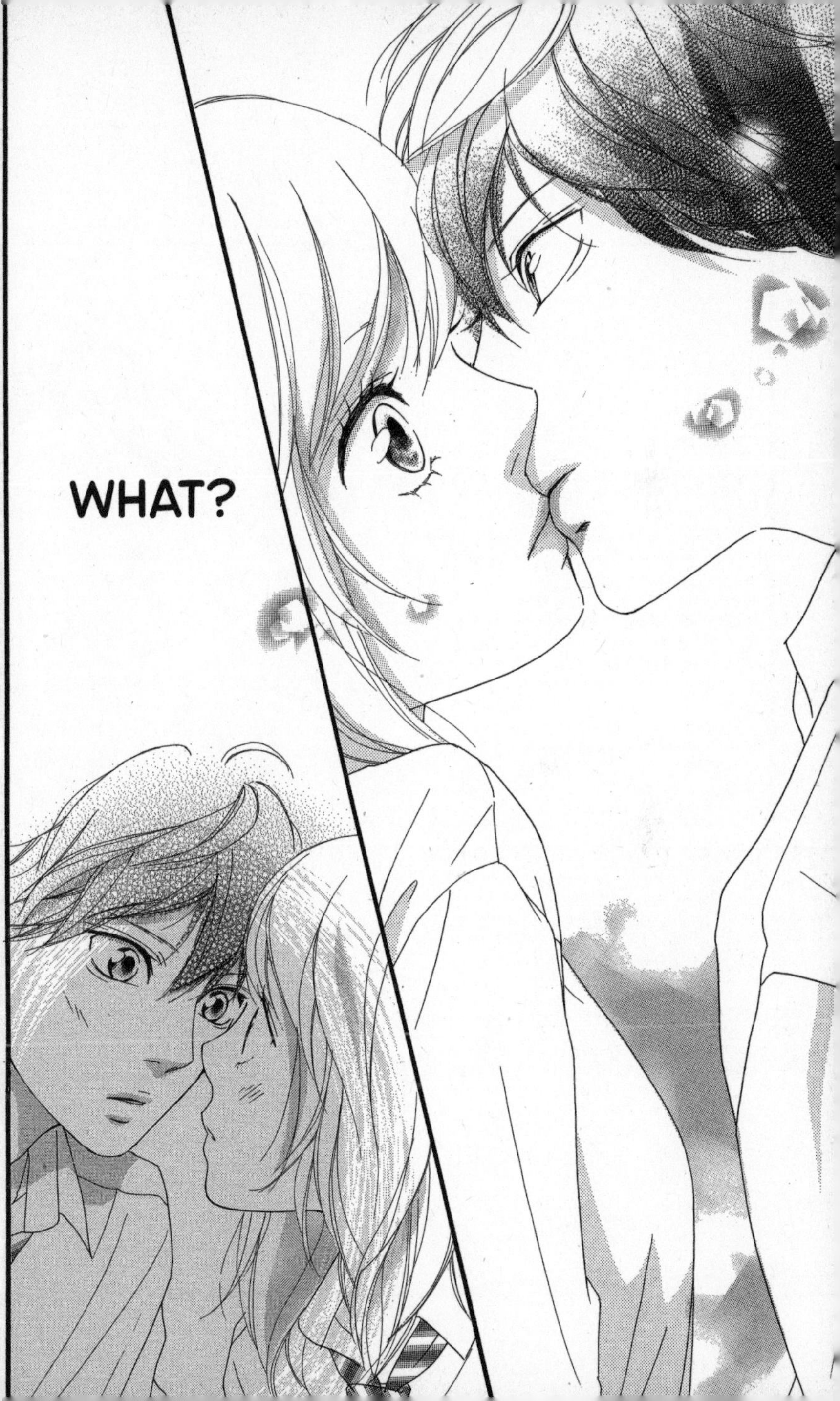
WHAT?

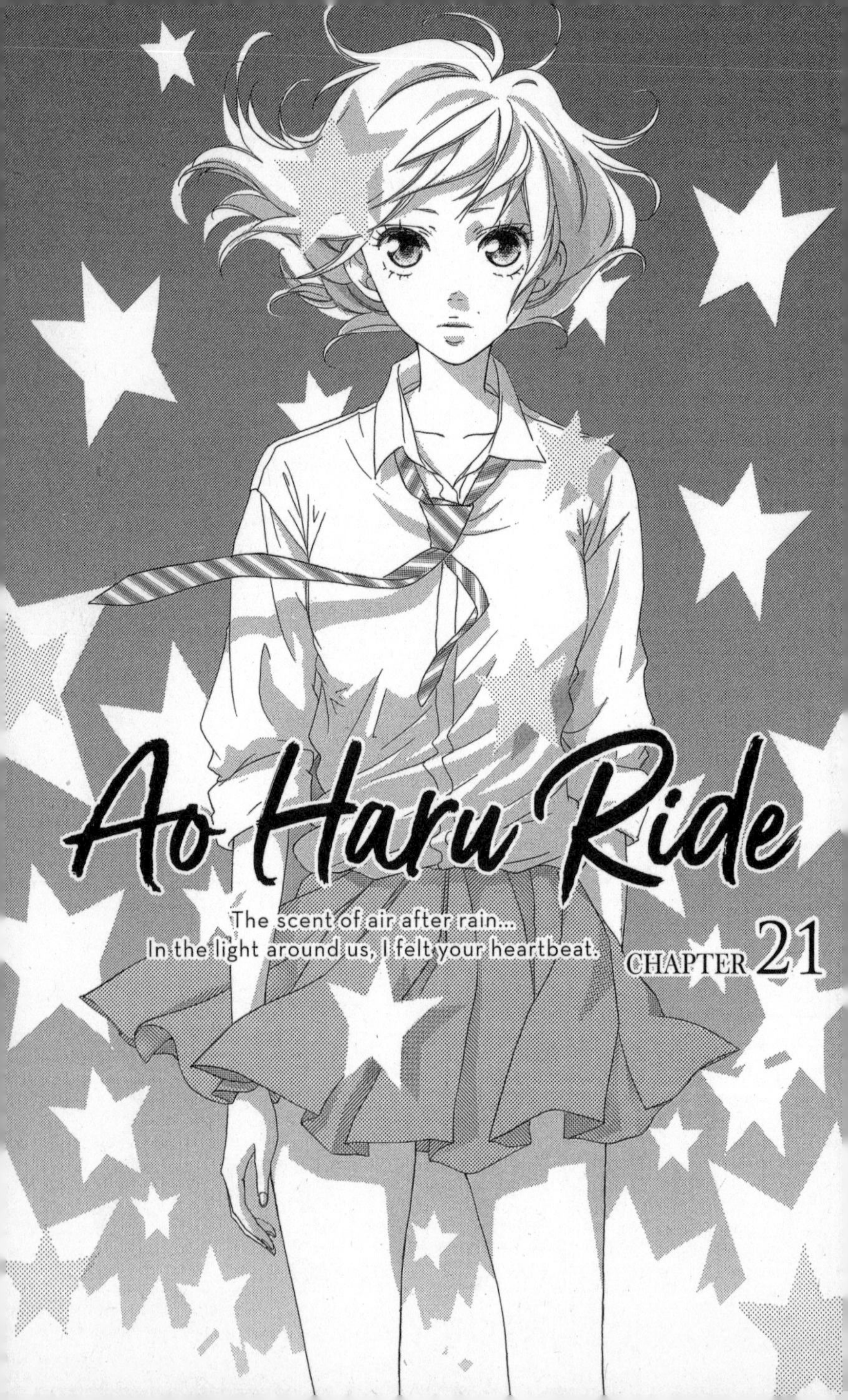
Ao Haru Ride
The scent of air after rain...
In the light around us, I felt your heartbeat.
CHAPTER 21

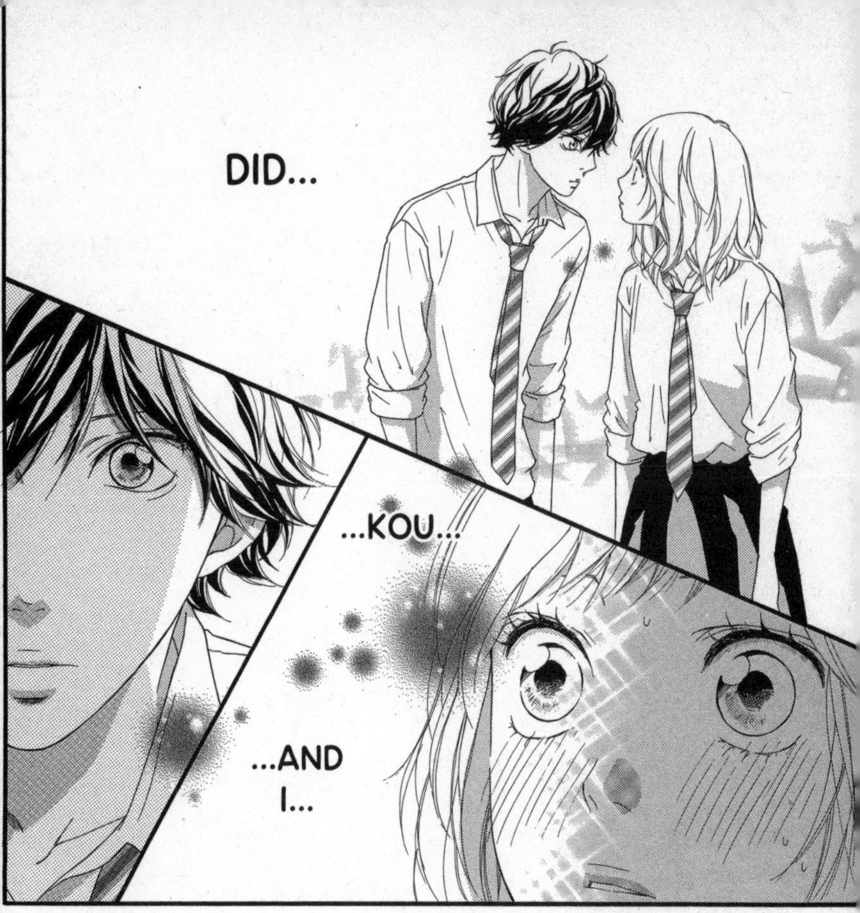
DID...
...KOU...
...AND
I...

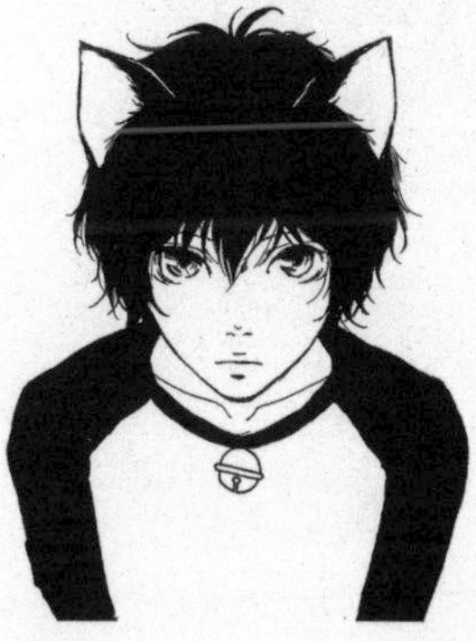

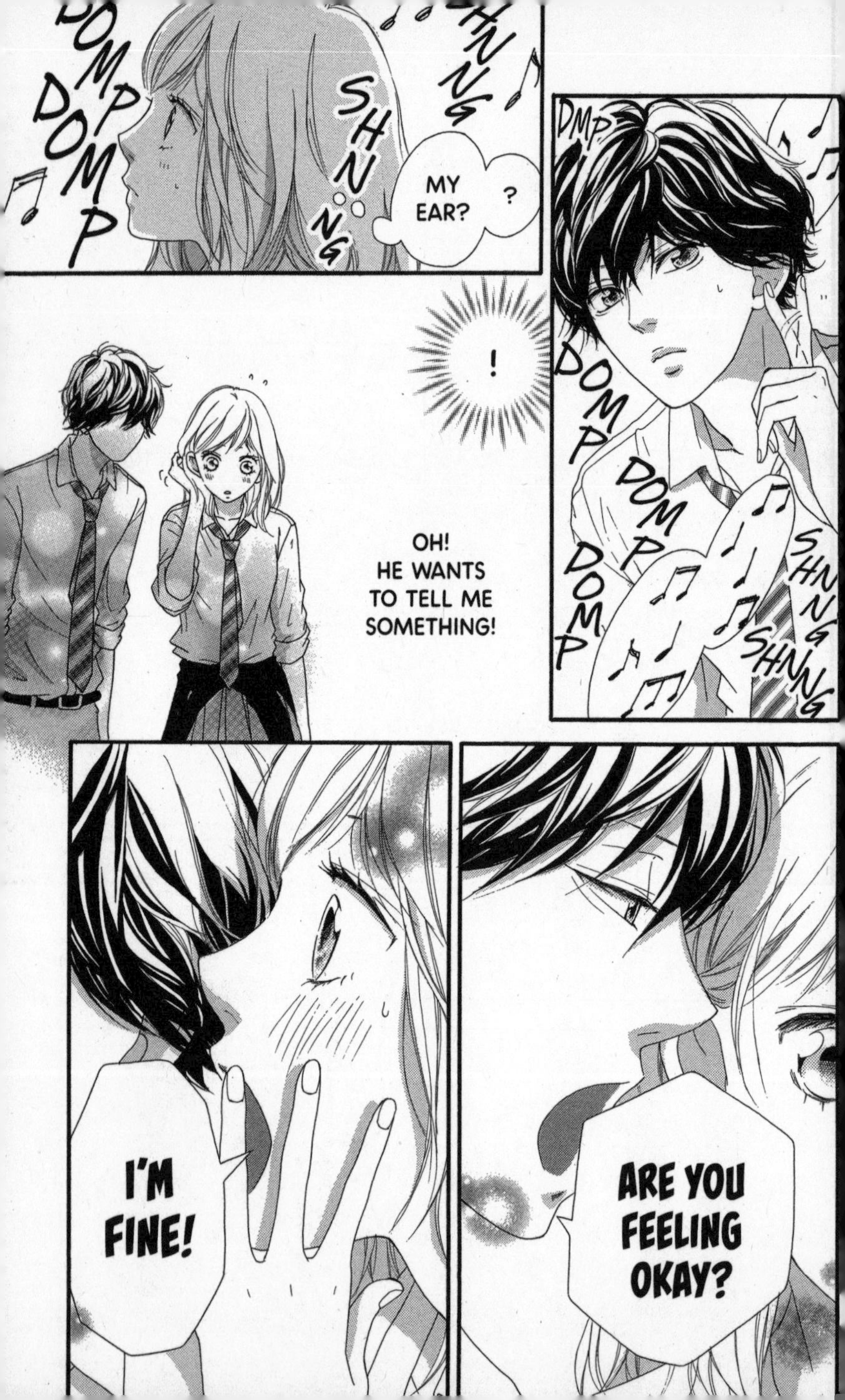
SHNNG
SHNNG
DOMP
DOMP
DOMP
MY EAR? ?
DMP
DOMP
DOMP
DOMP
SHNNG
SHNNG
!
OH! HE WANTS TO TELL ME SOMETHING!
ARE YOU FEELING OKAY?
I'M FINE!

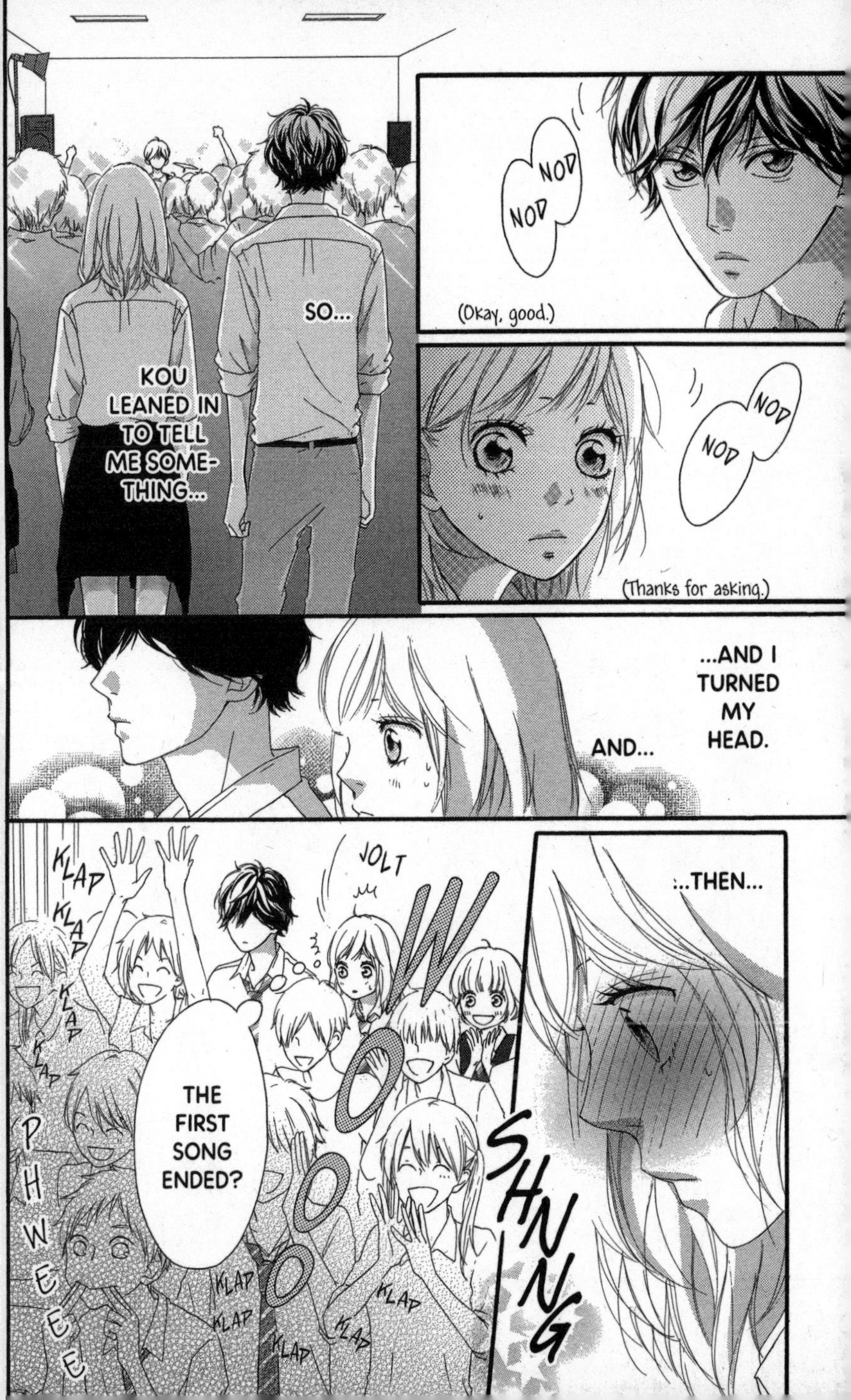
NOD
NOD
(Okay, good.)
NOD
NOD
(Thanks for asking.)
SO...
KOU LEANED IN TO TELL ME SOME-THING...
...AND I TURNED MY HEAD.
AND...
...THEN...
SHNG
JOLT
WOOOO
THE FIRST SONG ENDED?
KLAP KLAP KLAP KLAP KLAP
KLAP KLAP KLAP KLAP KLAP
PHWEEE

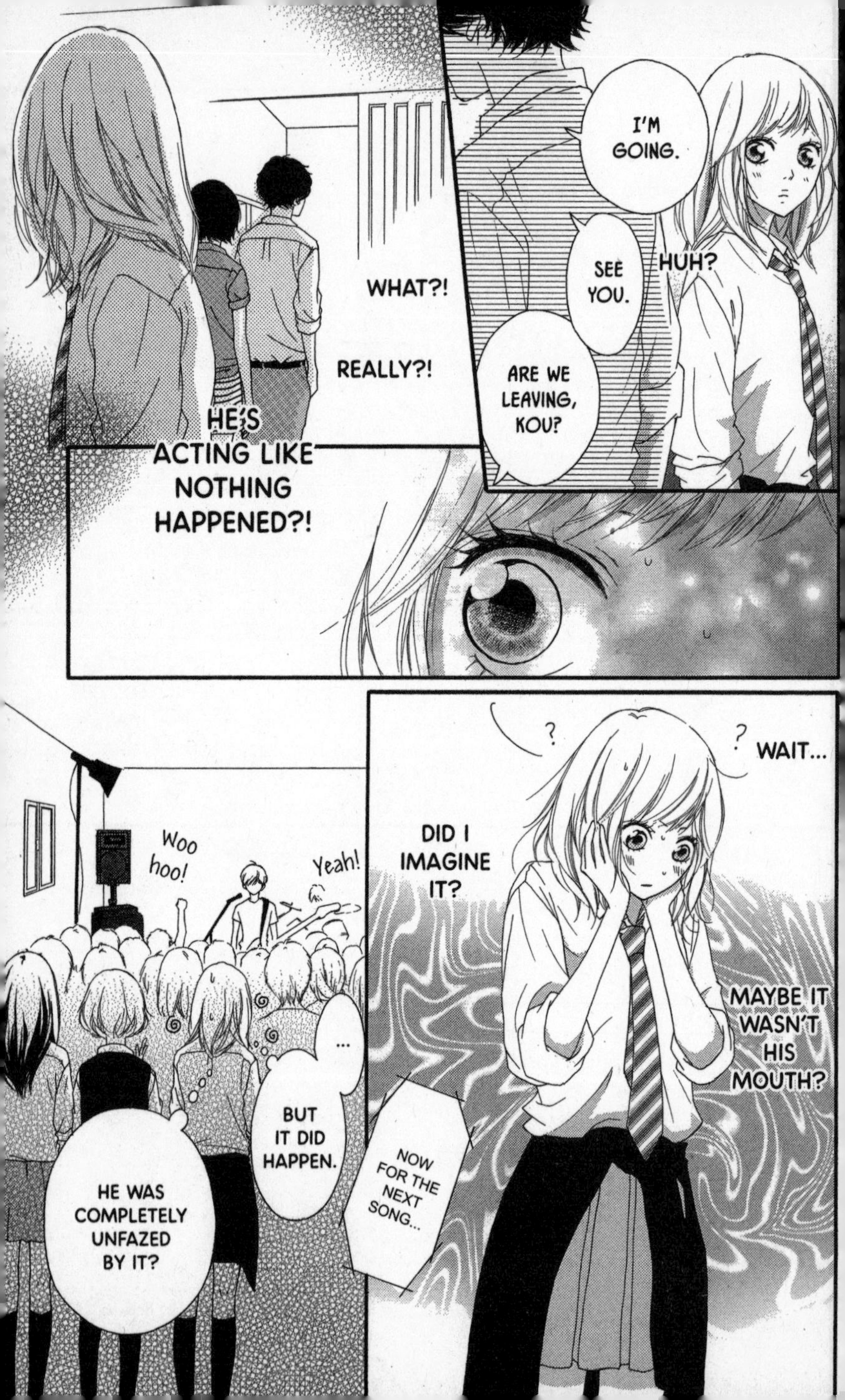
I'M GOING.
HUH?
SEE YOU.
ARE WE LEAVING, KOU?
WHAT?!
REALLY?!
HE'S ACTING LIKE NOTHING HAPPENED?!
WAIT...
?
?
MAYBE IT WASN'T HIS MOUTH?
DID I IMAGINE IT?
NOW FOR THE NEXT SONG...
...
BUT IT DID HAPPEN.
Yeah!
Woo hoo!
HE WAS COMPLETELY UNFAZED BY IT?

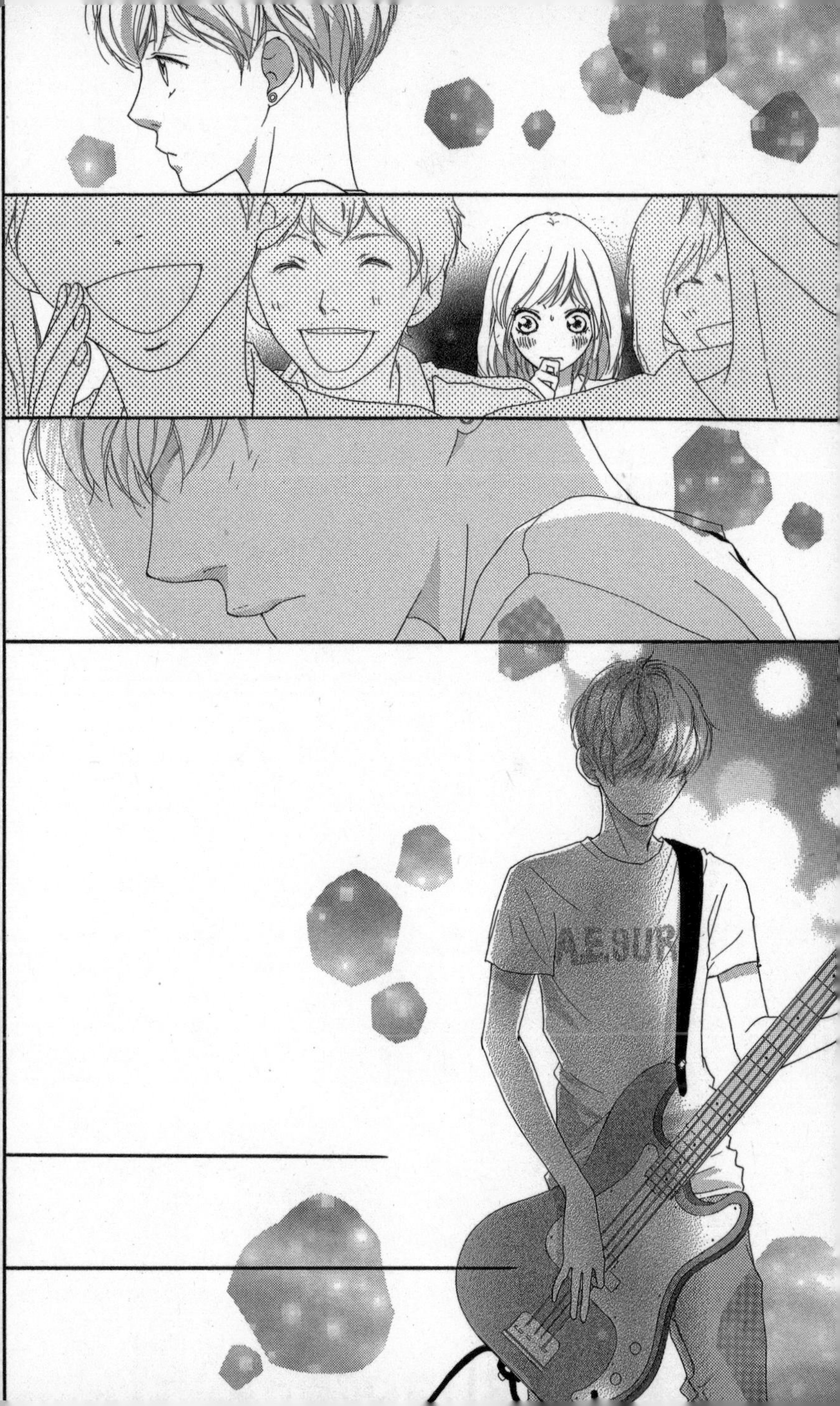

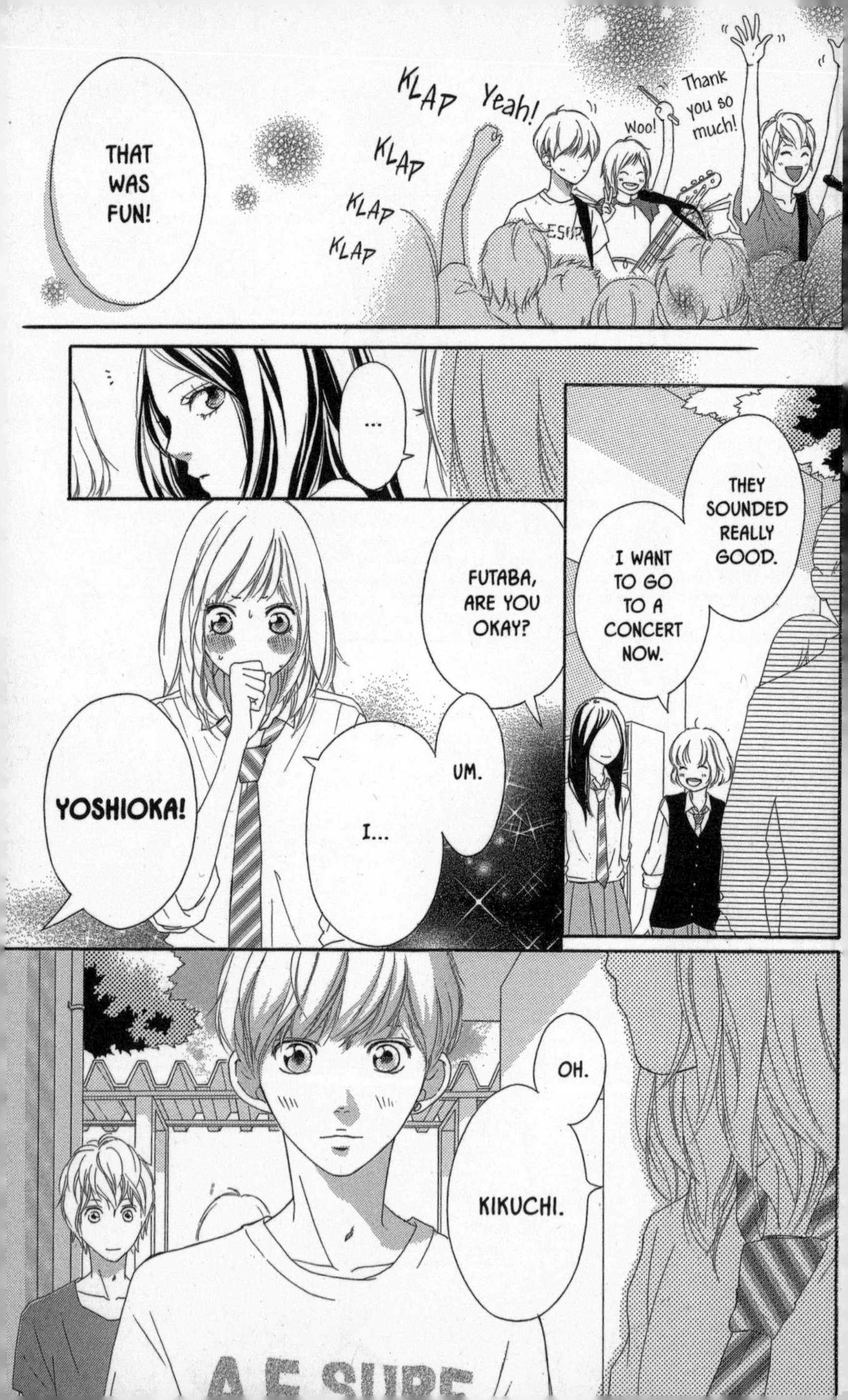
Thank you so much!
Woo!
Yeah!
KLAP
KLAP
KLAP
KLAP
THAT WAS FUN!
THEY SOUNDED REALLY GOOD.
I WANT TO GO TO A CONCERT NOW.
...
FUTABA, ARE YOU OKAY?
UM.
I...
YOSHIOKA!
OH.
KIKUCHI.

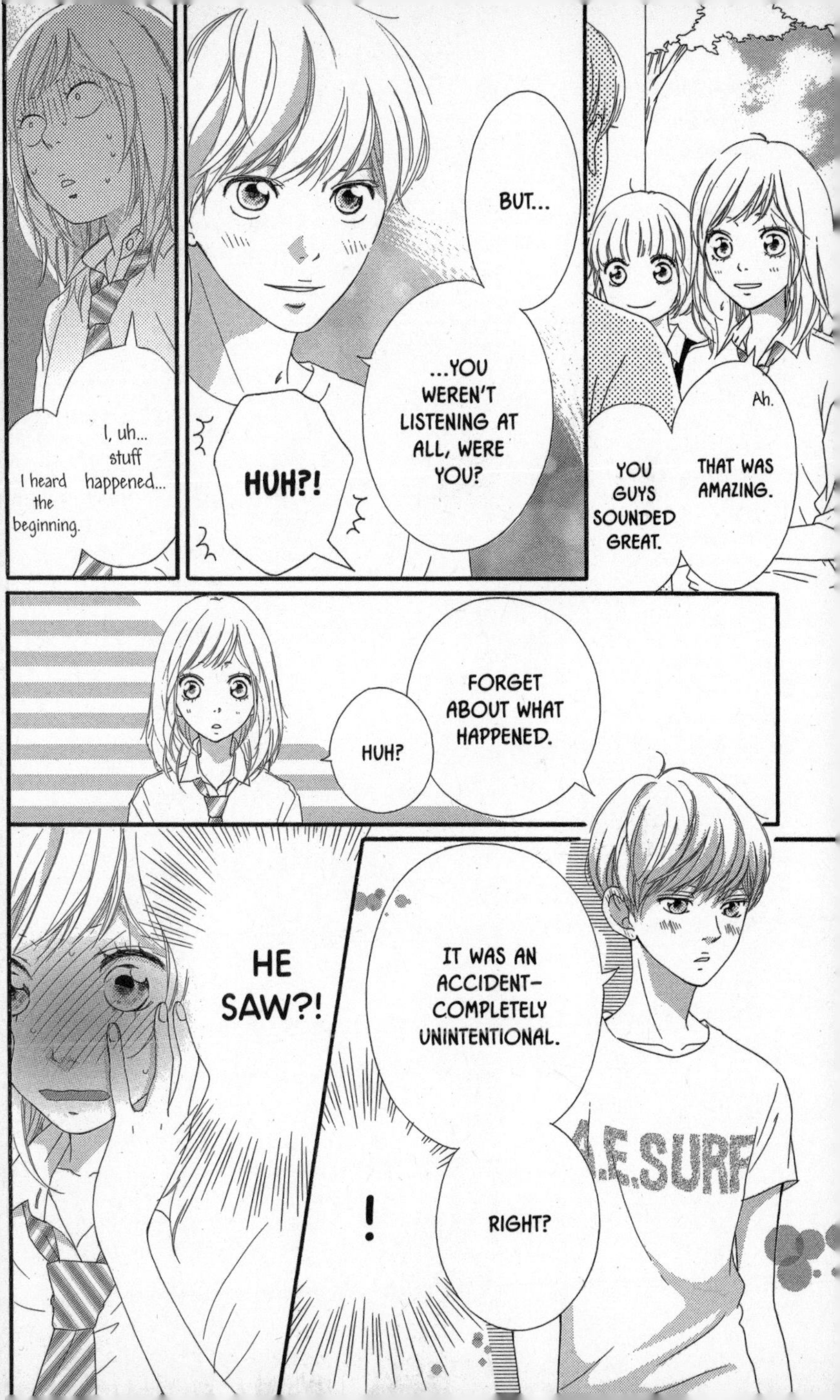
Ah.
THAT WAS AMAZING.
YOU GUYS SOUNDED GREAT.
BUT...
...YOU WEREN'T LISTENING AT ALL, WERE YOU?
HUH?!
I, uh... stuff happened...
I heard the beginning.
FORGET ABOUT WHAT HAPPENED.
HUH?
IT WAS AN ACCIDENT—COMPLETELY UNINTENTIONAL.
RIGHT?
!
HE SAW?!

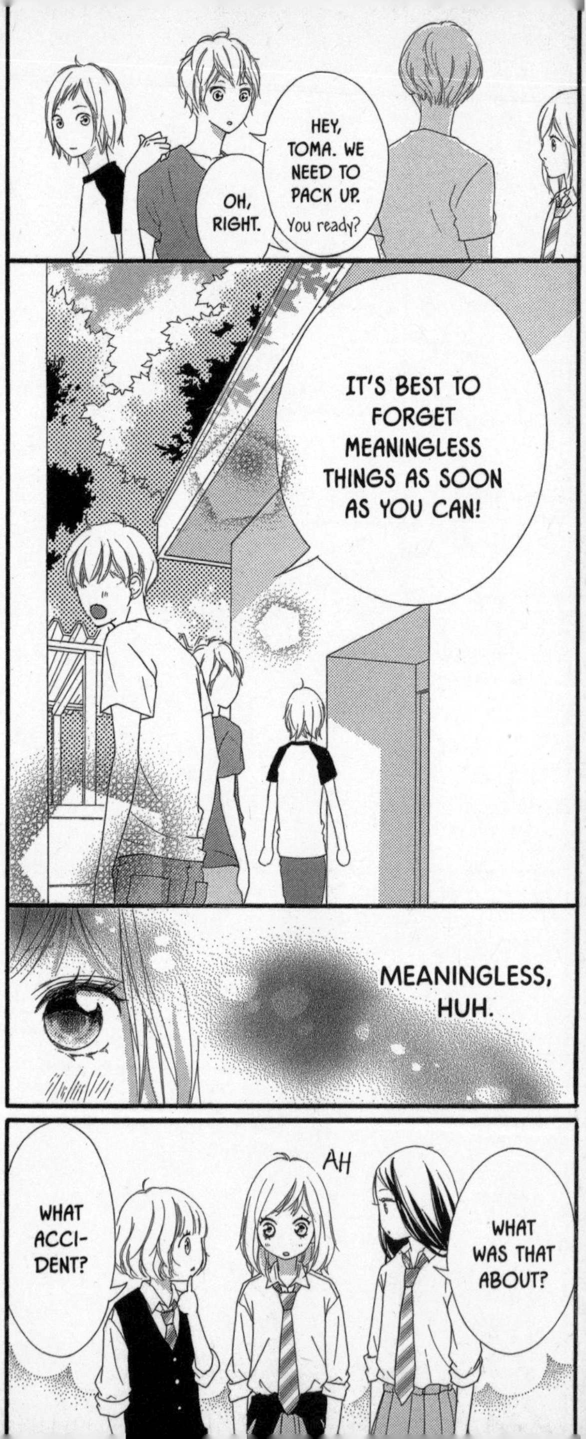
HEY, TOMA. WE NEED TO PACK UP. You ready?
OH, RIGHT.
IT'S BEST TO FORGET MEANINGLESS THINGS AS SOON AS YOU CAN!
MEANINGLESS, HUH.
WHAT WAS THAT ABOUT?
AH
WHAT ACCI-DENT?

The accidental kiss in *Ao Haru Ride* chapter 20... Well, um, it actually happened to me, and the way it happened was almost identical to Futaba's. Our teeth never hit—it was truly an accidental kiss. I was at a music event with a group of friends when a guy tried to tell me something, but our timing was off, and we accidentally kissed. Immediately afterward he talked into my ear, and everything went back to normal. In my case, we didn't have any feelings for each other, so love didn't bloom. It was truly just an accidental kiss. But looking back now, I think I must have been thrown off by it because otherwise I would've laughed after it happened. The fact that I didn't means I must've been pretty flustered. Ha ha.

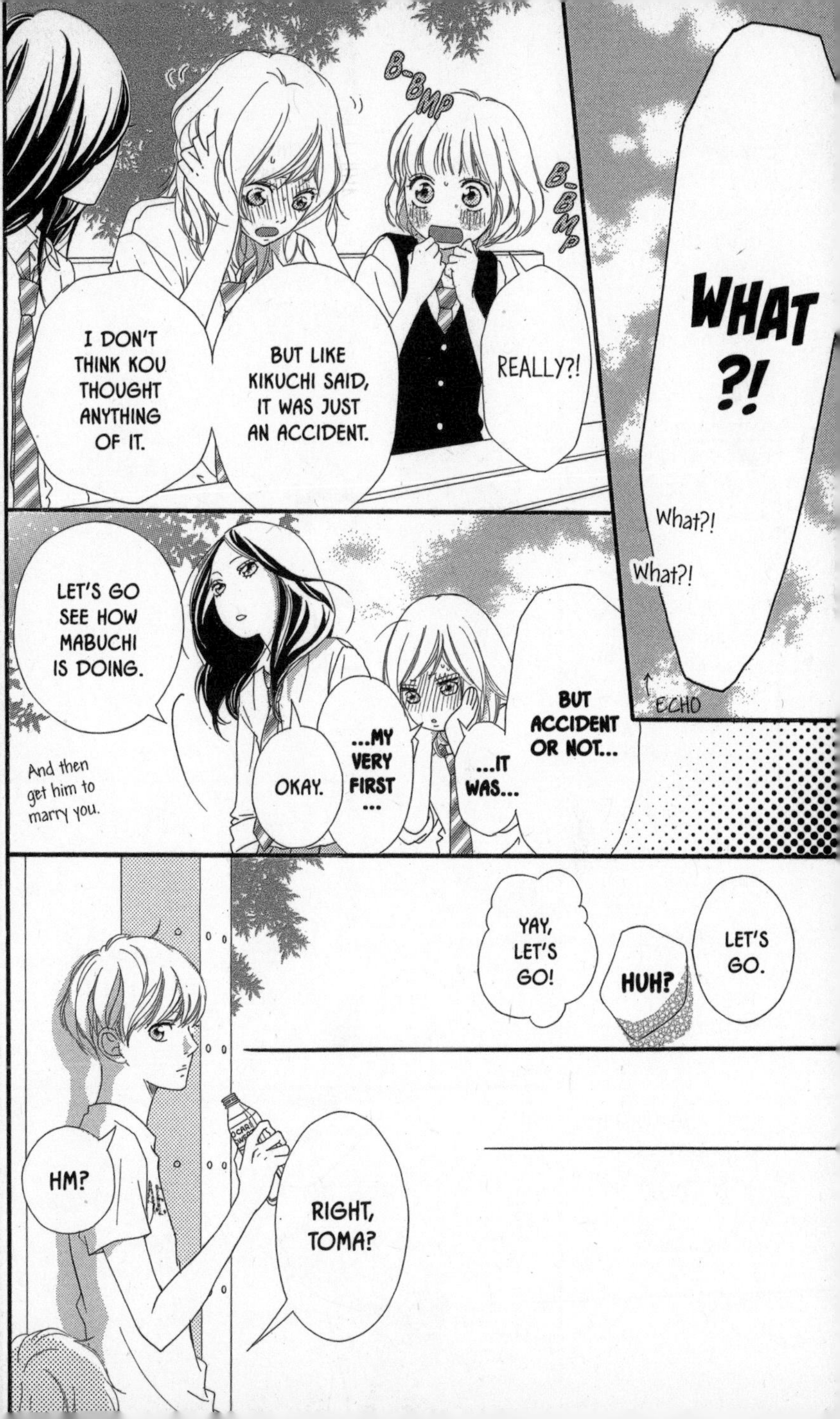
WHAT ?!
What?!
What?!
ECHO
B-BMP
B-BMP
REALLY?!
BUT LIKE KIKUCHI SAID, IT WAS JUST AN ACCIDENT.
I DON'T THINK KOU THOUGHT ANYTHING OF IT.
BUT ACCIDENT OR NOT...
...IT WAS...
...MY VERY FIRST ...
OKAY.
LET'S GO SEE HOW MABUCHI IS DOING.
And then get him to marry you.
LET'S GO.
HUH?
YAY, LET'S GO!
RIGHT, TOMA?
HM?

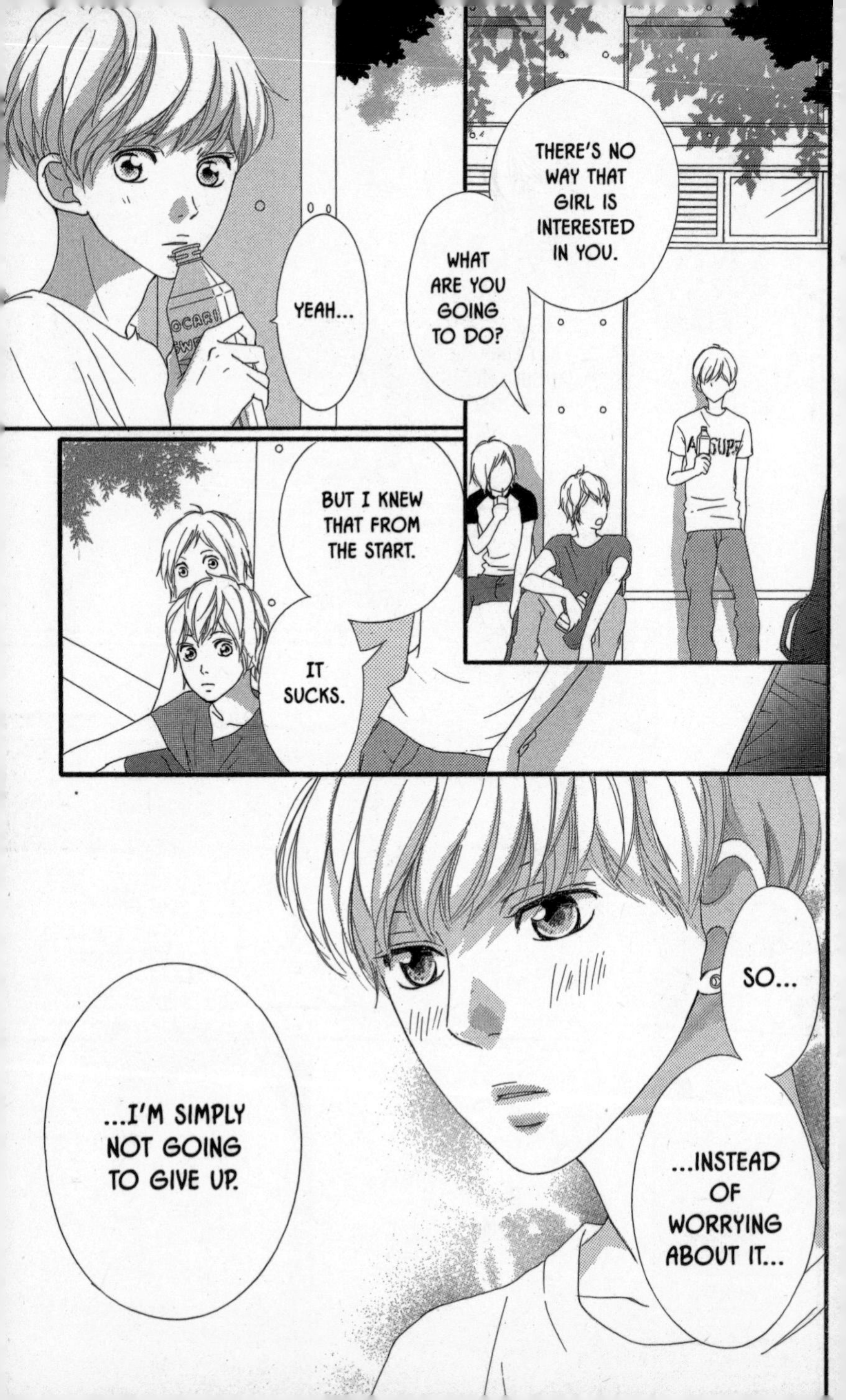
THERE'S NO WAY THAT GIRL IS INTERESTED IN YOU.
WHAT ARE YOU GOING TO DO?
YEAH...
BUT I KNEW THAT FROM THE START.
IT SUCKS.
SO...
...INSTEAD OF WORRYING ABOUT IT...
...I'M SIMPLY NOT GOING TO GIVE UP.

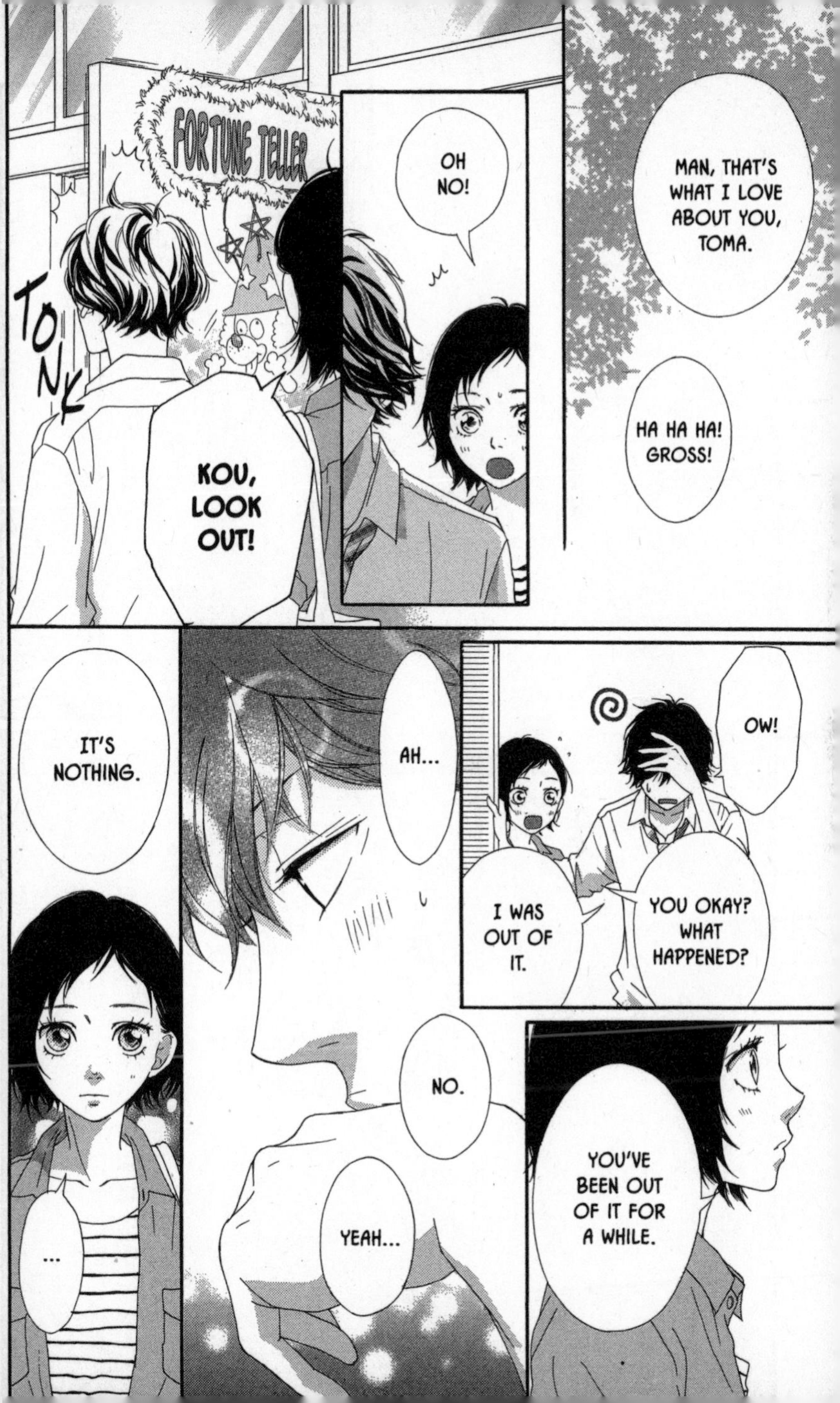
MAN, THAT'S WHAT I LOVE ABOUT YOU, TOMA.
HA HA HA! GROSS!
OH NO!
FORTUNE TELLER
TONK
KOU, LOOK OUT!
OW!
YOU OKAY? WHAT HAPPENED?
I WAS OUT OF IT.
YOU'VE BEEN OUT OF IT FOR A WHILE.
AH...
NO.
YEAH...
IT'S NOTHING.
...

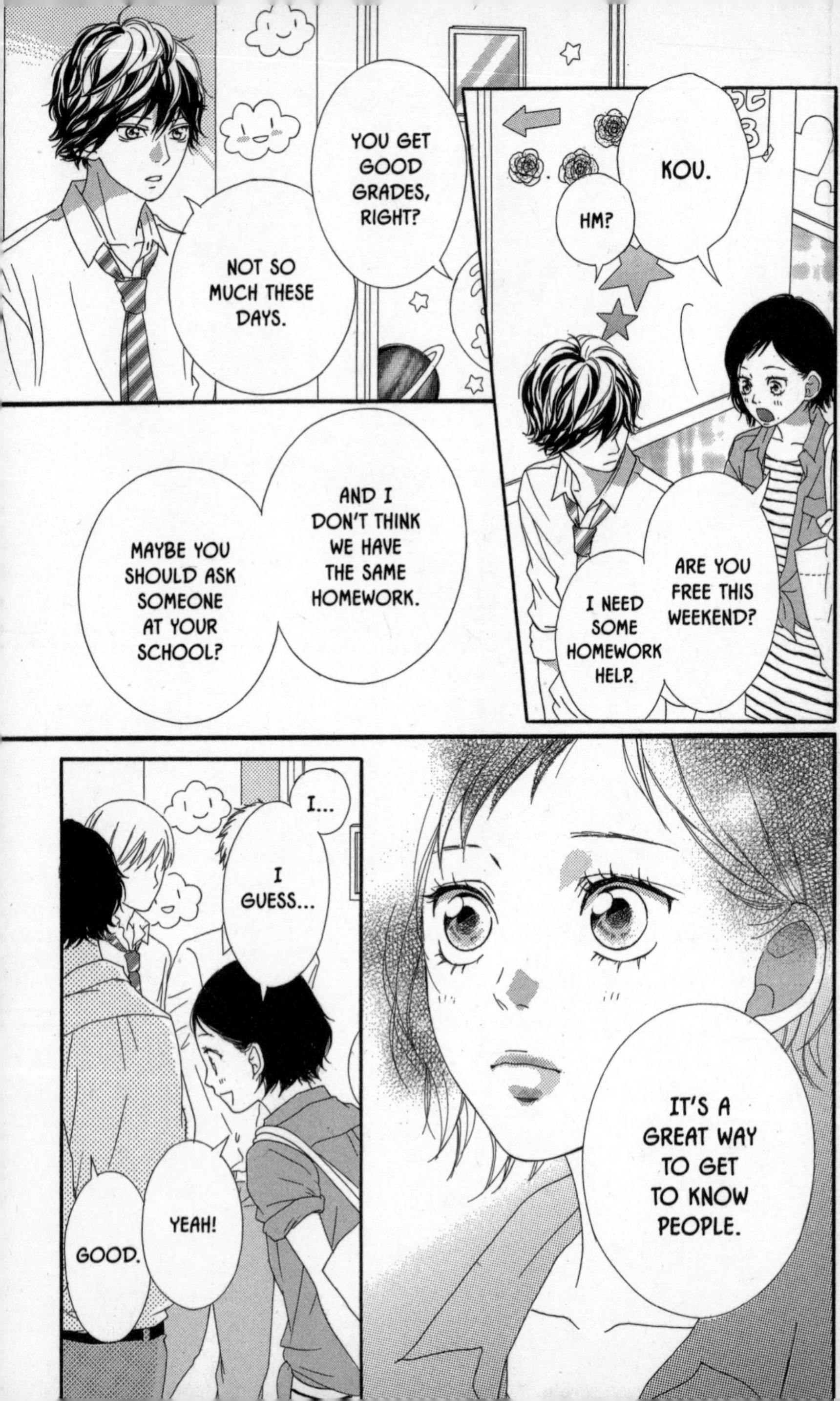
KOU.
HM?
ARE YOU FREE THIS WEEKEND?
I NEED SOME HOMEWORK HELP.
YOU GET GOOD GRADES, RIGHT?
NOT SO MUCH THESE DAYS.
AND I DON'T THINK WE HAVE THE SAME HOMEWORK.
MAYBE YOU SHOULD ASK SOMEONE AT YOUR SCHOOL?
IT'S A GREAT WAY TO GET TO KNOW PEOPLE.
I...
I GUESS...
YEAH!
GOOD.

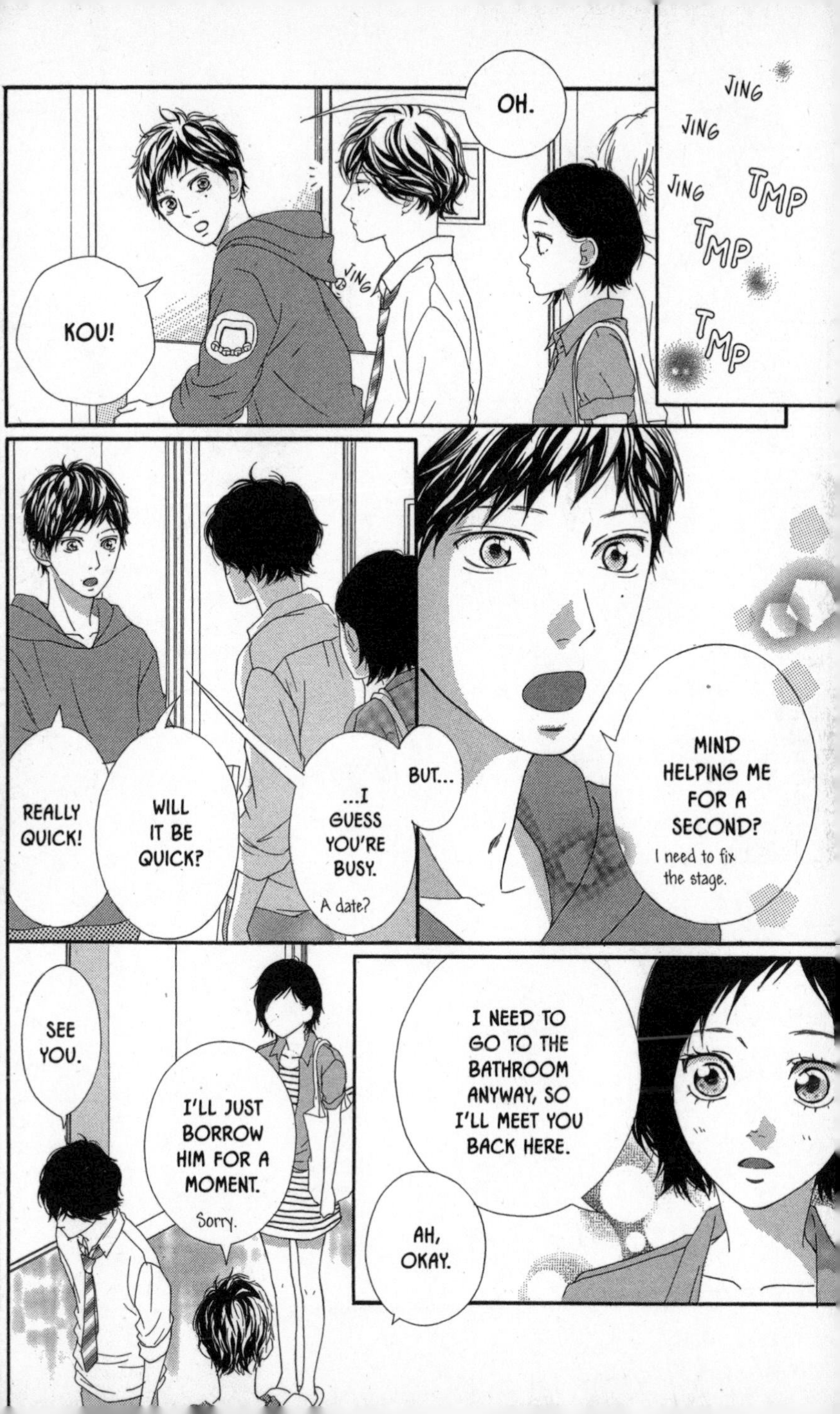
JING
JING
JING
TMP
TMP
TMP
OH.
JING
KOU!
MIND HELPING ME FOR A SECOND?
I need to fix the stage.
BUT...
...I GUESS YOU'RE BUSY.
A date?
WILL IT BE QUICK?
REALLY QUICK!
I NEED TO GO TO THE BATHROOM ANYWAY, SO I'LL MEET YOU BACK HERE.
AH, OKAY.
I'LL JUST BORROW HIM FOR A MOMENT.
Sorry.
SEE YOU.

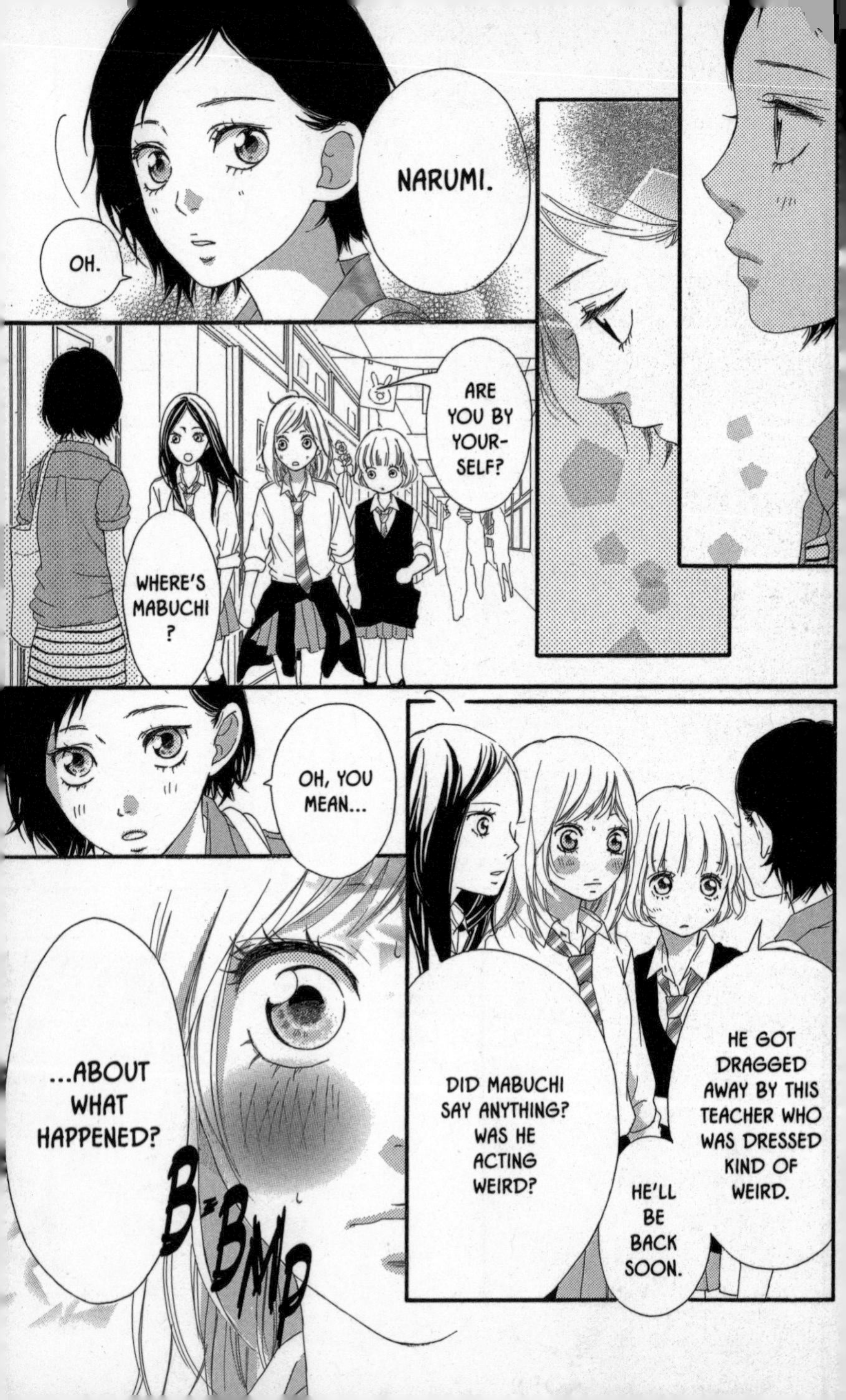
NARUMI.
OH.
ARE YOU BY YOURSELF?
WHERE'S MABUCHI?
HE GOT DRAGGED AWAY BY THIS TEACHER WHO WAS DRESSED KIND OF WEIRD.
HE'LL BE BACK SOON.
DID MABUCHI SAY ANYTHING? WAS HE ACTING WEIRD?
OH, YOU MEAN...
...ABOUT WHAT HAPPENED?
B-BMP

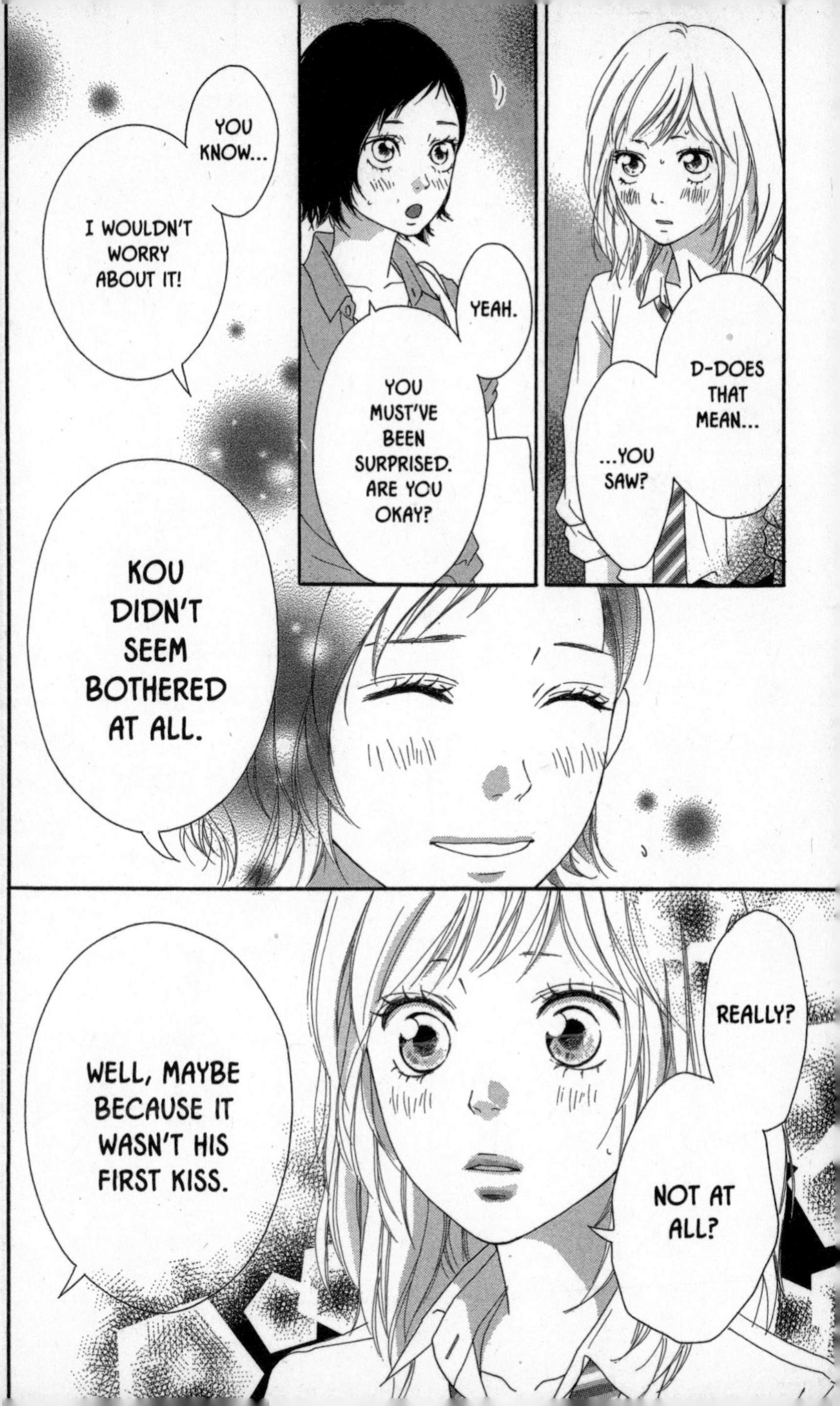
D-DOES THAT MEAN...
...YOU SAW?
YEAH.
YOU MUST'VE BEEN SURPRISED. ARE YOU OKAY?
YOU KNOW...
I WOULDN'T WORRY ABOUT IT!
KOU DIDN'T SEEM BOTHERED AT ALL.
REALLY?
NOT AT ALL?
WELL, MAYBE BECAUSE IT WASN'T HIS FIRST KISS.

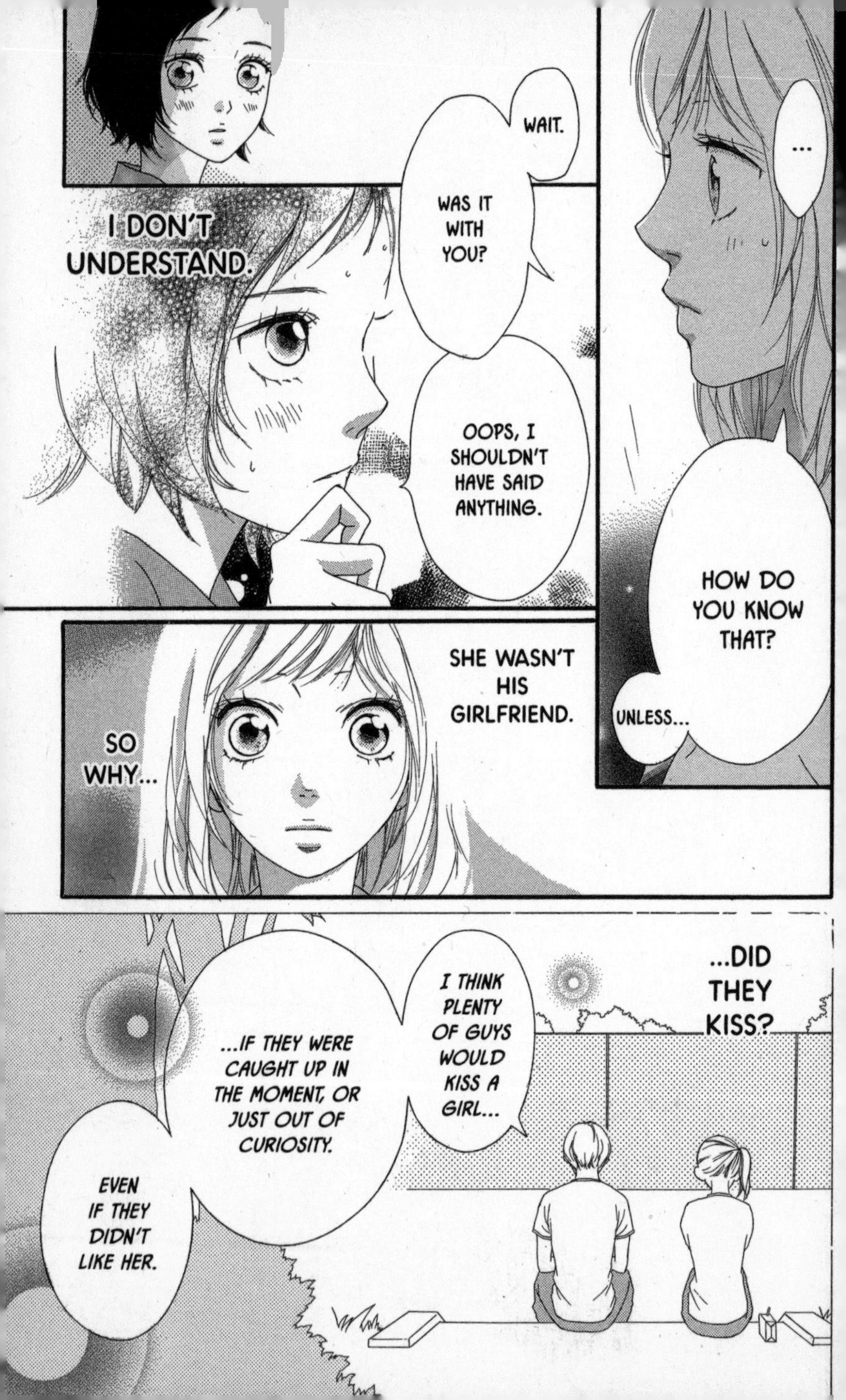
...
HOW DO YOU KNOW THAT?
UNLESS...
WAIT.
WAS IT WITH YOU?
OOPS, I SHOULDN'T HAVE SAID ANYTHING.
I DON'T UNDERSTAND.
SHE WASN'T HIS GIRLFRIEND.
SO WHY...
...DID THEY KISS?
I THINK PLENTY OF GUYS WOULD KISS A GIRL...
...IF THEY WERE CAUGHT UP IN THE MOMENT, OR JUST OUT OF CURIOSITY.
EVEN IF THEY DIDN'T LIKE HER.

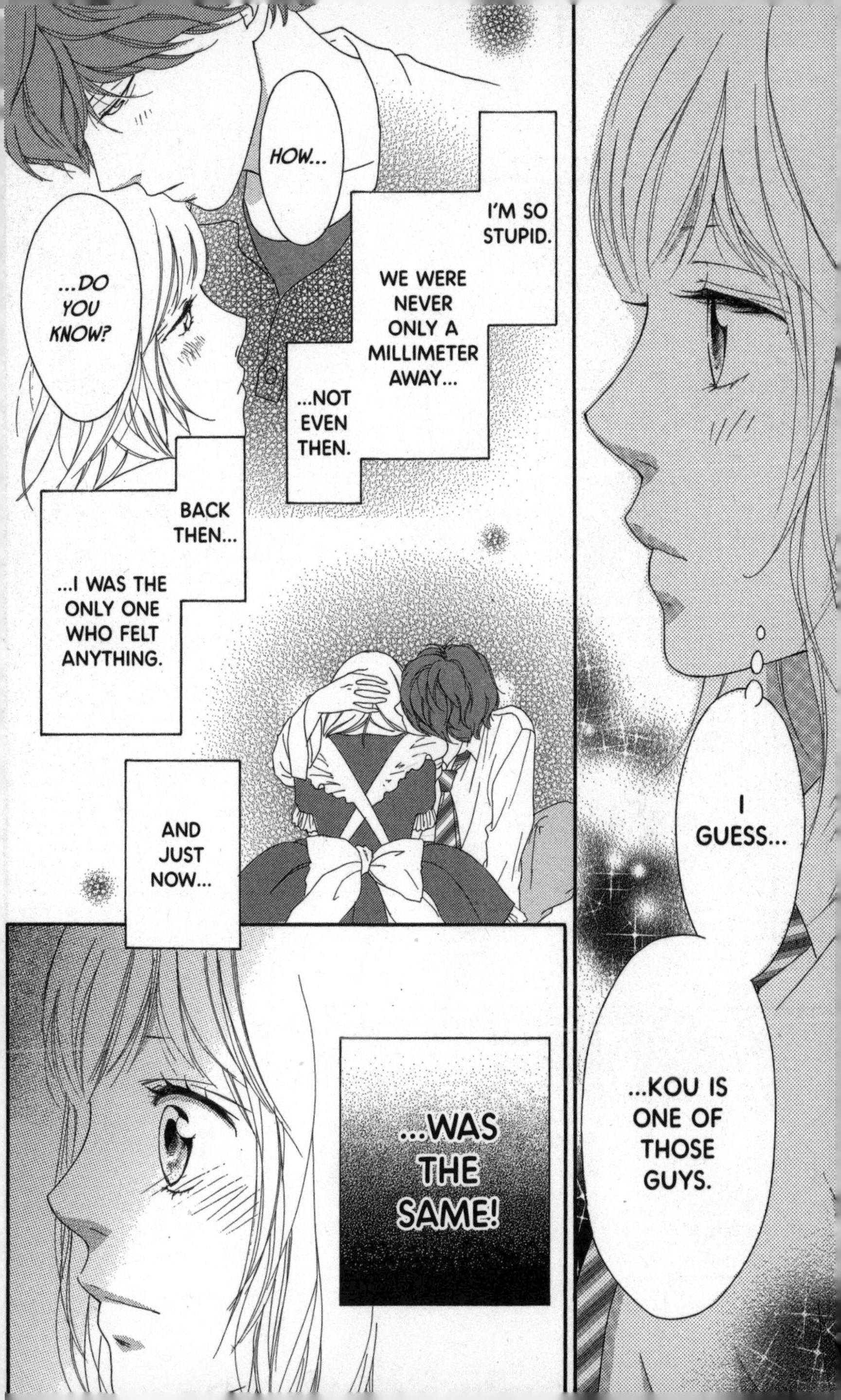
I GUESS...
...KOU IS ONE OF THOSE GUYS.
HOW...
...DO YOU KNOW?
I'M SO STUPID.
WE WERE NEVER ONLY A MILLIMETER AWAY...
...NOT EVEN THEN.
BACK THEN...
...I WAS THE ONLY ONE WHO FELT ANYTHING.
AND JUST NOW...
...WAS THE SAME!

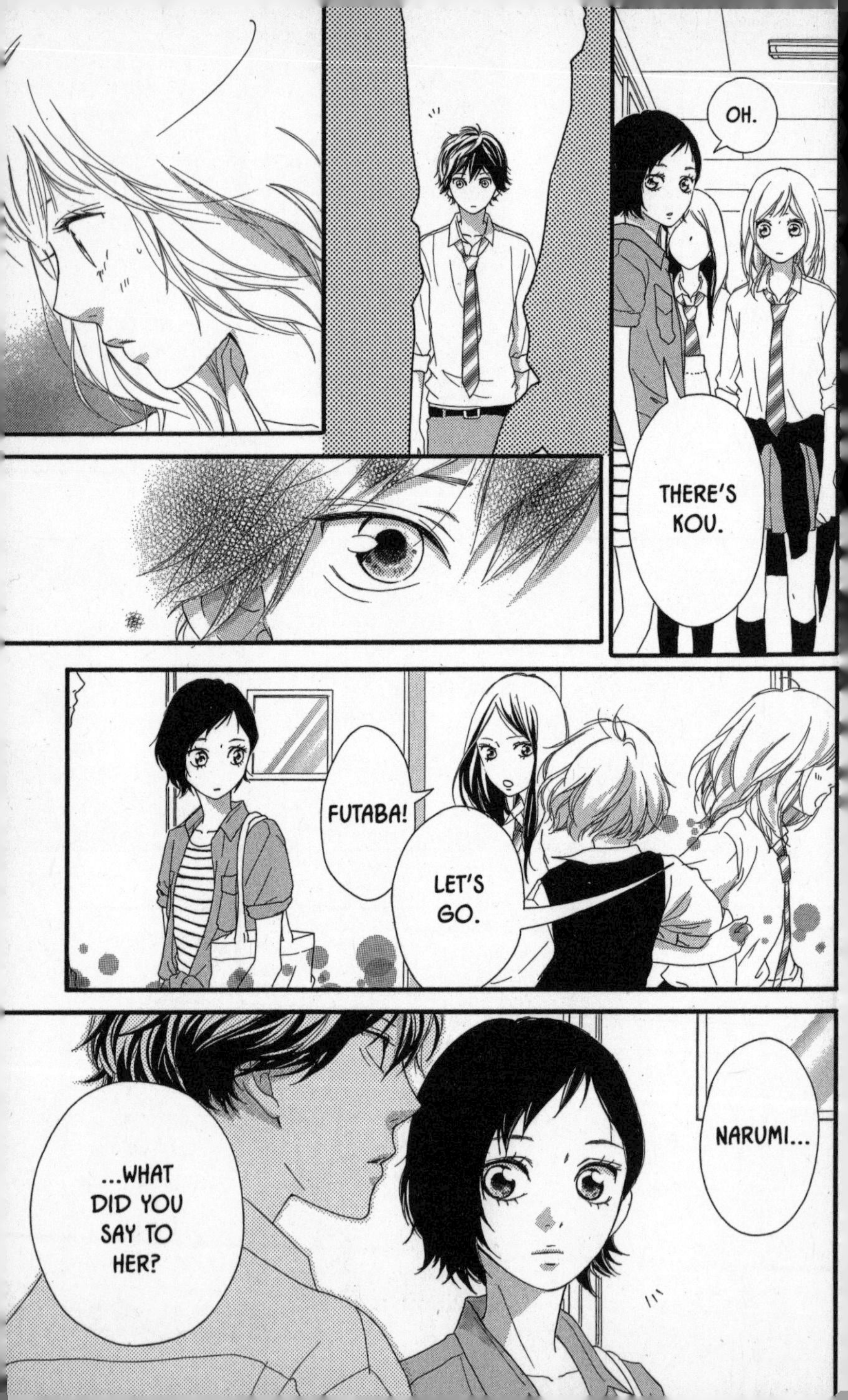
OH.
THERE'S KOU.
FUTABA!
LET'S GO.
NARUMI...
...WHAT DID YOU SAY TO HER?

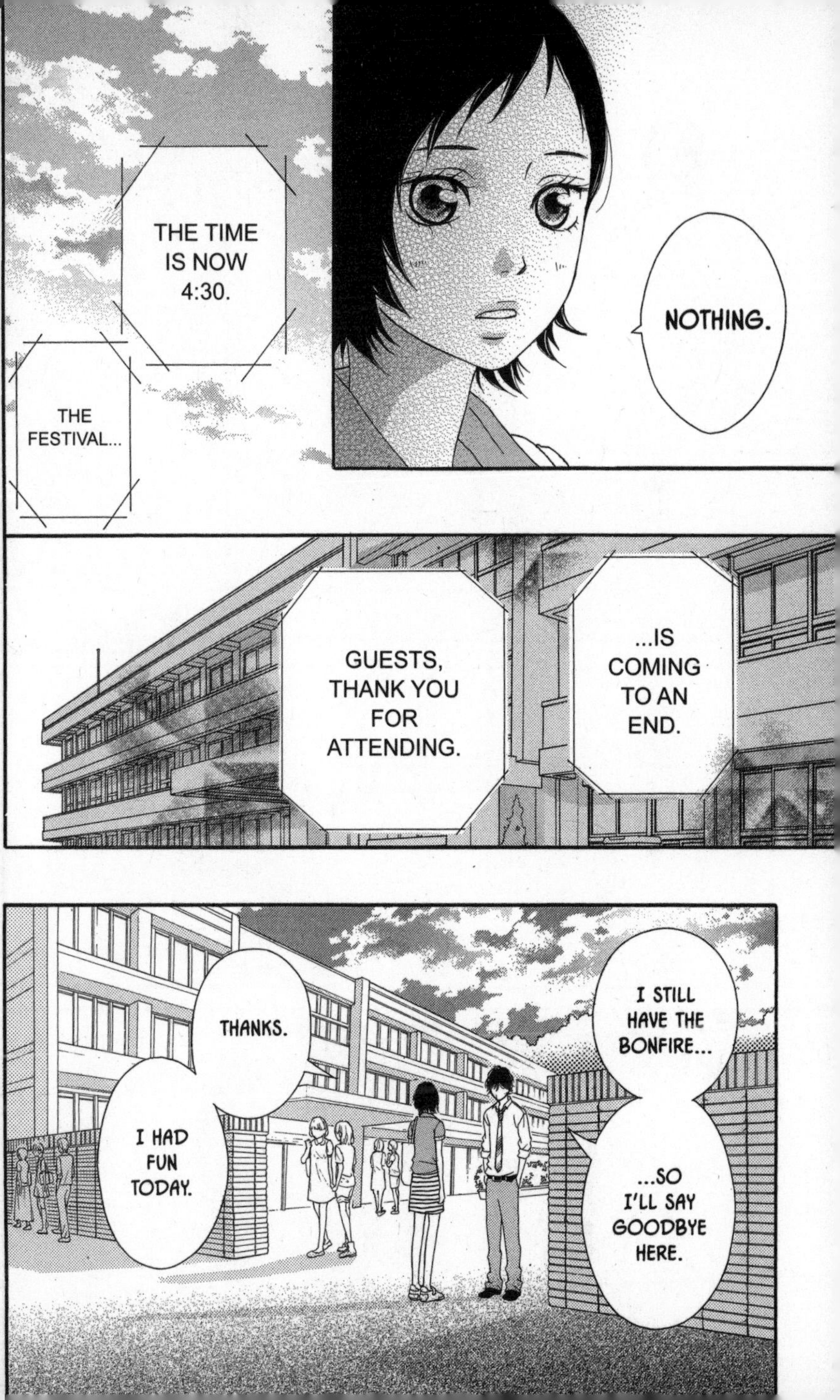
NOTHING.
THE TIME IS NOW 4:30.
THE FESTIVAL...
...IS COMING TO AN END.
GUESTS, THANK YOU FOR ATTENDING.
I STILL HAVE THE BONFIRE...
...SO I'LL SAY GOODBYE HERE.
THANKS.
I HAD FUN TODAY.

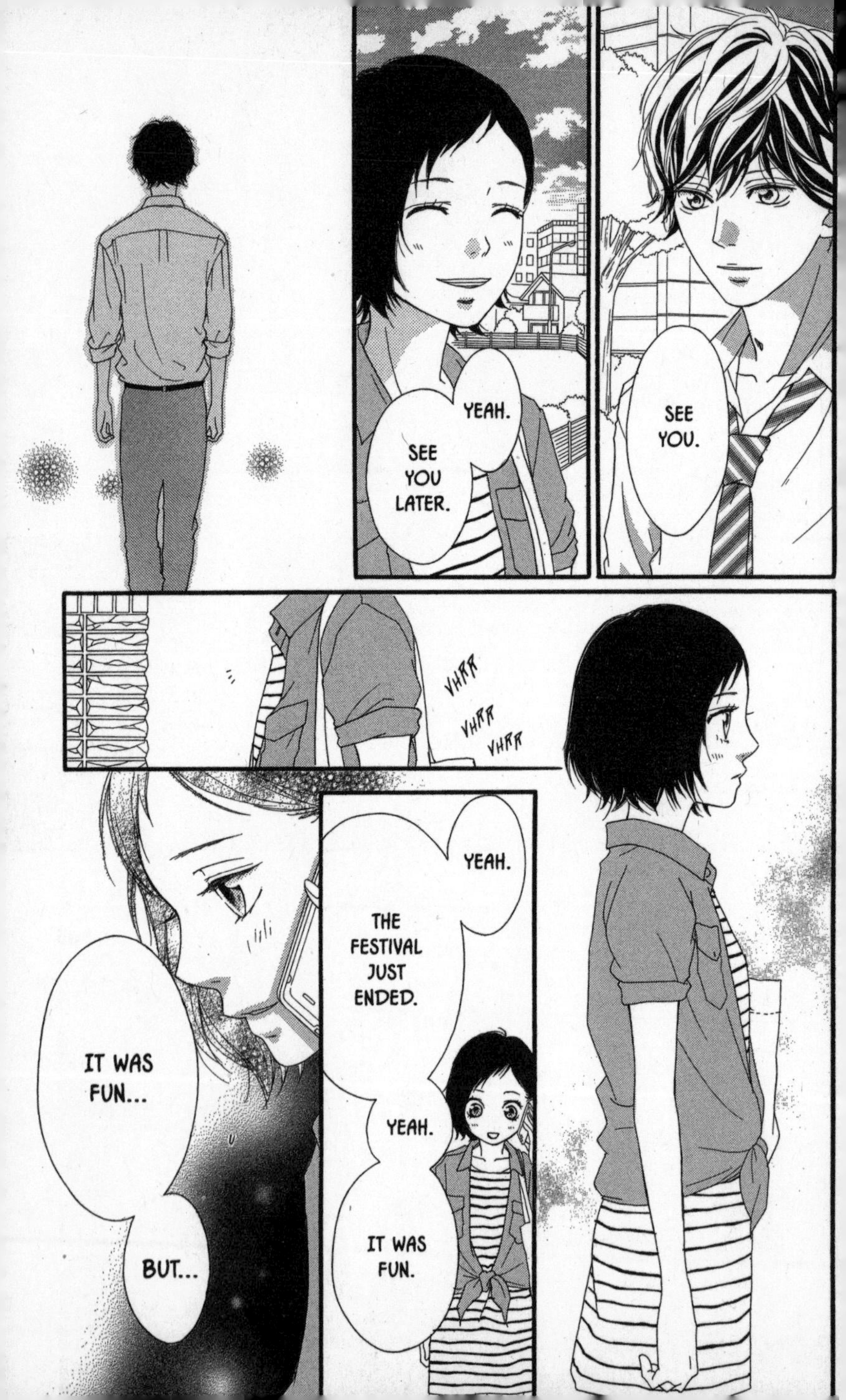
SEE YOU.
YEAH.
SEE YOU LATER.
VHRR
VHRR
VHRR
YEAH.
THE FESTIVAL JUST ENDED.
YEAH.
IT WAS FUN.
IT WAS FUN...
BUT...

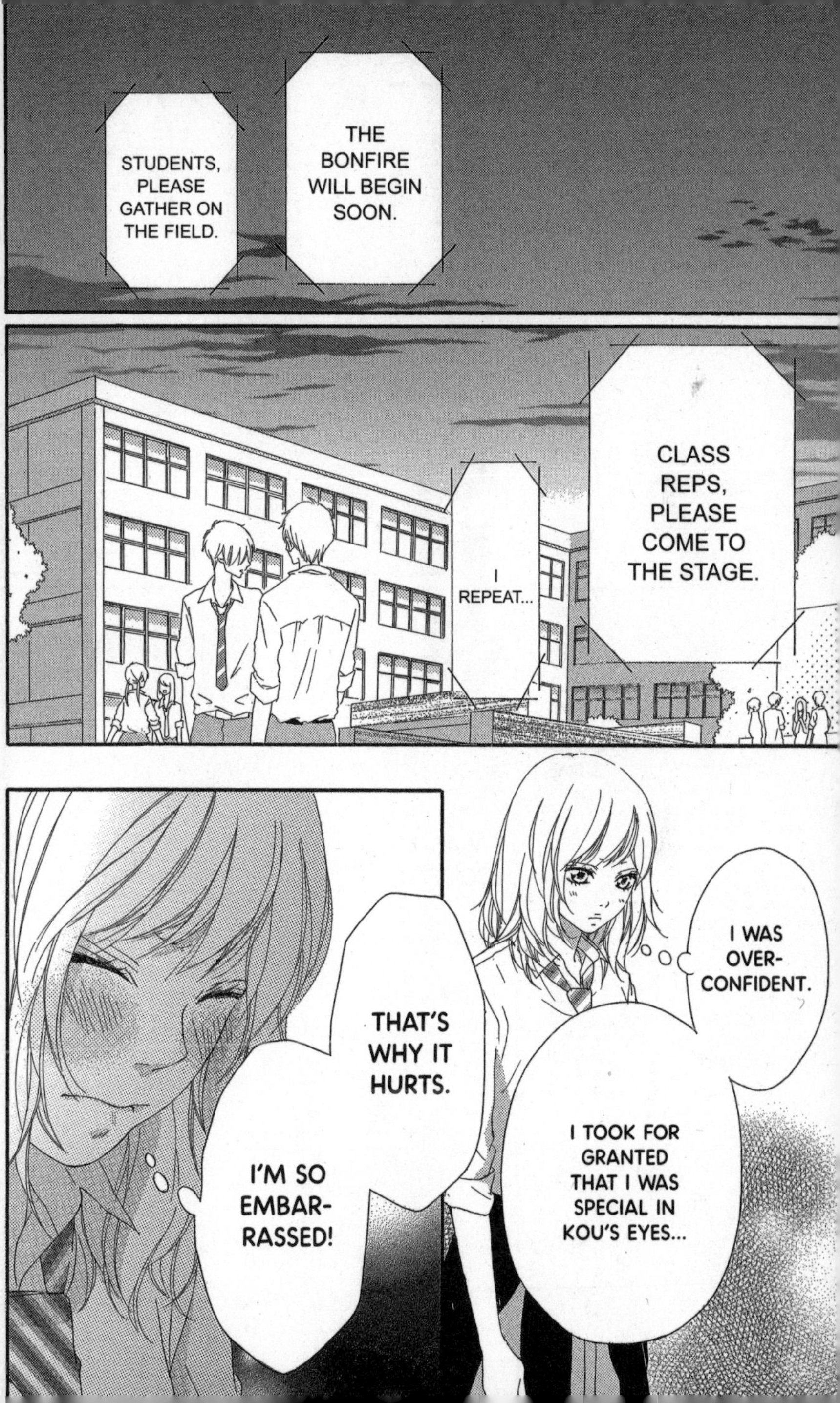
THE BONFIRE WILL BEGIN SOON.
STUDENTS, PLEASE GATHER ON THE FIELD.
CLASS REPS, PLEASE COME TO THE STAGE.
I REPEAT...
I WAS OVER-CONFIDENT.
I TOOK FOR GRANTED THAT I WAS SPECIAL IN KOU'S EYES...
THAT'S WHY IT HURTS.
I'M SO EMBAR-RASSED!

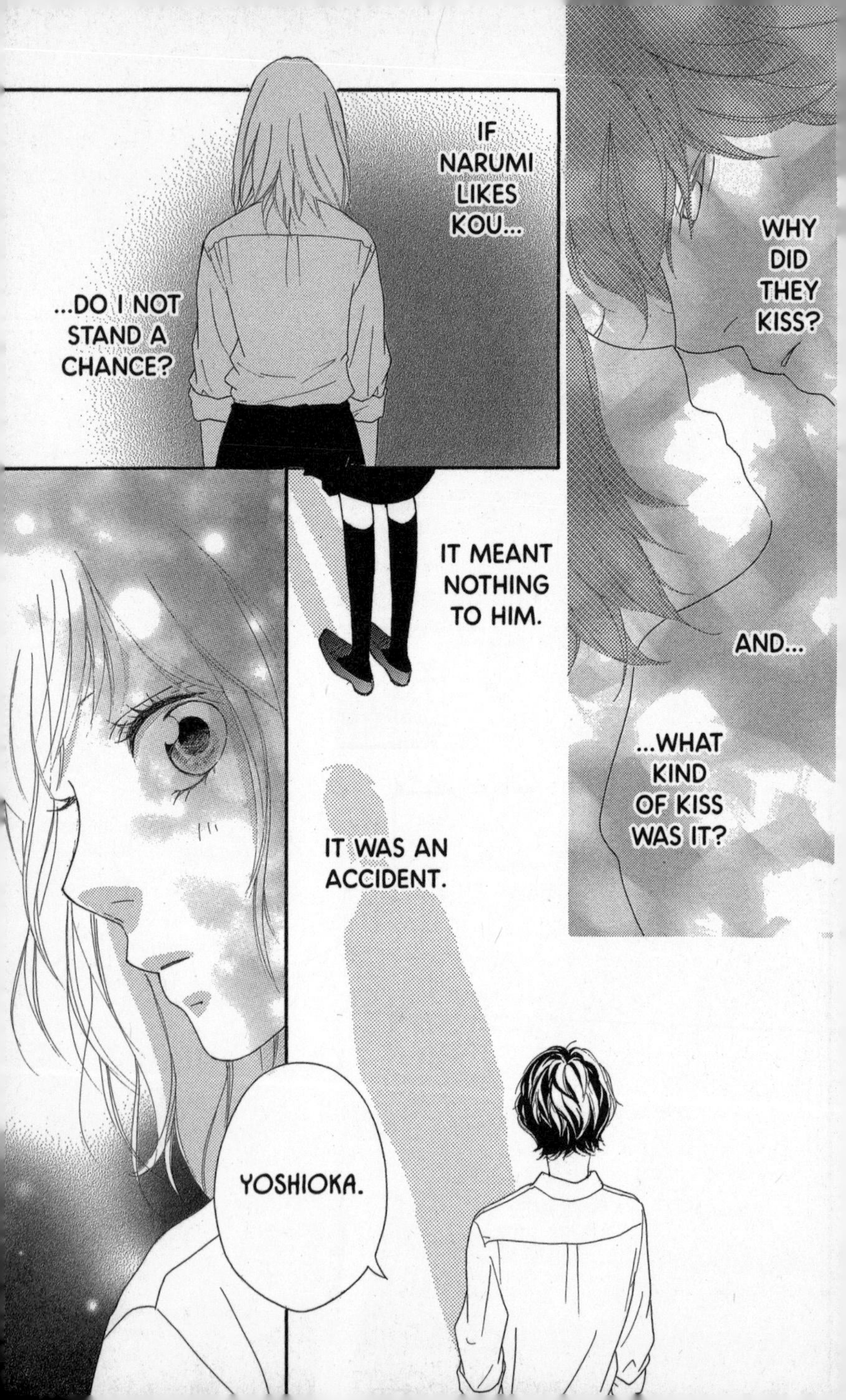
WHY DID THEY KISS?
AND...
...WHAT KIND OF KISS WAS IT?
IF NARUMI LIKES KOU...
...DO I NOT STAND A CHANCE?
IT MEANT NOTHING TO HIM.
IT WAS AN ACCIDENT.
YOSHIOKA.

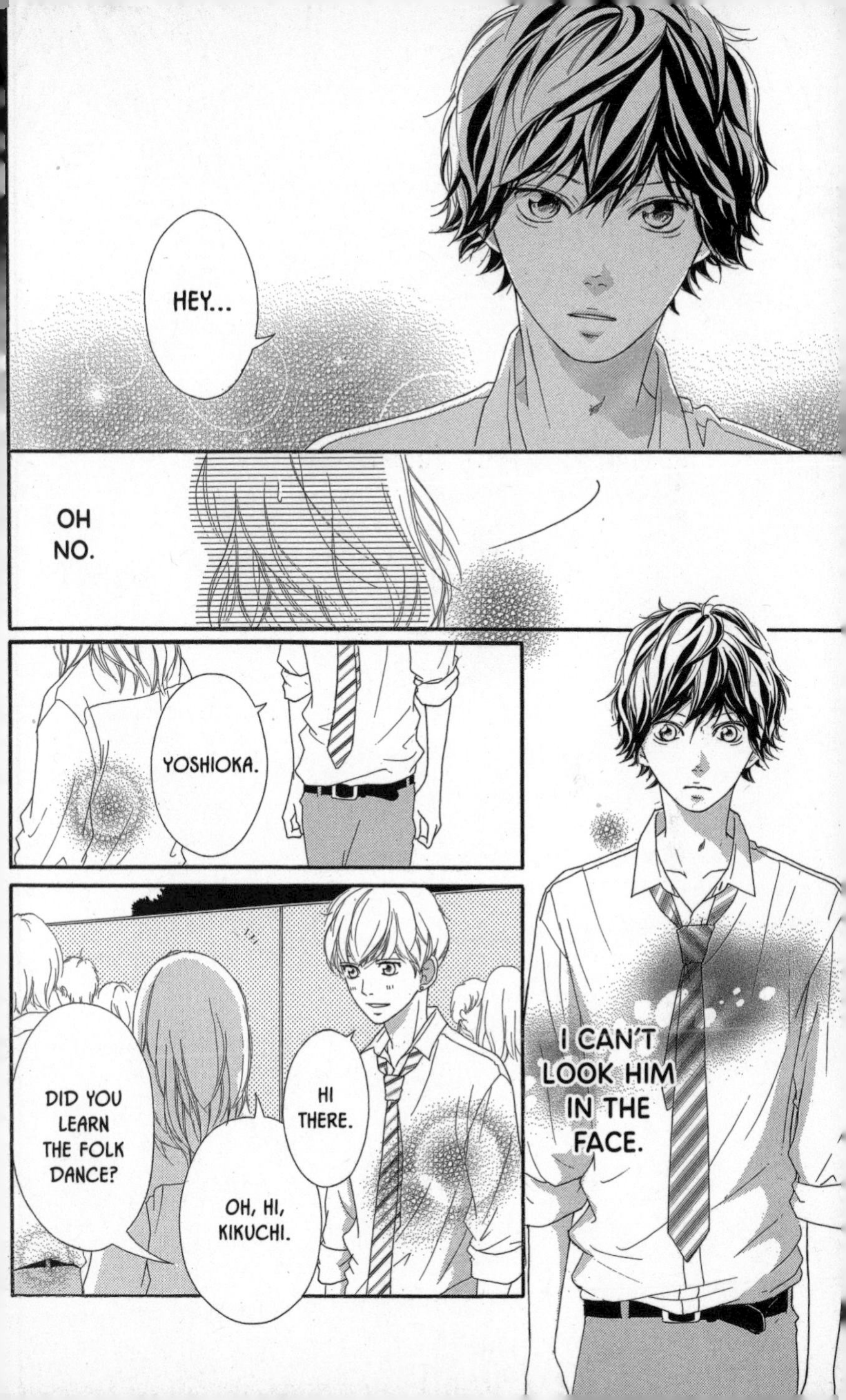
HEY...
OH NO.
I CAN'T LOOK HIM IN THE FACE.
YOSHIOKA.
HI THERE.
OH, HI, KIKUCHI.
DID YOU LEARN THE FOLK DANCE?

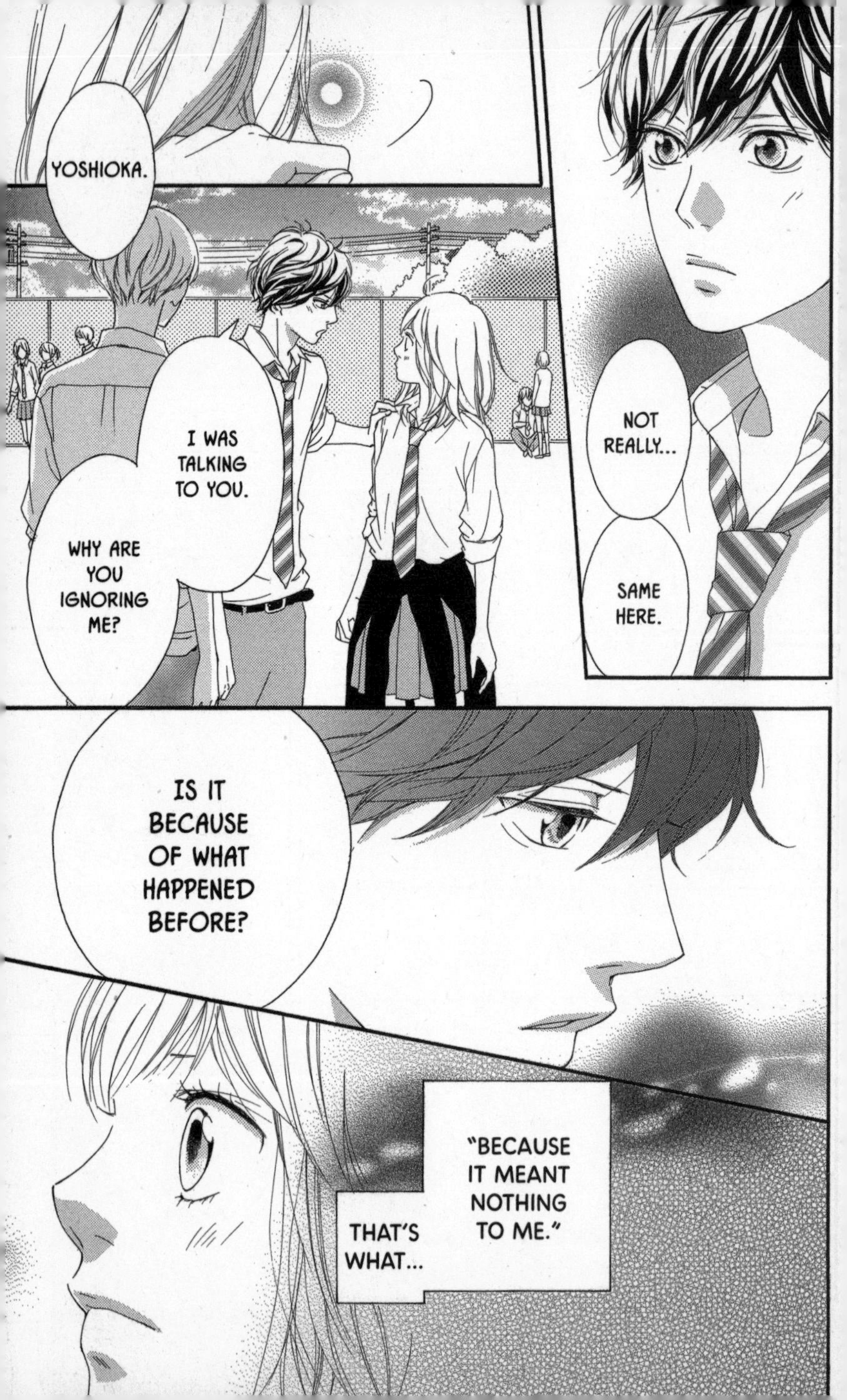
NOT REALLY...
SAME HERE.
YOSHIOKA.
I WAS TALKING TO YOU.
WHY ARE YOU IGNORING ME?
IS IT BECAUSE OF WHAT HAPPENED BEFORE?
"BECAUSE IT MEANT NOTHING TO ME."
THAT'S WHAT...

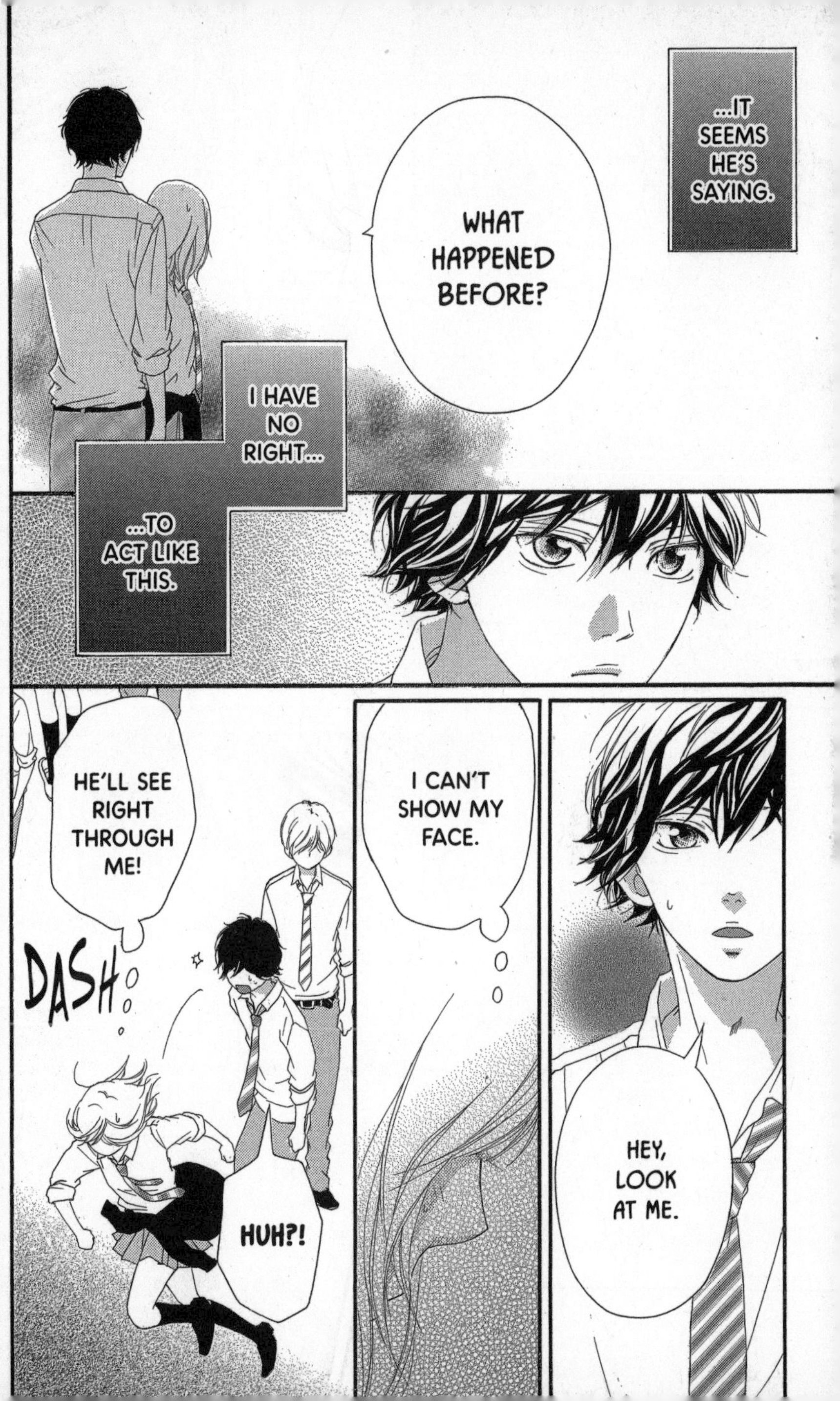
...IT SEEMS HE'S SAYING.
WHAT HAPPENED BEFORE?
I HAVE NO RIGHT...
...TO ACT LIKE THIS.
HEY, LOOK AT ME.
I CAN'T SHOW MY FACE.
HE'LL SEE RIGHT THROUGH ME!
DASH
HUH?!

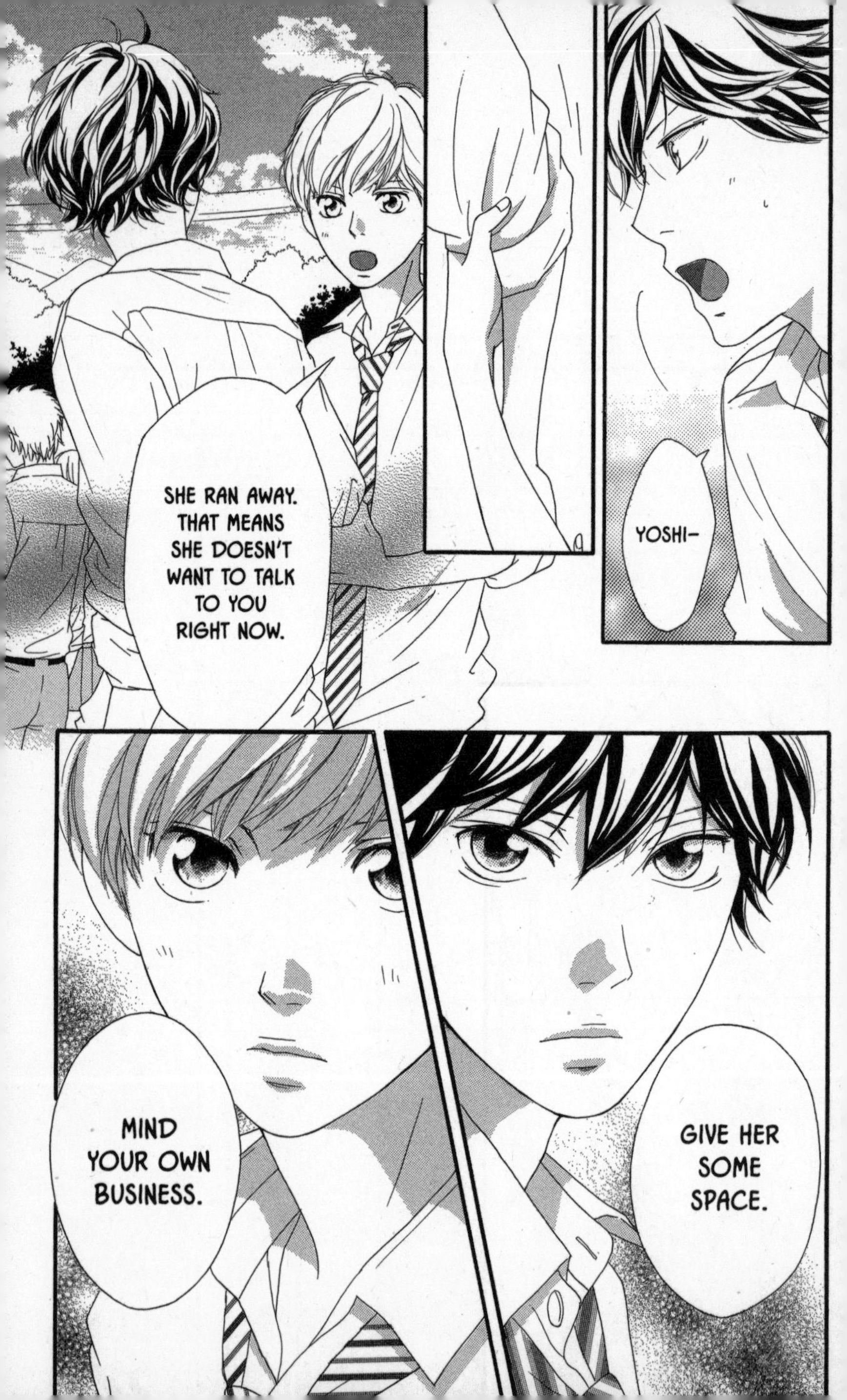
YOSHI-
SHE RAN AWAY. THAT MEANS SHE DOESN'T WANT TO TALK TO YOU RIGHT NOW.
GIVE HER SOME SPACE.
MIND YOUR OWN BUSINESS.

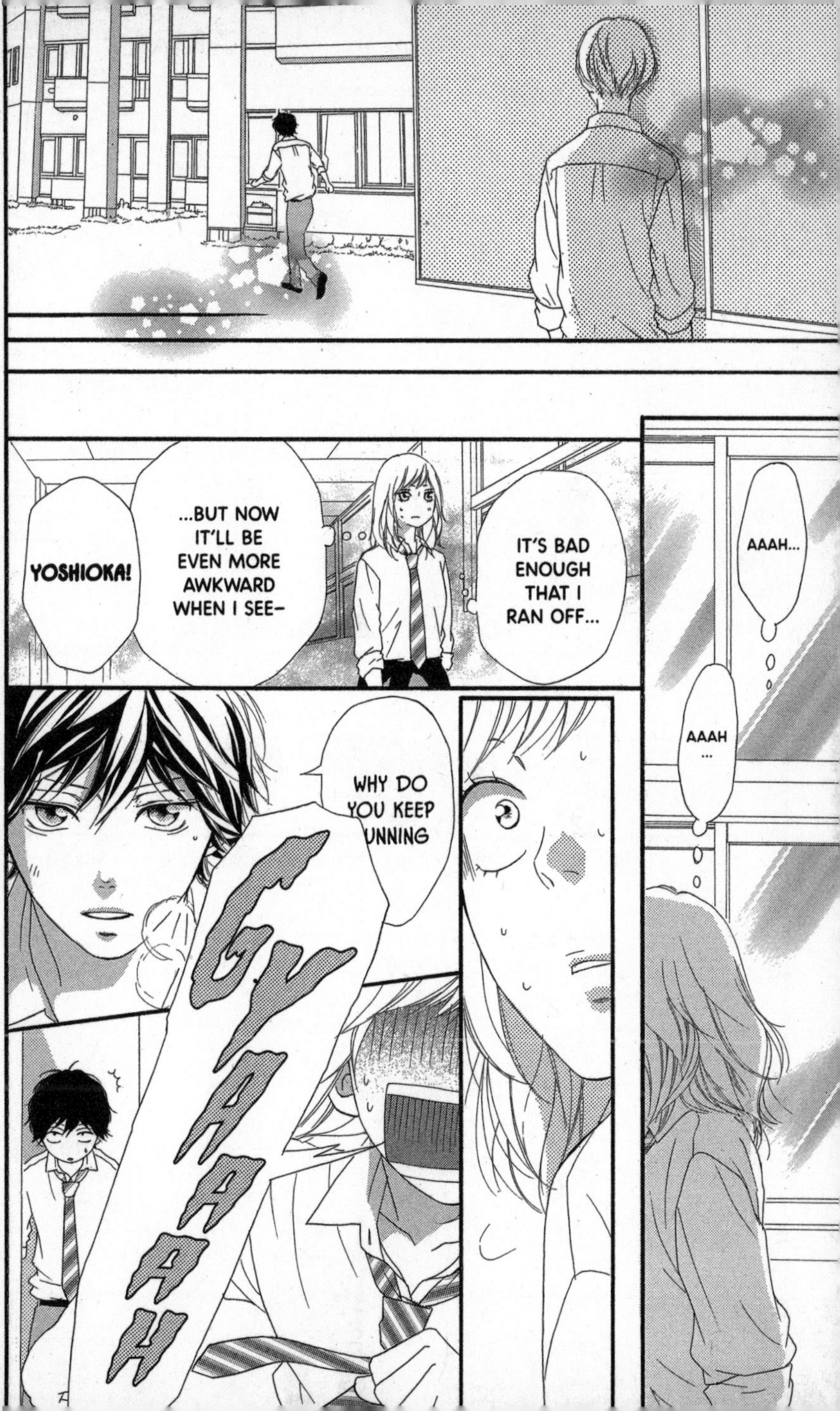
AAAH...
AAAH ...
IT'S BAD ENOUGH THAT I RAN OFF...
...BUT NOW IT'LL BE EVEN MORE AWKWARD WHEN I SEE–
YOSHIOKA!
WHY DO YOU KEEP UNNING
GYAAAAAH

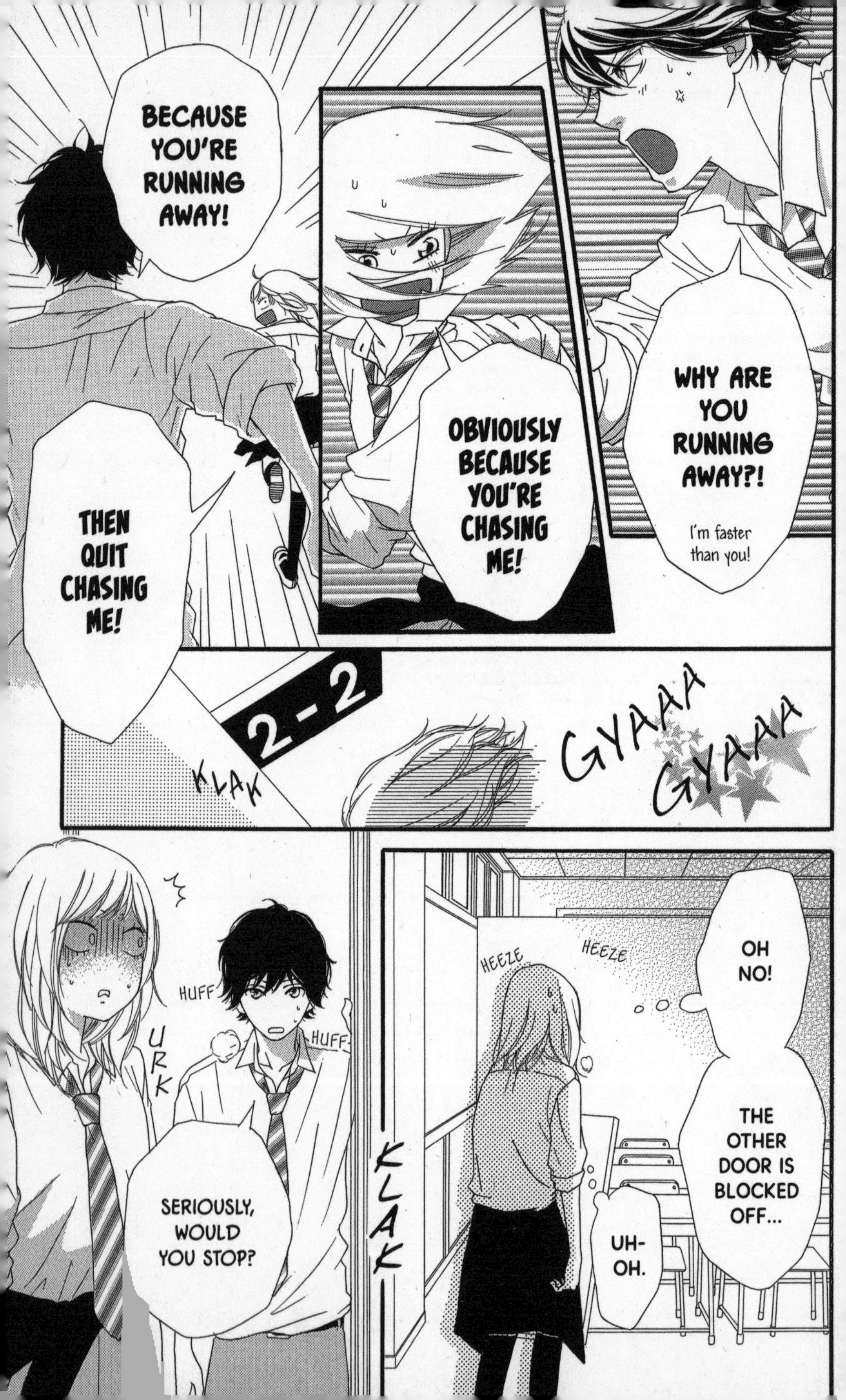
WHY ARE YOU RUNNING AWAY?!
I'm faster than you!
OBVIOUSLY BECAUSE YOU'RE CHASING ME!
BECAUSE YOU'RE RUNNING AWAY!
THEN QUIT CHASING ME!
GYAAA
GYAAA
2-2
KLAK
OH NO!
THE OTHER DOOR IS BLOCKED OFF...
HEEZE
HEEZE
UH-OH.
KLAK
HUFF
HUFF
URK
SERIOUSLY, WOULD YOU STOP?

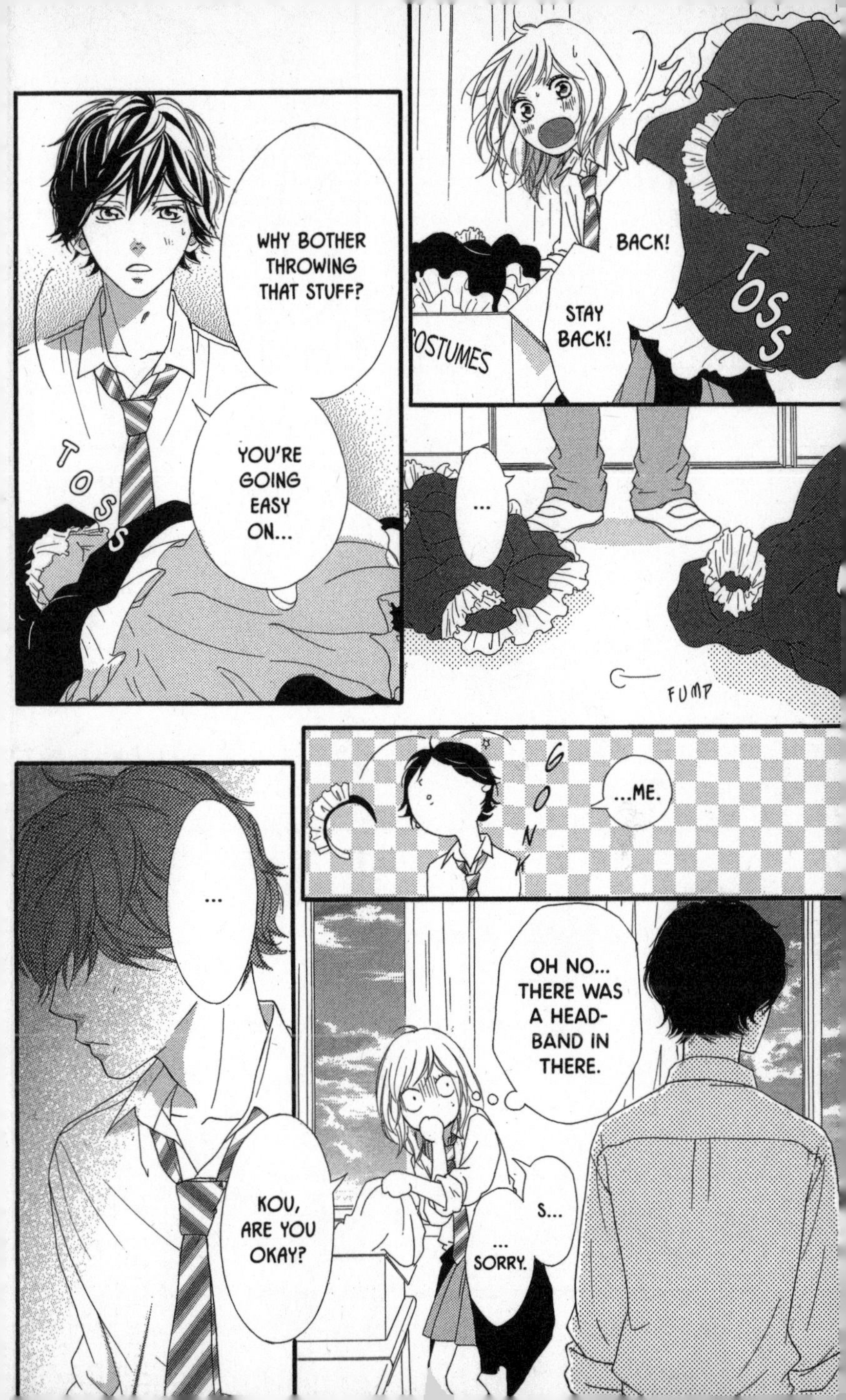
BACK!
STAY BACK!
TOSS
OSTUMES
...
FUMP
WHY BOTHER THROWING THAT STUFF?
TOSS
YOU'RE GOING EASY ON...
GONK
...ME.
OH NO... THERE WAS A HEAD-BAND IN THERE.
S...
... SORRY.
...
KOU, ARE YOU OKAY?

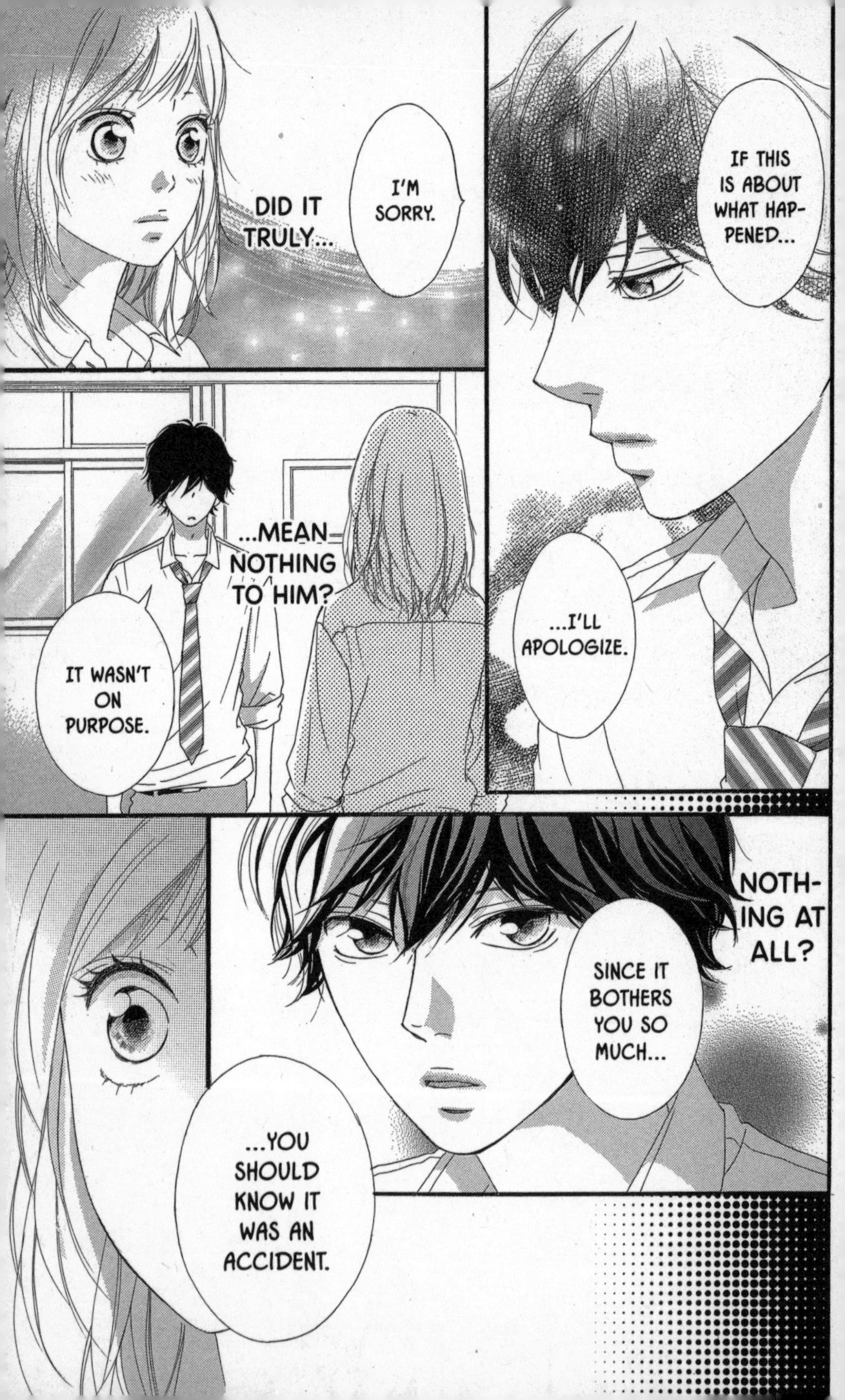
IF THIS IS ABOUT WHAT HAP-PENED...
...I'LL APOLOGIZE.
I'M SORRY.
DID IT TRULY...
...MEAN NOTHING TO HIM?
IT WASN'T ON PURPOSE.
NOTH-ING AT ALL?
SINCE IT BOTHERS YOU SO MUCH...
...YOU SHOULD KNOW IT WAS AN ACCIDENT.

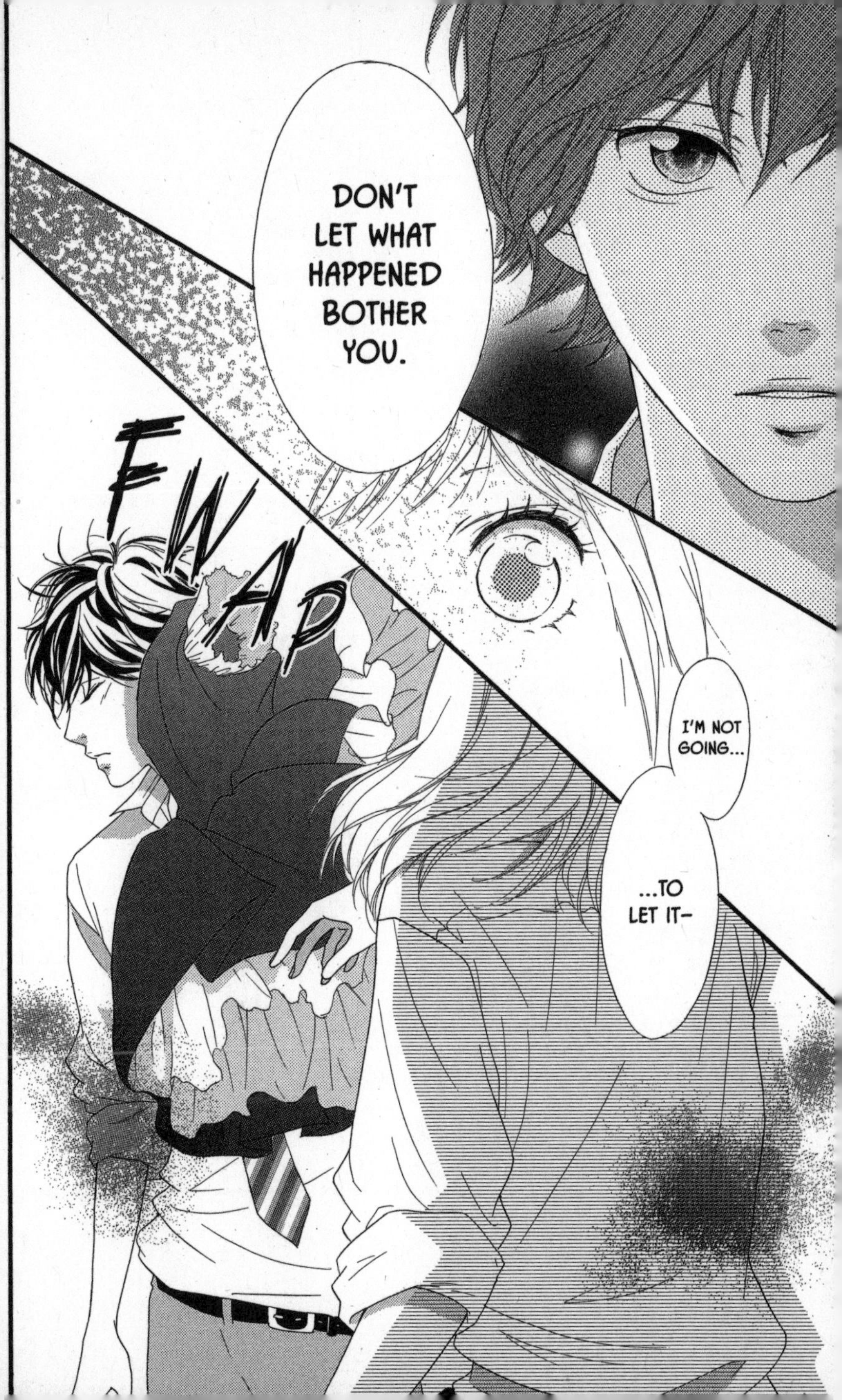
DON'T LET WHAT HAPPENED BOTHER YOU.
I'M NOT GOING...
...TO LET IT–
FWAP

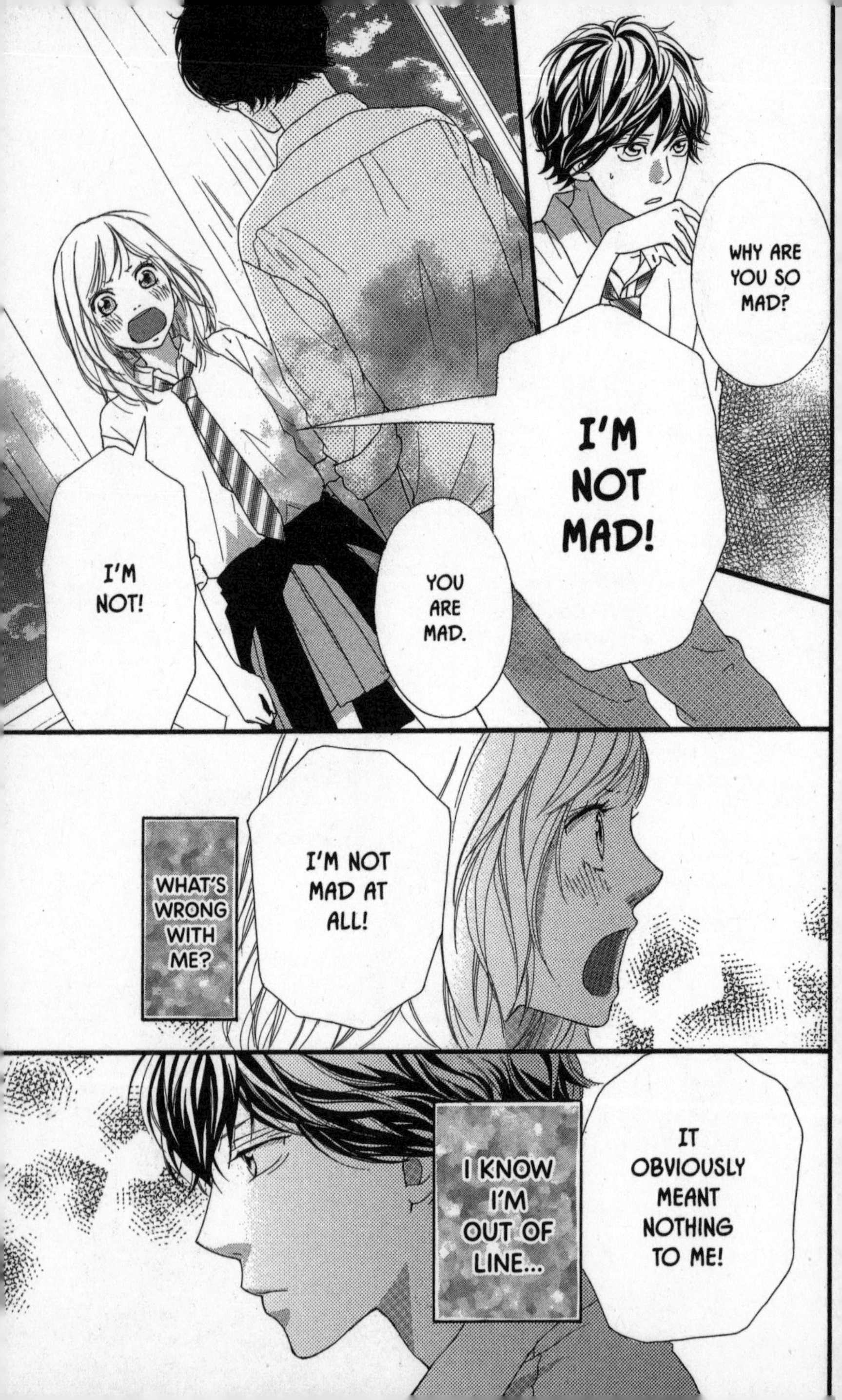
WHY ARE YOU SO MAD?
I'M NOT MAD!
YOU ARE MAD.
I'M NOT!
I'M NOT MAD AT ALL!
WHAT'S WRONG WITH ME?
IT OBVIOUSLY MEANT NOTHING TO ME!
I KNOW I'M OUT OF LINE...

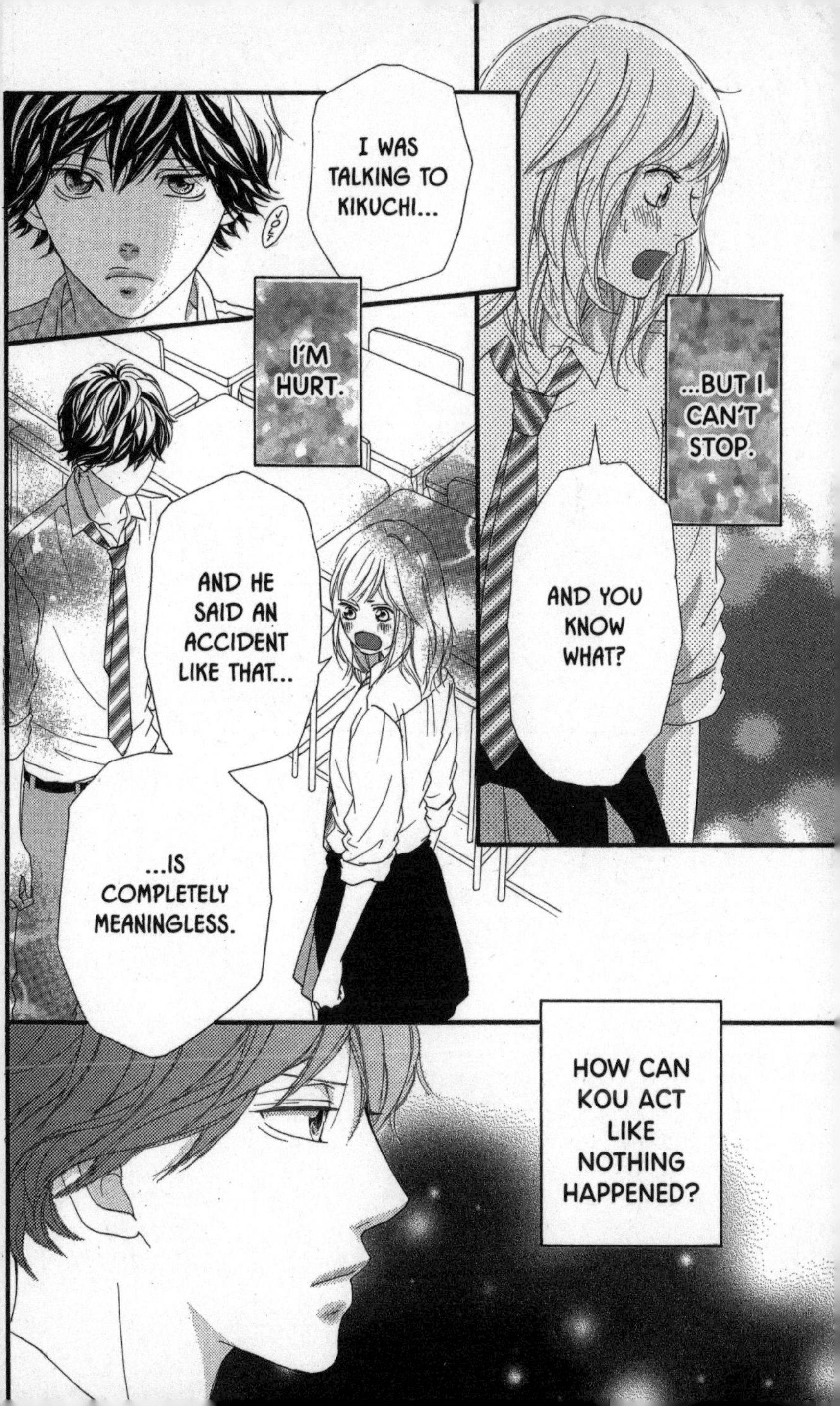
...BUT I CAN'T STOP.
AND YOU KNOW WHAT?
I WAS TALKING TO KIKUCHI...
I'M HURT.
AND HE SAID AN ACCIDENT LIKE THAT...
...IS COMPLETELY MEANINGLESS.
HOW CAN KOU ACT LIKE NOTHING HAPPENED?

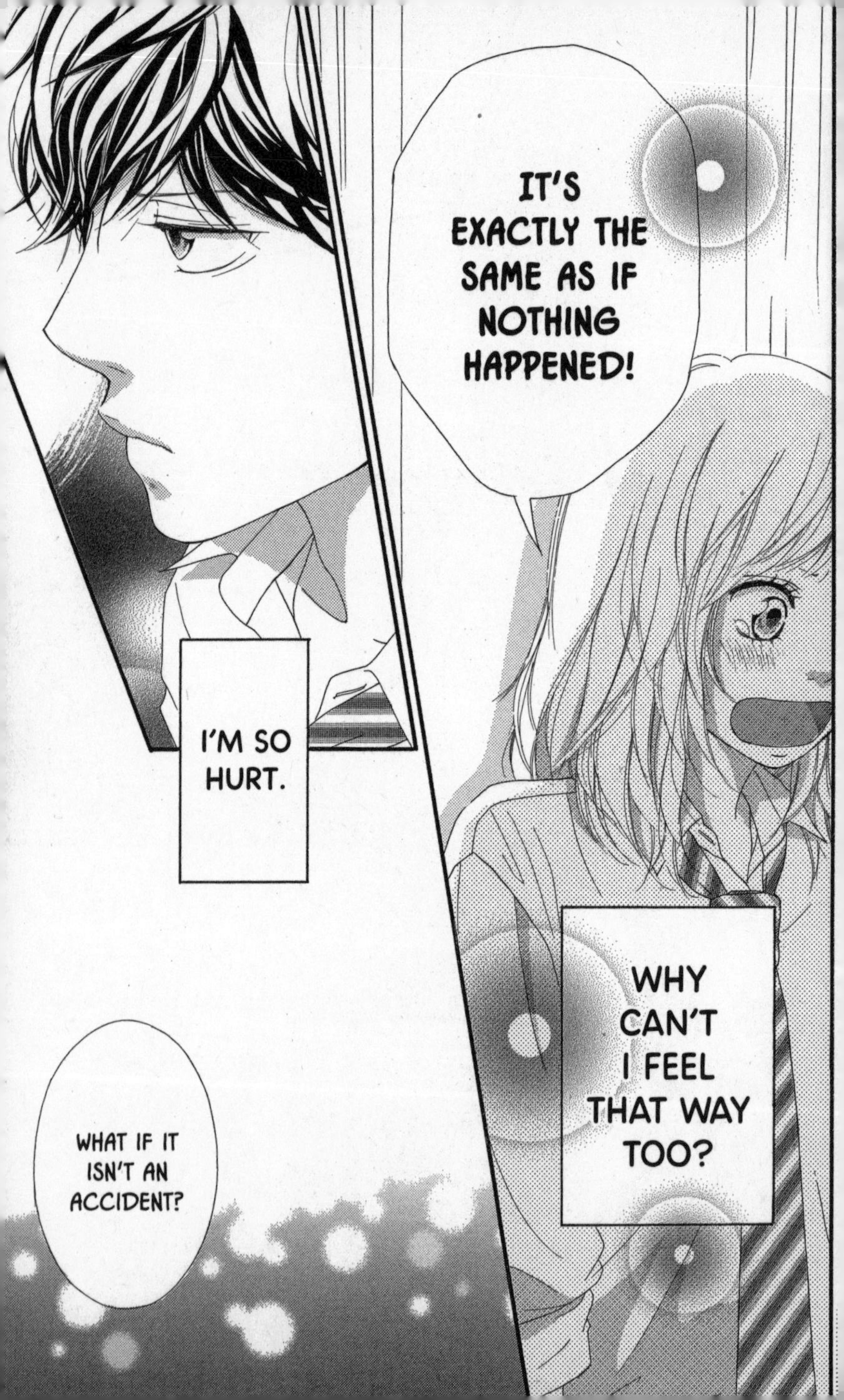
IT'S EXACTLY THE SAME AS IF NOTHING HAPPENED!
WHY CAN'T I FEEL THAT WAY TOO?
I'M SO HURT.
WHAT IF IT ISN'T AN ACCIDENT?

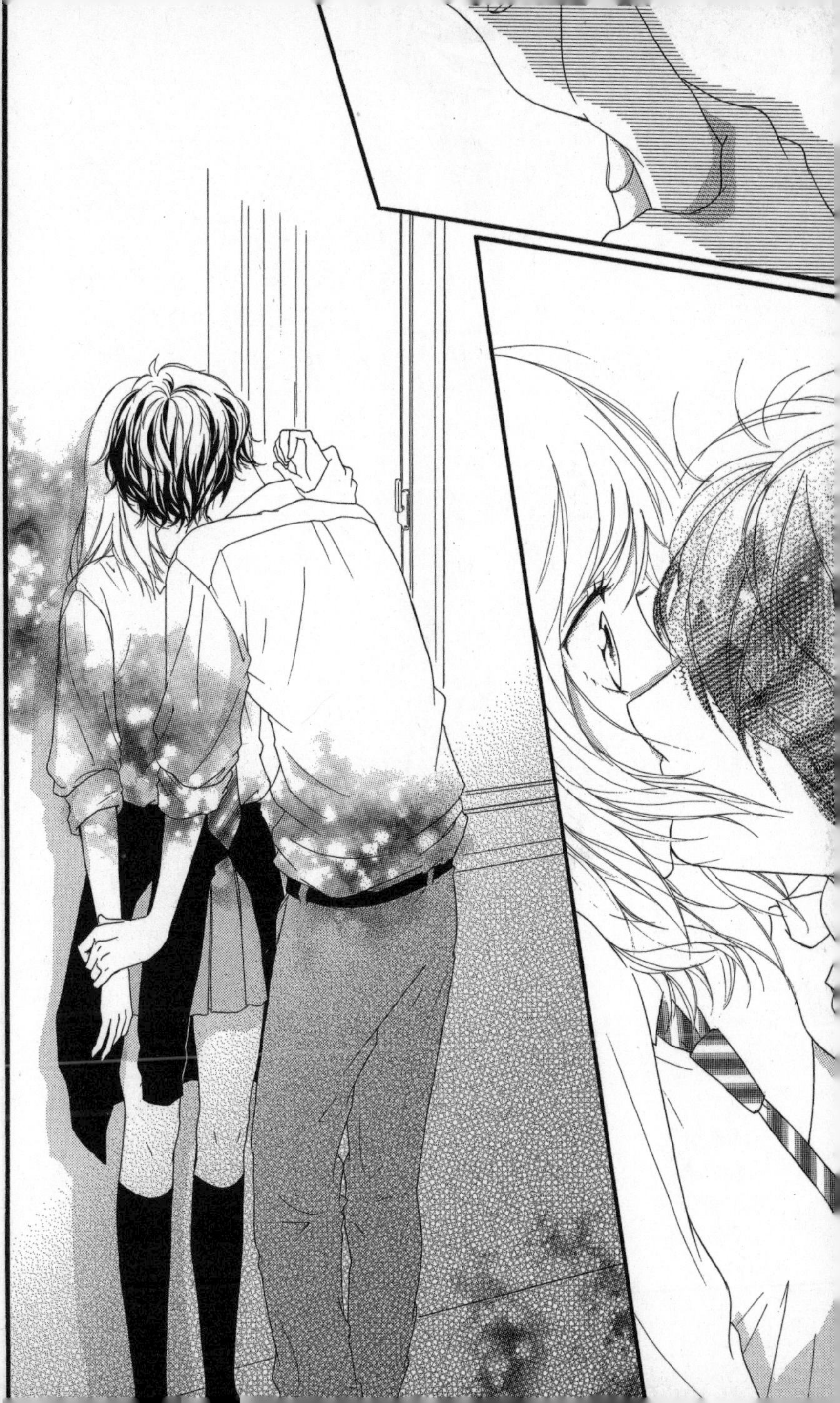

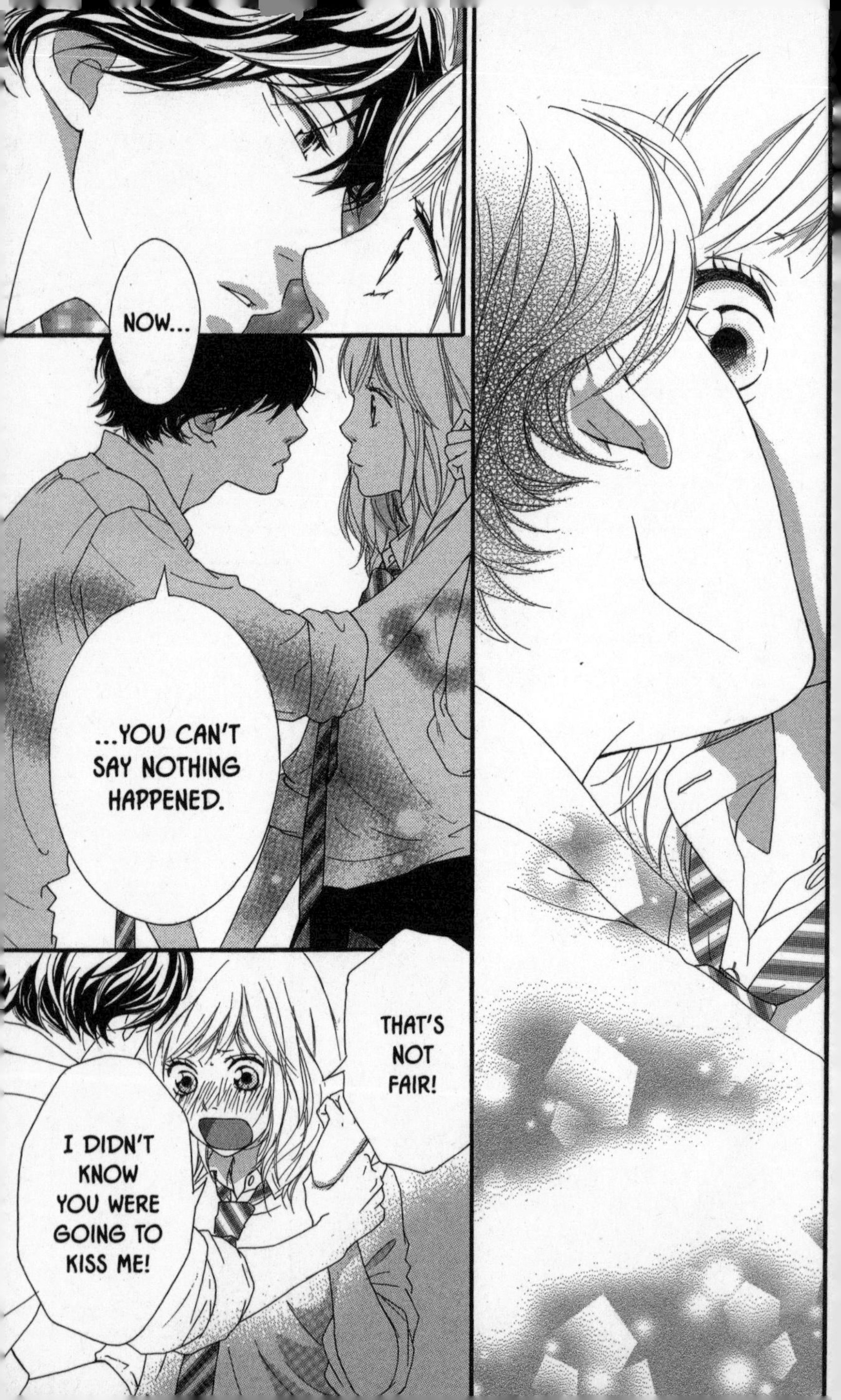
NOW...
...YOU CAN'T SAY NOTHING HAPPENED.
THAT'S NOT FAIR!
I DIDN'T KNOW YOU WERE GOING TO KISS ME!

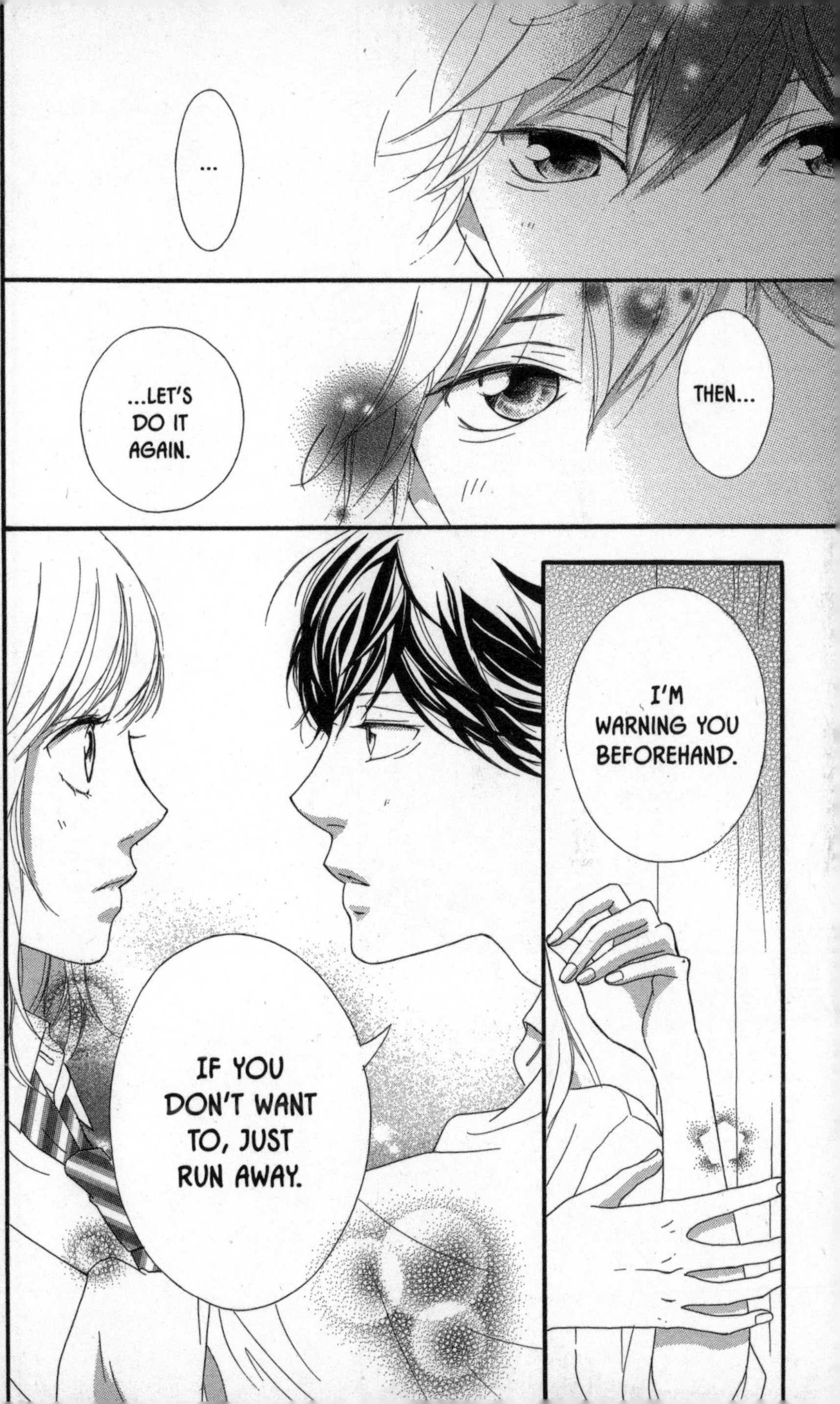
...
THEN...
...LET'S DO IT AGAIN.
I'M WARNING YOU BEFOREHAND.
IF YOU DON'T WANT TO, JUST RUN AWAY.

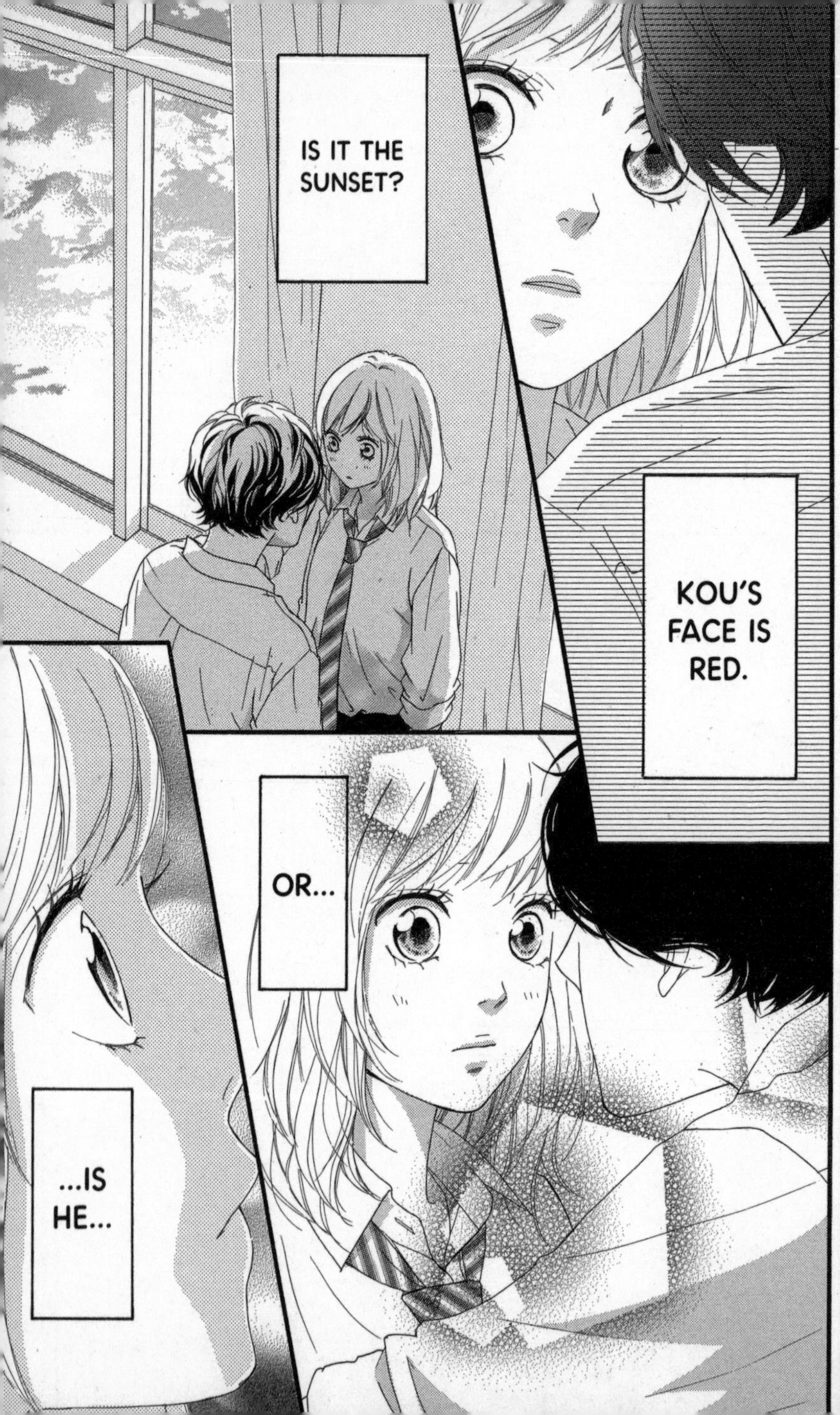
KOU'S FACE IS RED.
IS IT THE SUNSET?
OR...
...IS HE...

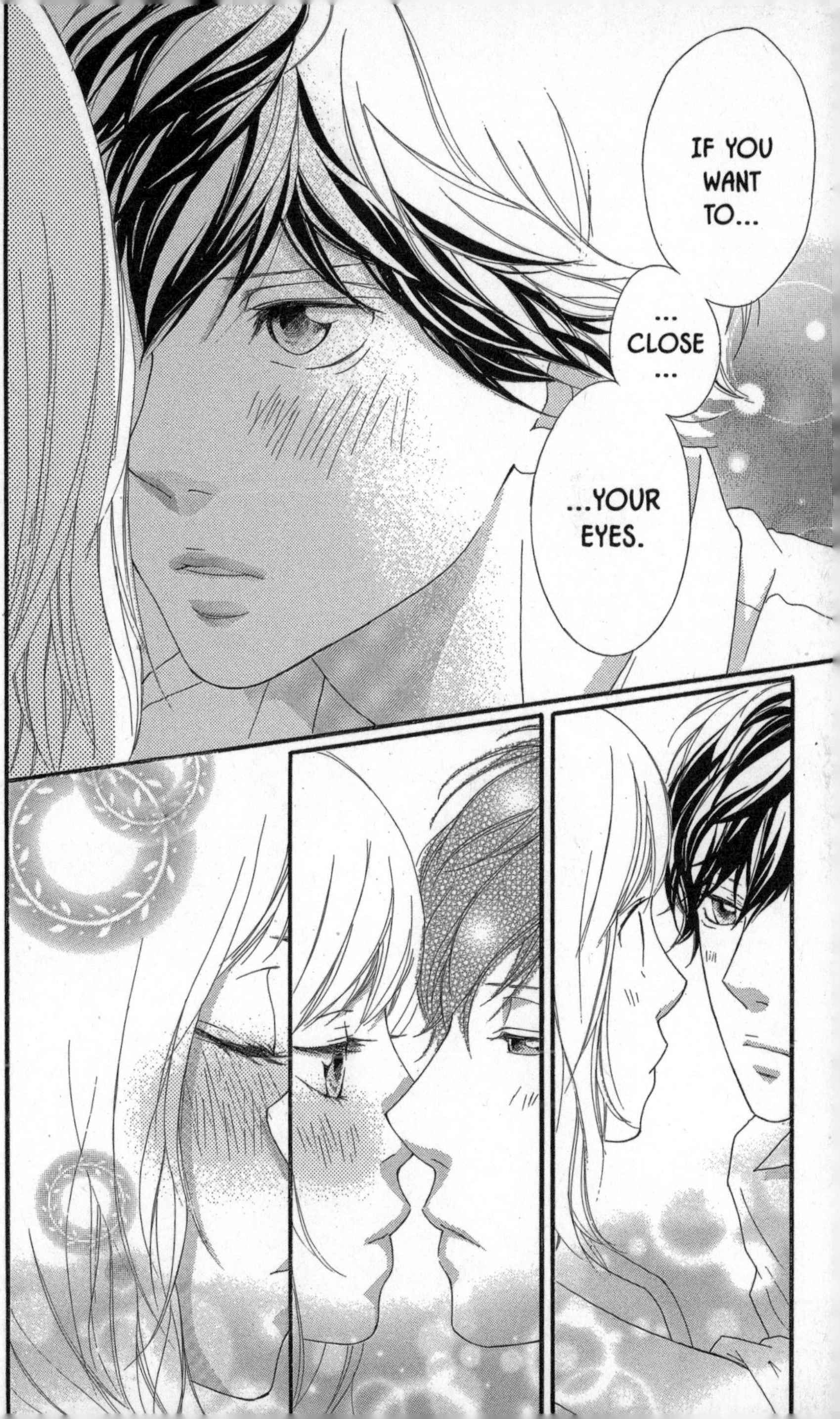
IF YOU WANT TO...
...CLOSE...
...YOUR EYES.

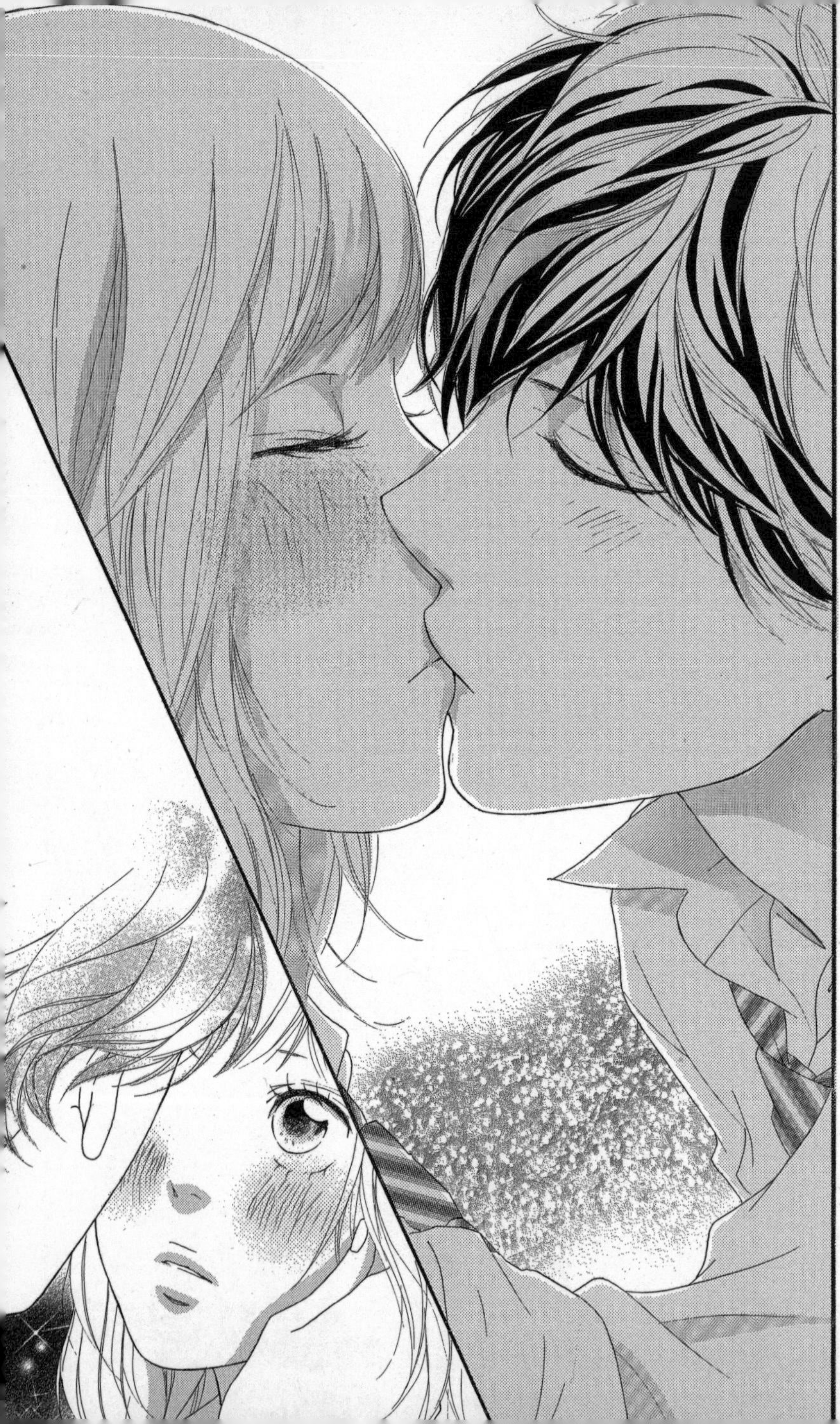

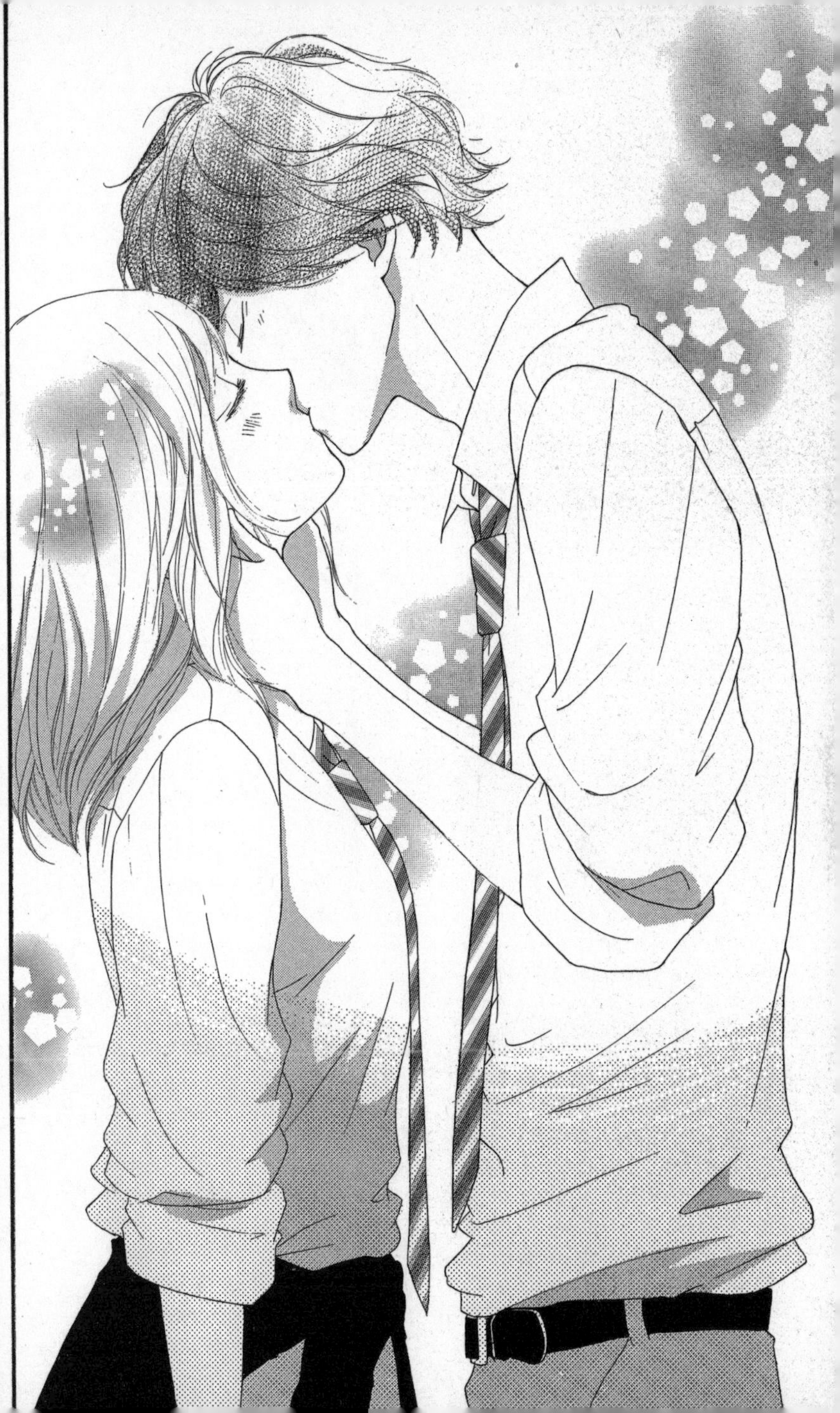

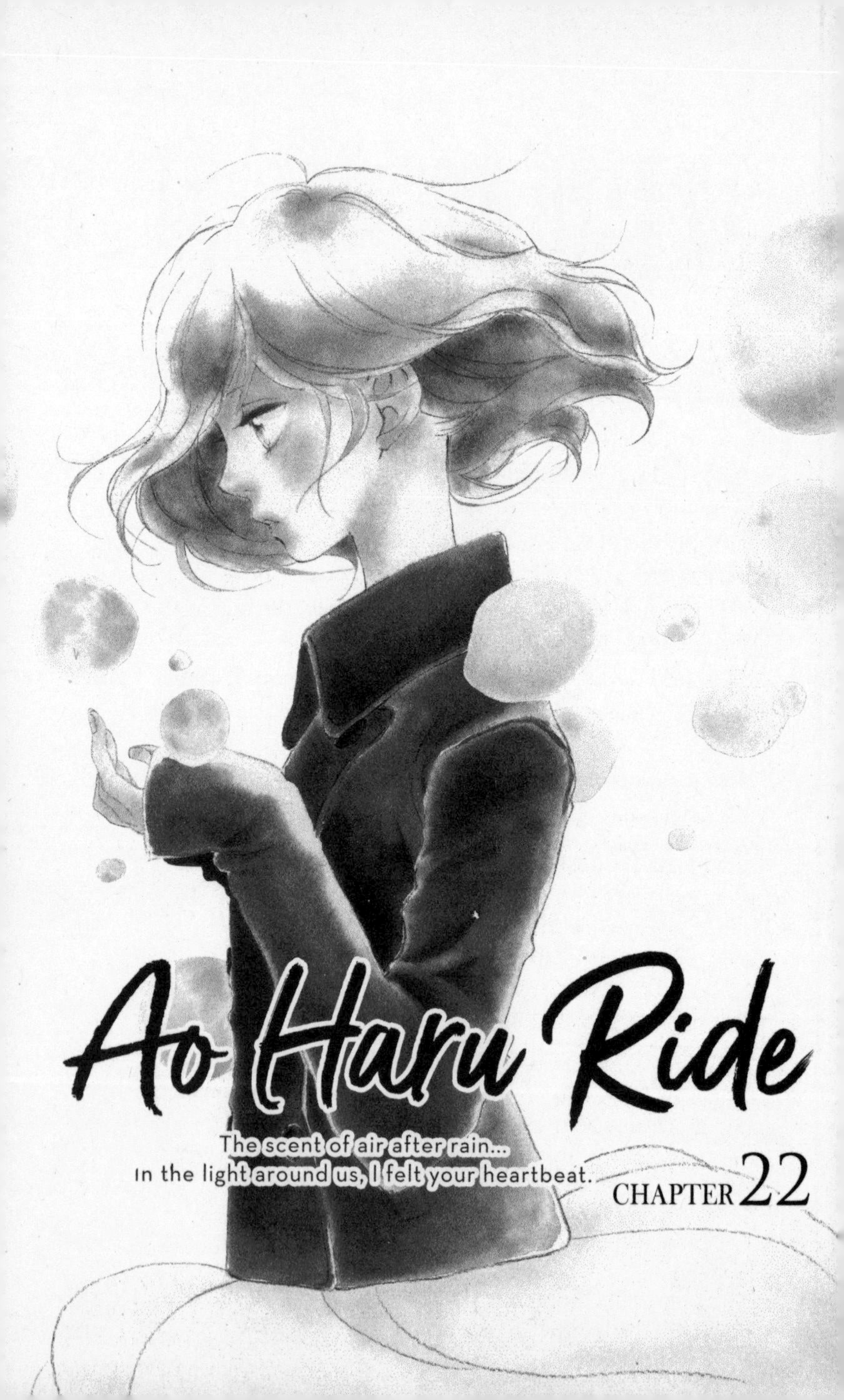
Ao Haru Ride
The scent of air after rain...
In the light around us, I felt your heartbeat.
CHAPTER 22

AO HARU RIDE Behind the Scenes

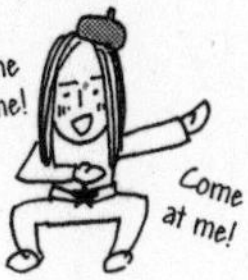
Come at me!
Come at me!

I love receiving your letters. They make me so happy.
Thank you for sending them. 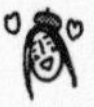 Fwah! ♡

A few of you wrote that Toma's necktie is different from his classmates'. Well, his friends' neckties are also different, and there are a total of three patterns. If you're wondering why, it's because their school allows kids to choose between three different neckties... At least, that's the story I'm going with. The truth is that the screentone I use for the neckties has three patterns printed on it, and because I was using just one of the patterns (Futaba's), I ended up with way too many of the others. It drove me crazy. So when Toma appeared, I gave him a different necktie to try to use up some of the excess screentone. And of course, because it's me we're talking about, I sometimes mess up and use the wrong pattern, so now the school has a policy that allows kids to

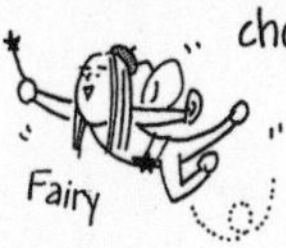
Fairy

choose between three different neckties. That's the ~~escape route~~ story I'm going with. If you ever notice a character wearing a necktie that is different from their usual one, please just assume that they were in a different mood that day. And if you notice a character's necktie pattern change between manga panels, please just assume that they were suddenly in a different mood and decided to change. Thanks.

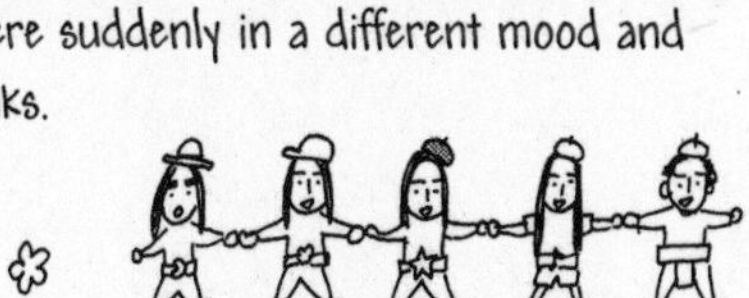
Can you find me?

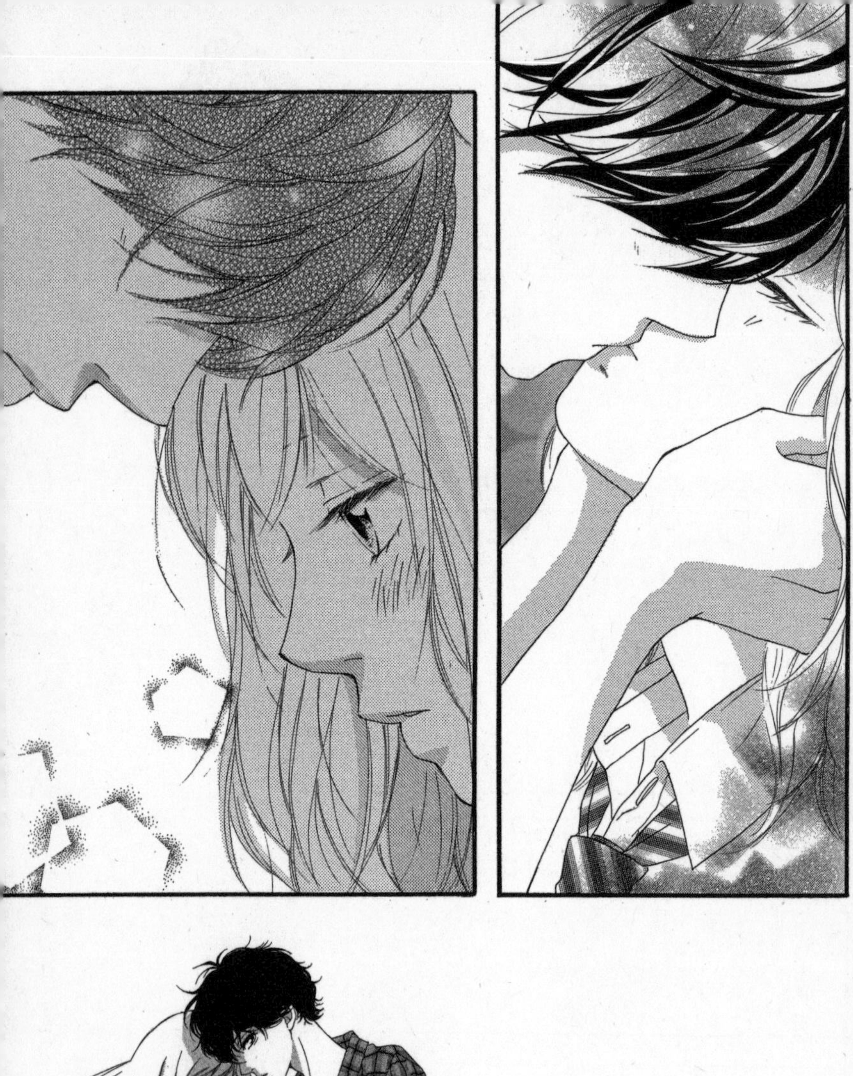

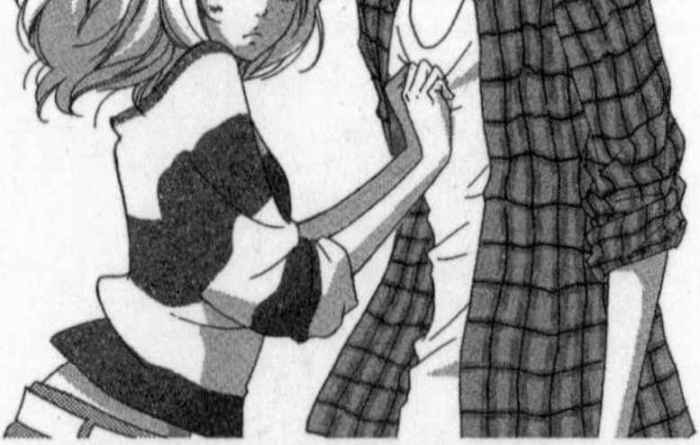

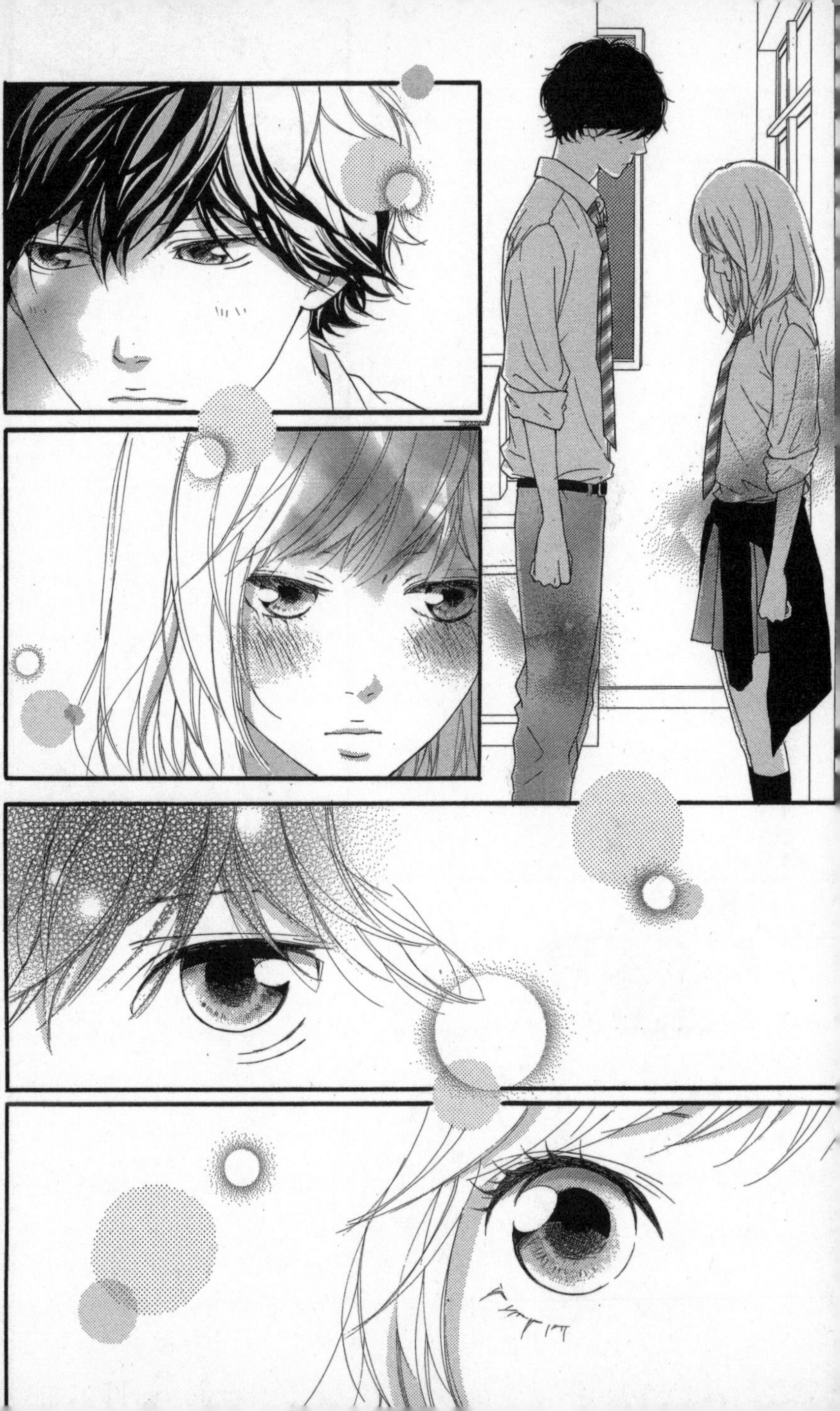

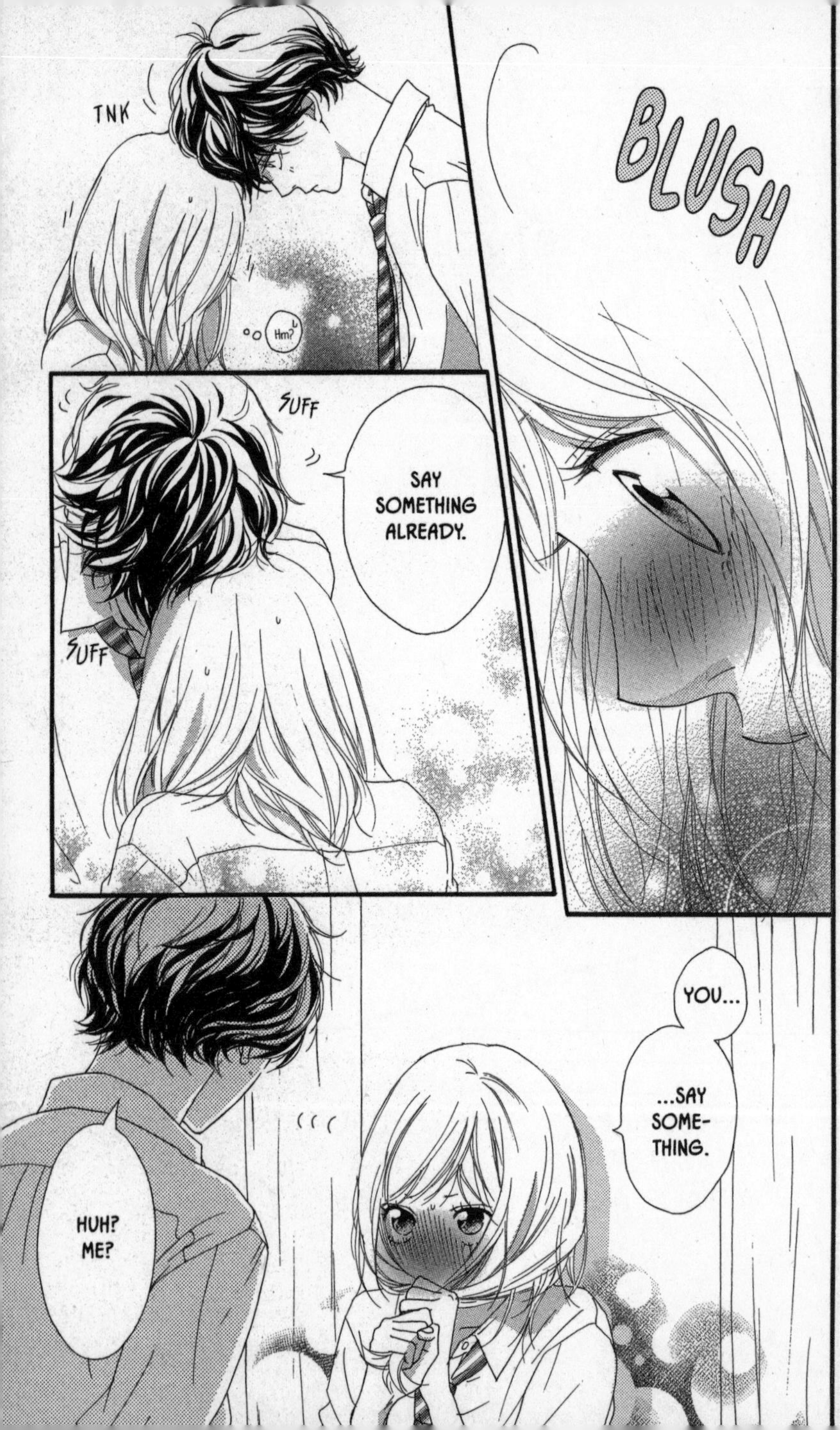
BLUSH
TNK
Hm?
SUFF
SAY SOMETHING ALREADY.
SUFF
YOU...
...SAY SOME-THING.
HUH? ME?

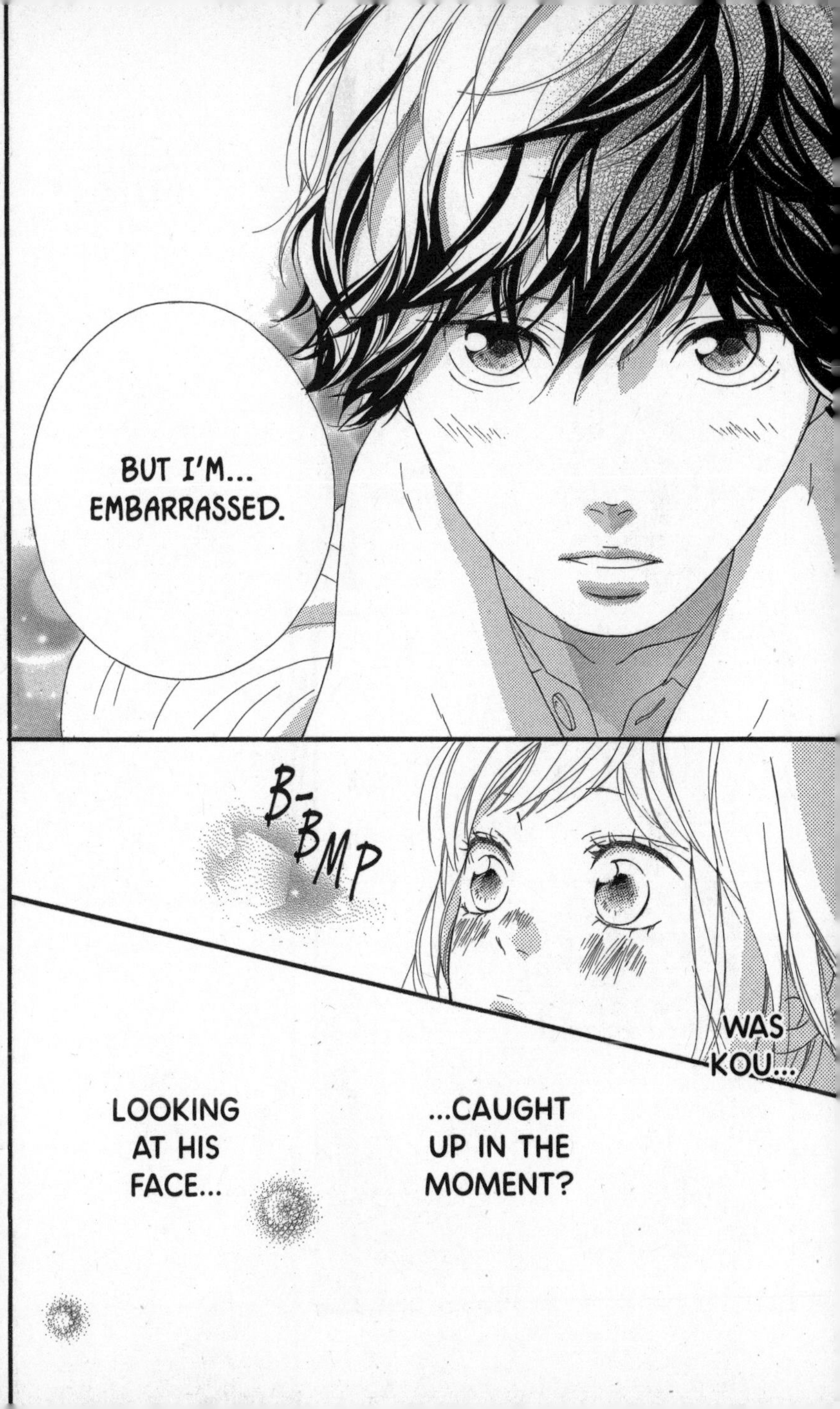
BUT I'M... EMBARRASSED.
B-BMP
WAS KOU...
...CAUGHT UP IN THE MOMENT?
LOOKING AT HIS FACE...

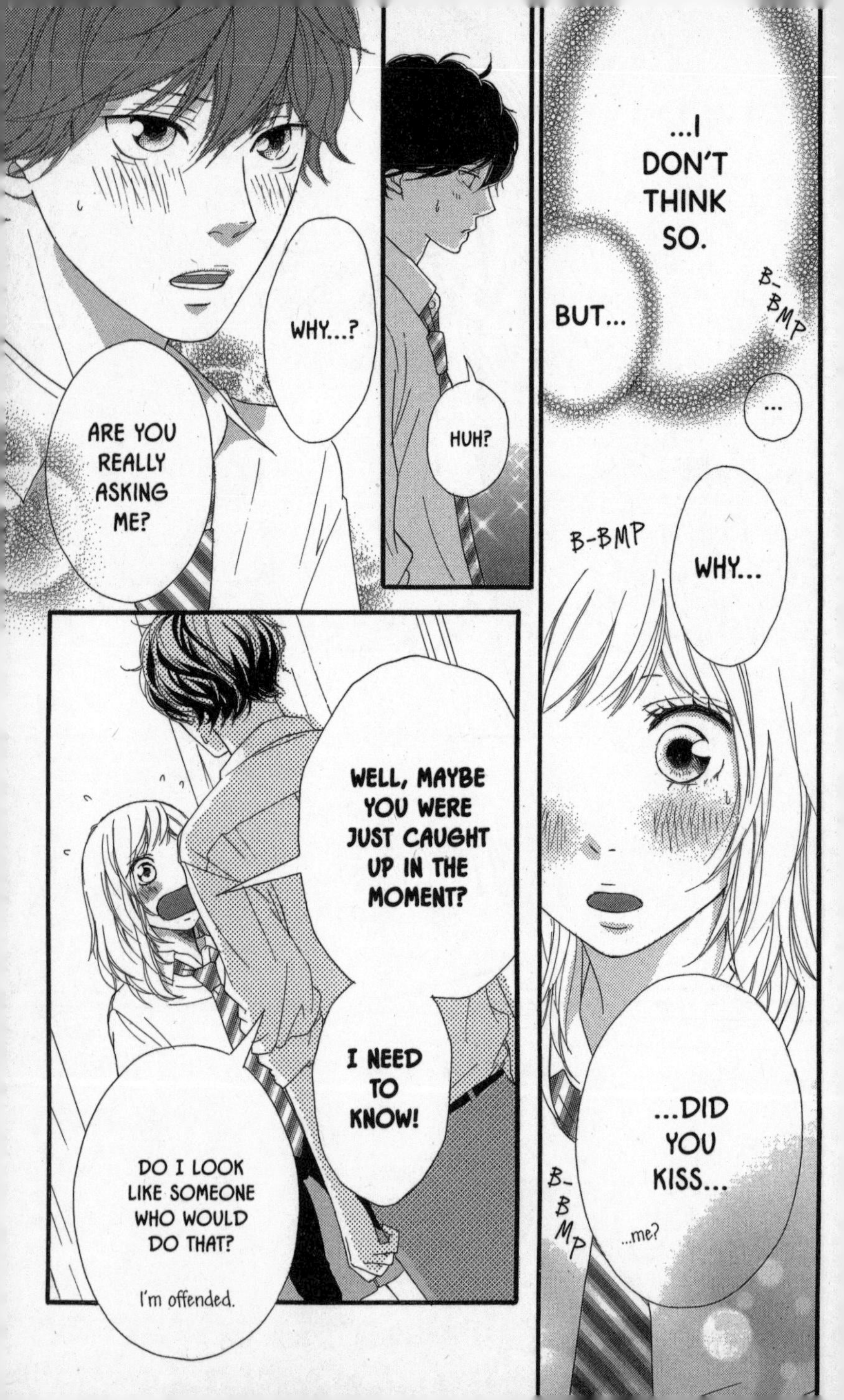
...I DON'T THINK SO.
BUT...
B-BMP
...
B-BMP
WHY...
...DID YOU KISS...
B-BMP
...me?
HUH?
WHY...?
ARE YOU REALLY ASKING ME?
WELL, MAYBE YOU WERE JUST CAUGHT UP IN THE MOMENT?
I NEED TO KNOW!
DO I LOOK LIKE SOMEONE WHO WOULD DO THAT?
I'm offended.

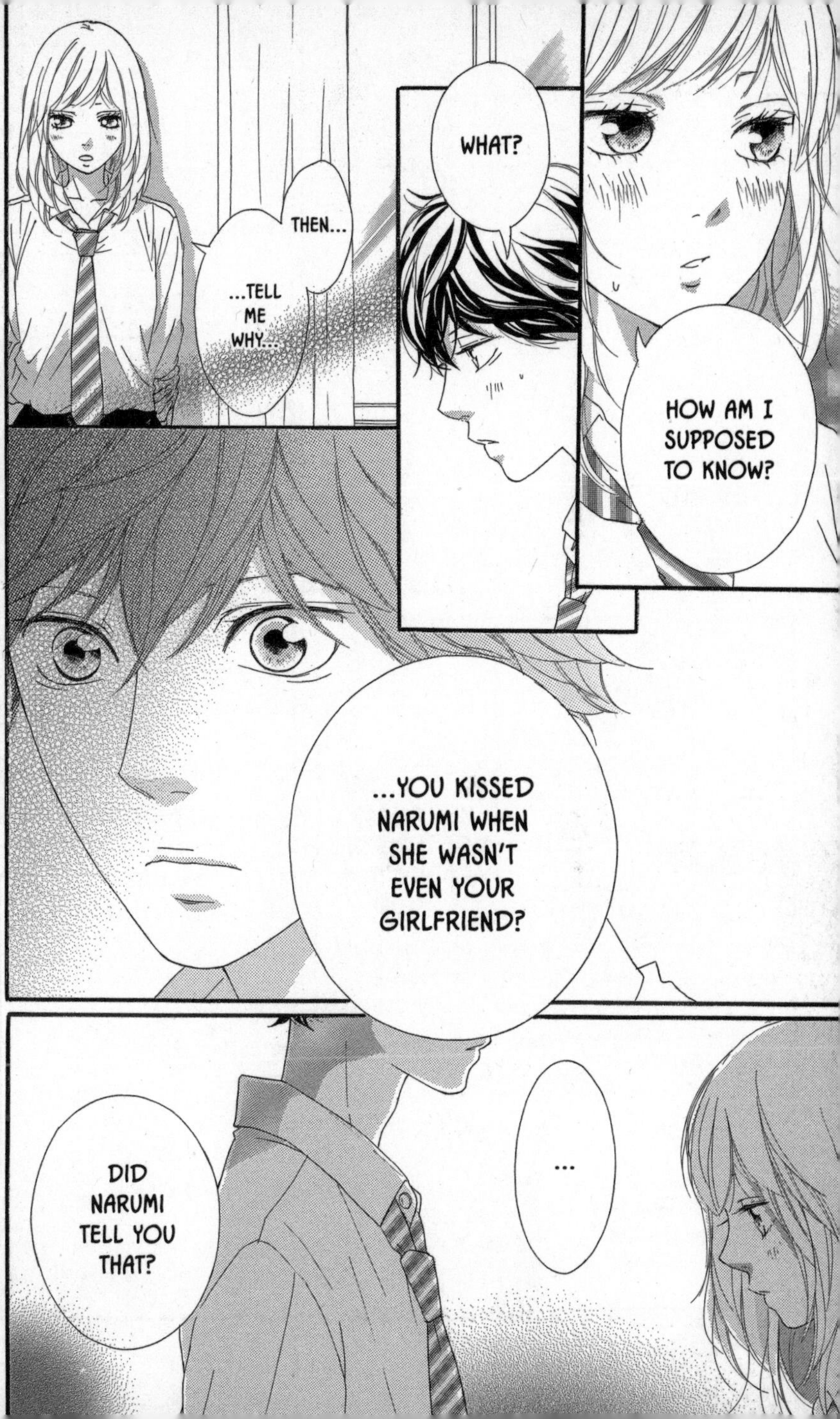
HOW AM I SUPPOSED TO KNOW?
WHAT?
THEN...
...TELL ME WHY...
...YOU KISSED NARUMI WHEN SHE WASN'T EVEN YOUR GIRLFRIEND?
...
DID NARUMI TELL YOU THAT?

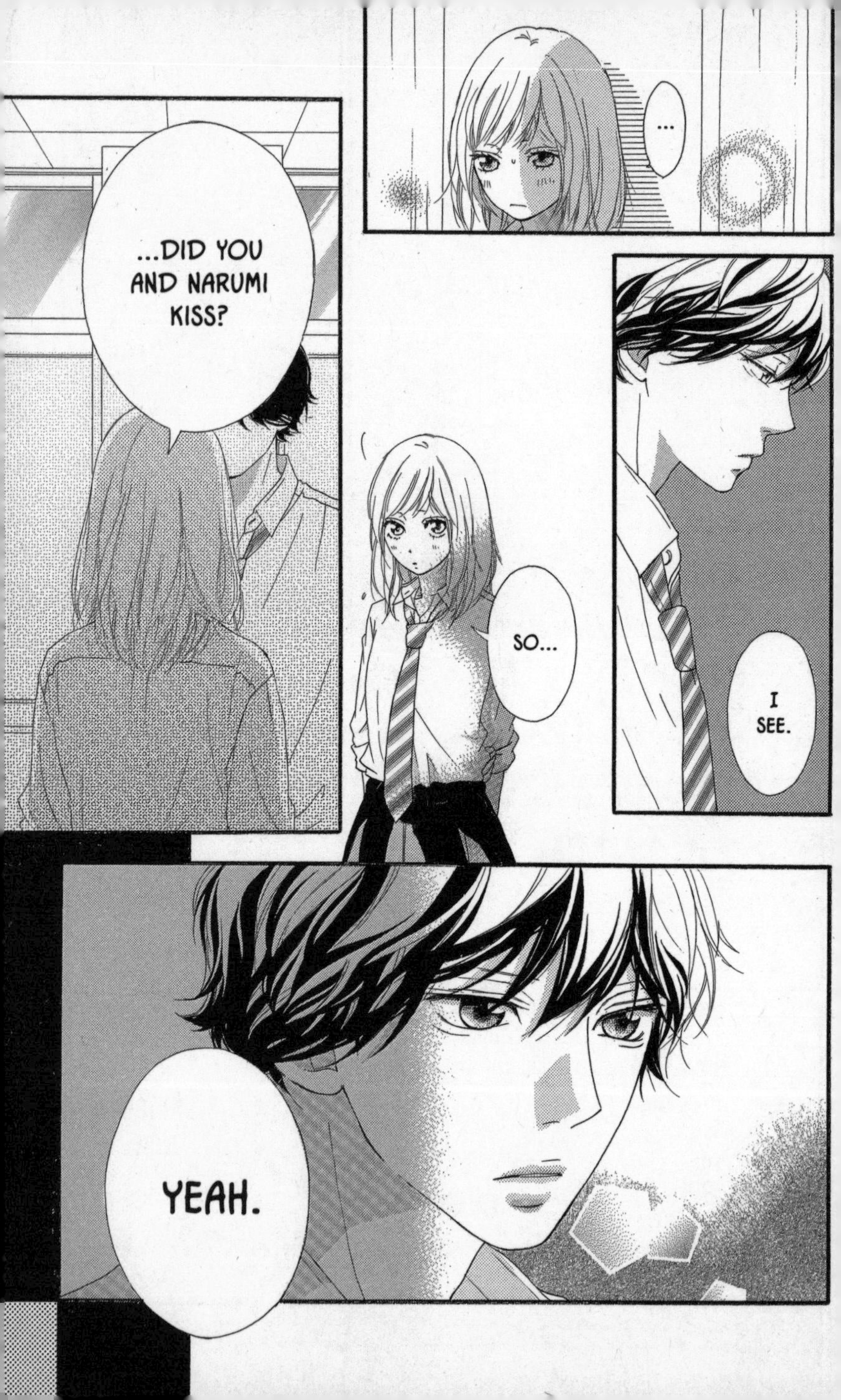
...
...DID YOU AND NARUMI KISS?
I SEE.
SO...
YEAH.

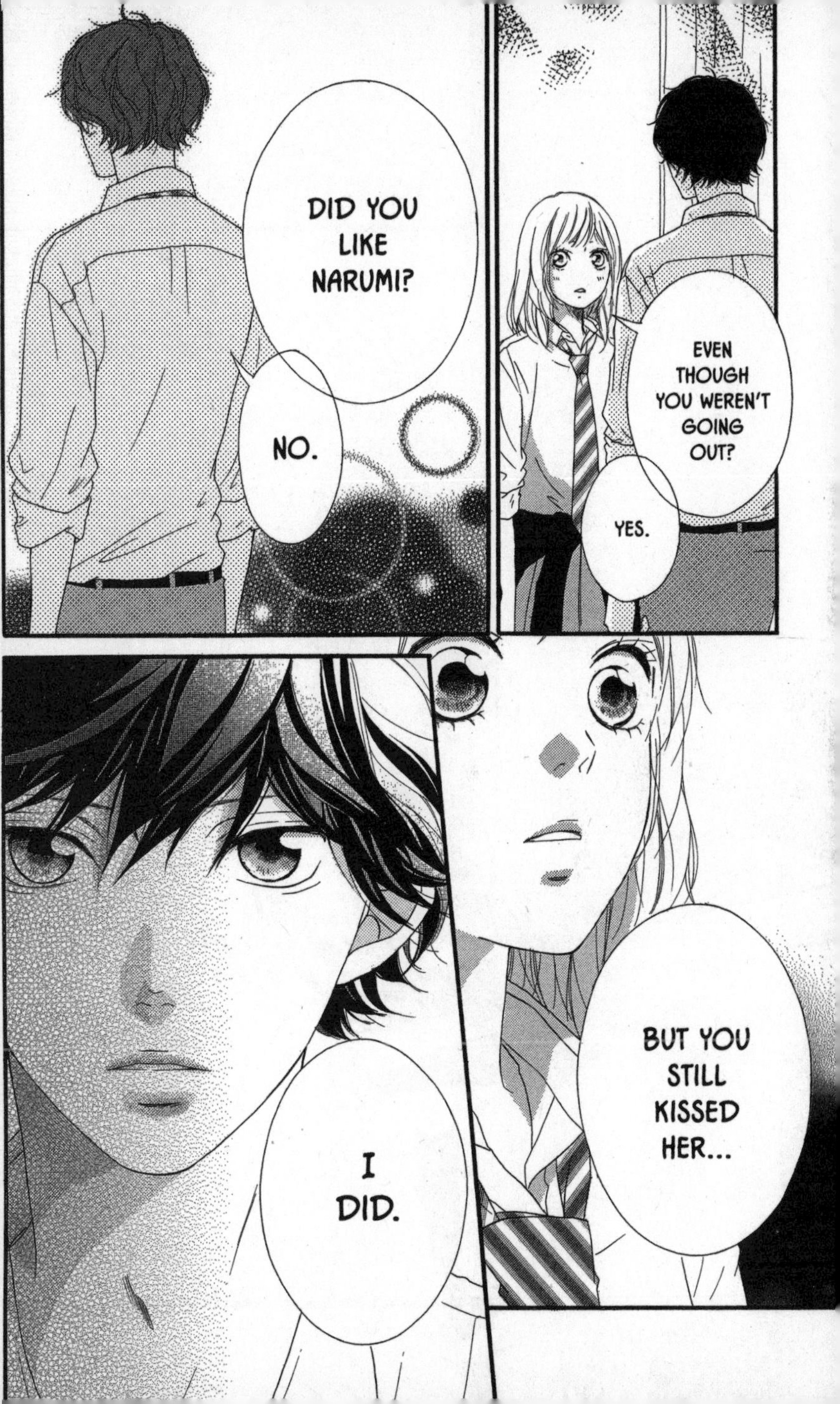
EVEN THOUGH YOU WEREN'T GOING OUT?
YES.
DID YOU LIKE NARUMI?
NO.
BUT YOU STILL KISSED HER...
I DID.

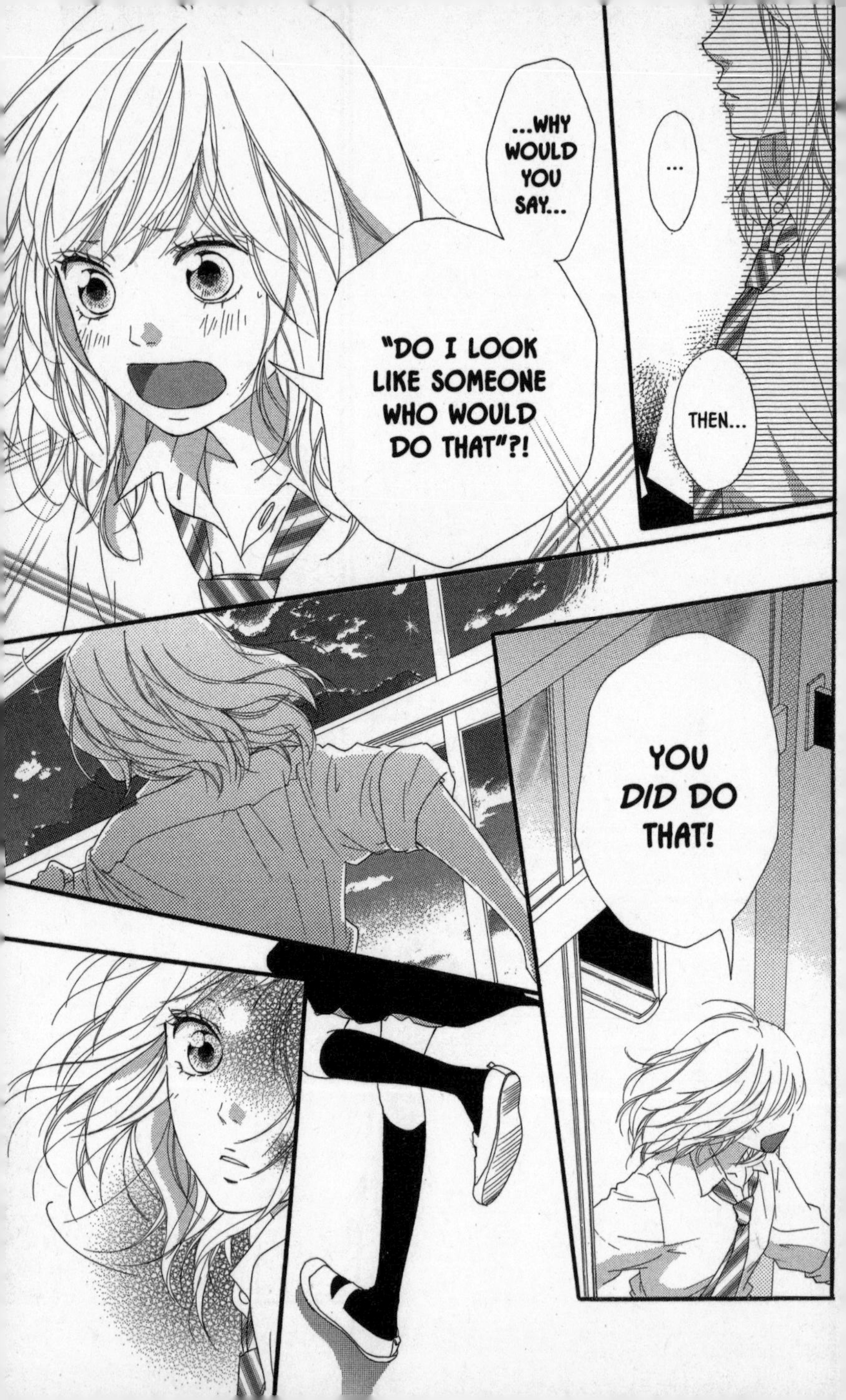
...
THEN...
...WHY WOULD YOU SAY...
"DO I LOOK LIKE SOMEONE WHO WOULD DO THAT"?!
YOU *DID* DO THAT!

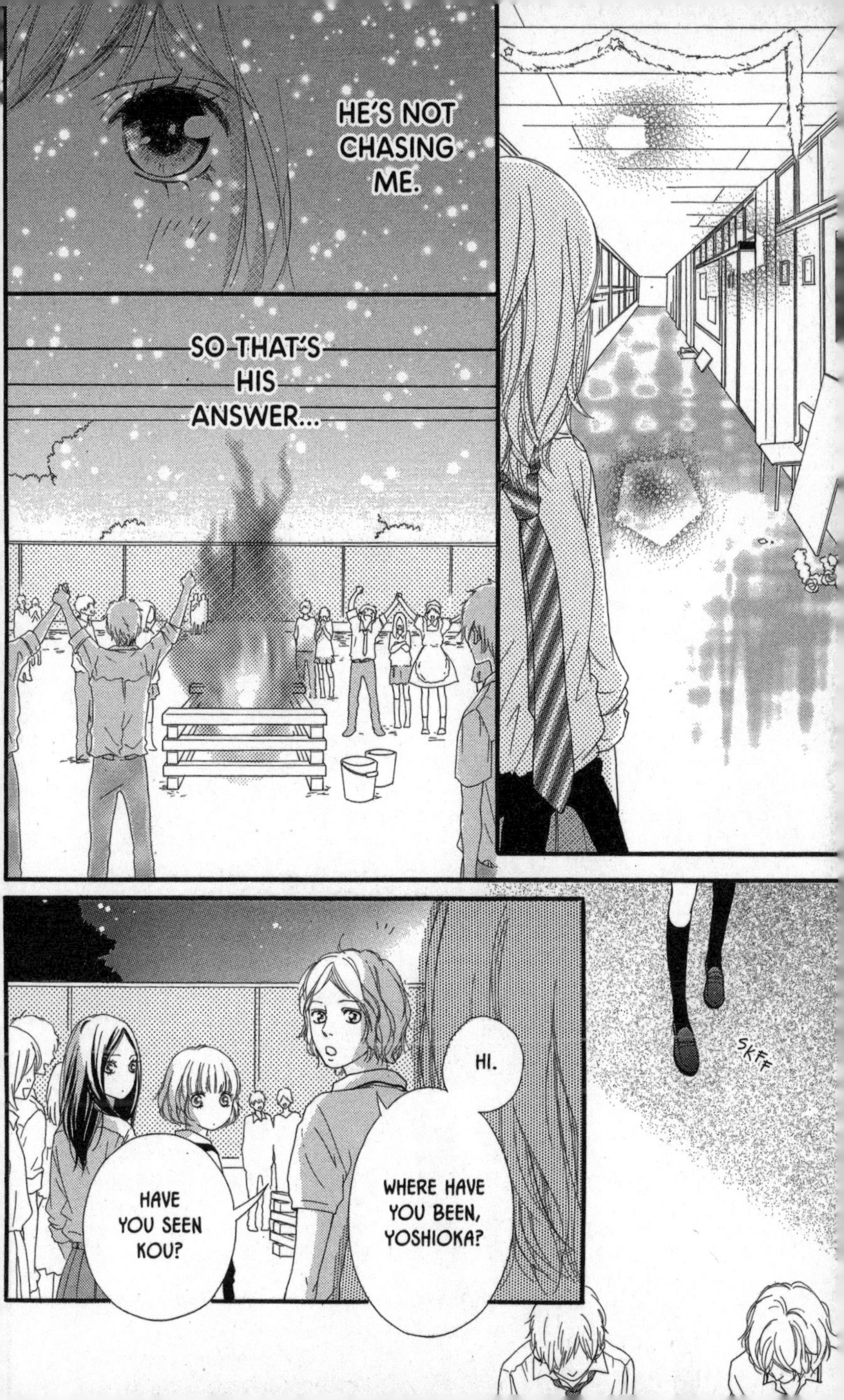
HE'S NOT CHASING ME.
SO THAT'S HIS ANSWER...
SKFF
HI.
WHERE HAVE YOU BEEN, YOSHIOKA?
HAVE YOU SEEN KOU?

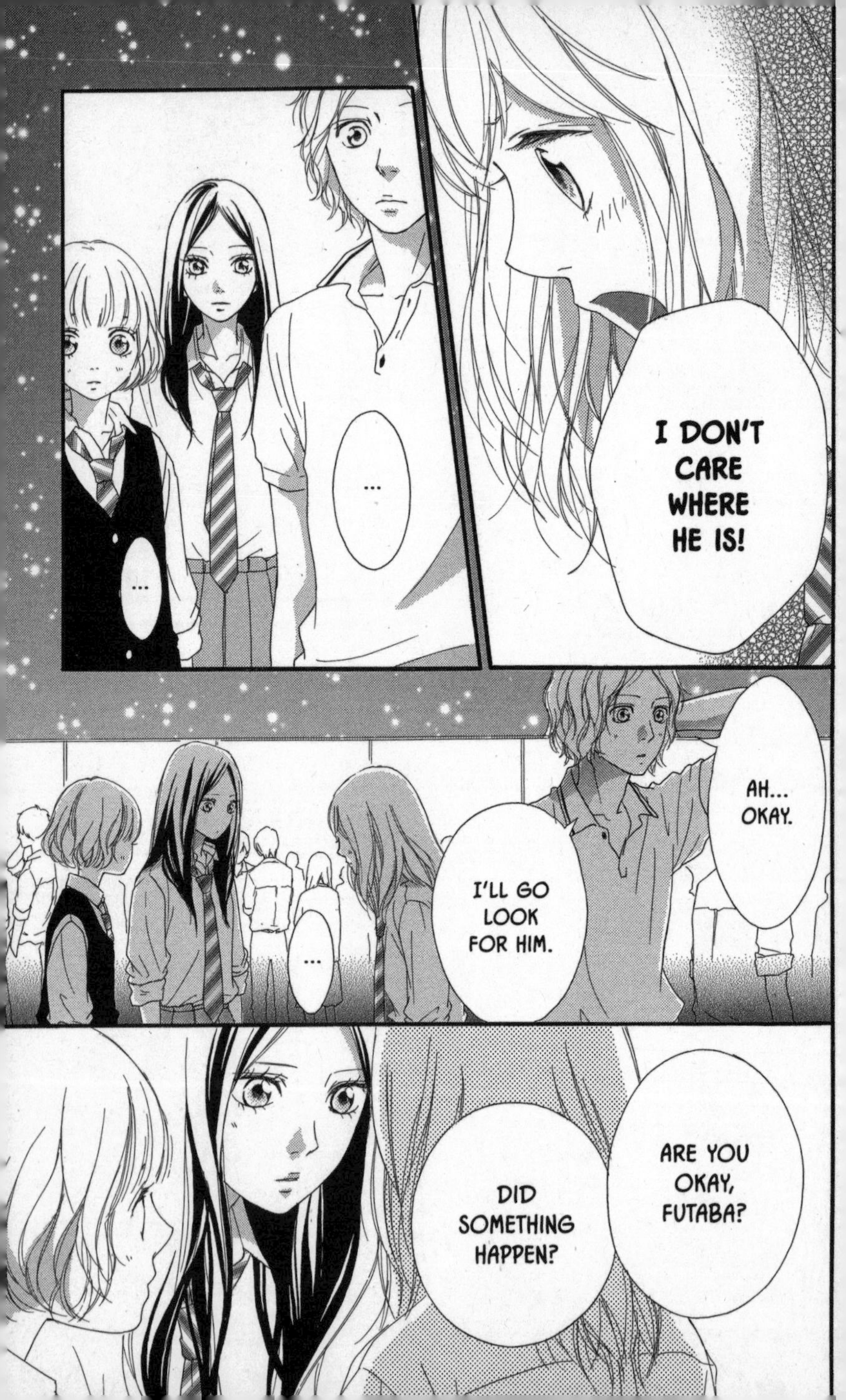
I DON'T CARE WHERE HE IS!
...
...
AH... OKAY.
I'LL GO LOOK FOR HIM.
...
ARE YOU OKAY, FUTABA?
DID SOMETHING HAPPEN?

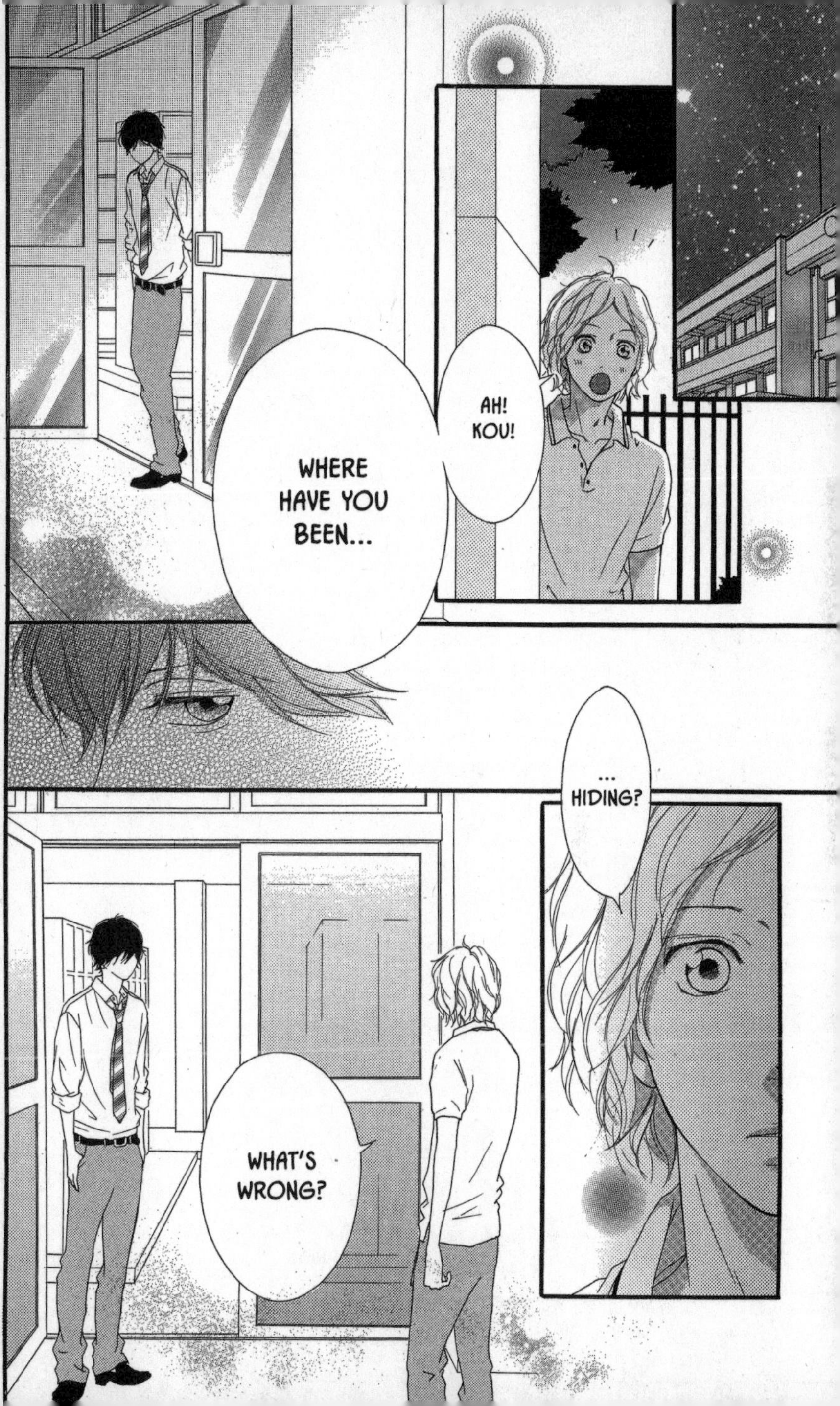
AH! KOU!
WHERE HAVE YOU BEEN...
... HIDING?
WHAT'S WRONG?

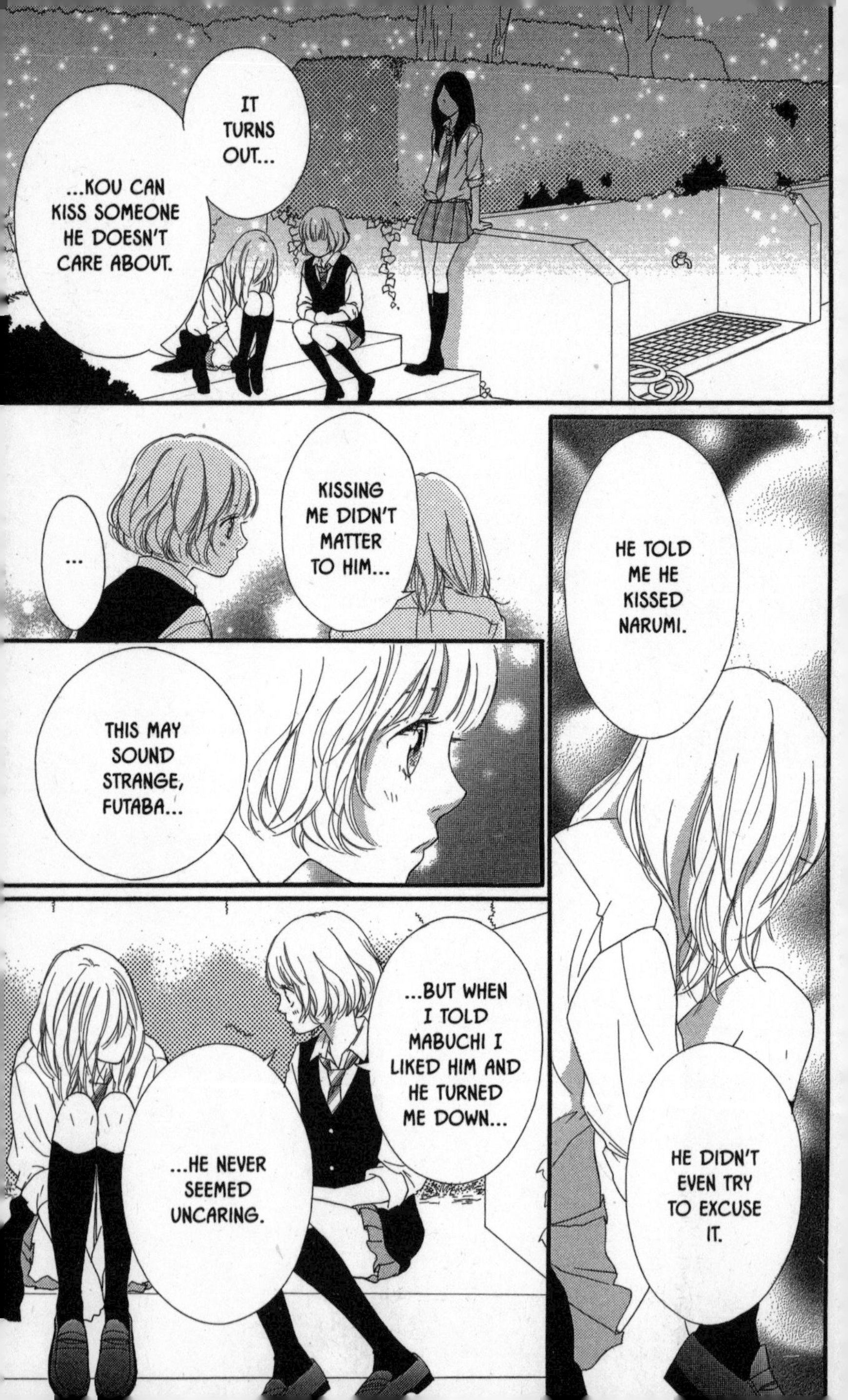
IT TURNS OUT...
...KOU CAN KISS SOMEONE HE DOESN'T CARE ABOUT.
HE TOLD ME HE KISSED NARUMI.
HE DIDN'T EVEN TRY TO EXCUSE IT.
KISSING ME DIDN'T MATTER TO HIM...
...
THIS MAY SOUND STRANGE, FUTABA...
...BUT WHEN I TOLD MABUCHI I LIKED HIM AND HE TURNED ME DOWN...
...HE NEVER SEEMED UNCARING.

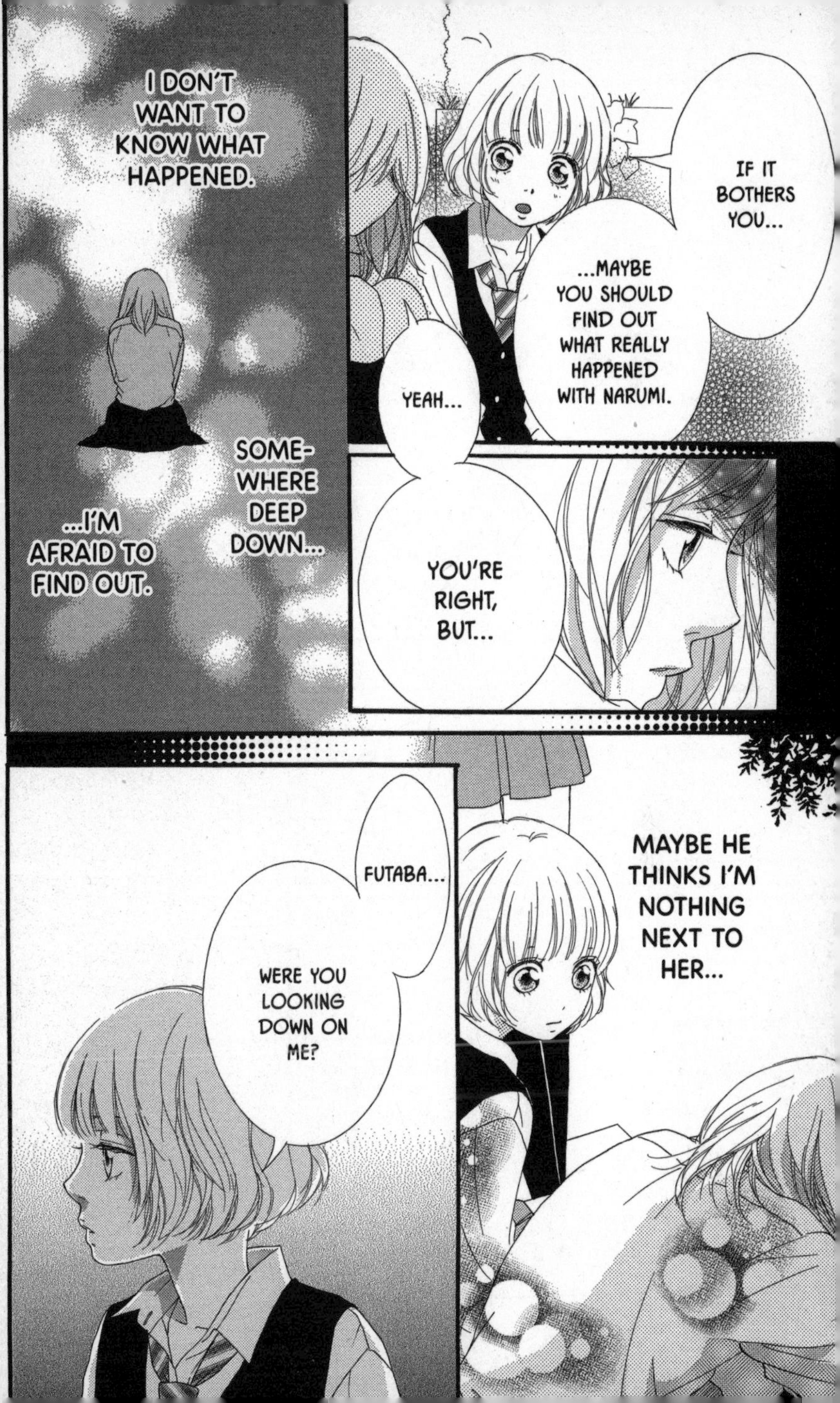
IF IT BOTHERS YOU...
...MAYBE YOU SHOULD FIND OUT WHAT REALLY HAPPENED WITH NARUMI.
YEAH...
YOU'RE RIGHT, BUT...
I DON'T WANT TO KNOW WHAT HAPPENED.
SOME-WHERE DEEP DOWN...
...I'M AFRAID TO FIND OUT.
MAYBE HE THINKS I'M NOTHING NEXT TO HER...
FUTABA...
WERE YOU LOOKING DOWN ON ME?

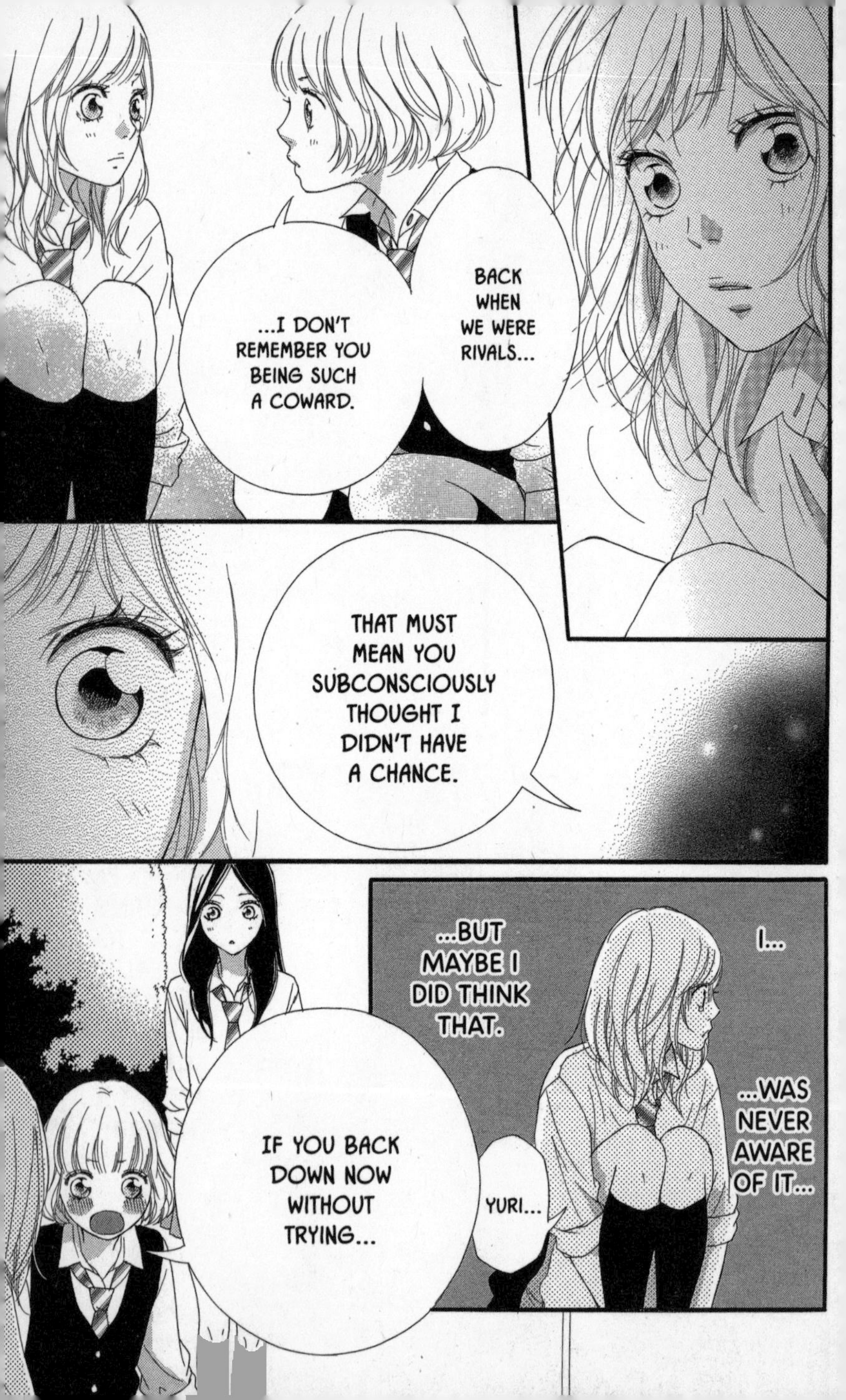
BACK WHEN WE WERE RIVALS...
...I DON'T REMEMBER YOU BEING SUCH A COWARD.
THAT MUST MEAN YOU SUBCONSCIOUSLY THOUGHT I DIDN'T HAVE A CHANCE.
I...
...WAS NEVER AWARE OF IT...
...BUT MAYBE I DID THINK THAT.
YURI...
IF YOU BACK DOWN NOW WITHOUT TRYING...

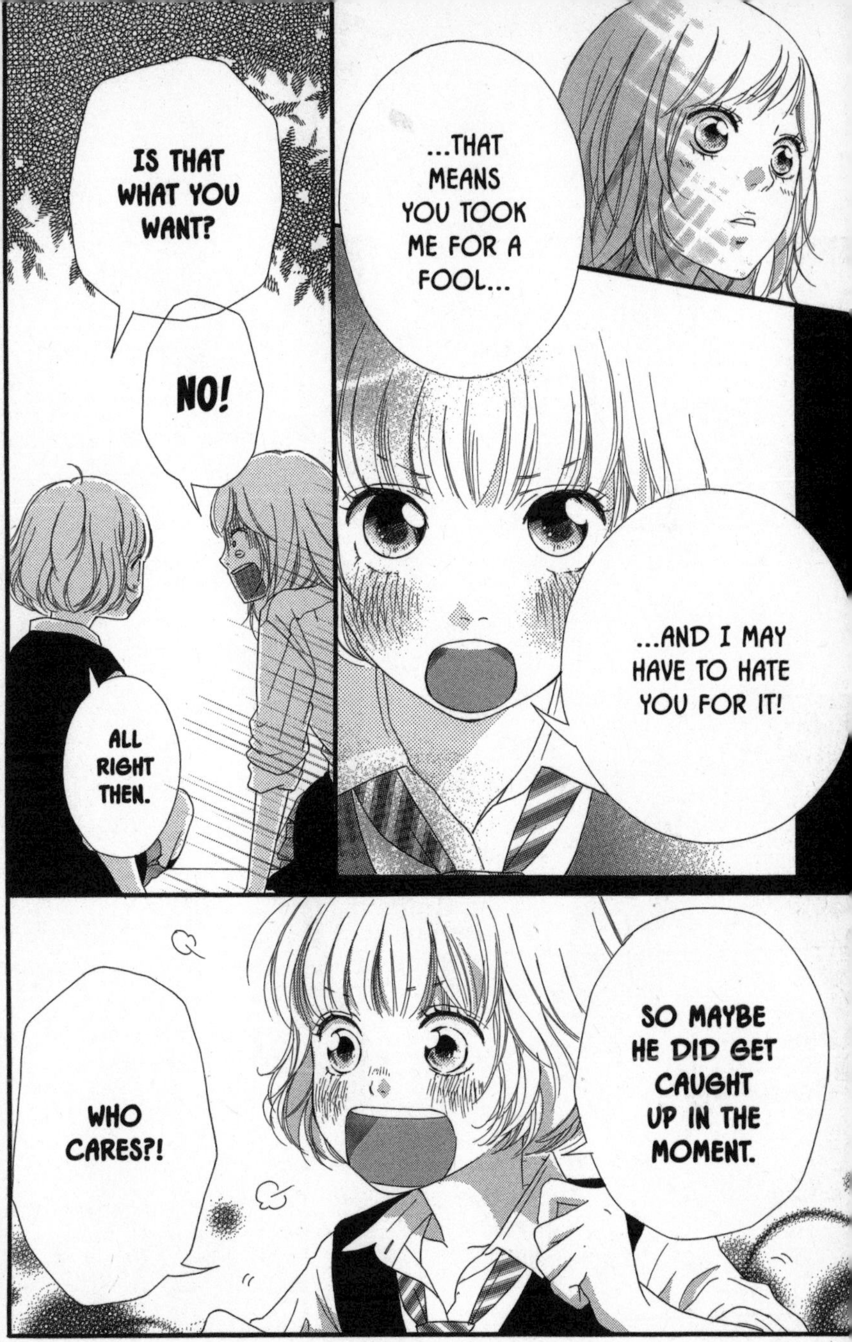
...THAT MEANS YOU TOOK ME FOR A FOOL...
...AND I MAY HAVE TO HATE YOU FOR IT!
IS THAT WHAT YOU WANT?
NO!
ALL RIGHT THEN.
SO MAYBE HE DID GET CAUGHT UP IN THE MOMENT.
WHO CARES?!

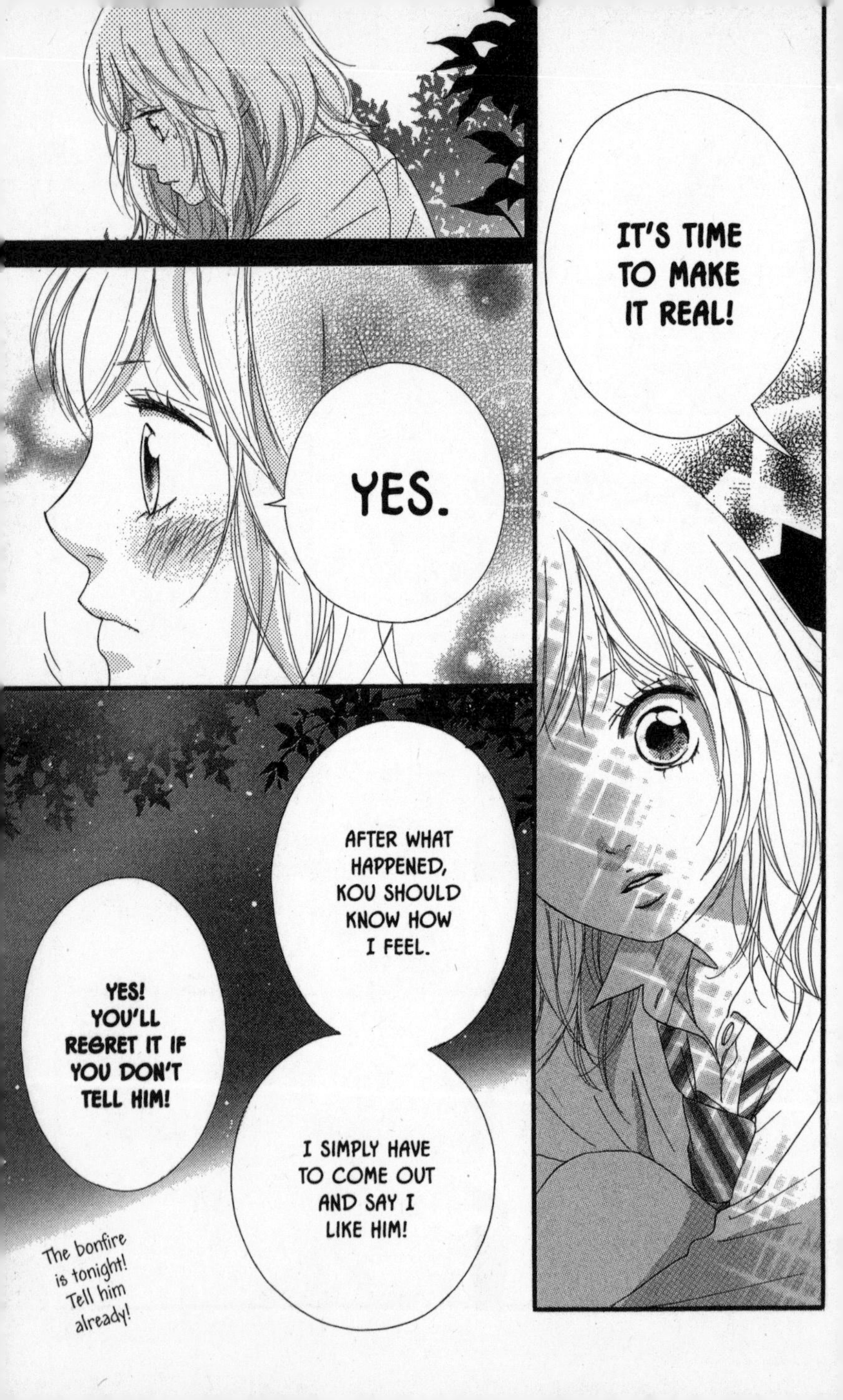

IT'S TIME TO MAKE IT REAL!
YES.
AFTER WHAT HAPPENED, KOU SHOULD KNOW HOW I FEEL.
I SIMPLY HAVE TO COME OUT AND SAY I LIKE HIM!
YES! YOU'LL REGRET IT IF YOU DON'T TELL HIM!
The bonfire is tonight! Tell him already!

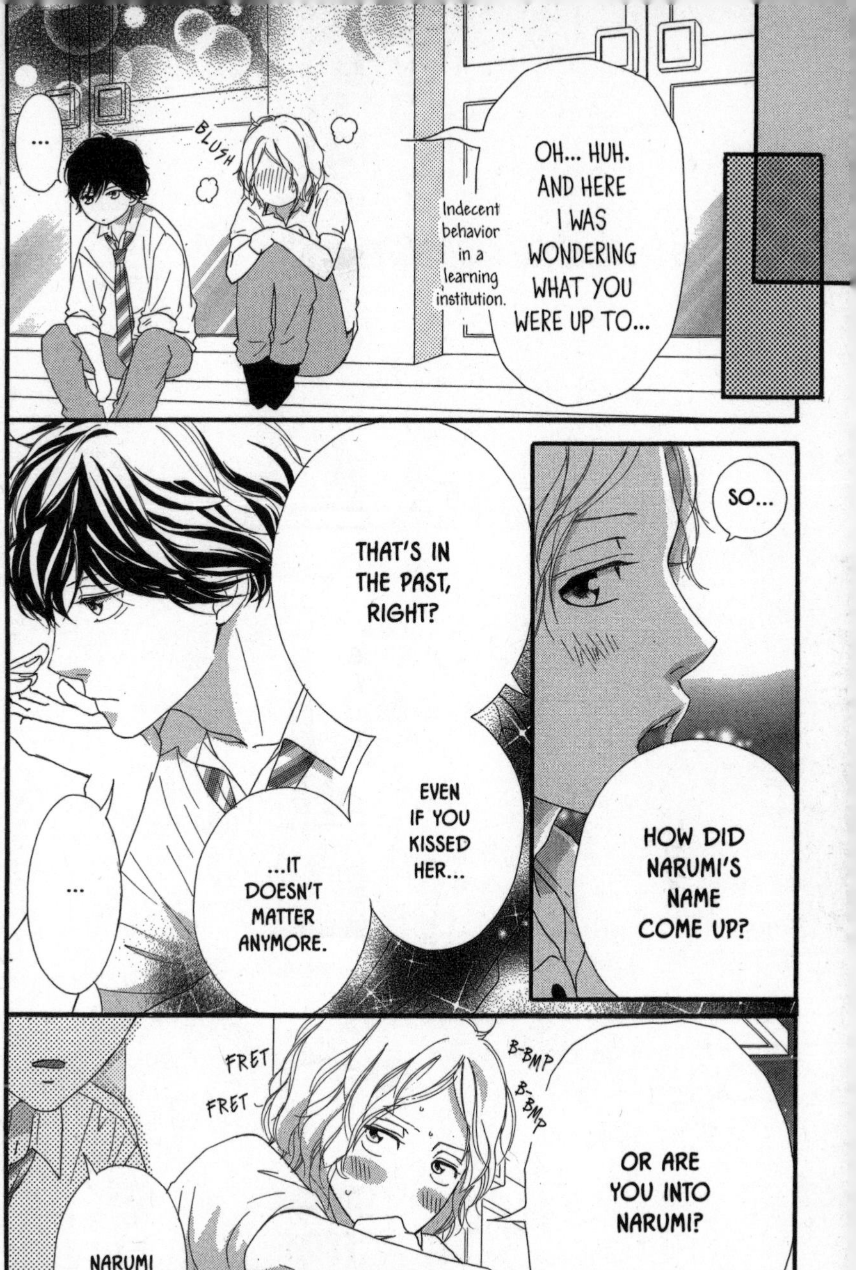
OH... HUH. AND HERE I WAS WONDERING WHAT YOU WERE UP TO...
Indecent behavior in a learning institution.
BLUSH
...
SO...
HOW DID NARUMI'S NAME COME UP?
THAT'S IN THE PAST, RIGHT?
EVEN IF YOU KISSED HER...
...IT DOESN'T MATTER ANYMORE.
...
B-BMP
B-BMP
OR ARE YOU INTO NARUMI?
FRET
FRET
NARUMI IS...

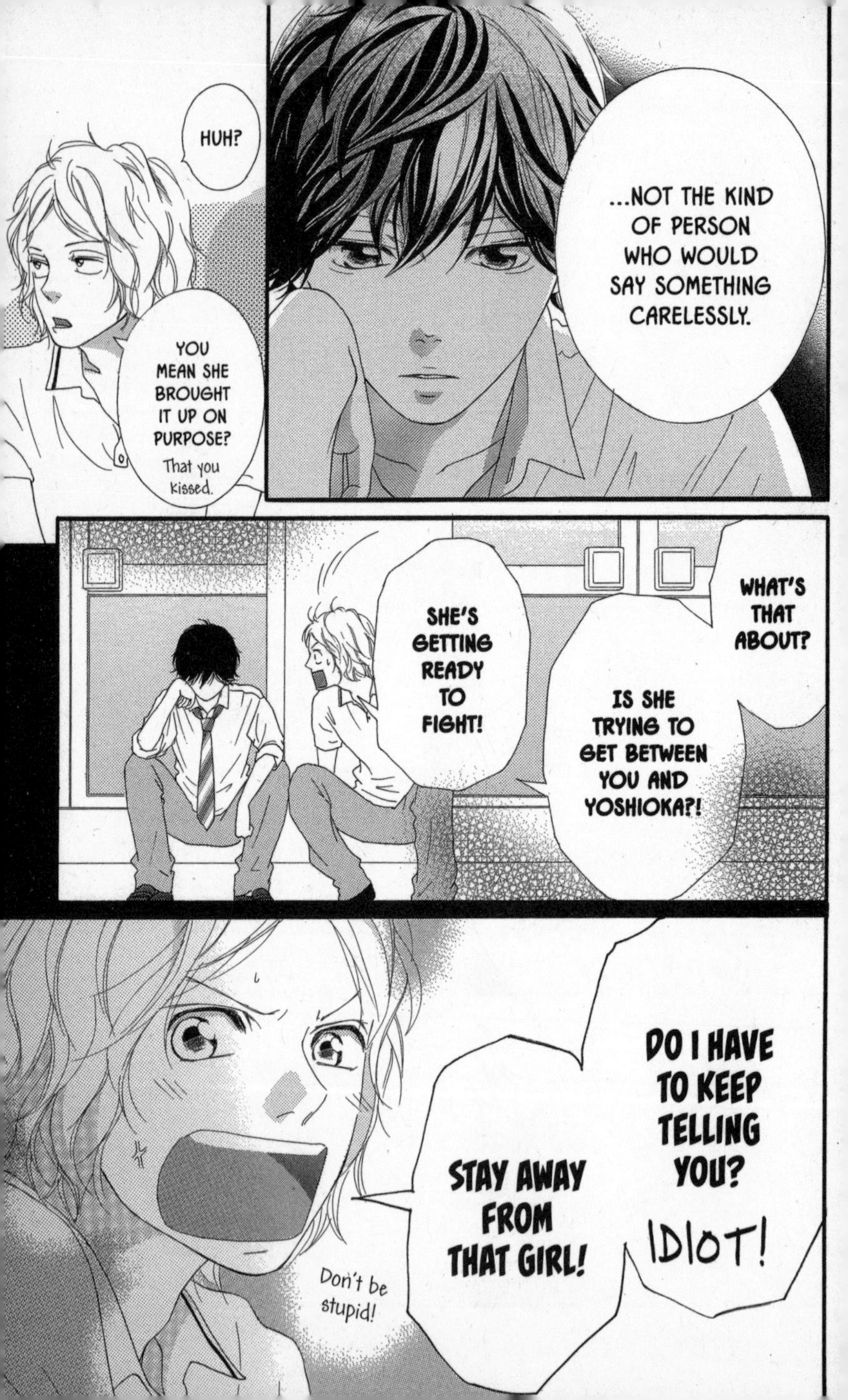
...NOT THE KIND OF PERSON WHO WOULD SAY SOMETHING CARELESSLY.
HUH?
YOU MEAN SHE BROUGHT IT UP ON PURPOSE?
That you kissed.
WHAT'S THAT ABOUT?
IS SHE TRYING TO GET BETWEEN YOU AND YOSHIOKA?!
SHE'S GETTING READY TO FIGHT!
DO I HAVE TO KEEP TELLING YOU?
IDIOT!
STAY AWAY FROM THAT GIRL!
Don't be stupid!

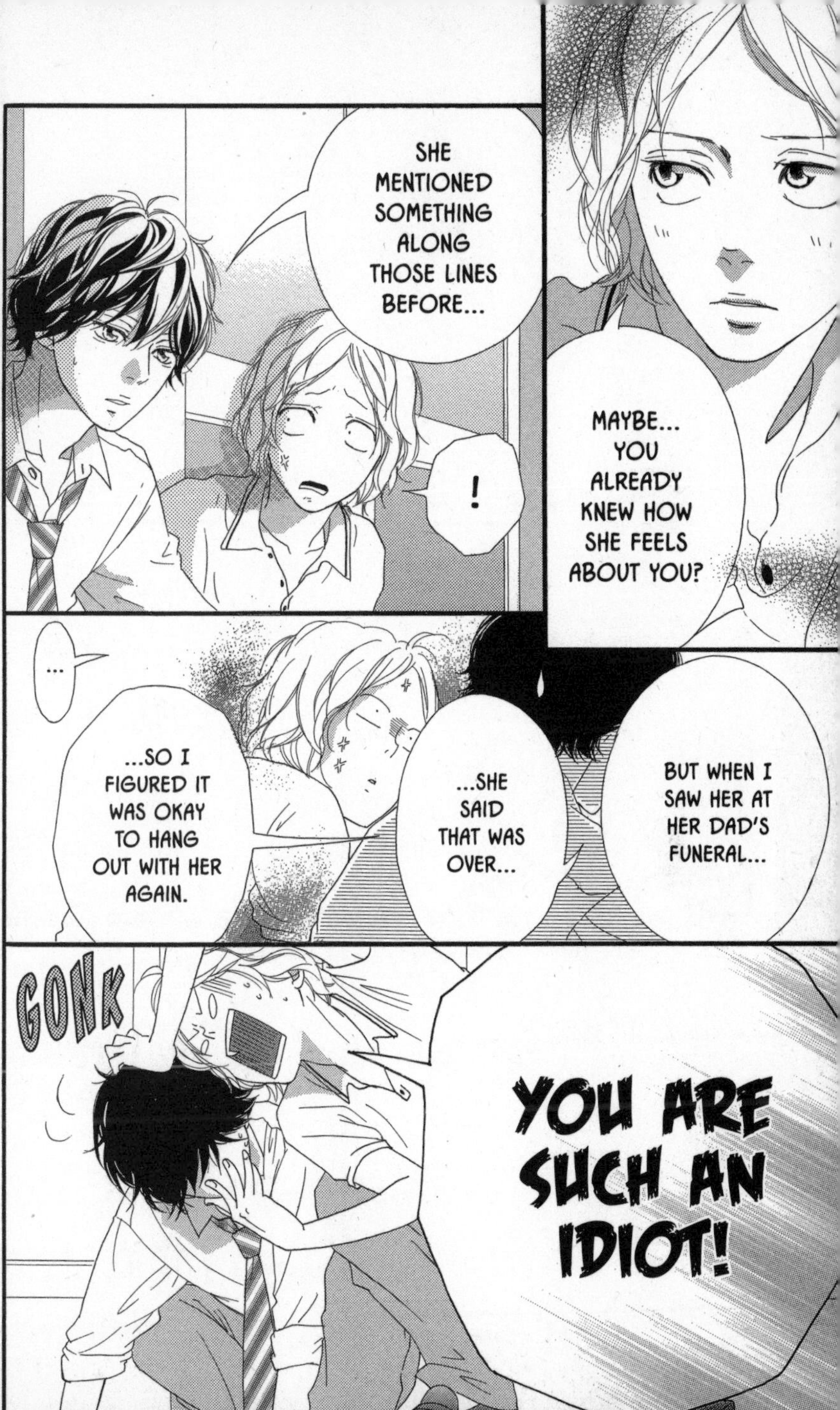
MAYBE... YOU ALREADY KNEW HOW SHE FEELS ABOUT YOU?
SHE MENTIONED SOMETHING ALONG THOSE LINES BEFORE...
!
BUT WHEN I SAW HER AT HER DAD'S FUNERAL...
...SHE SAID THAT WAS OVER...
...SO I FIGURED IT WAS OKAY TO HANG OUT WITH HER AGAIN.
...
YOU ARE SUCH AN IDIOT!
GONK

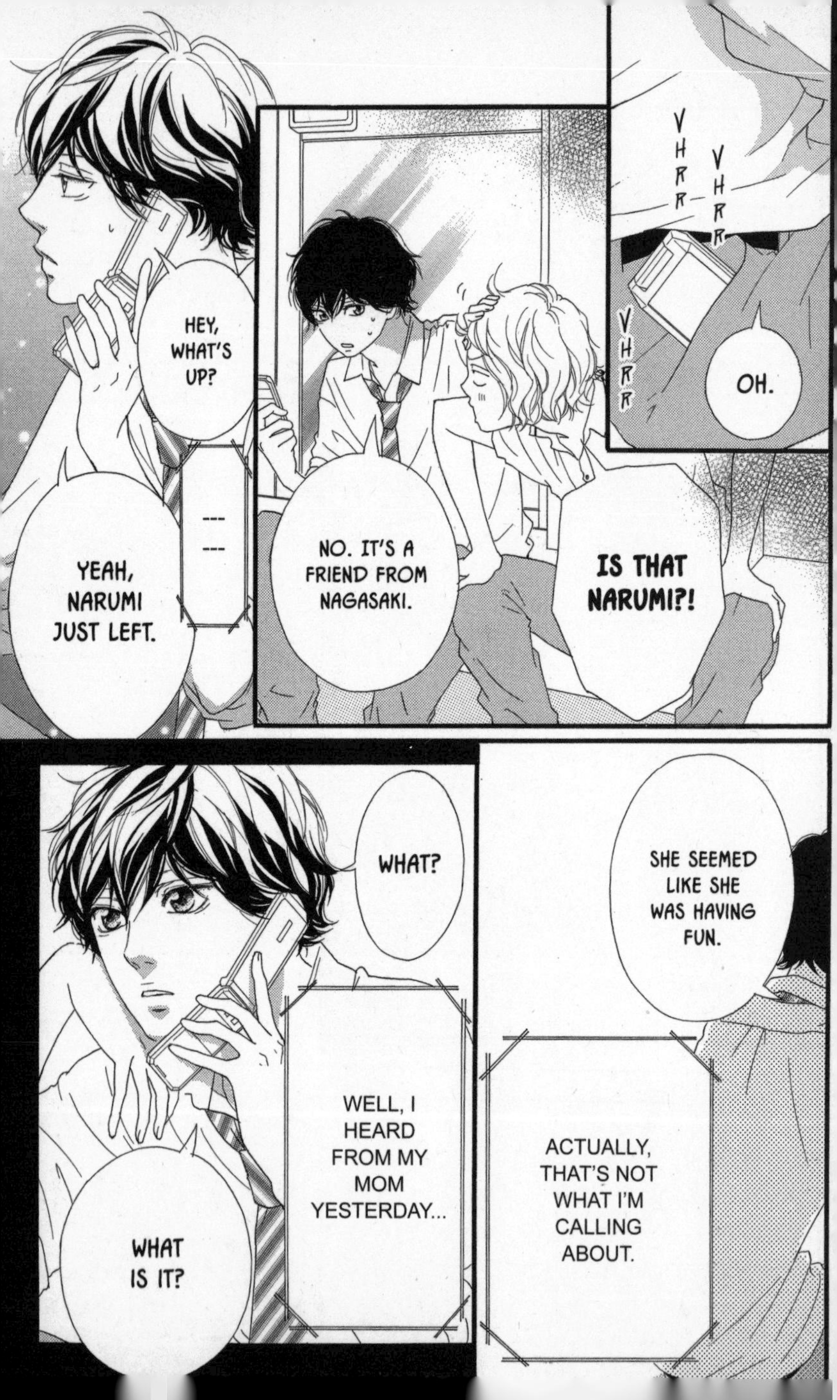
VHRR VHRR
VHRR
OH.
IS THAT NARUMI?!
NO. IT'S A FRIEND FROM NAGASAKI.
HEY, WHAT'S UP?

YEAH, NARUMI JUST LEFT.
SHE SEEMED LIKE SHE WAS HAVING FUN.
ACTUALLY, THAT'S NOT WHAT I'M CALLING ABOUT.
WHAT?
WELL, I HEARD FROM MY MOM YESTERDAY...
WHAT IS IT?

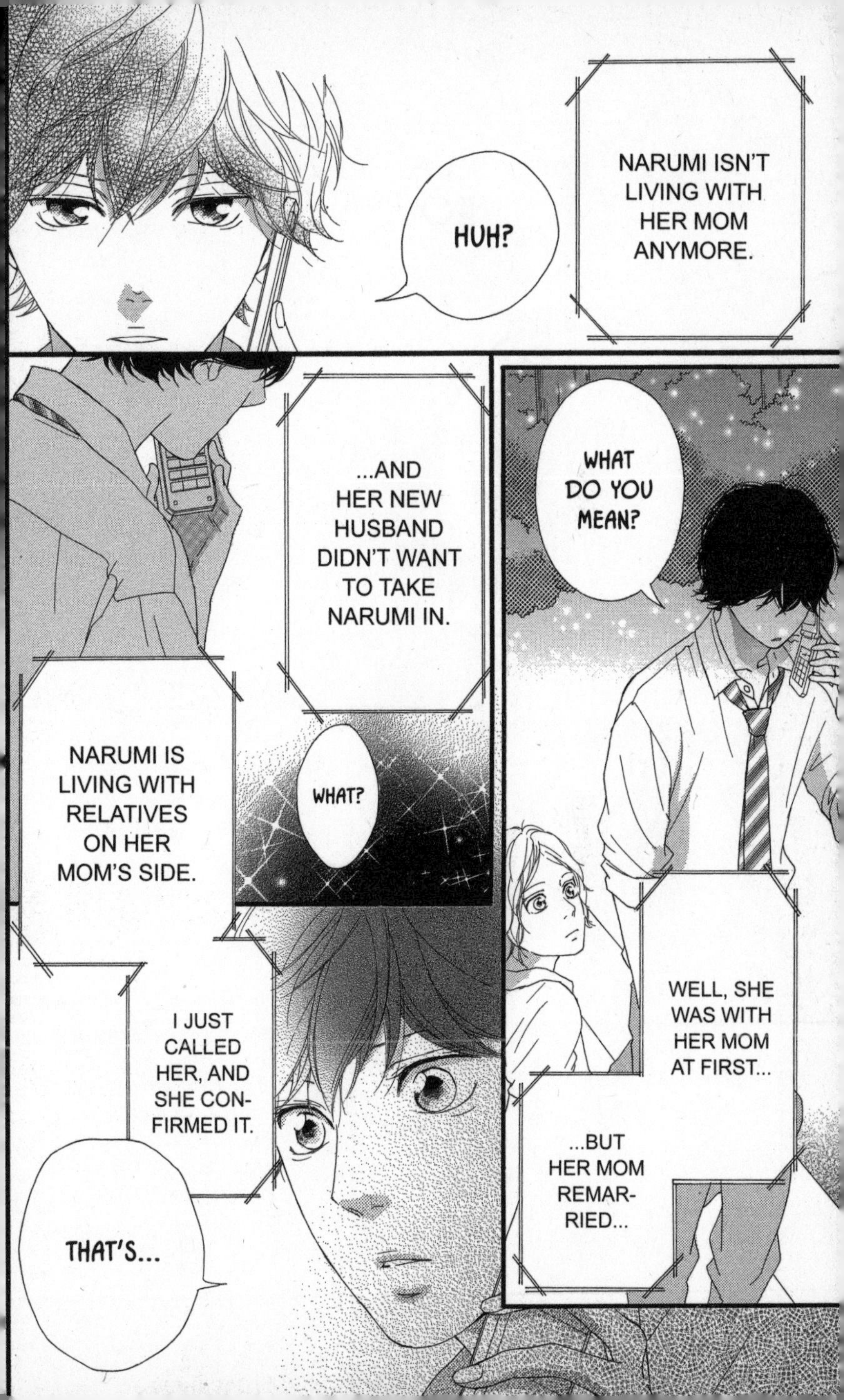
NARUMI ISN'T LIVING WITH HER MOM ANYMORE.
HUH?
WHAT DO YOU MEAN?
WELL, SHE WAS WITH HER MOM AT FIRST...
...BUT HER MOM REMAR-RIED...
...AND HER NEW HUSBAND DIDN'T WANT TO TAKE NARUMI IN.
WHAT?
NARUMI IS LIVING WITH RELATIVES ON HER MOM'S SIDE.
I JUST CALLED HER, AND SHE CON-FIRMED IT.
THAT'S...

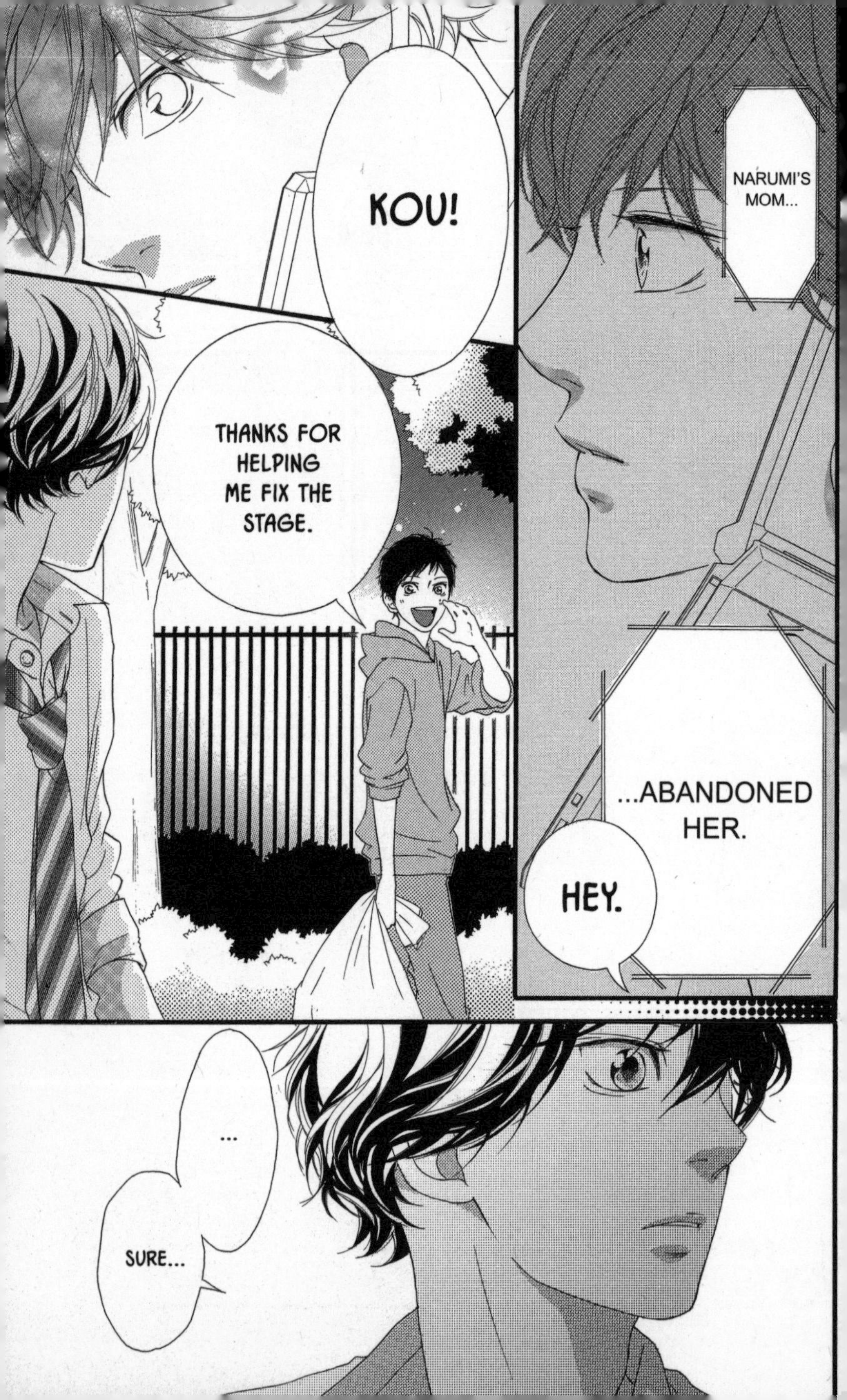
NARUMI'S MOM...
...ABANDONED HER.
HEY.
KOU!
THANKS FOR HELPING ME FIX THE STAGE.
...
SURE...

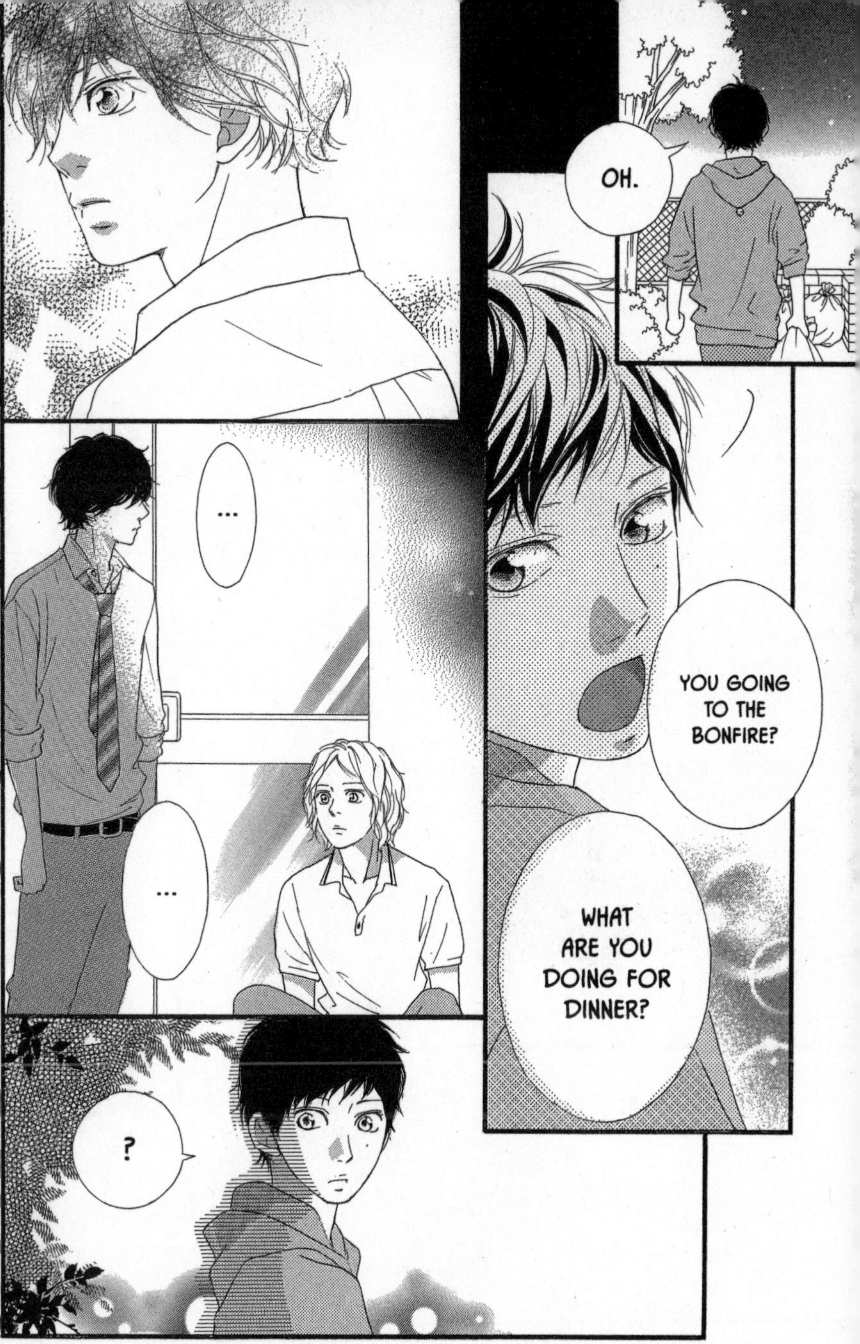
OH.
YOU GOING TO THE BONFIRE?
WHAT ARE YOU DOING FOR DINNER?
...
...
?

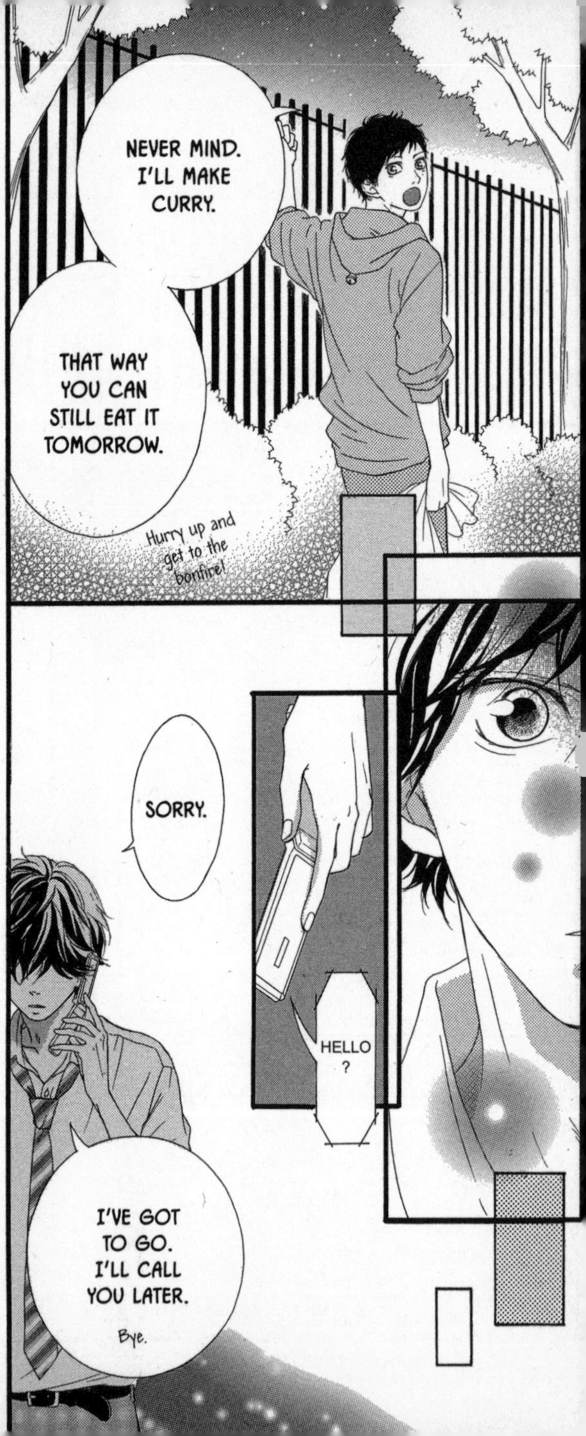
NEVER MIND. I'LL MAKE CURRY.
THAT WAY YOU CAN STILL EAT IT TOMORROW.
Hurry up and get to the bonfire!
HELLO?
SORRY.
I'VE GOT TO GO. I'LL CALL YOU LATER.
Bye.

As I wrote in the last volume, I recently moved my work area into a slightly bigger room, and I'd just like to say that I really appreciate the open space. Before I would work myself into a frenzy to meet a deadline, and the added pressure of the small space would send me spinning—Argh! I'm truly glad to be in this new room, even though moving was a pain. At the same time, when I think about how much work my assistants do, I think I should try to make space for another person, which means losing the open space. And I want another large desk... I suppose I need a work area that is ginormous. And you know, I think I'm going to make that my goal. Which means I need to work harder! And when I meet all my goals, I think I'll change the chairs again. I just upgraded my chairs, but right after doing so I found another style that I liked even more. I hope these dreams become reality.

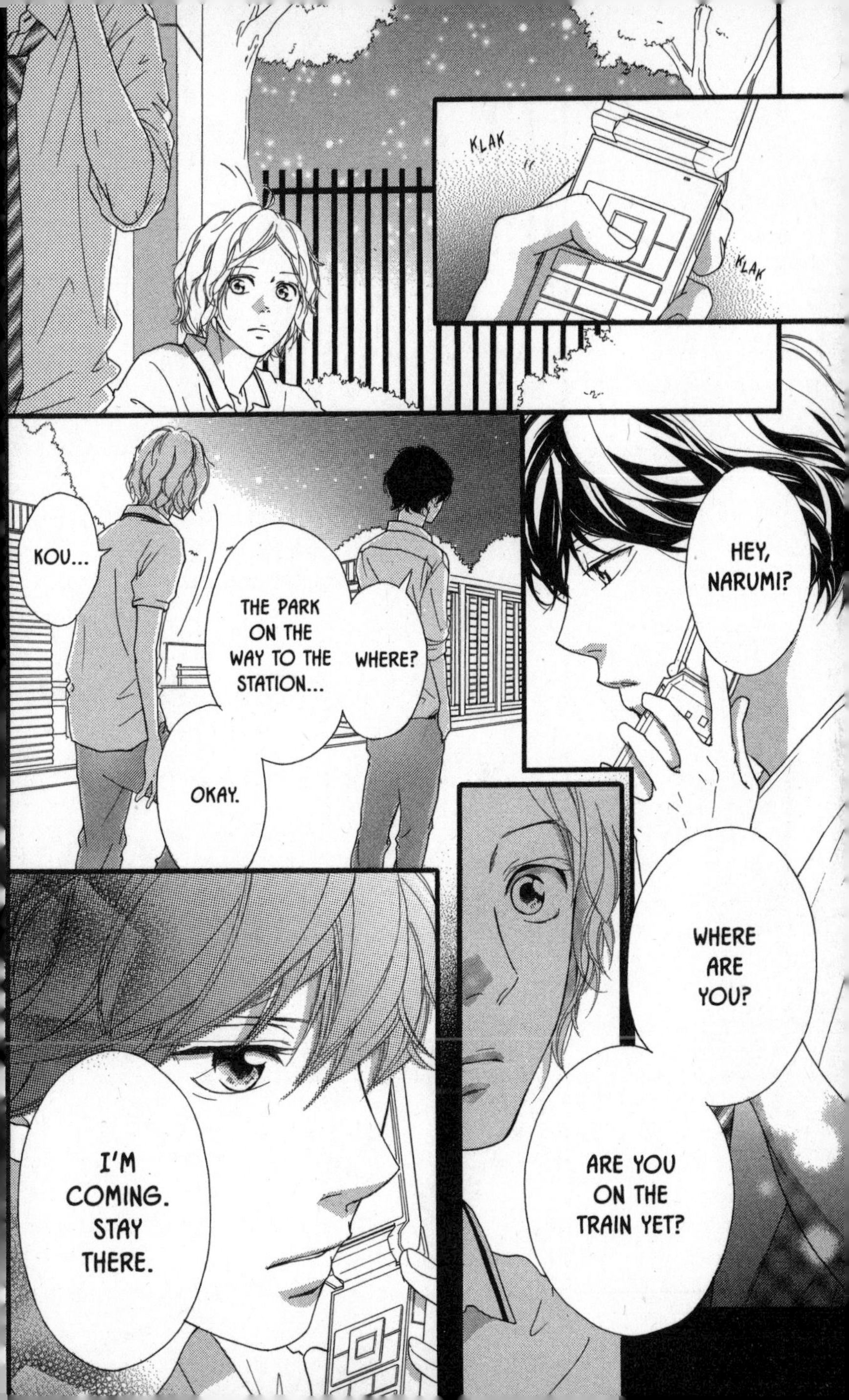
KLAK
KLAK
HEY, NARUMI?
WHERE ARE YOU?
ARE YOU ON THE TRAIN YET?
WHERE?
THE PARK ON THE WAY TO THE STATION...
KOU...
OKAY.
I'M COMING. STAY THERE.

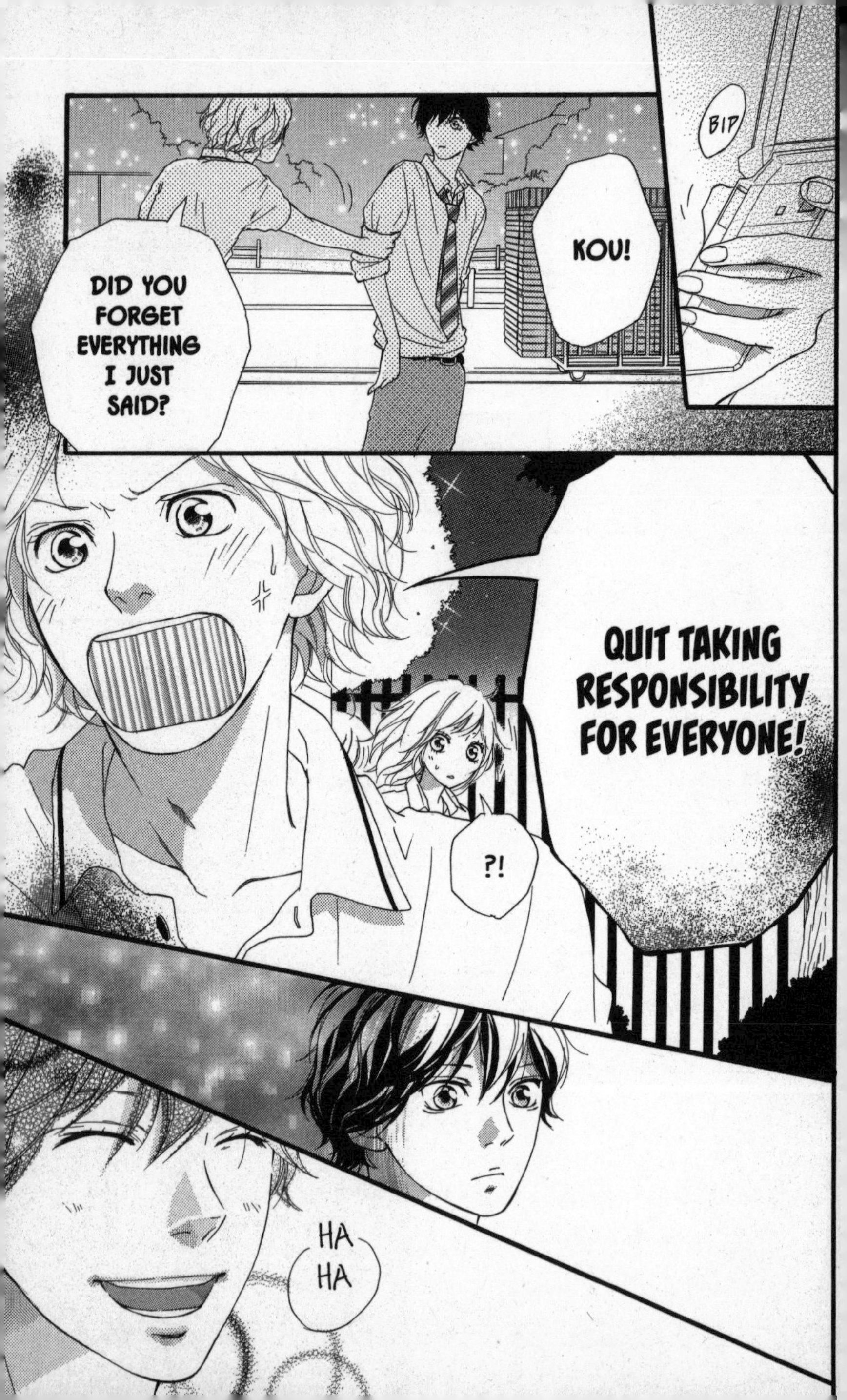
BIP
KOU!
DID YOU FORGET EVERYTHING I JUST SAID?
QUIT TAKING RESPONSIBILITY FOR EVERYONE!
?!
HA HA

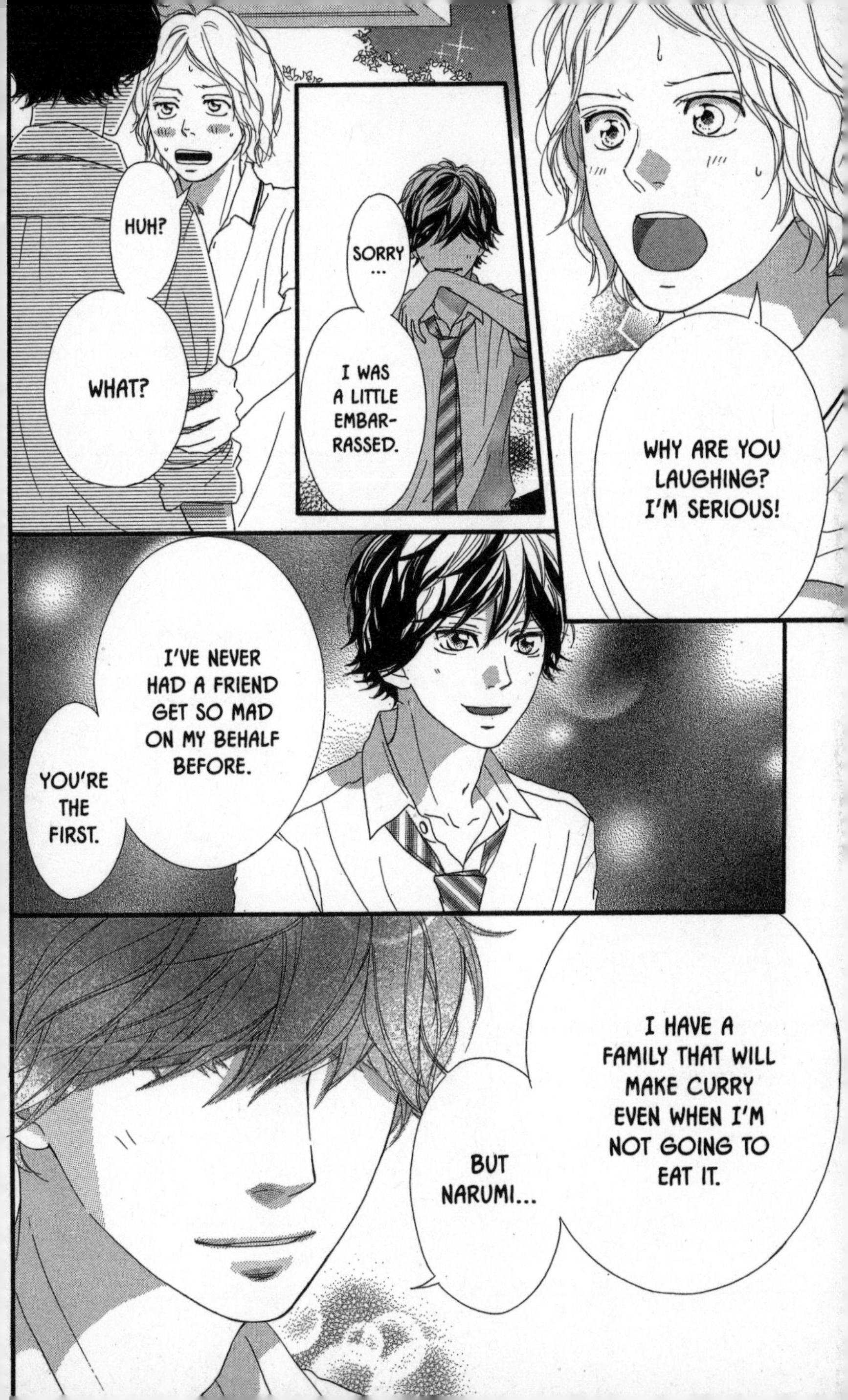
WHY ARE YOU LAUGHING? I'M SERIOUS!
SORRY ...
I WAS A LITTLE EMBARRASSED.
HUH?
WHAT?
I'VE NEVER HAD A FRIEND GET SO MAD ON MY BEHALF BEFORE.
YOU'RE THE FIRST.
I HAVE A FAMILY THAT WILL MAKE CURRY EVEN WHEN I'M NOT GOING TO EAT IT.
BUT NARUMI...

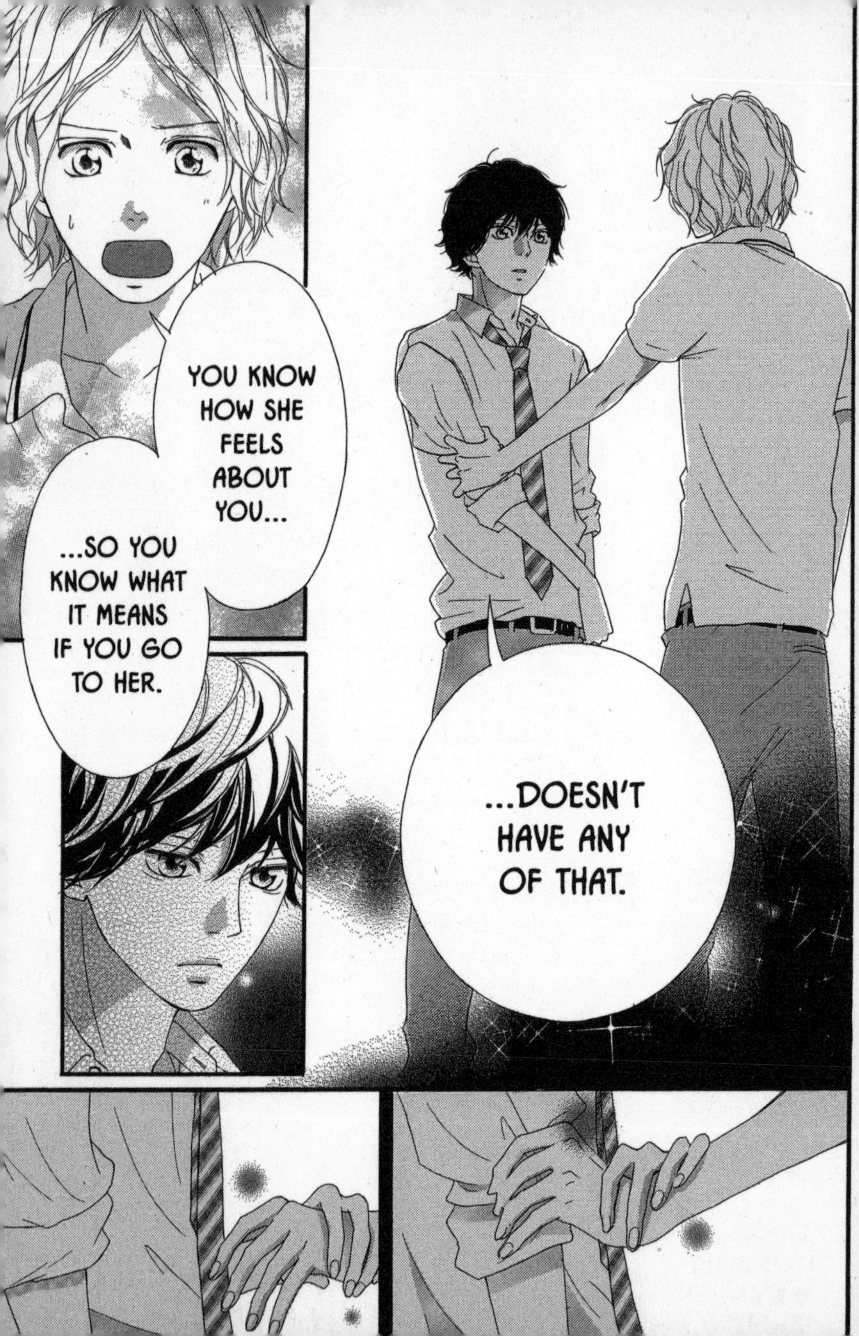
...DOESN'T HAVE ANY OF THAT.
YOU KNOW HOW SHE FEELS ABOUT YOU...
...SO YOU KNOW WHAT IT MEANS IF YOU GO TO HER.

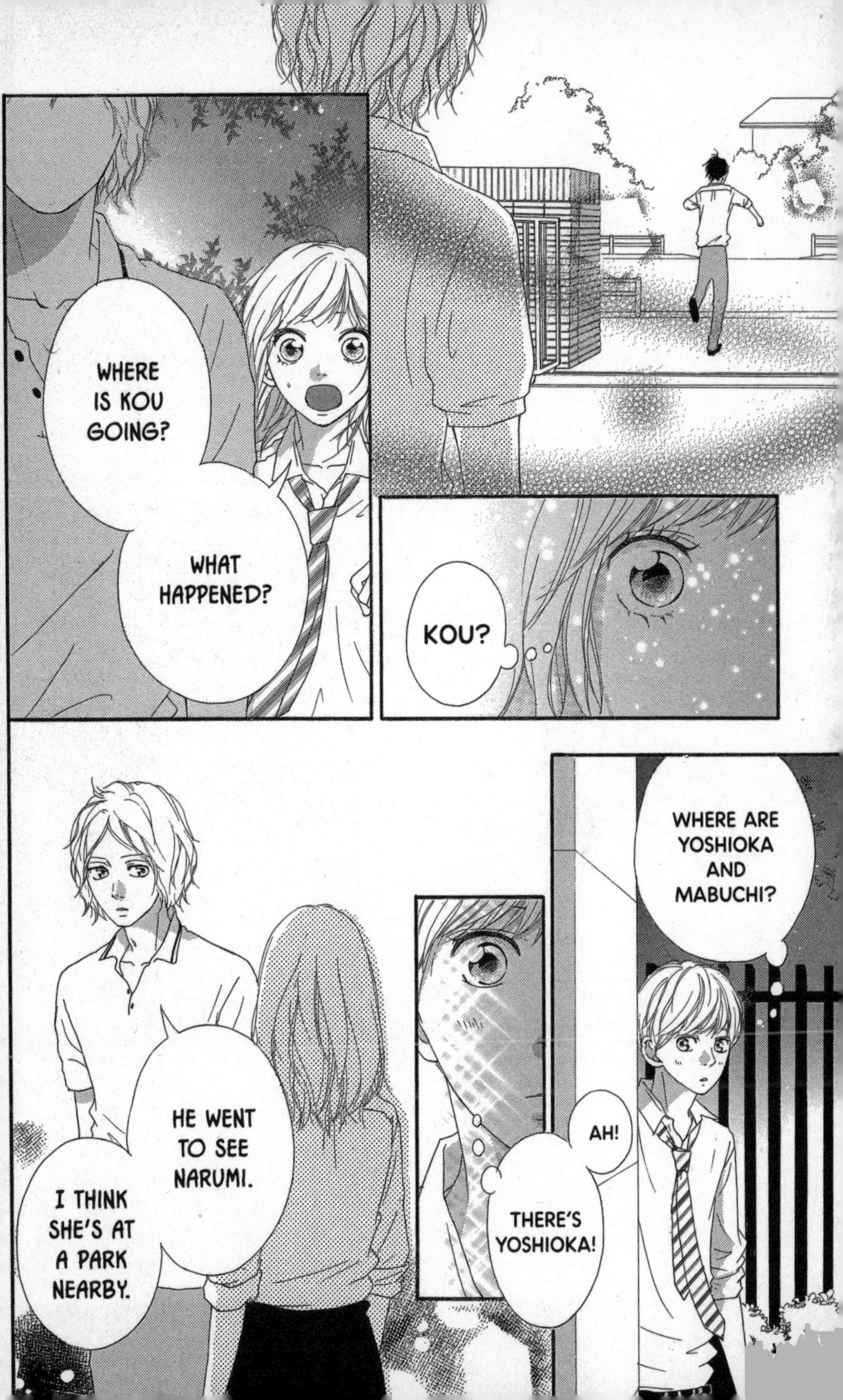
KOU?
WHERE IS KOU GOING?
WHAT HAPPENED?
WHERE ARE YOSHIOKA AND MABUCHI?
AH!
THERE'S YOSHIOKA!
HE WENT TO SEE NARUMI.
I THINK SHE'S AT A PARK NEARBY.

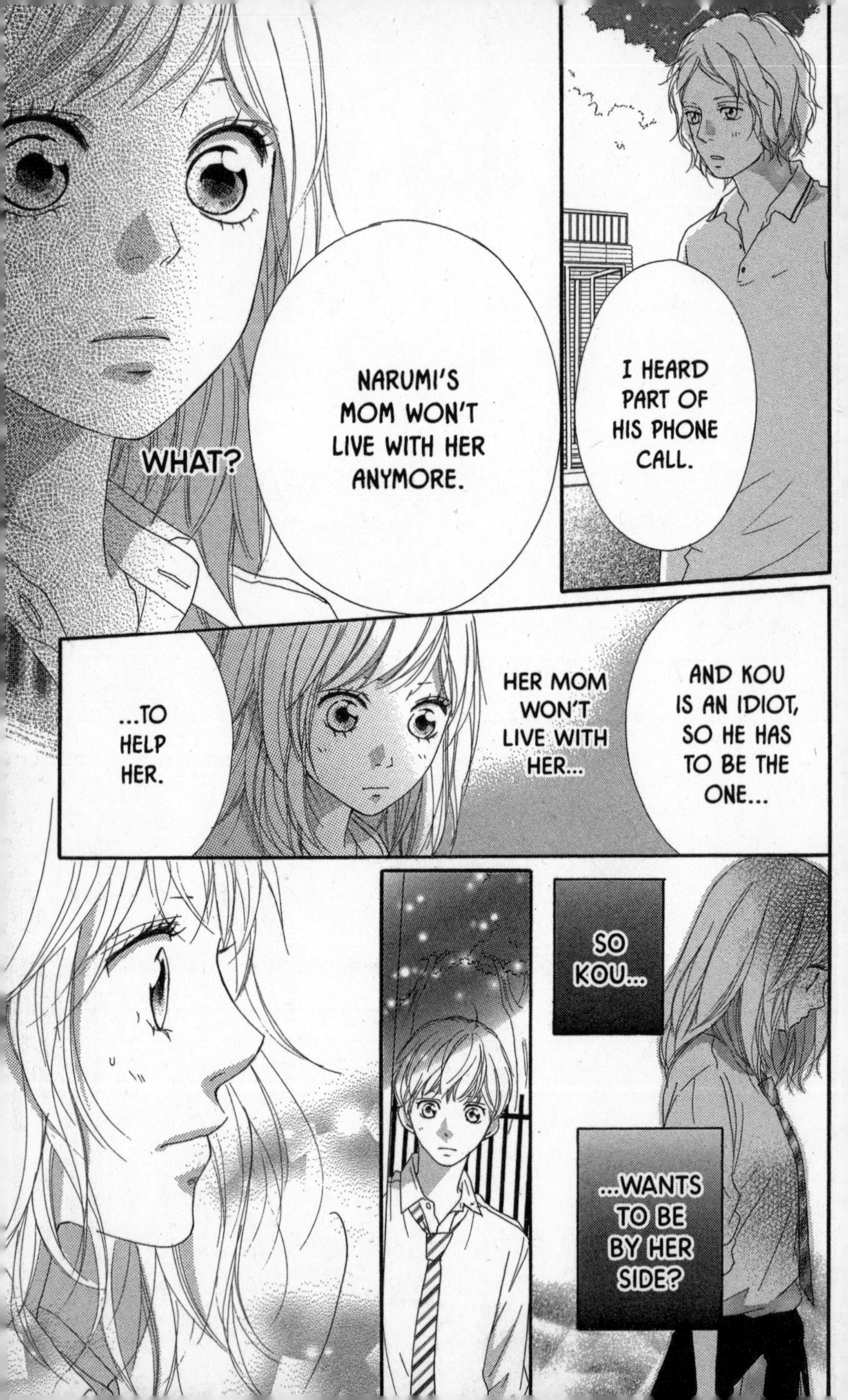
I HEARD PART OF HIS PHONE CALL.
NARUMI'S MOM WON'T LIVE WITH HER ANYMORE.
WHAT?
AND KOU IS AN IDIOT, SO HE HAS TO BE THE ONE...
HER MOM WON'T LIVE WITH HER...
...TO HELP HER.
SO KOU...
...WANTS TO BE BY HER SIDE?

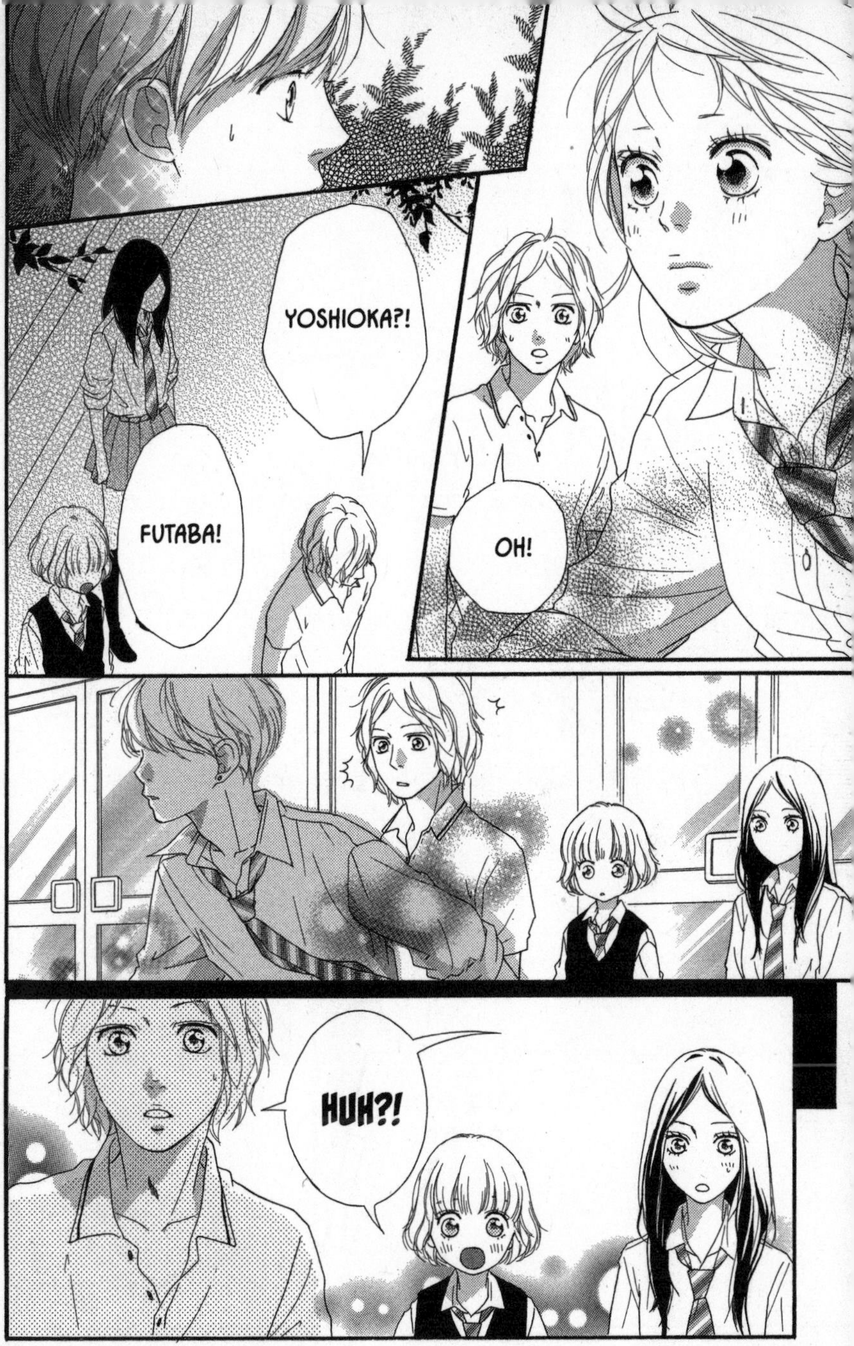
OH!
YOSHIOKA?!
FUTABA!
HUH?!

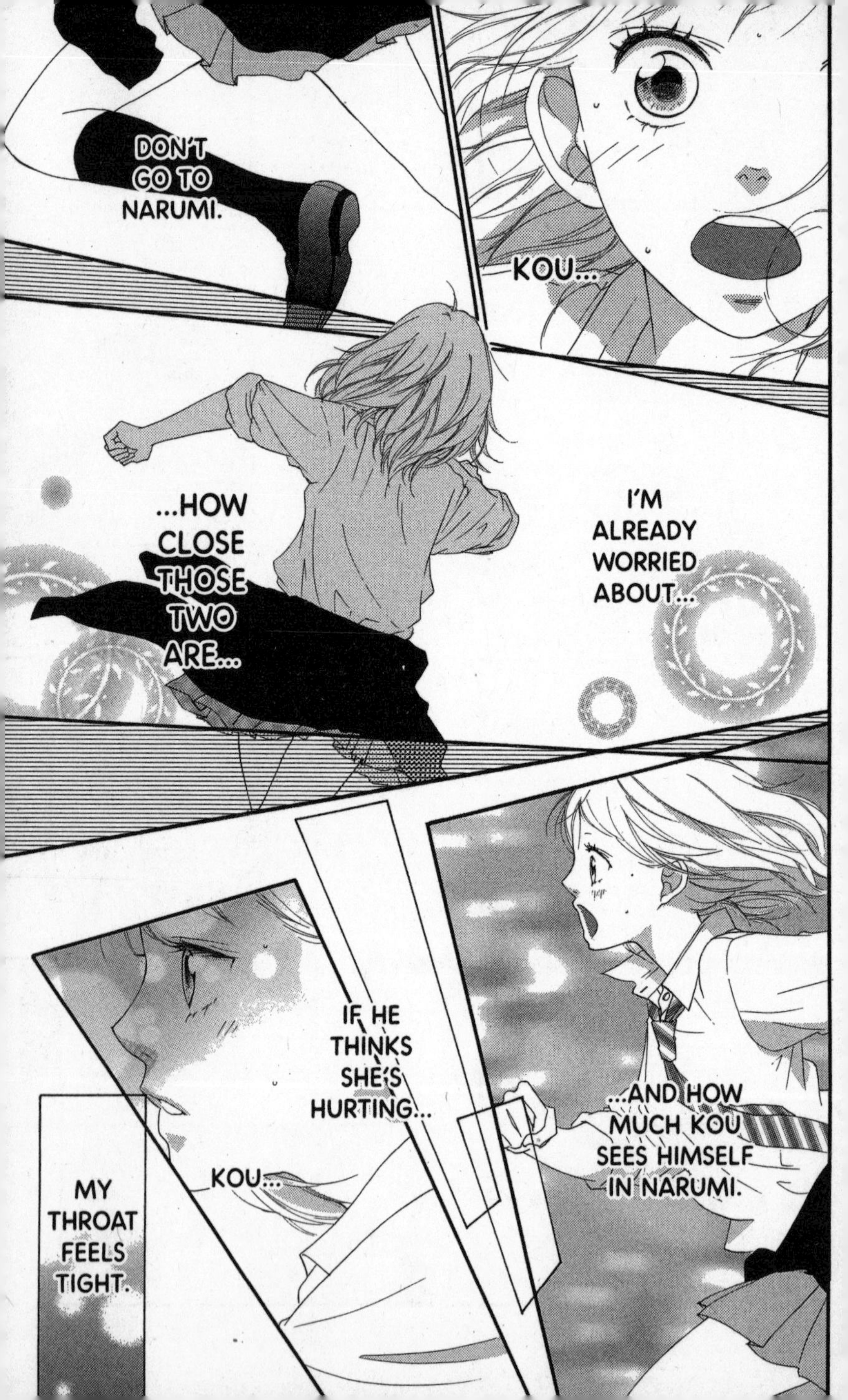
KOU...
DON'T GO TO NARUMI.
I'M ALREADY WORRIED ABOUT...
...HOW CLOSE THOSE TWO ARE...
...AND HOW MUCH KOU SEES HIMSELF IN NARUMI.
IF HE THINKS SHE'S HURTING...
KOU...
MY THROAT FEELS TIGHT.

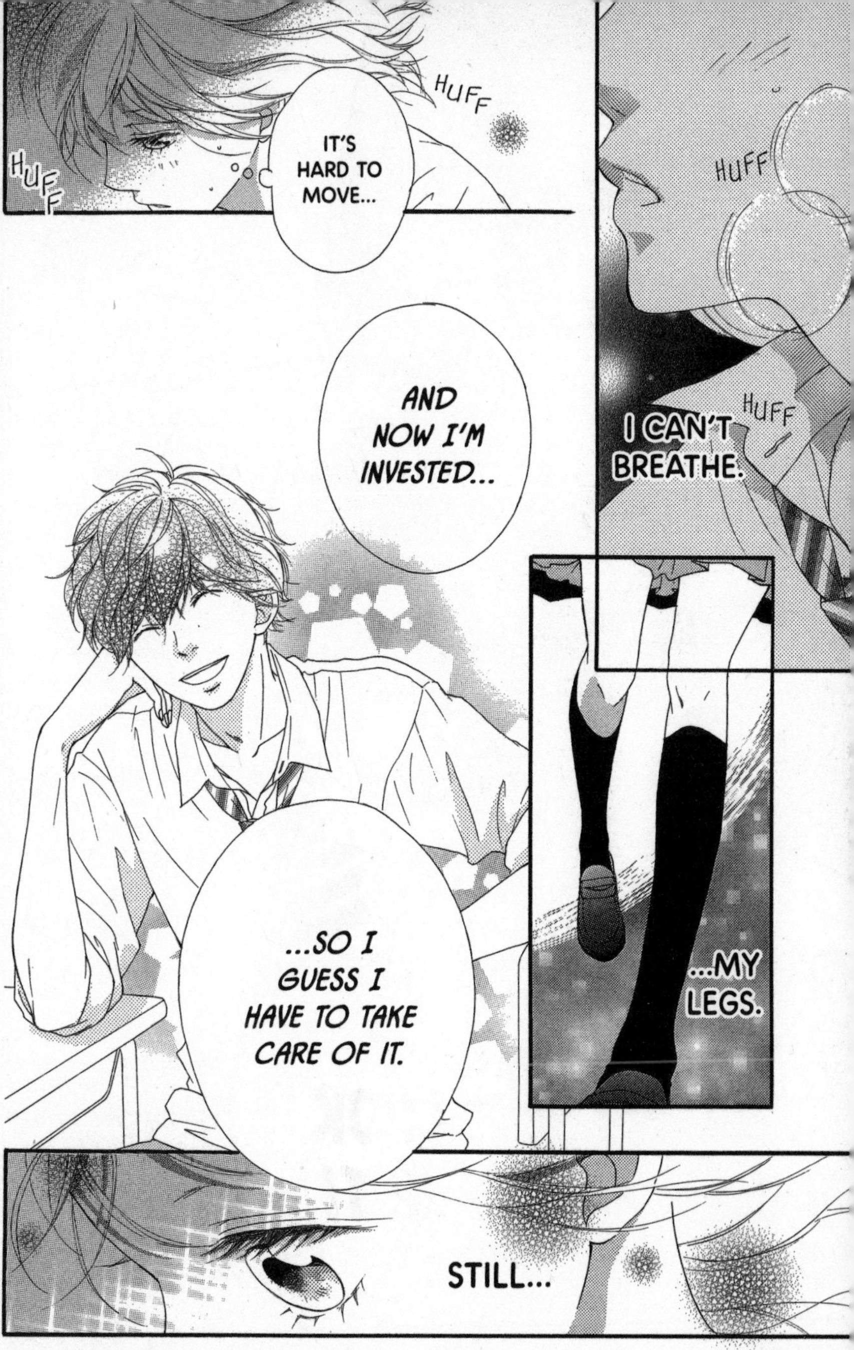
HUFF
HUFF
I CAN'T BREATHE.
HUFF
IT'S HARD TO MOVE...
HUFF
...MY LEGS.
AND NOW I'M INVESTED...
...SO I GUESS I HAVE TO TAKE CARE OF IT.
STILL...

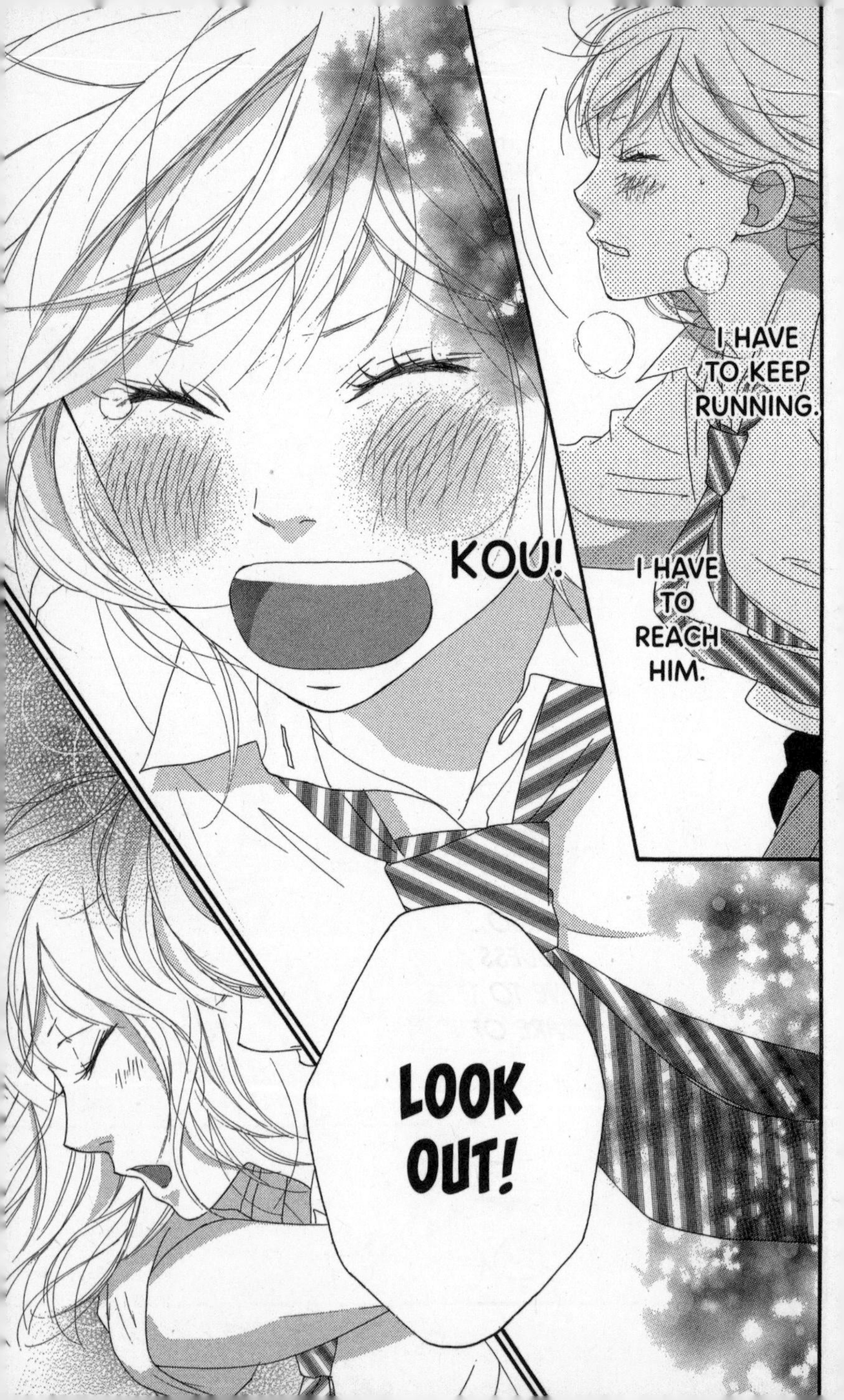
I HAVE TO KEEP RUNNING.
I HAVE TO REACH HIM.
KOU!
LOOK OUT!

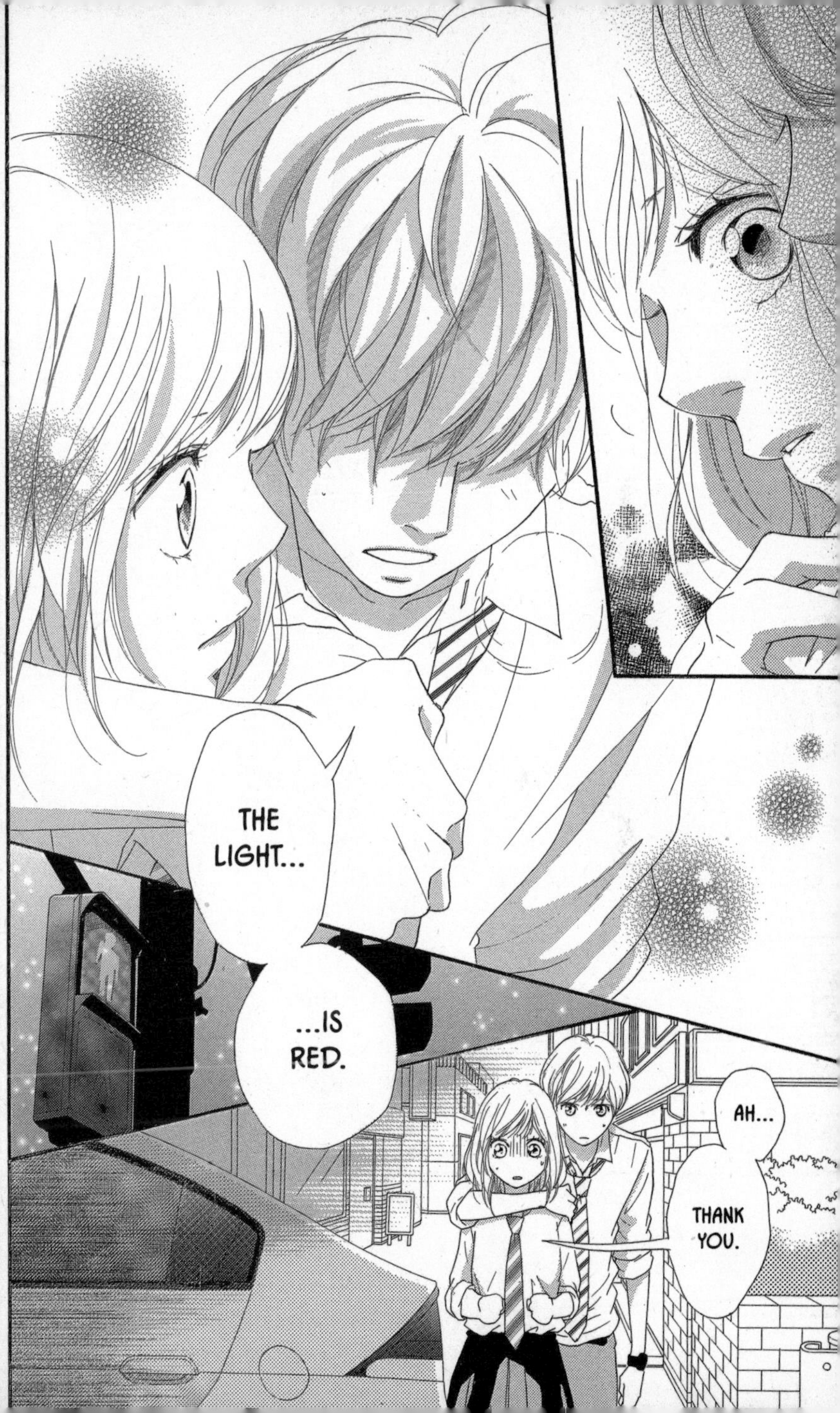
THE LIGHT...
...IS RED.
AH...
THANK YOU.

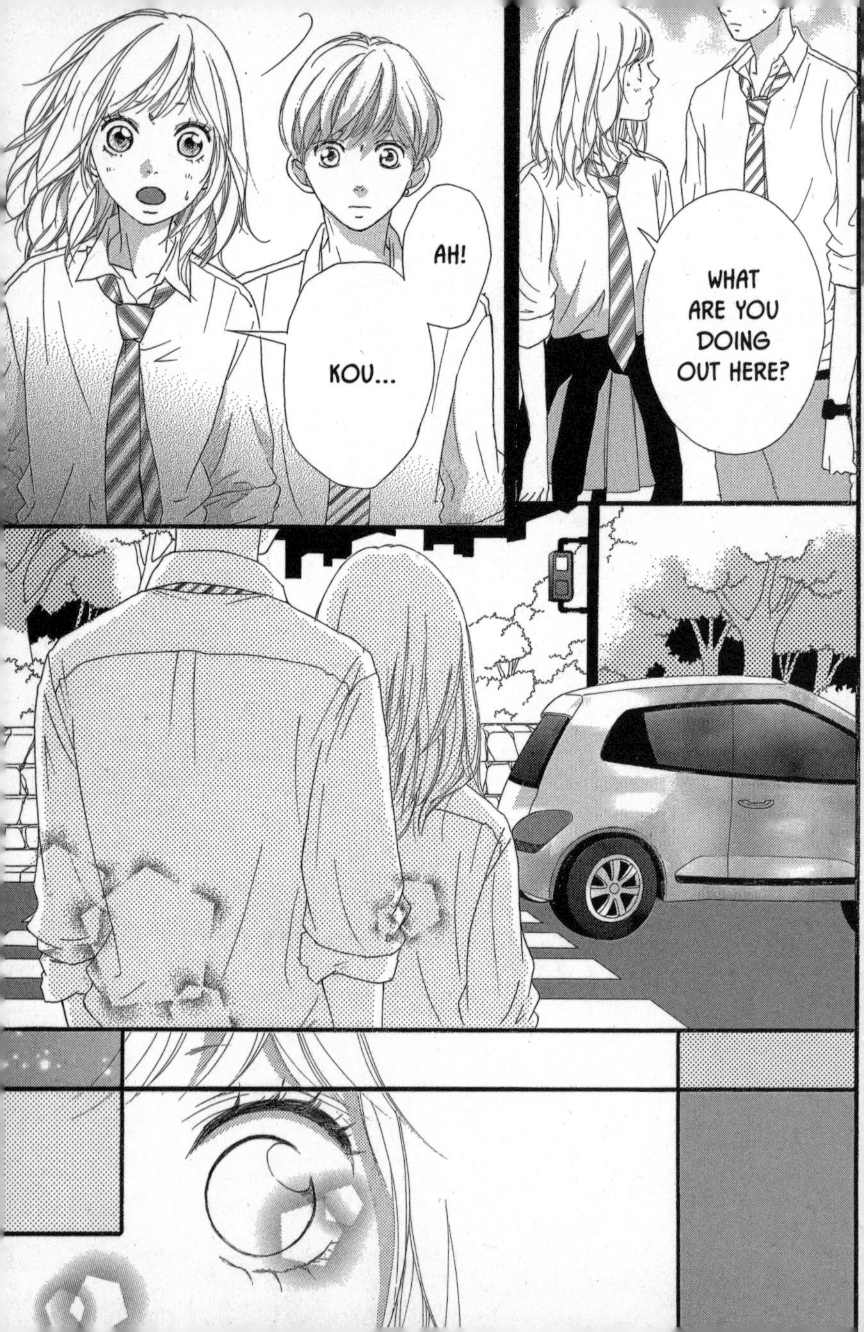
WHAT ARE YOU DOING OUT HERE?
AH!
KOU...

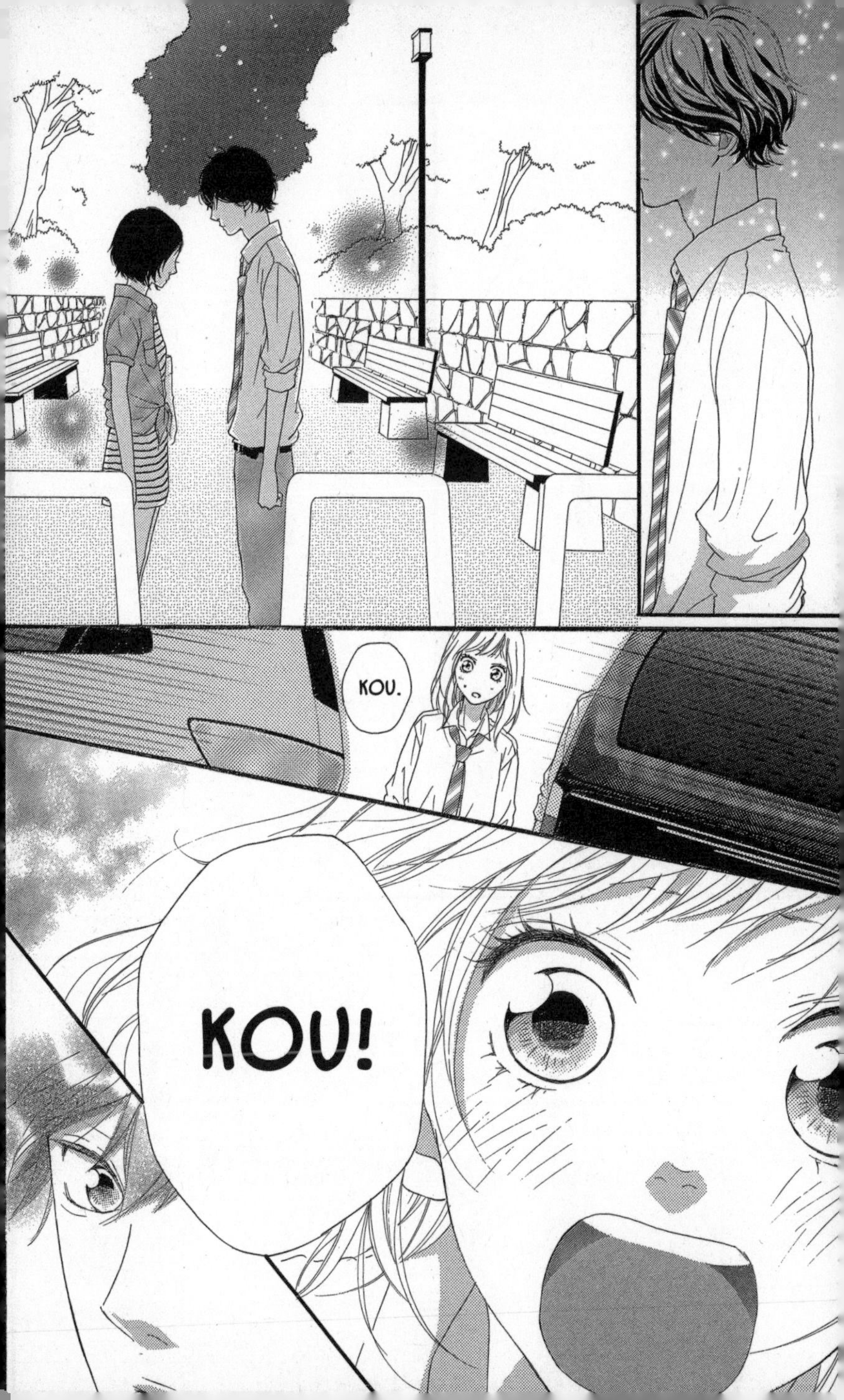
KOU.
KOU!

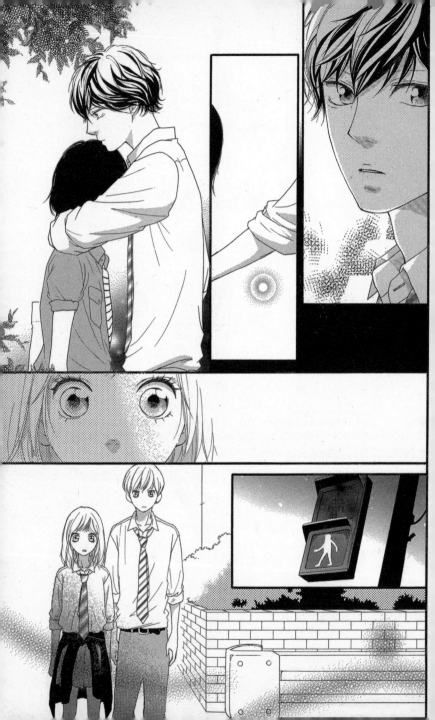

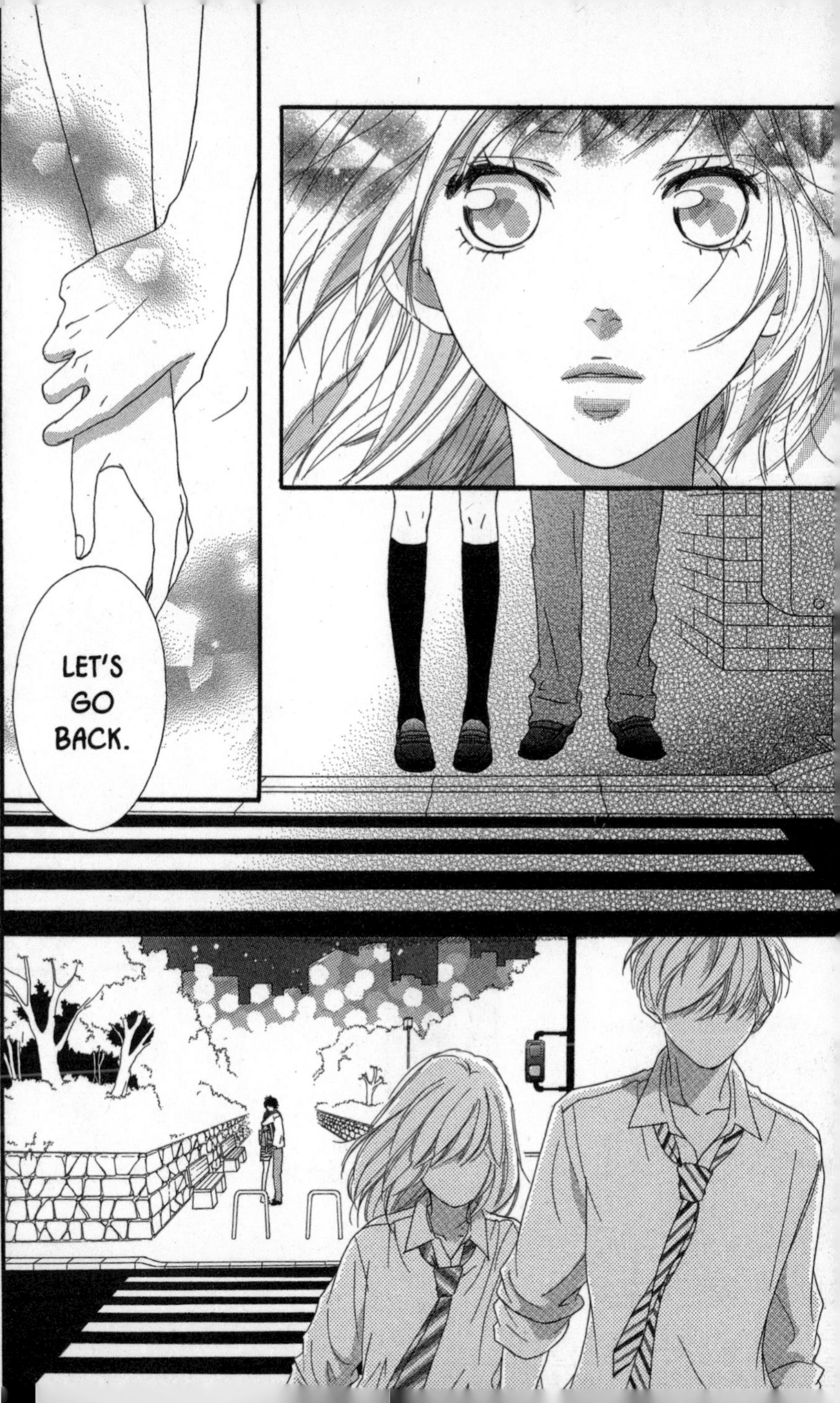
LET'S GO BACK.

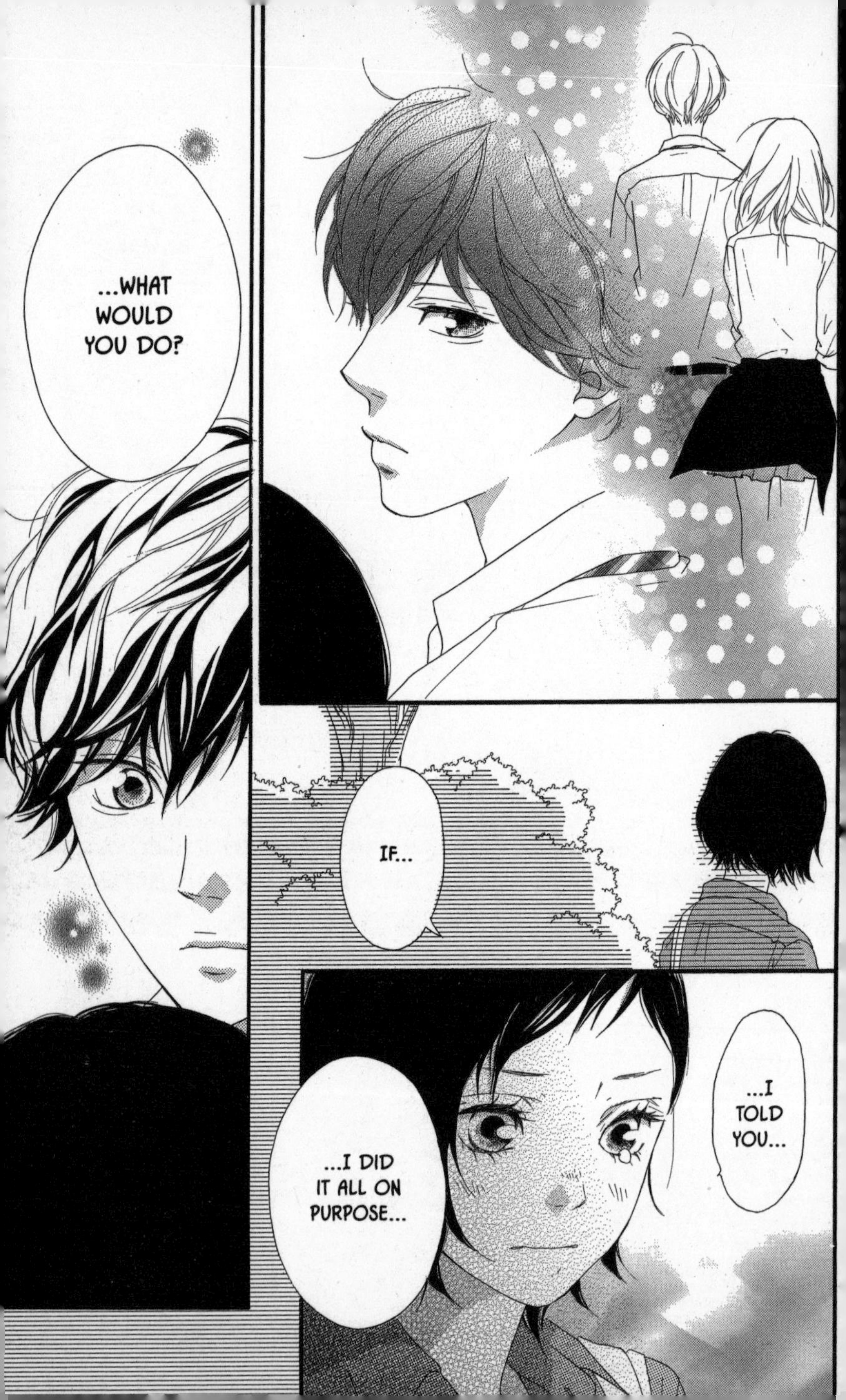
IF...
...I TOLD YOU...
...I DID IT ALL ON PURPOSE...
...WHAT WOULD YOU DO?

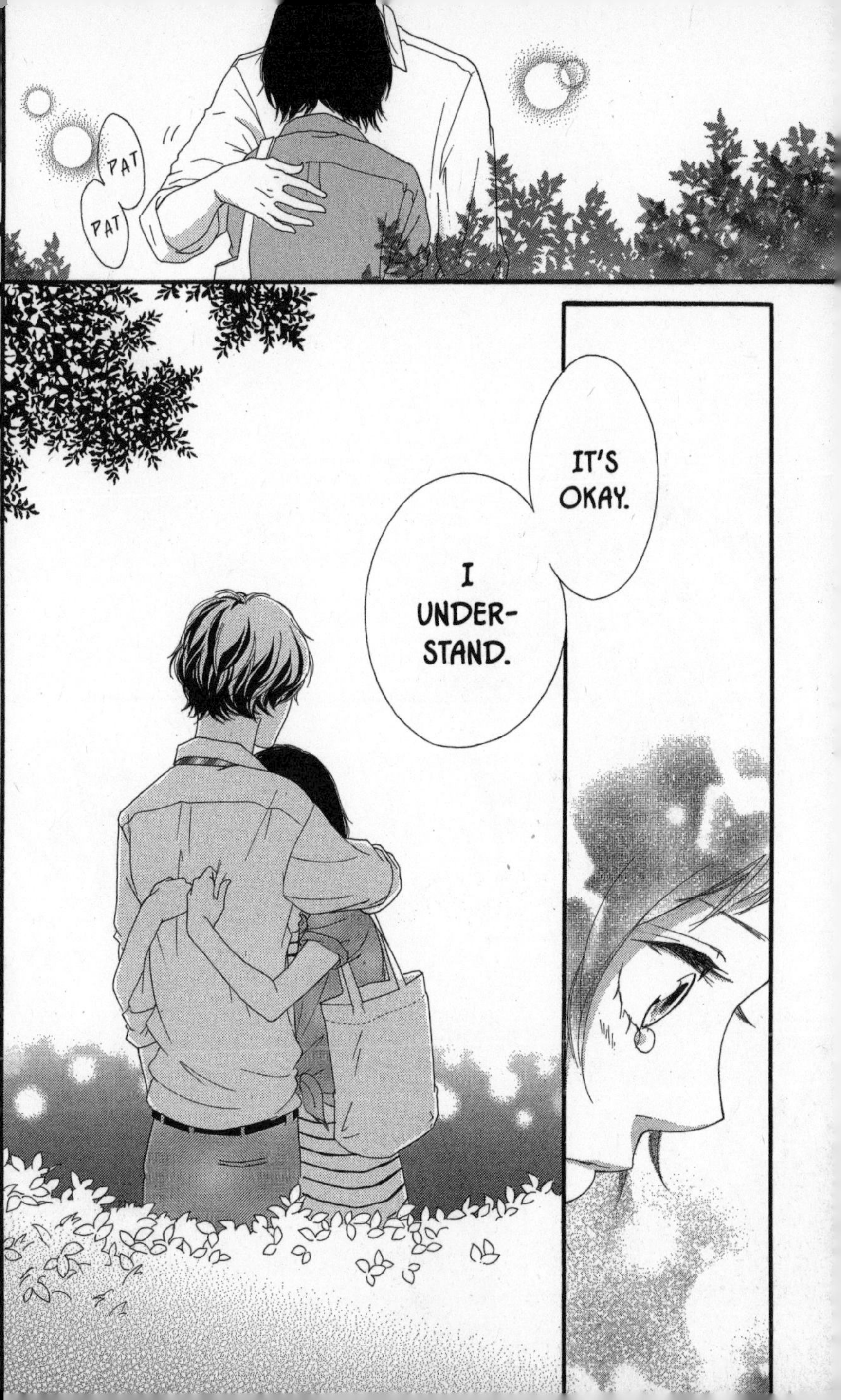
PAT PAT
IT'S OKAY.
I UNDER-STAND.

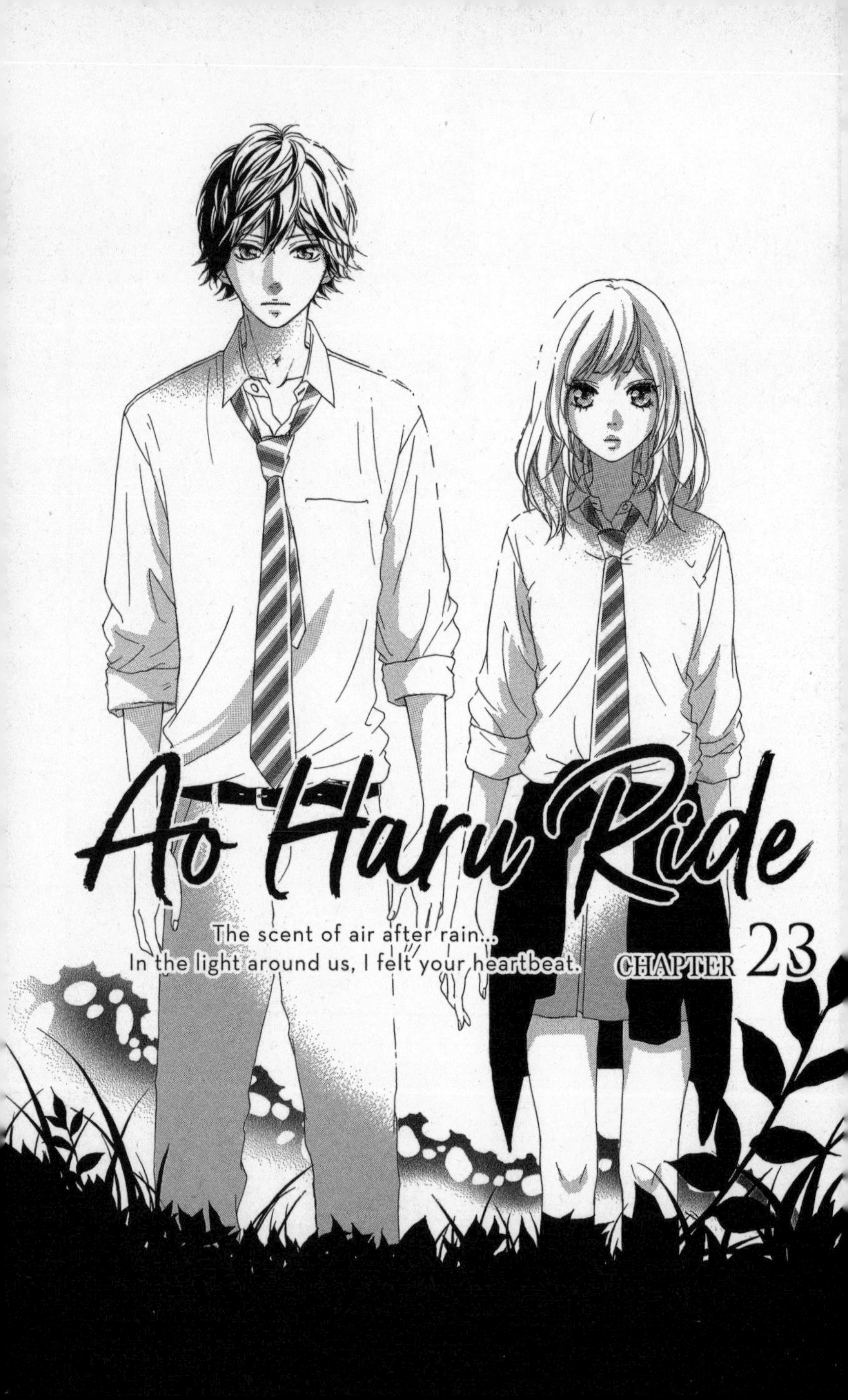

Ao Haru Ride
The scent of air after rain...
In the light around us, I felt your heartbeat.
CHAPTER 23

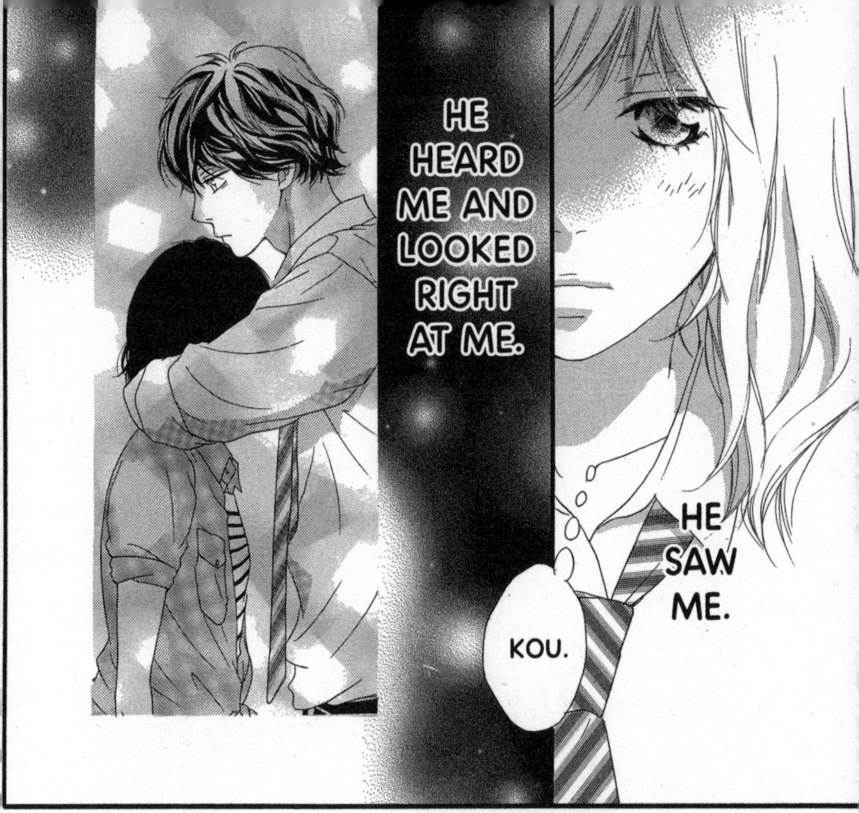
HE SAW ME.
KOU.
HE HEARD ME AND LOOKED RIGHT AT ME.

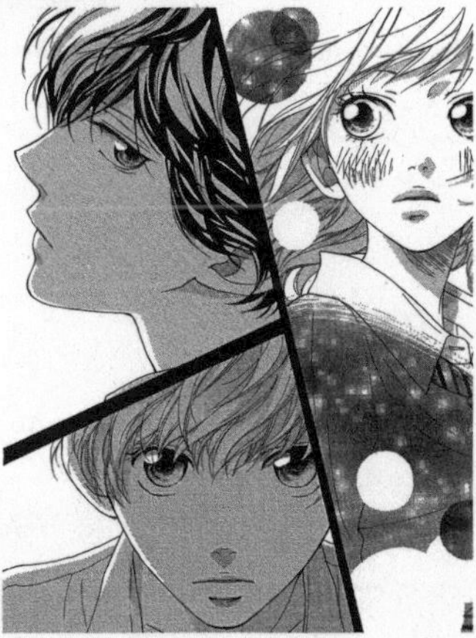

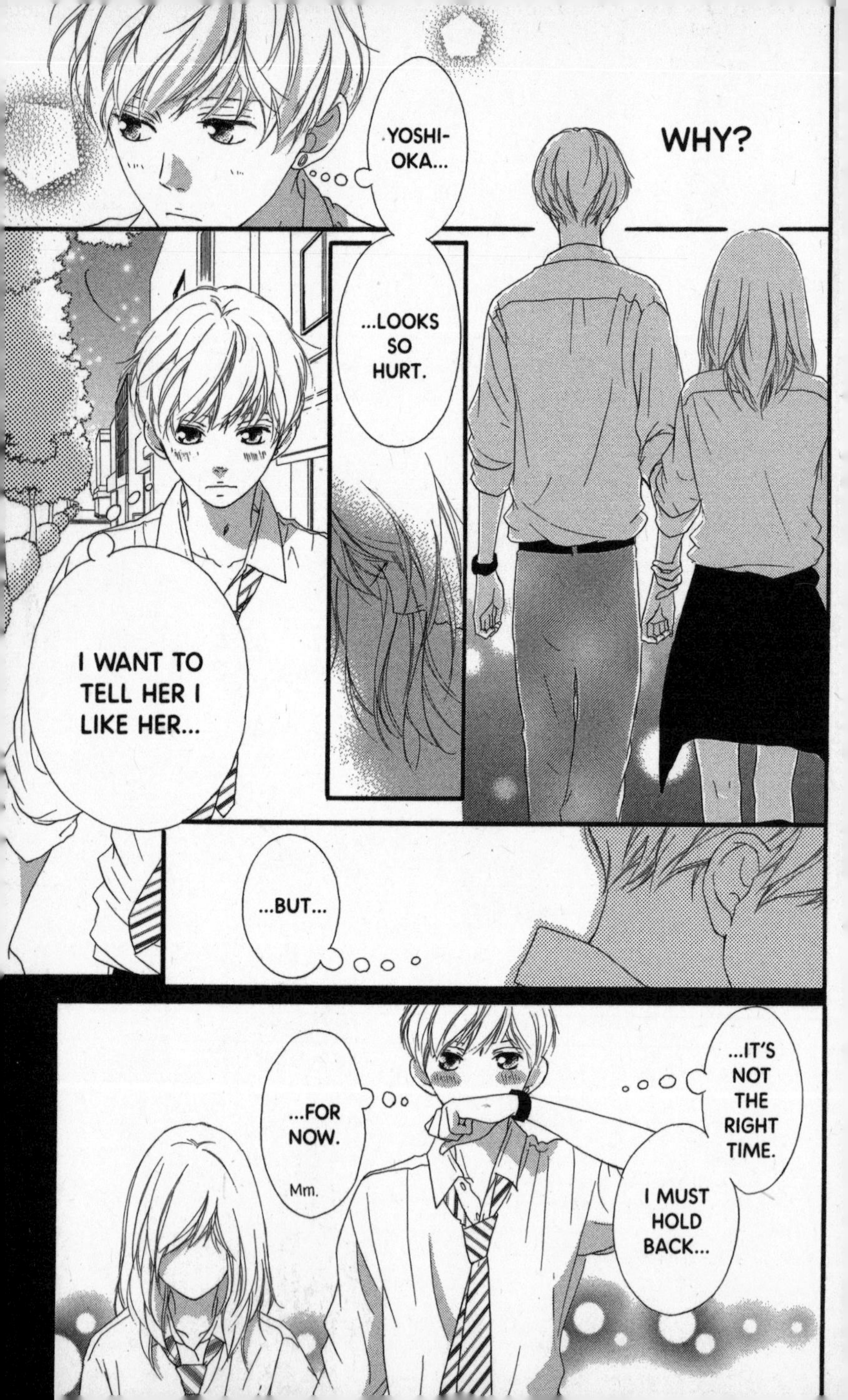
WHY?
YOSHI-OKA...
...LOOKS SO HURT.
I WANT TO TELL HER I LIKE HER...
...BUT...
...IT'S NOT THE RIGHT TIME.
I MUST HOLD BACK...
...FOR NOW.
Mm.

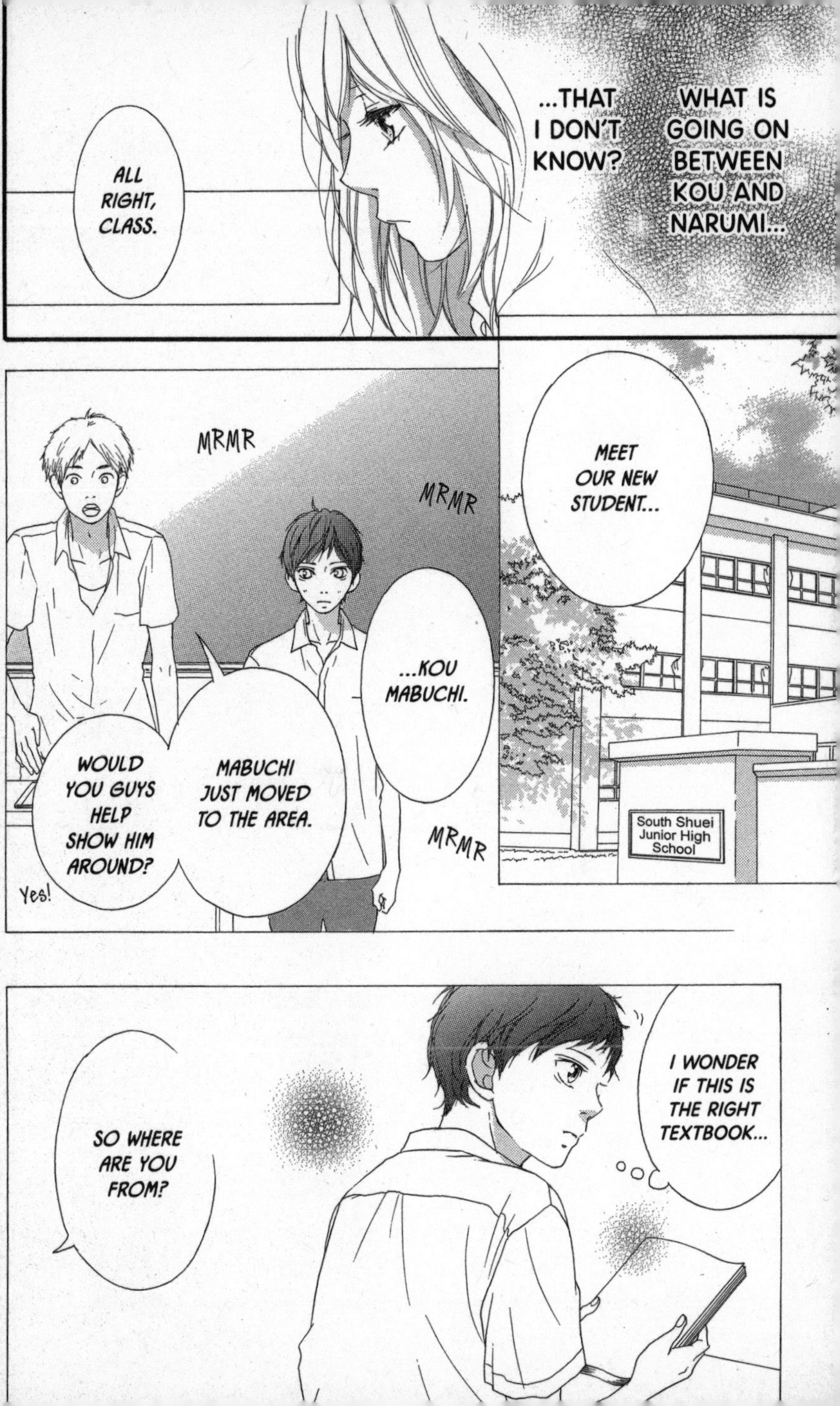
WHAT IS GOING ON BETWEEN KOU AND NARUMI...
...THAT I DON'T KNOW?
ALL RIGHT, CLASS.
MEET OUR NEW STUDENT...
South Shuei Junior High School
...KOU MABUCHI.
MRMR
MRMR
MRMR
MABUCHI JUST MOVED TO THE AREA.
WOULD YOU GUYS HELP SHOW HIM AROUND?
Yes!
I WONDER IF THIS IS THE RIGHT TEXTBOOK...
SO WHERE ARE YOU FROM?

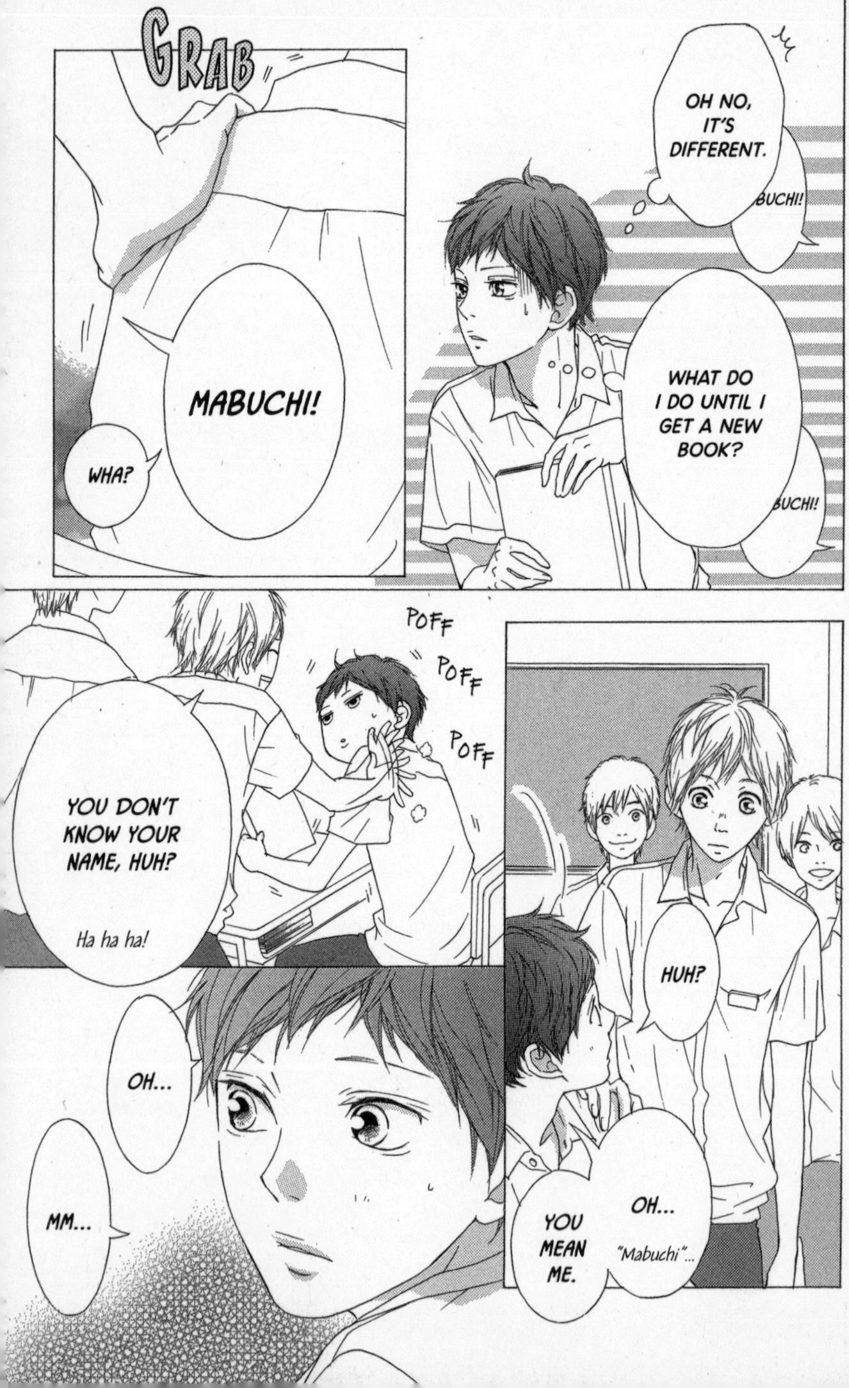
OH NO, IT'S DIFFERENT.
BUCHI!
WHAT DO I DO UNTIL I GET A NEW BOOK?
BUCHI!
GRAB
MABUCHI!
WHA?
HUH?
OH...
"Mabuchi"...
YOU MEAN ME.
POFF
POFF
POFF
YOU DON'T KNOW YOUR NAME, HUH?
Ha ha ha!
OH...
MM...

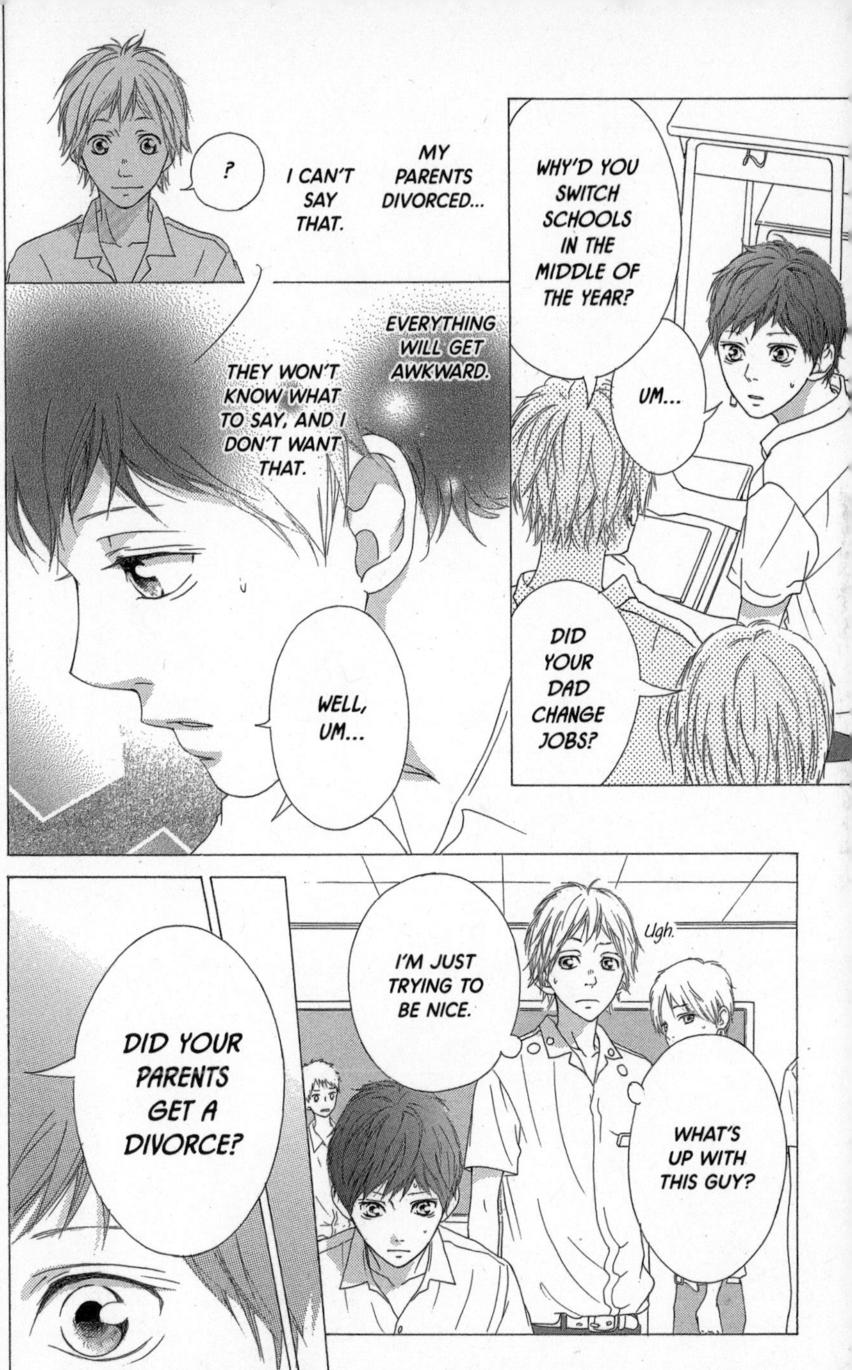
WHY'D YOU SWITCH SCHOOLS IN THE MIDDLE OF THE YEAR?
UM...
DID YOUR DAD CHANGE JOBS?
?
MY PARENTS DIVORCED...
I CAN'T SAY THAT.
EVERYTHING WILL GET AWKWARD.
THEY WON'T KNOW WHAT TO SAY, AND I DON'T WANT THAT.
WELL, UM...
I'M JUST TRYING TO BE NICE.
Ugh.
WHAT'S UP WITH THIS GUY?
DID YOUR PARENTS GET A DIVORCE?

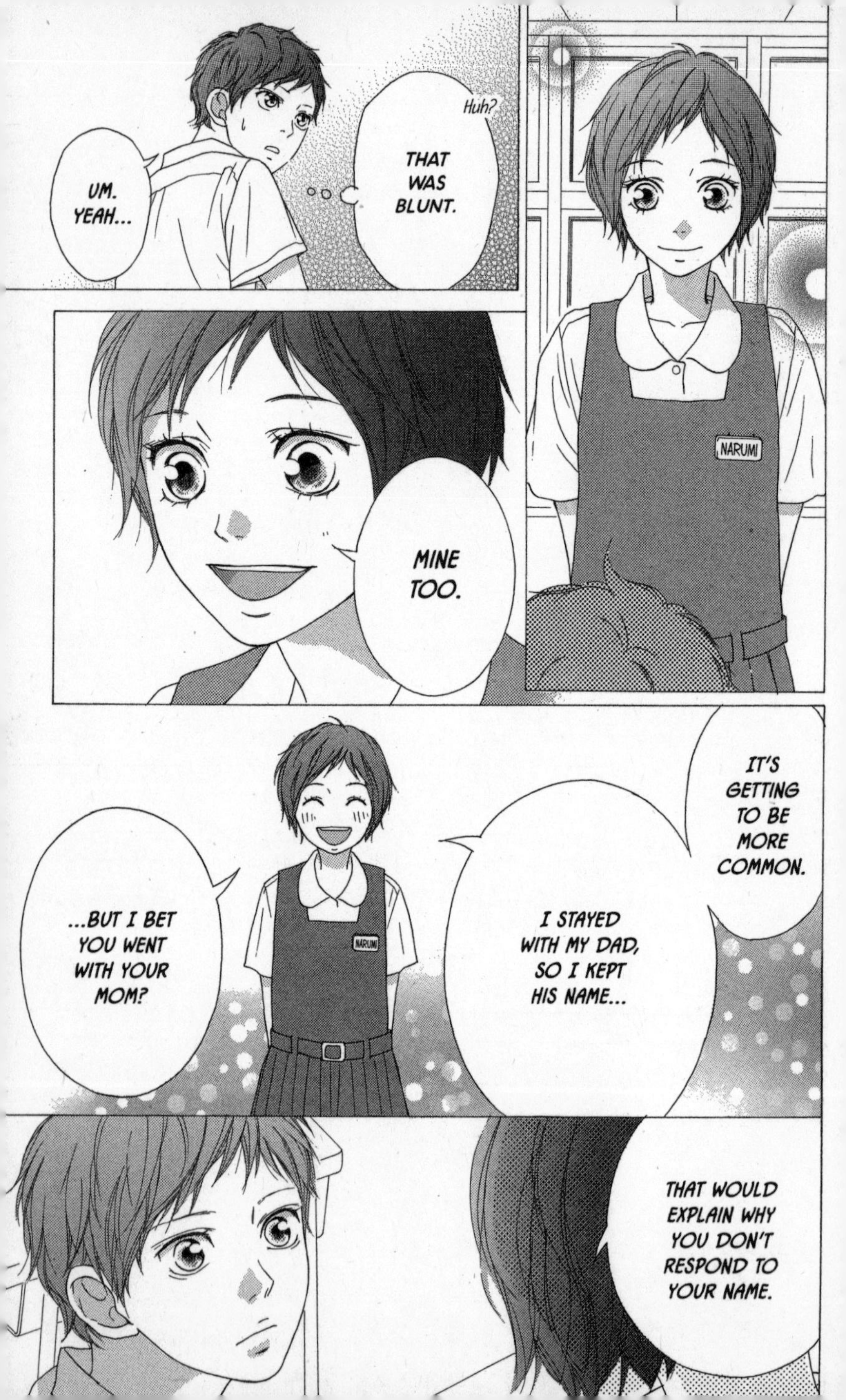

NARUMI
Huh?
THAT WAS BLUNT.
UM. YEAH...
MINE TOO.
IT'S GETTING TO BE MORE COMMON.
I STAYED WITH MY DAD, SO I KEPT HIS NAME...
NARUMI
...BUT I BET YOU WENT WITH YOUR MOM?
THAT WOULD EXPLAIN WHY YOU DON'T RESPOND TO YOUR NAME.

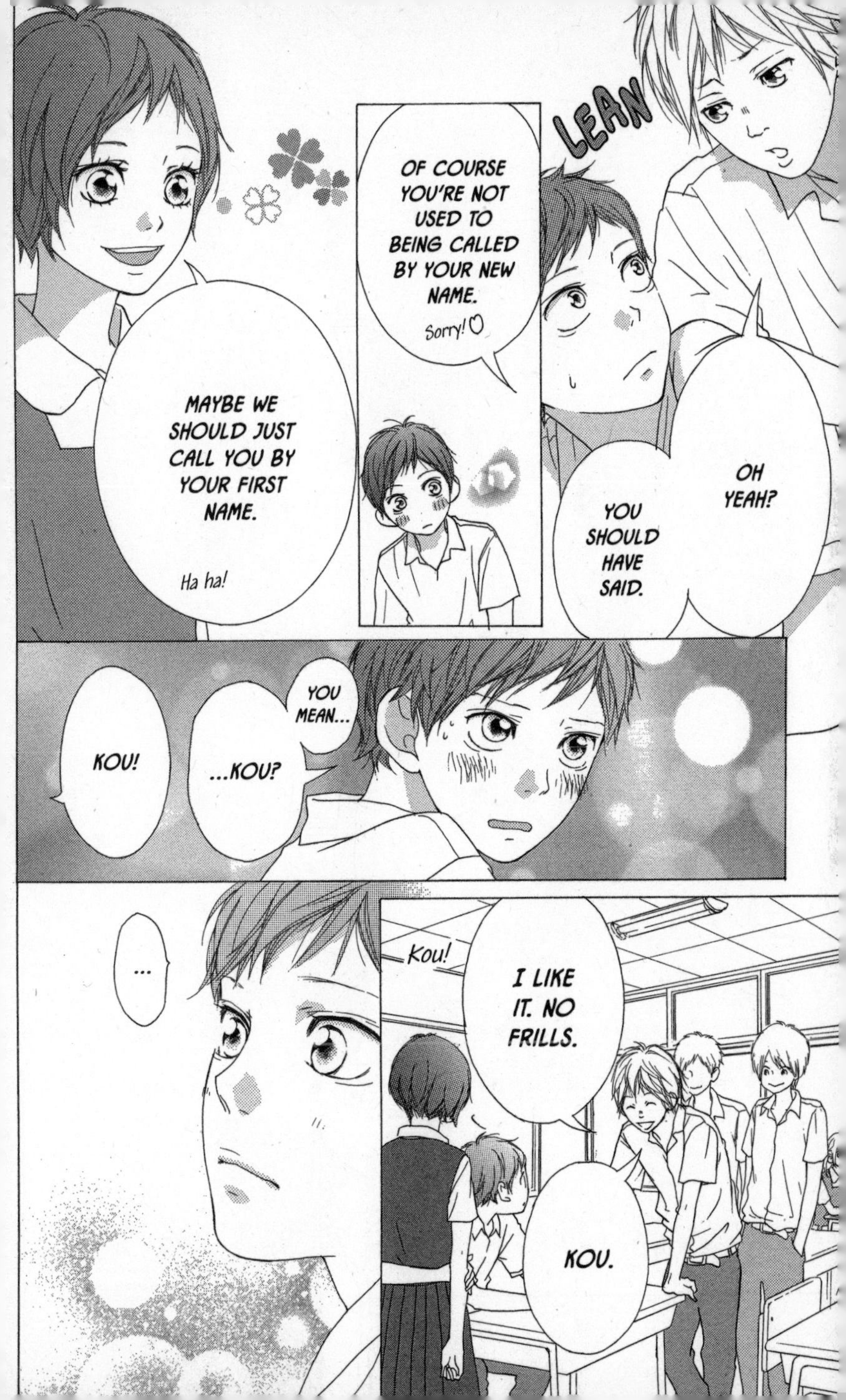
LEAN
OH YEAH?
YOU SHOULD HAVE SAID.
OF COURSE YOU'RE NOT USED TO BEING CALLED BY YOUR NEW NAME.
Sorry!♡
MAYBE WE SHOULD JUST CALL YOU BY YOUR FIRST NAME.
Ha ha!
YOU MEAN...
...KOU?
KOU!
I LIKE IT. NO FRILLS.
Kou!
KOU.
...

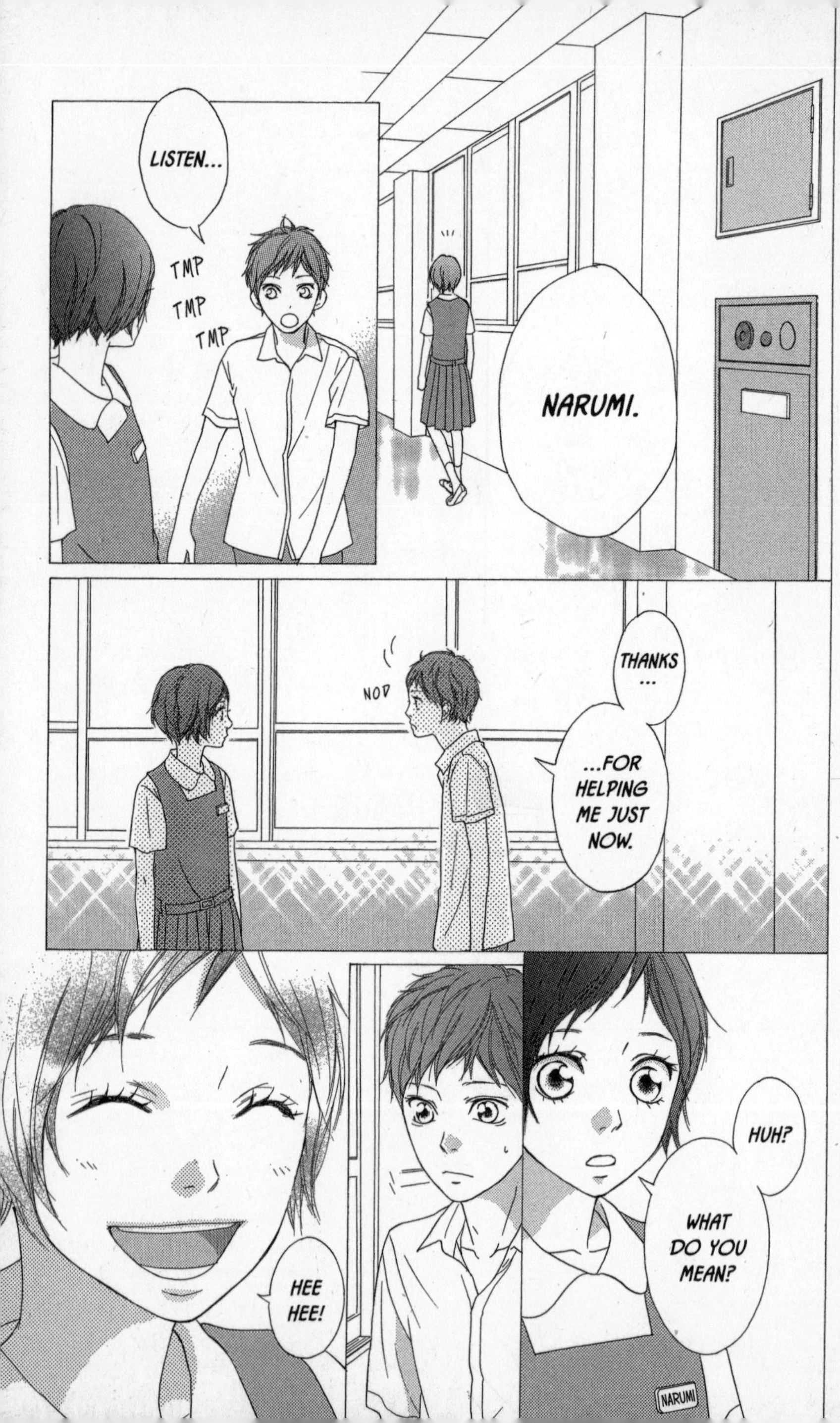
NARUMI.
LISTEN...
TMP
TMP
TMP
THANKS...
...FOR HELPING ME JUST NOW.
NOD
HUH?
WHAT DO YOU MEAN?
NARUMI
HEE HEE!

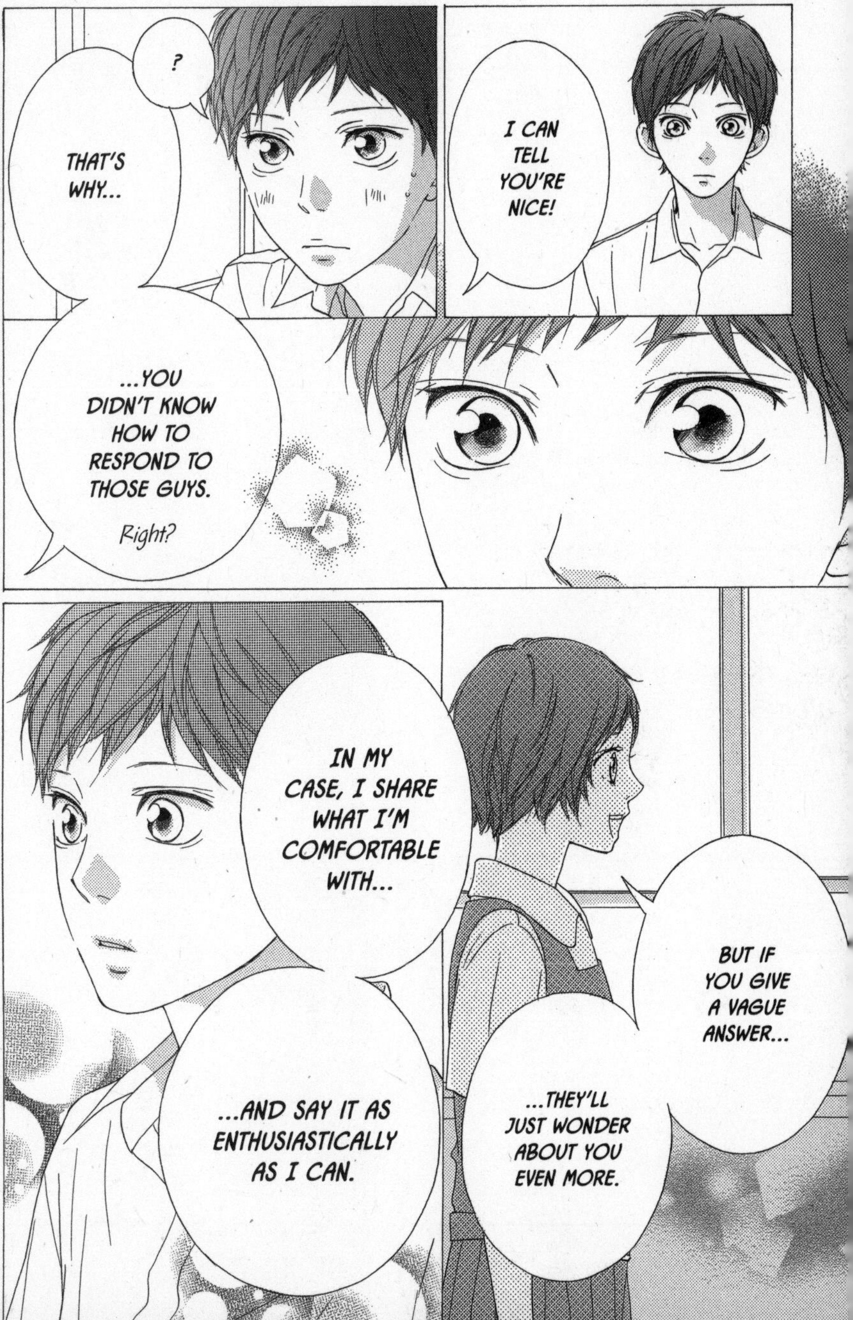
I CAN TELL YOU'RE NICE!
?
THAT'S WHY...
...YOU DIDN'T KNOW HOW TO RESPOND TO THOSE GUYS.
Right?
BUT IF YOU GIVE A VAGUE ANSWER...
...THEY'LL JUST WONDER ABOUT YOU EVEN MORE.
IN MY CASE, I SHARE WHAT I'M COMFORTABLE WITH...
...AND SAY IT AS ENTHUSIASTICALLY AS I CAN.

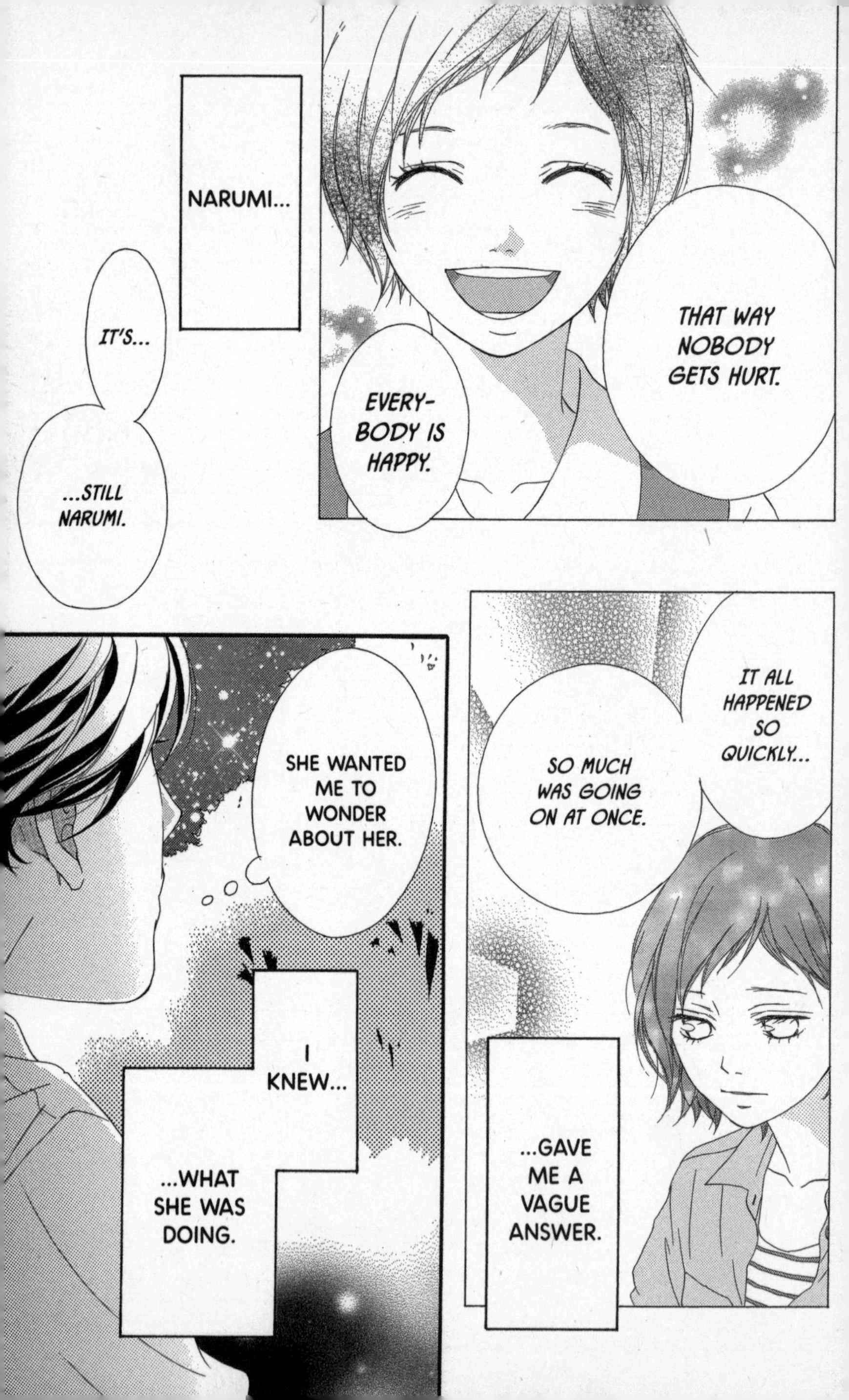
THAT WAY NOBODY GETS HURT.
EVERY-BODY IS HAPPY.
NARUMI...
IT'S...
...STILL NARUMI.
IT ALL HAPPENED SO QUICKLY...
SO MUCH WAS GOING ON AT ONCE.
...GAVE ME A VAGUE ANSWER.
SHE WANTED ME TO WONDER ABOUT HER.
I KNEW...
...WHAT SHE WAS DOING.

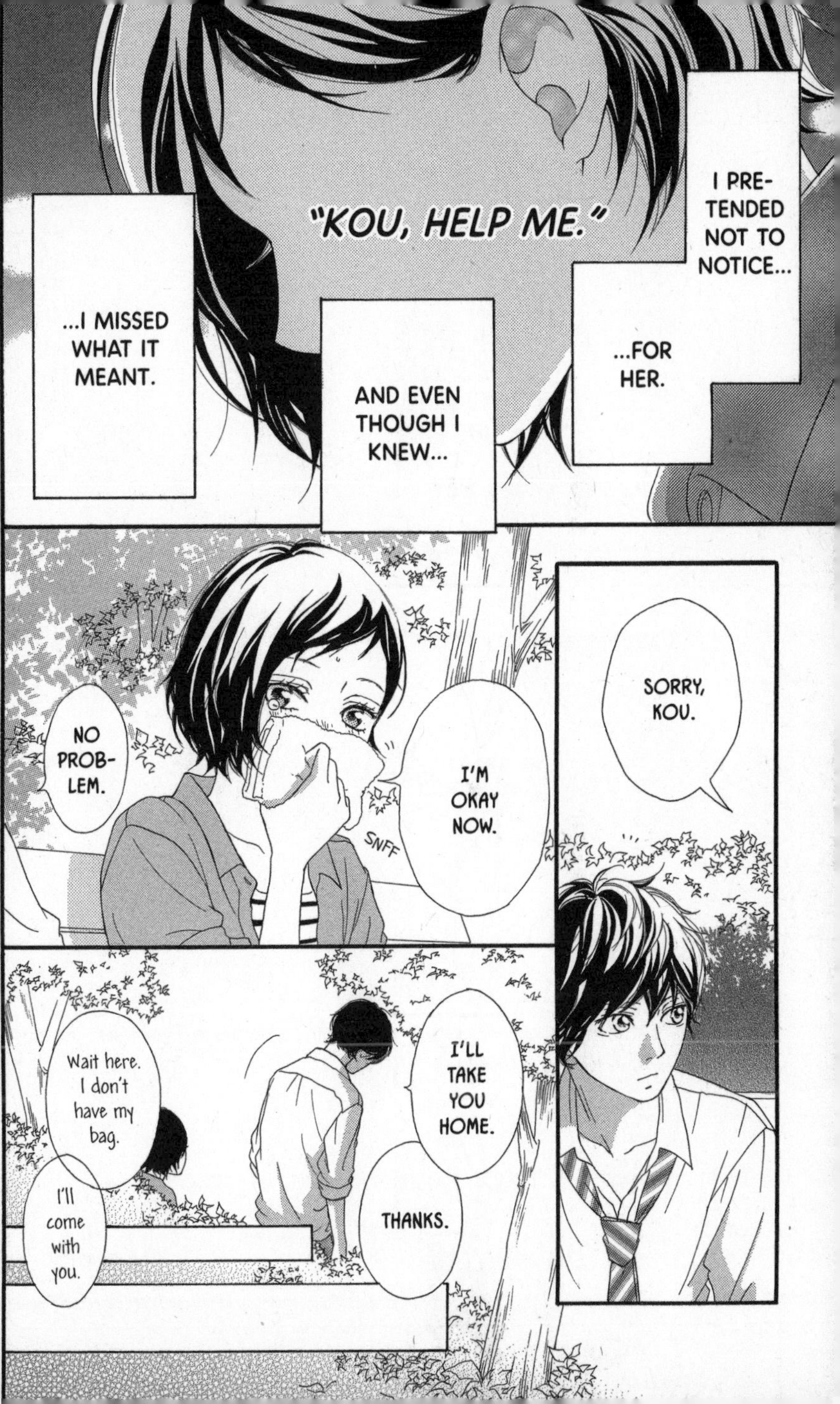
I PRE-TENDED NOT TO NOTICE...
"KOU, HELP ME."
...FOR HER.
AND EVEN THOUGH I KNEW...
...I MISSED WHAT IT MEANT.
SORRY, KOU.
I'M OKAY NOW.
SNFF
NO PROB-LEM.
I'LL TAKE YOU HOME.
THANKS.
Wait here. I don't have my bag.
I'll come with you.

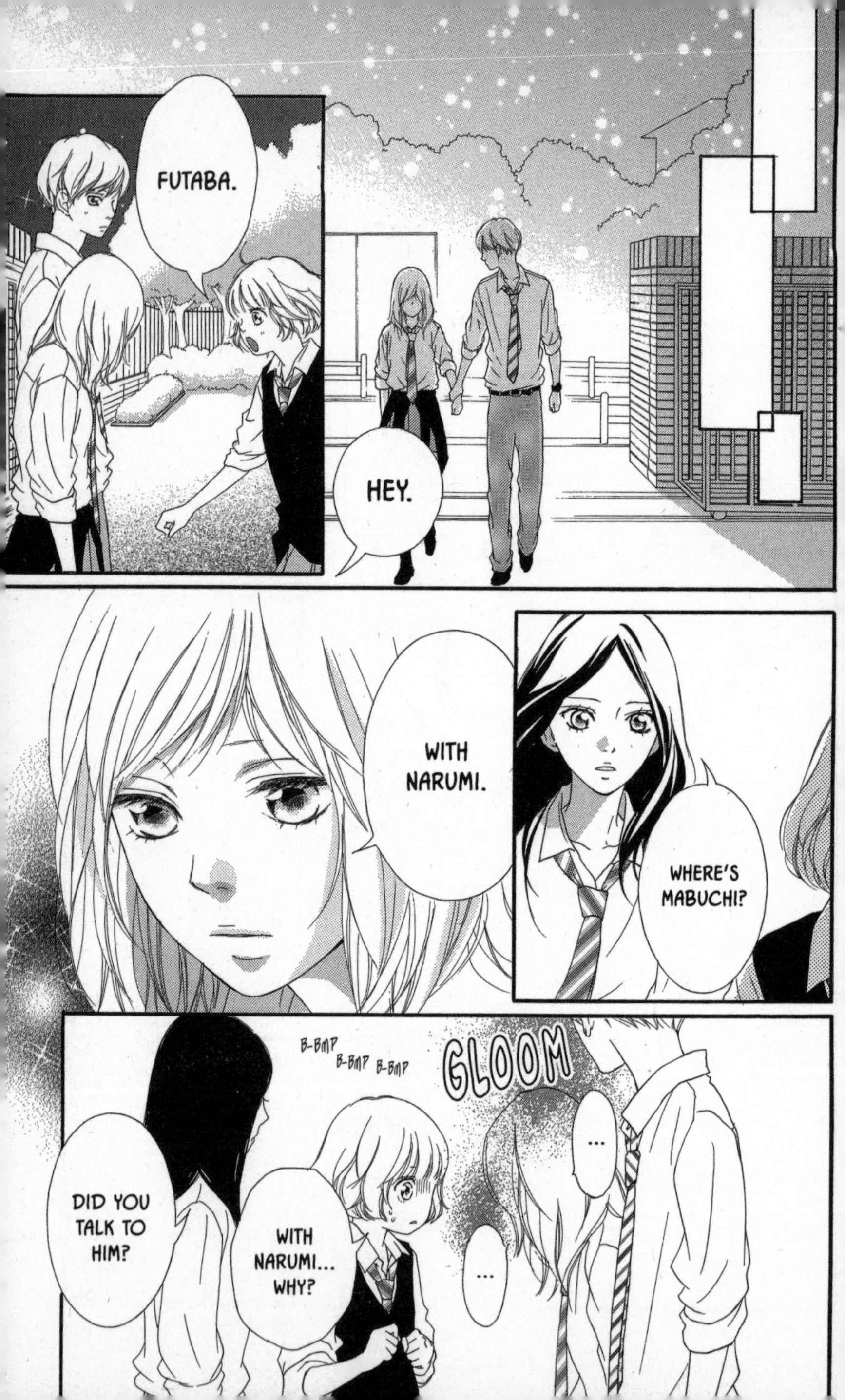
HEY.
FUTABA.
WHERE'S MABUCHI?
WITH NARUMI.
GLOOM
...
B-BMP B-BMP B-BMP
...
WITH NARUMI... WHY?
DID YOU TALK TO HIM?

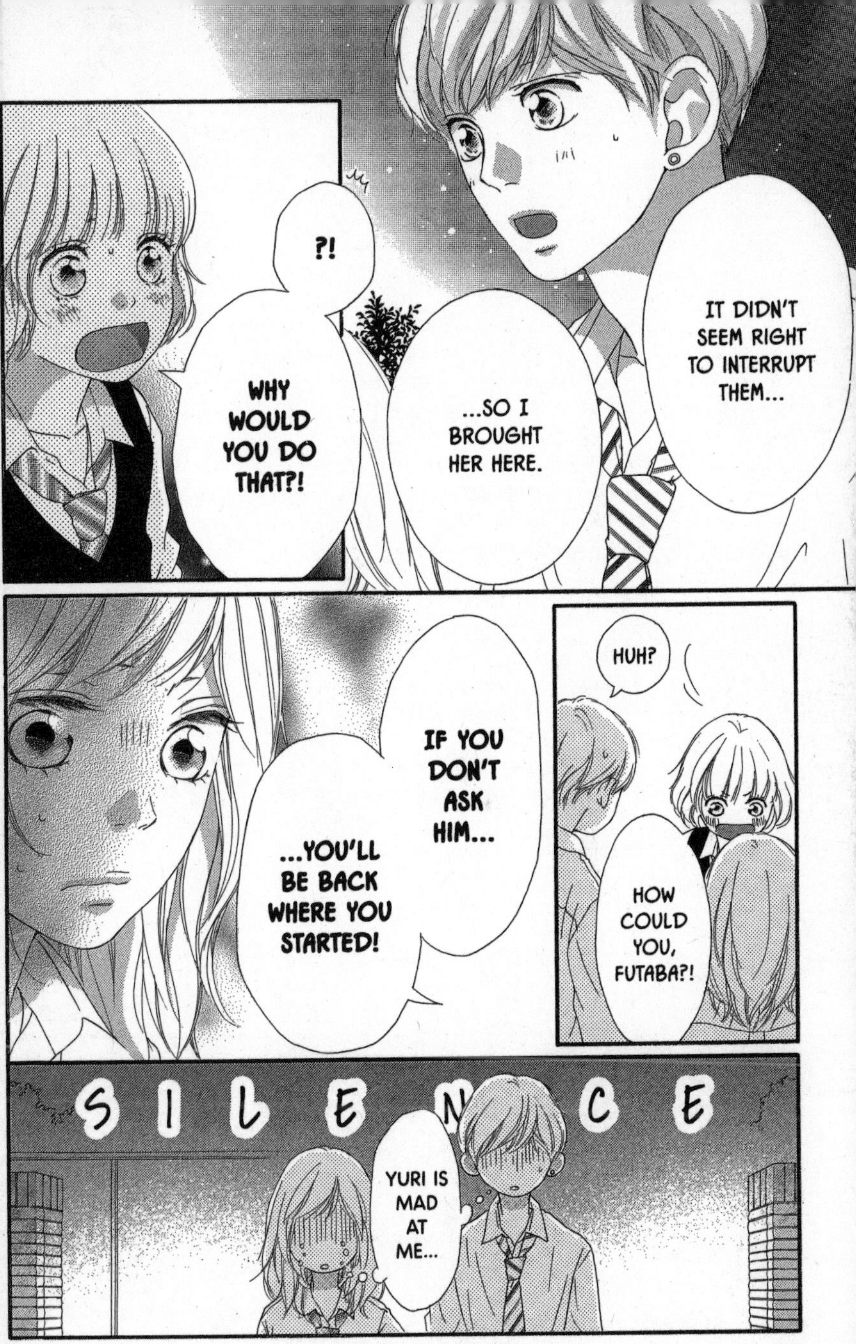
IT DIDN'T SEEM RIGHT TO INTERRUPT THEM...
...SO I BROUGHT HER HERE.
?!
WHY WOULD YOU DO THAT?!
HUH?
HOW COULD YOU, FUTABA?!
IF YOU DON'T ASK HIM...
...YOU'LL BE BACK WHERE YOU STARTED!
SILENCE
YURI IS MAD AT ME...

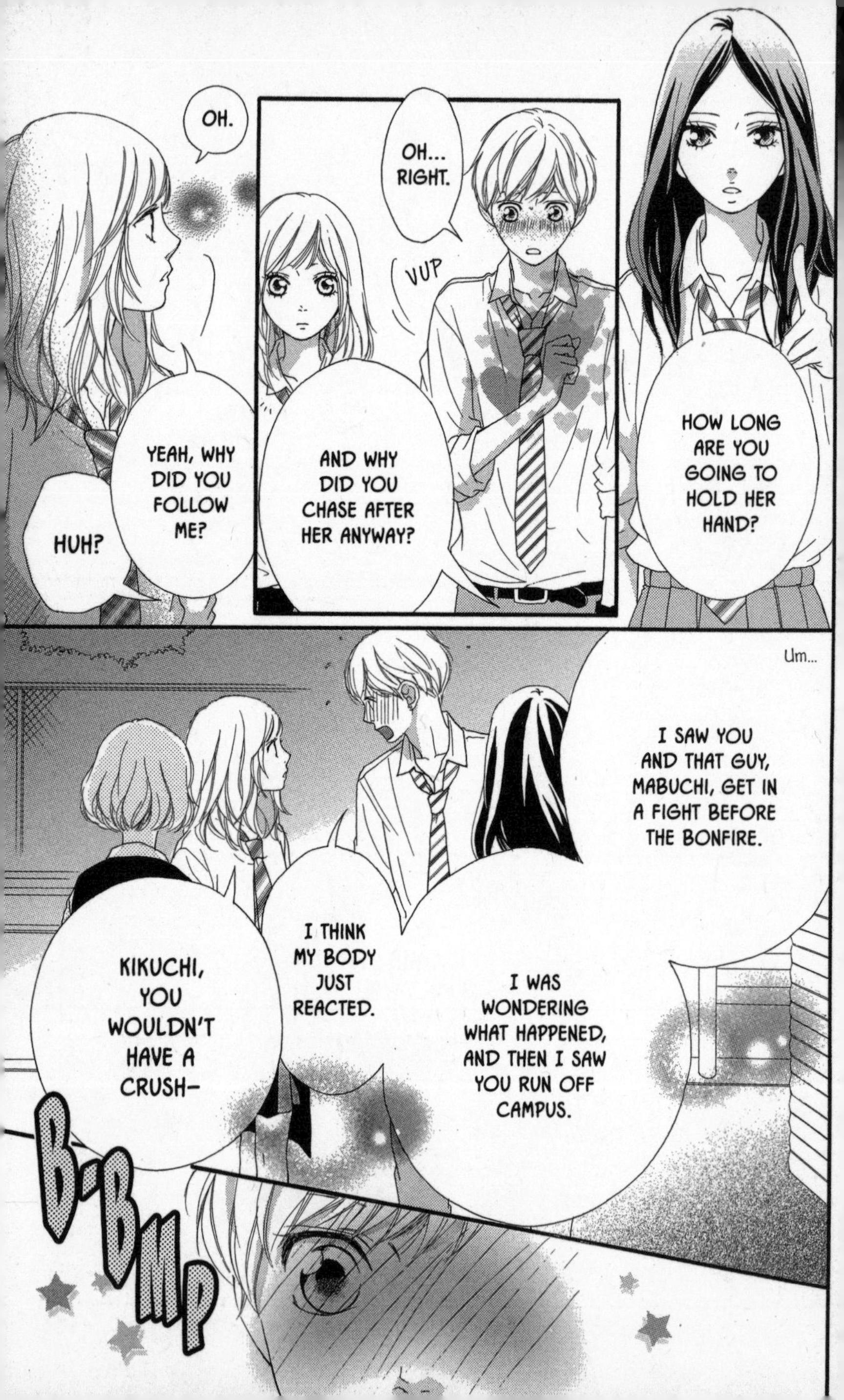
HOW LONG ARE YOU GOING TO HOLD HER HAND?
OH... RIGHT.
VUP
AND WHY DID YOU CHASE AFTER HER ANYWAY?
OH.
YEAH, WHY DID YOU FOLLOW ME?
HUH?
Um...
I SAW YOU AND THAT GUY, MABUCHI, GET IN A FIGHT BEFORE THE BONFIRE.
I WAS WONDERING WHAT HAPPENED, AND THEN I SAW YOU RUN OFF CAMPUS.
I THINK MY BODY JUST REACTED.
KIKUCHI, YOU WOULDN'T HAVE A CRUSH–
B-BMP

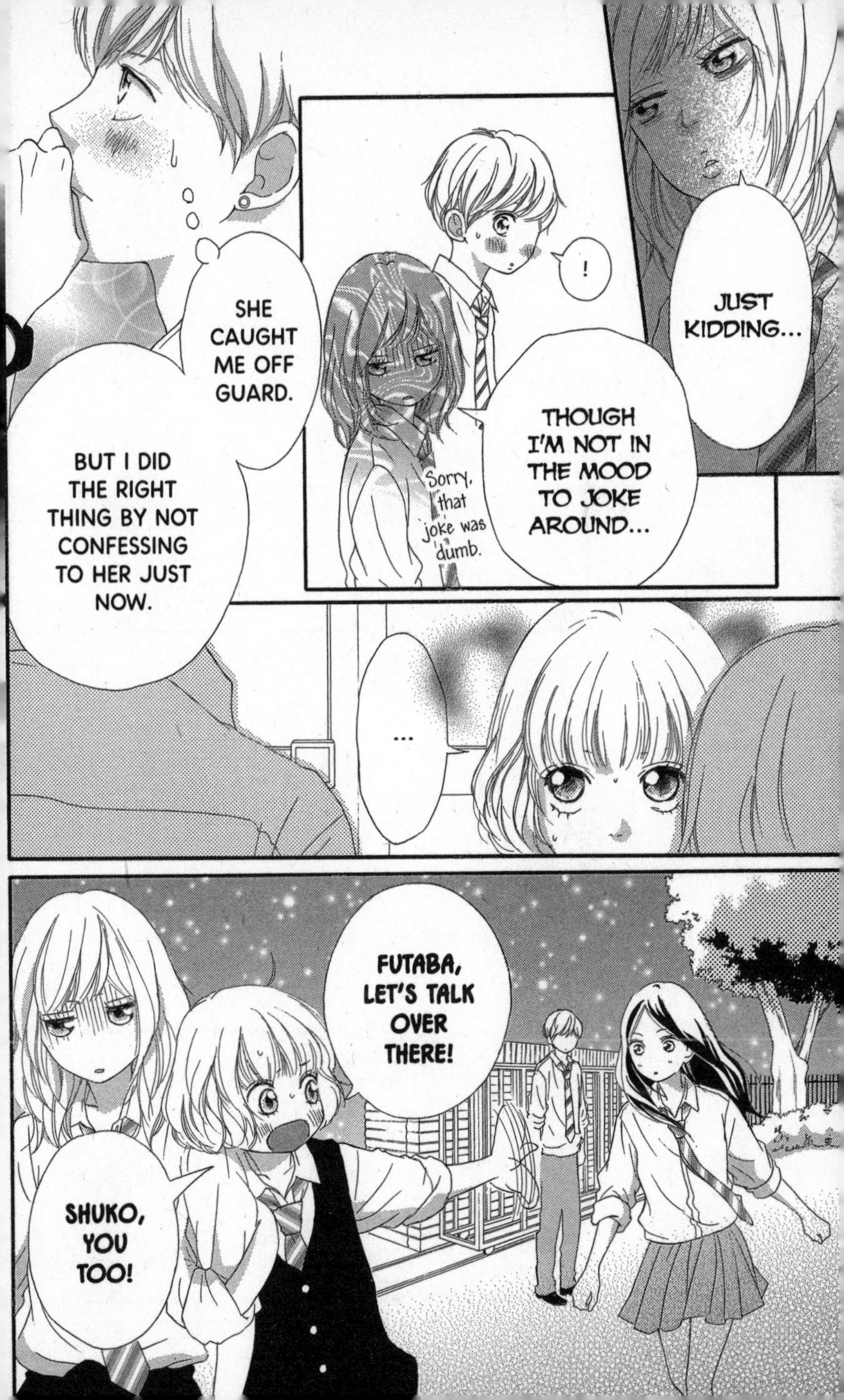
JUST KIDDING...
!
THOUGH I'M NOT IN THE MOOD TO JOKE AROUND...
Sorry, that joke was dumb.
SHE CAUGHT ME OFF GUARD.
BUT I DID THE RIGHT THING BY NOT CONFESSING TO HER JUST NOW.
...
FUTABA, LET'S TALK OVER THERE!
SHUKO, YOU TOO!

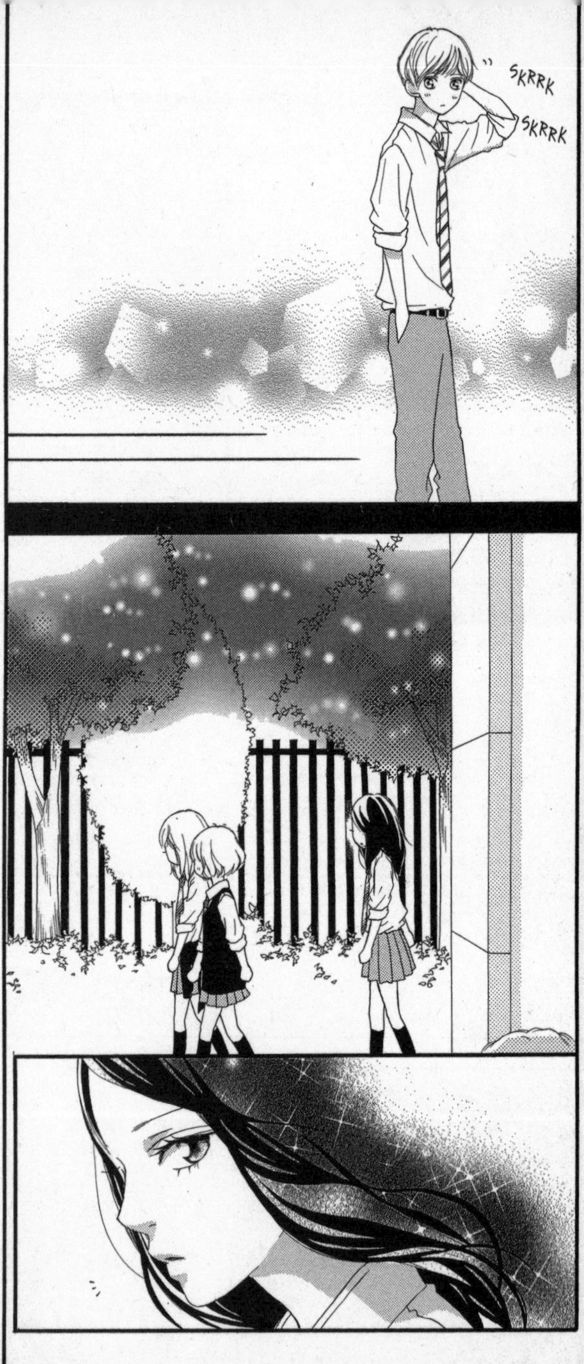
SKRRK
SKRRK

When I think about my mistakes and other embarrassing things I've done in the past, I can't help but let out an "Argh" or "Aaaah" or some other sound. It's as if I'm using sound to erase the memory and any thoughts tied to it. Nobody taught me to do this, and it comes out rather naturally, so I assumed it was a common thing. But one day I told my assistants about it and they laughed. No one said they did it too... What?! Am I the only one who feels the need to reject my embarrassing past? No, there are others. There have to be others. If you can relate, please, please send me a note saying so.

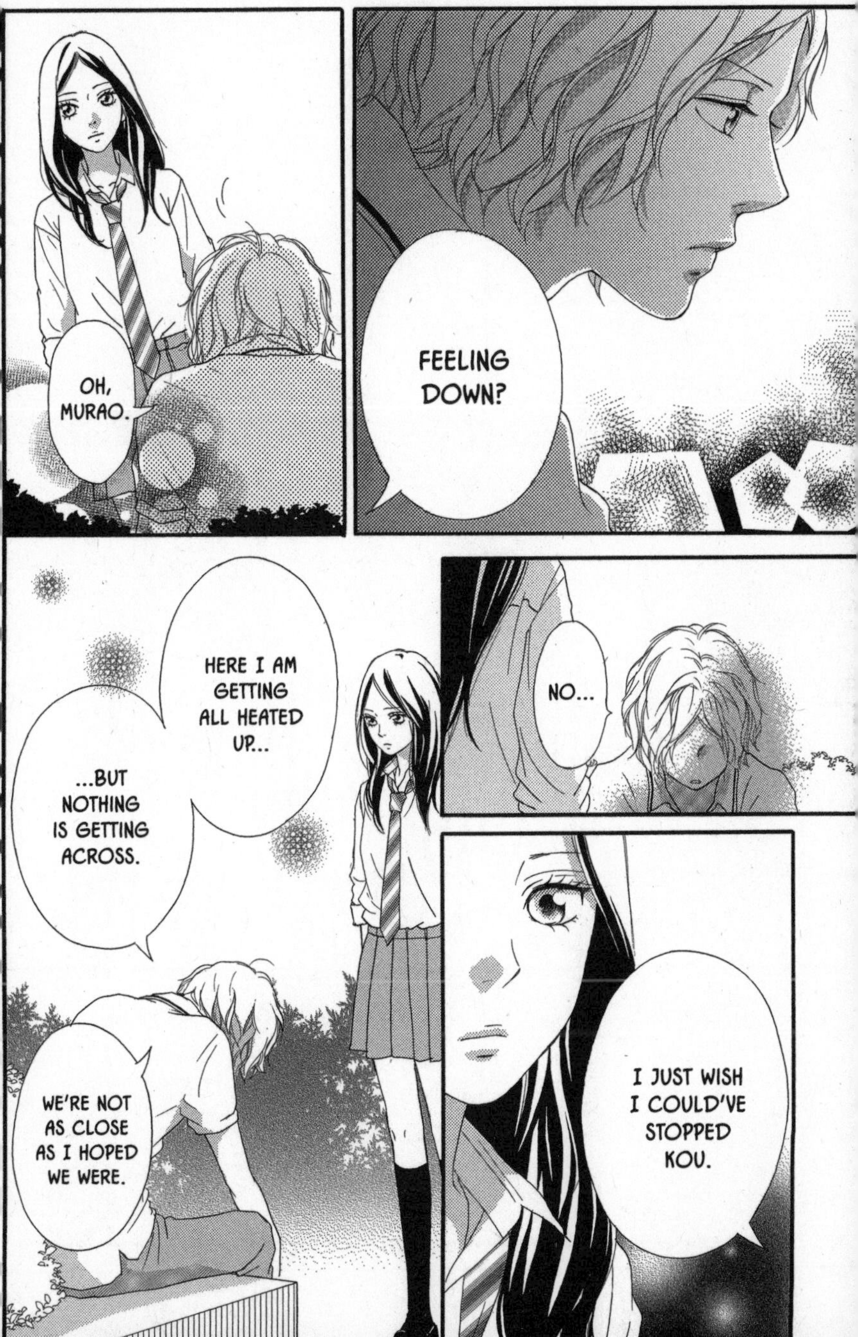
FEELING DOWN?
OH, MURAO.
NO...
I JUST WISH I COULD'VE STOPPED KOU.
HERE I AM GETTING ALL HEATED UP...
...BUT NOTHING IS GETTING ACROSS.
WE'RE NOT AS CLOSE AS I HOPED WE WERE.

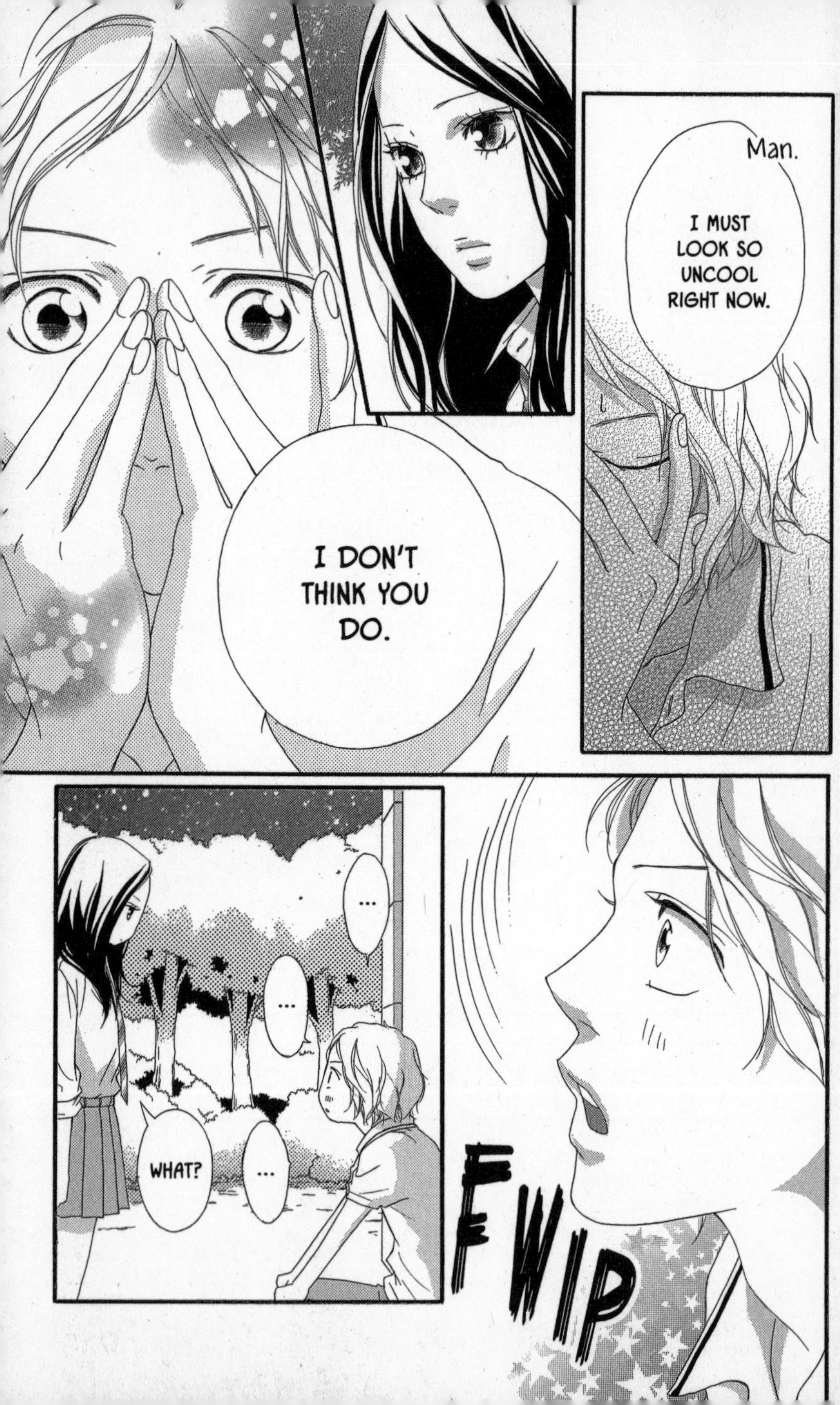

Man.
I MUST LOOK SO UNCOOL RIGHT NOW.
I DON'T THINK YOU DO.
FWIP
...
...
...
WHAT?

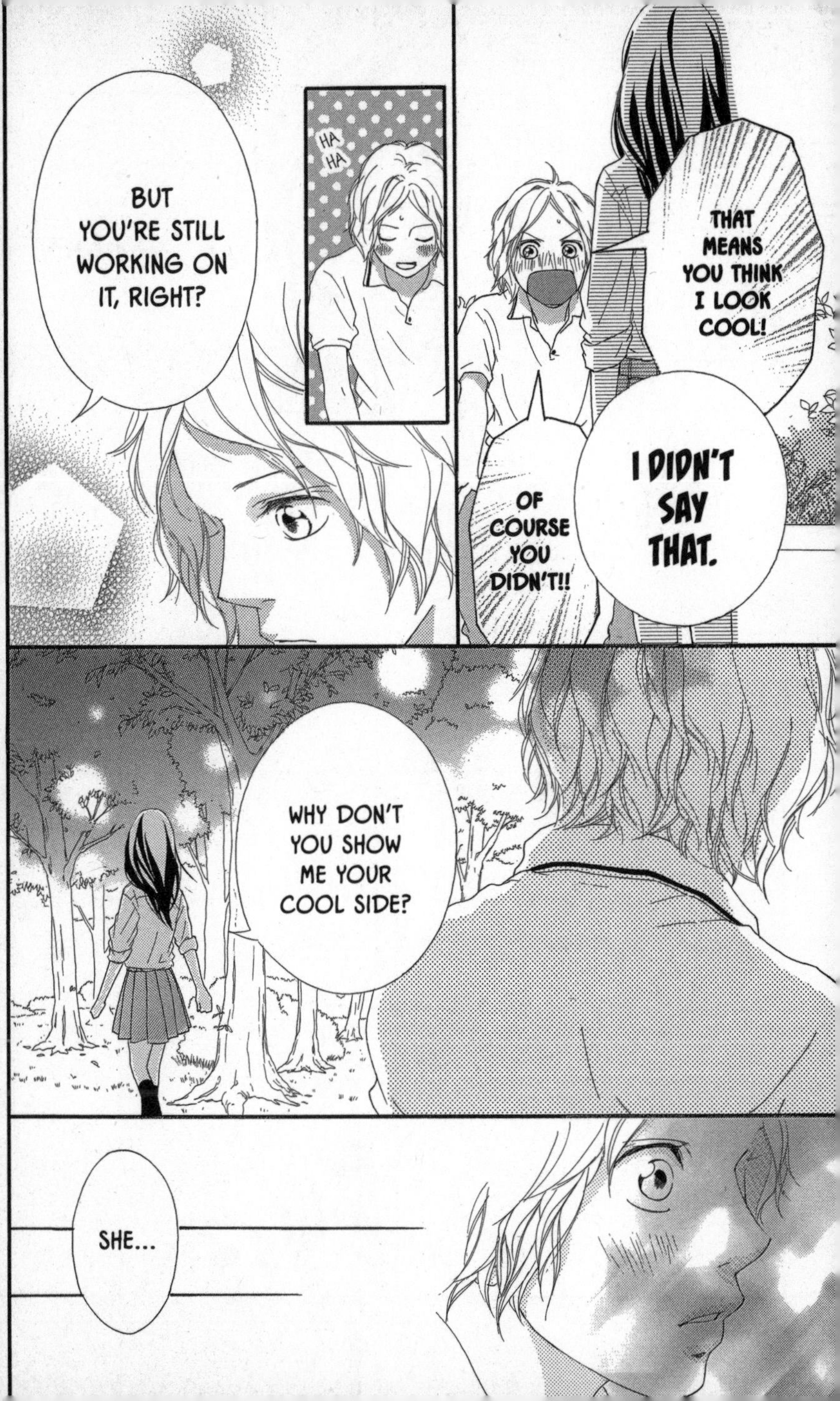
THAT MEANS YOU THINK I LOOK COOL!
I DIDN'T SAY THAT.
OF COURSE YOU DIDN'T!!
HA HA
BUT YOU'RE STILL WORKING ON IT, RIGHT?
WHY DON'T YOU SHOW ME YOUR COOL SIDE?
SHE...

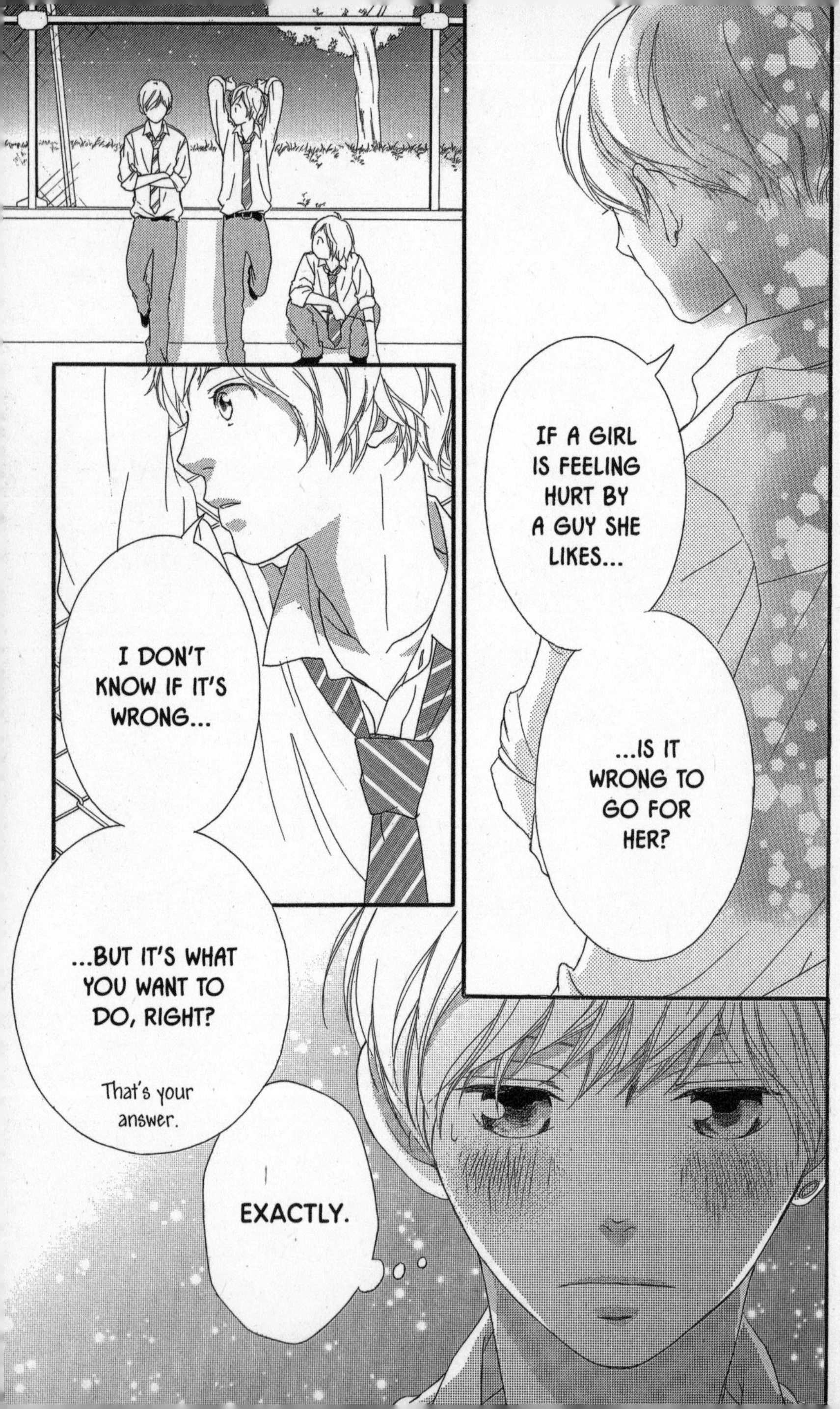
IF A GIRL IS FEELING HURT BY A GUY SHE LIKES...
...IS IT WRONG TO GO FOR HER?
I DON'T KNOW IF IT'S WRONG...
...BUT IT'S WHAT YOU WANT TO DO, RIGHT?
That's your answer.
EXACTLY.

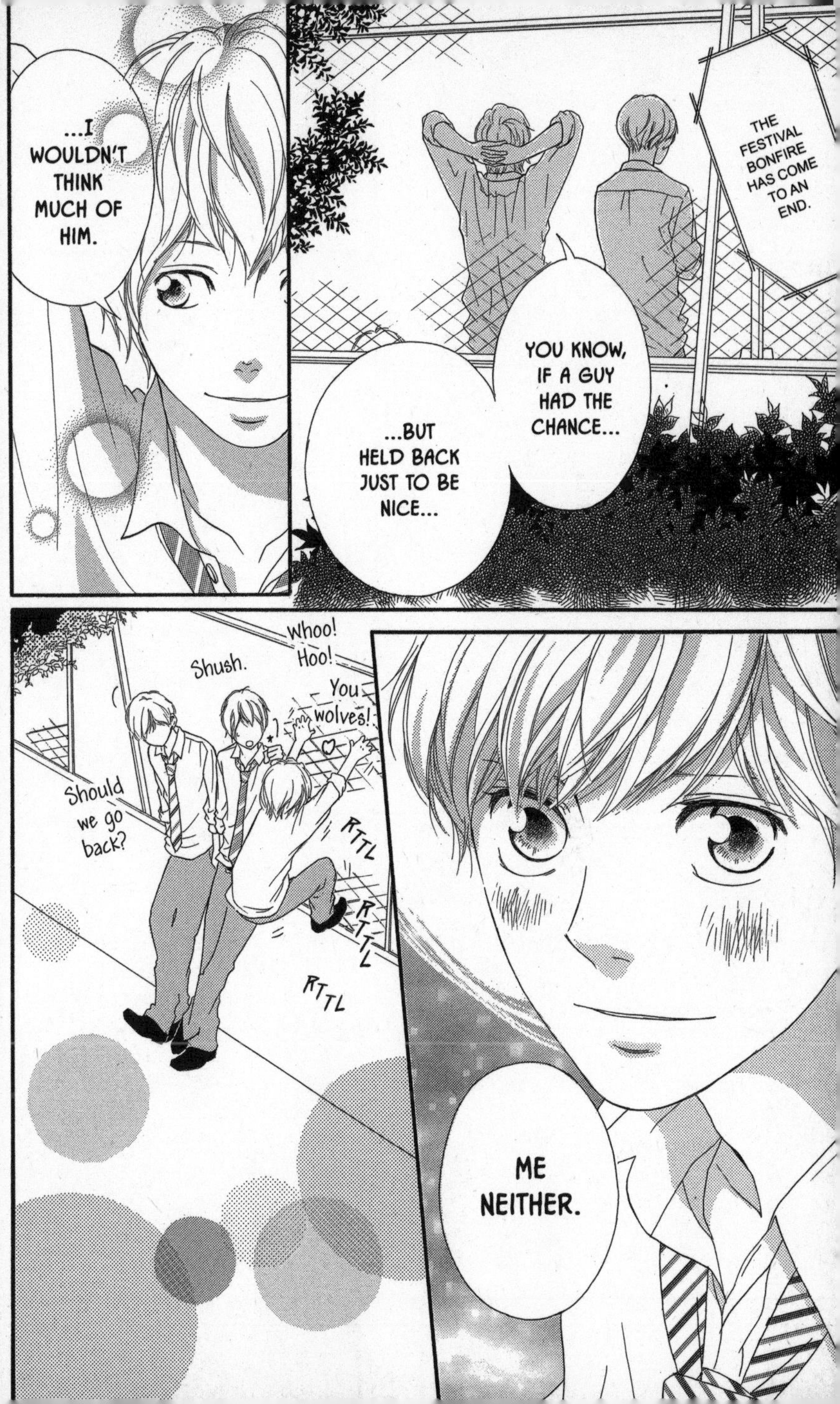
THE FESTIVAL BONFIRE HAS COME TO AN END.
YOU KNOW, IF A GUY HAD THE CHANCE...
...BUT HELD BACK JUST TO BE NICE...
...I WOULDN'T THINK MUCH OF HIM.
ME NEITHER.
Whoo! Hoo!
You wolves!
Shush.
RTTL
RTTL
RTTL
Should we go back?

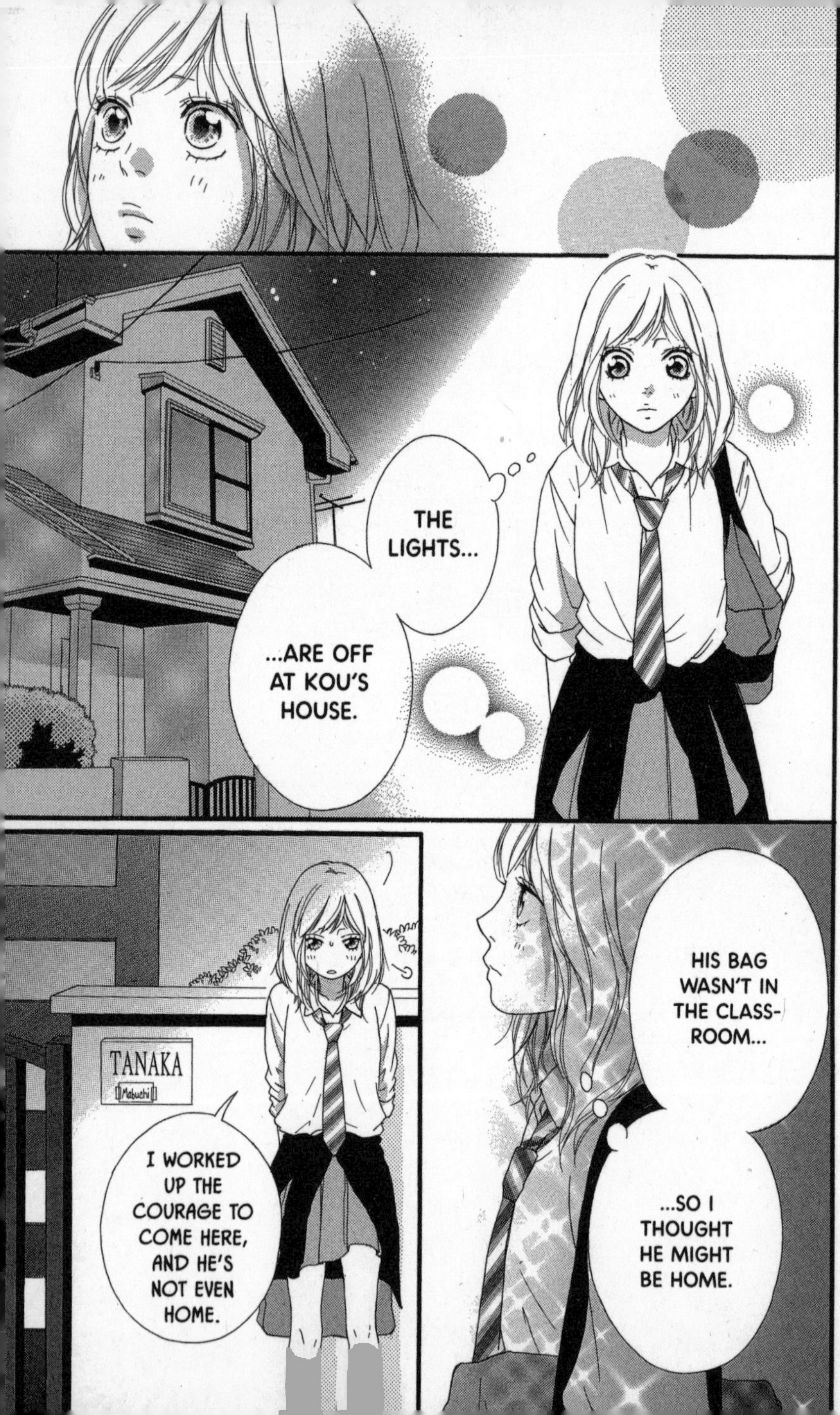
THE LIGHTS...
...ARE OFF AT KOU'S HOUSE.
HIS BAG WASN'T IN THE CLASSROOM...
...SO I THOUGHT HE MIGHT BE HOME.
TANAKA
Mabuchi
I WORKED UP THE COURAGE TO COME HERE, AND HE'S NOT EVEN HOME.

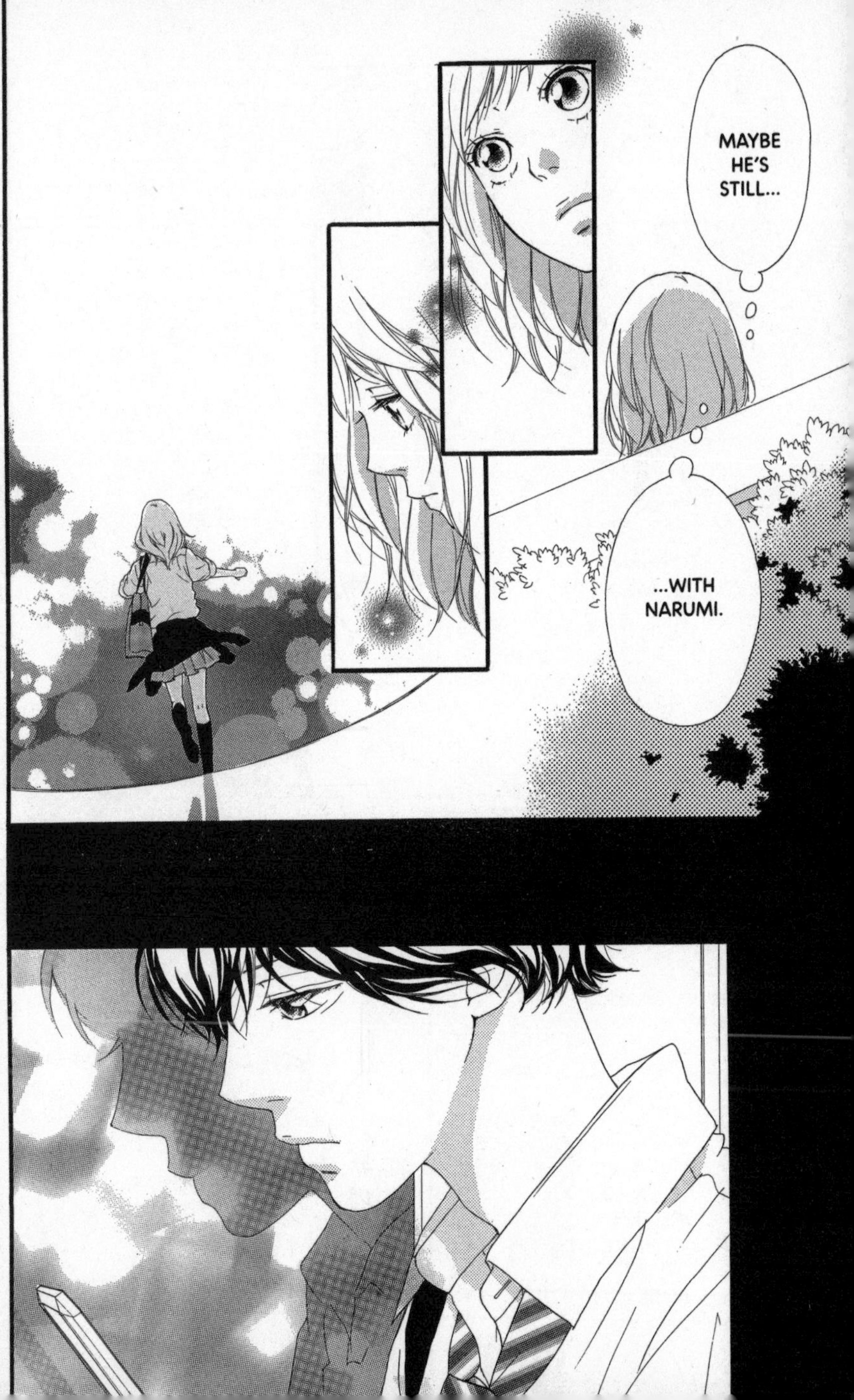
MAYBE HE'S STILL...
...WITH NARUMI.

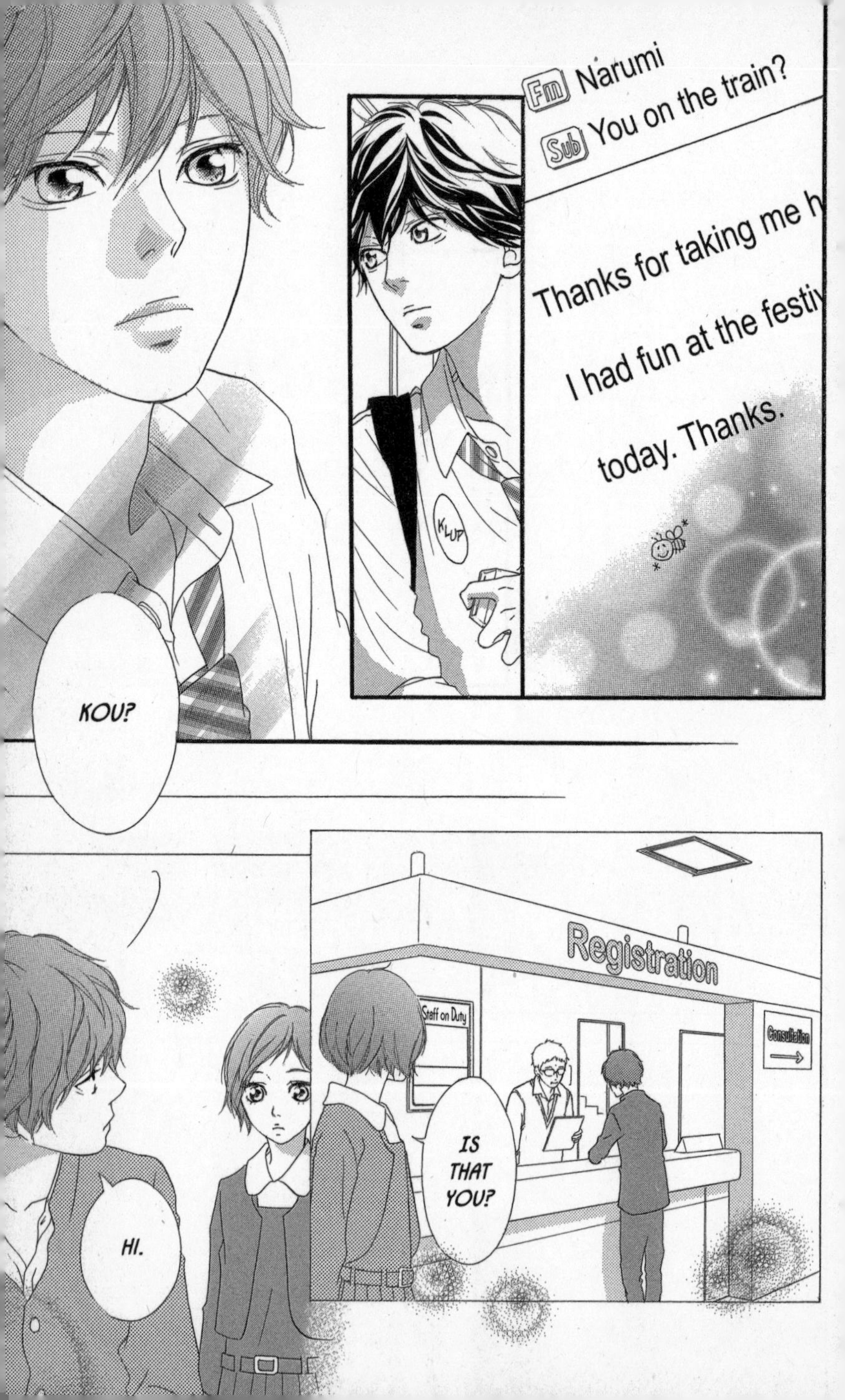
Fm Narumi
Sub You on the train?
Thanks for taking me h
I had fun at the festi
today. Thanks.
KLUP
KOU?
Registration
Staff on Duty
Consultation
IS THAT YOU?
HI.

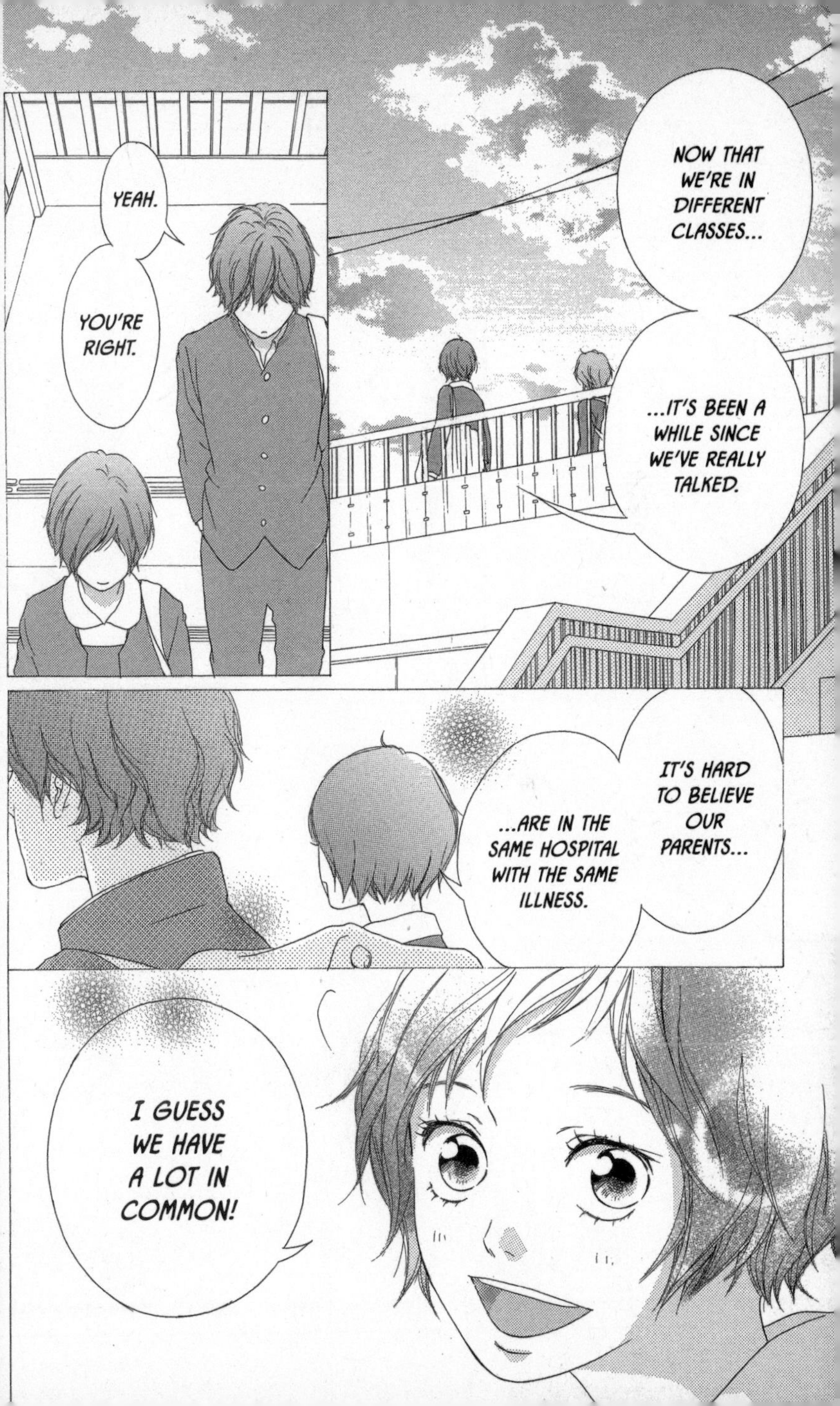
NOW THAT WE'RE IN DIFFERENT CLASSES...
...IT'S BEEN A WHILE SINCE WE'VE REALLY TALKED.
YEAH.
YOU'RE RIGHT.
IT'S HARD TO BELIEVE OUR PARENTS...
...ARE IN THE SAME HOSPITAL WITH THE SAME ILLNESS.
I GUESS WE HAVE A LOT IN COMMON!

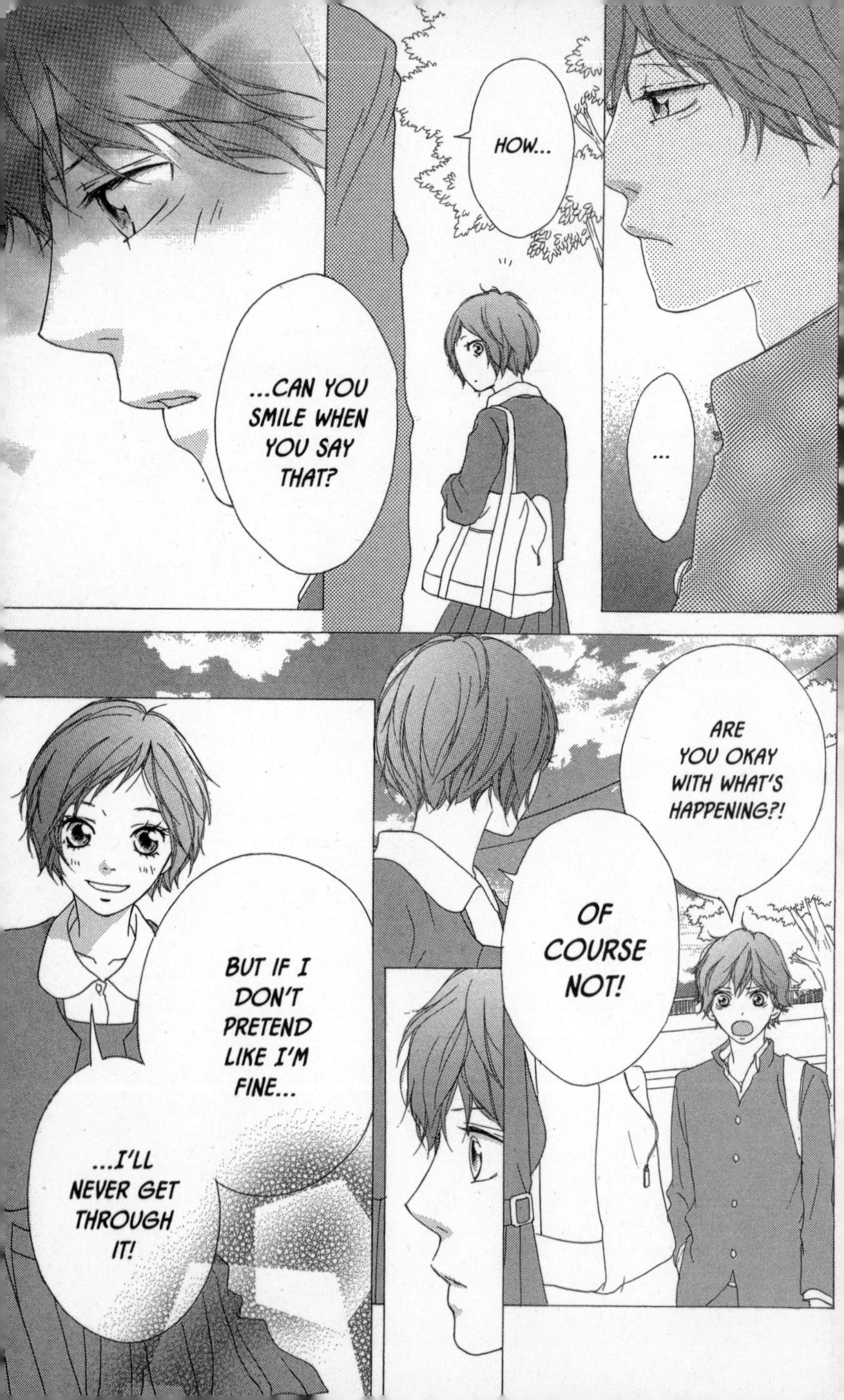
...
HOW...
...CAN YOU SMILE WHEN YOU SAY THAT?
ARE YOU OKAY WITH WHAT'S HAPPENING?!
OF COURSE NOT!
BUT IF I DON'T PRETEND LIKE I'M FINE...
...I'LL NEVER GET THROUGH IT!

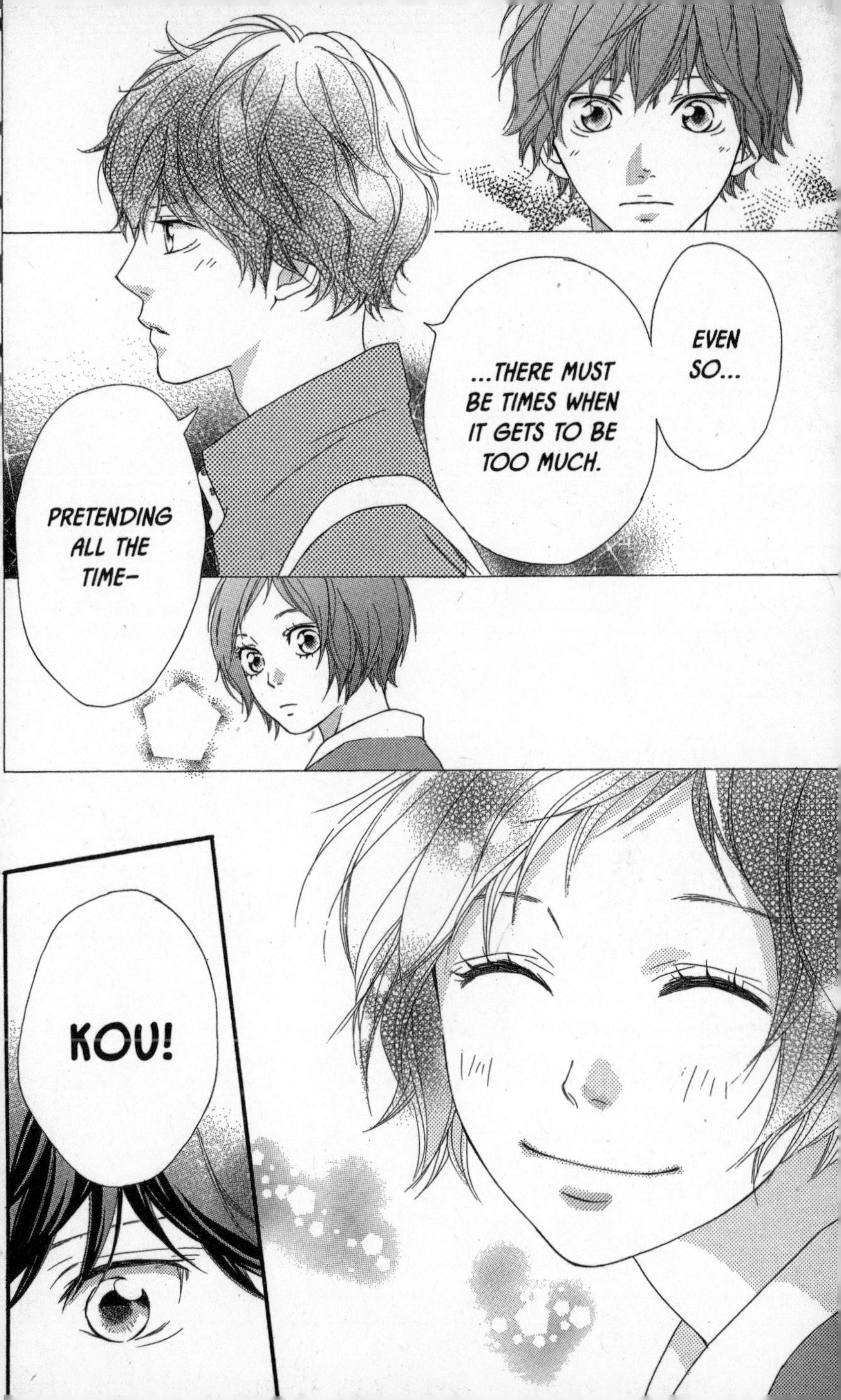
EVEN SO...
...THERE MUST BE TIMES WHEN IT GETS TO BE TOO MUCH.
PRETENDING ALL THE TIME—
KOU!

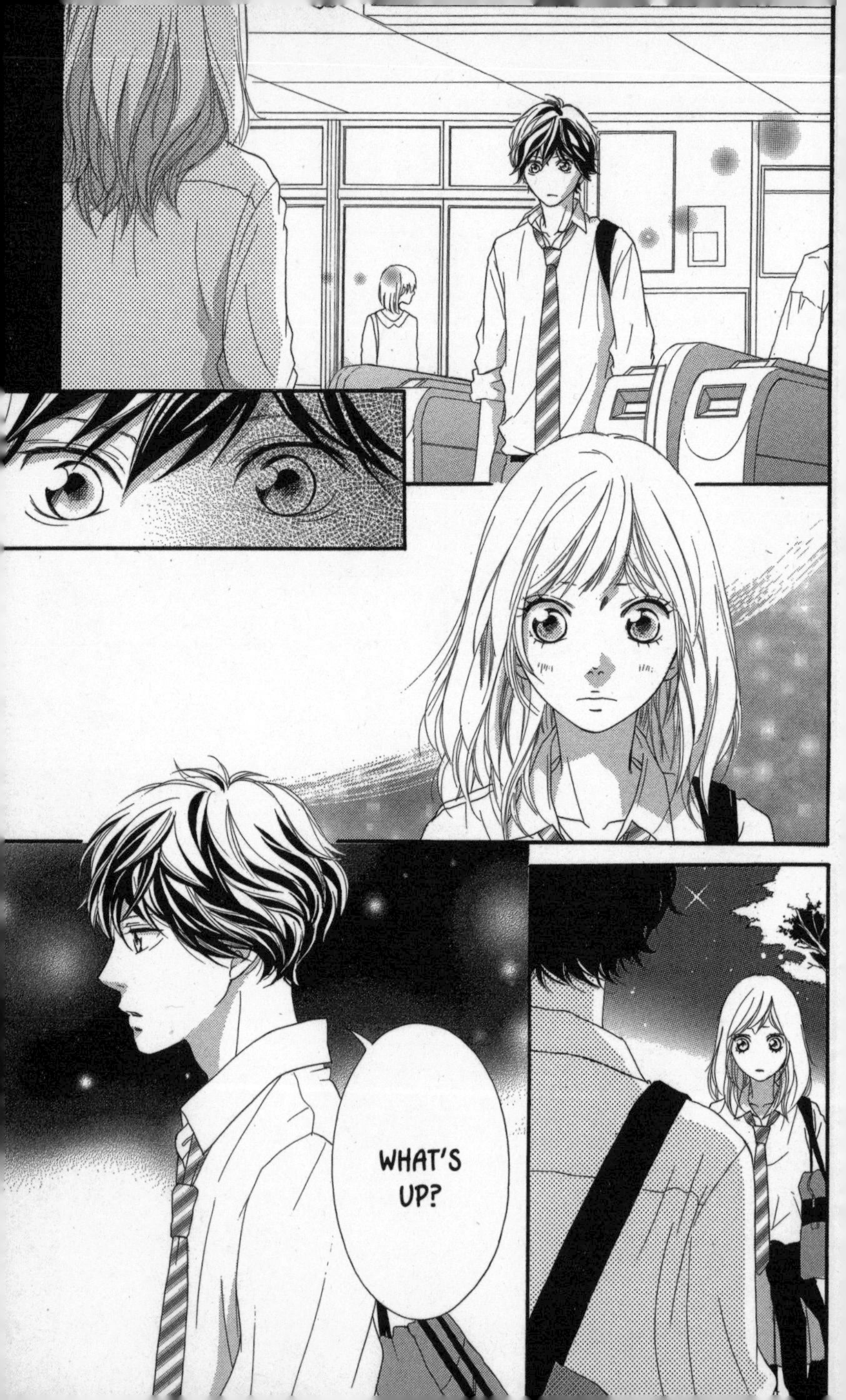
WHAT'S UP?

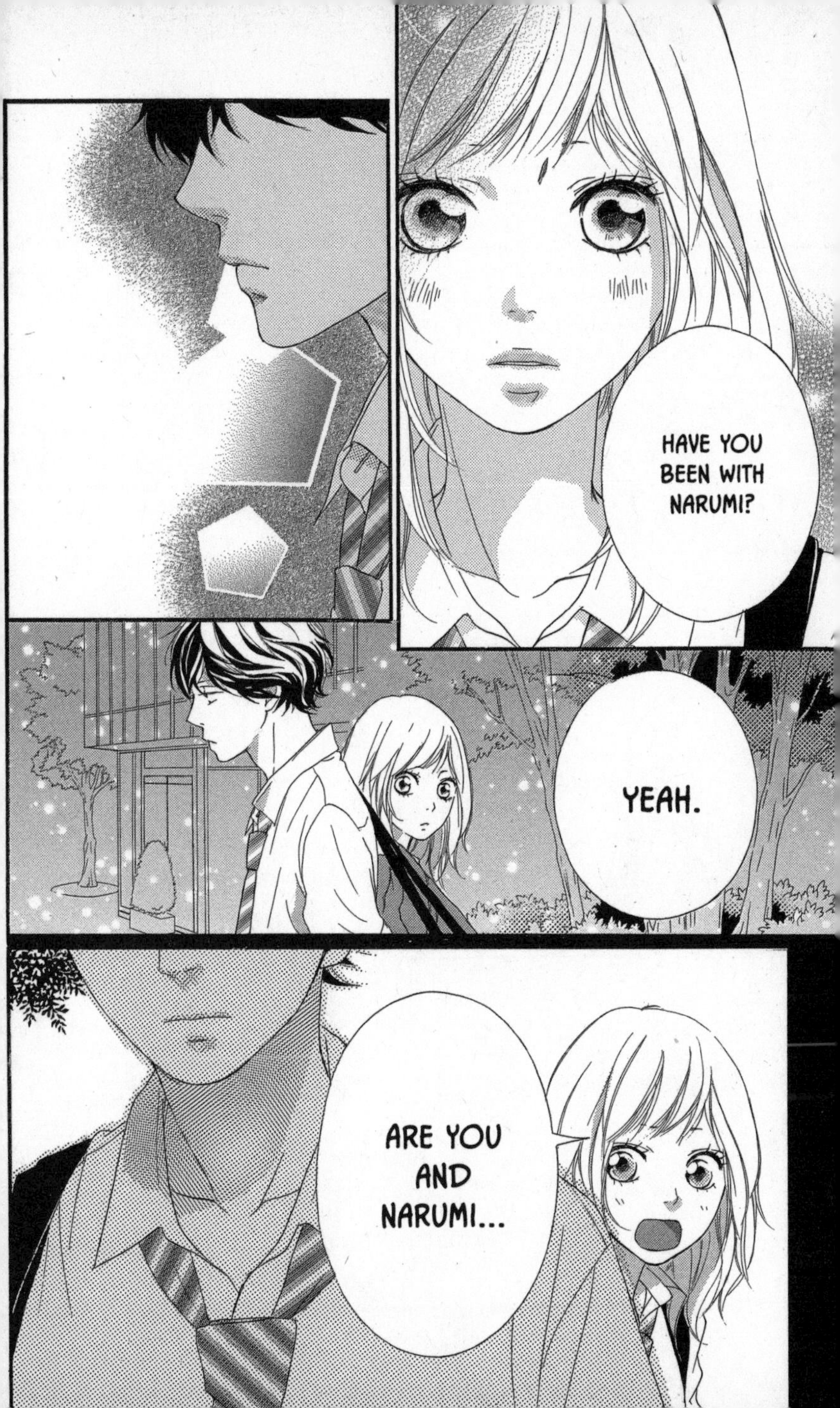
HAVE YOU BEEN WITH NARUMI?
YEAH.
ARE YOU AND NARUMI...

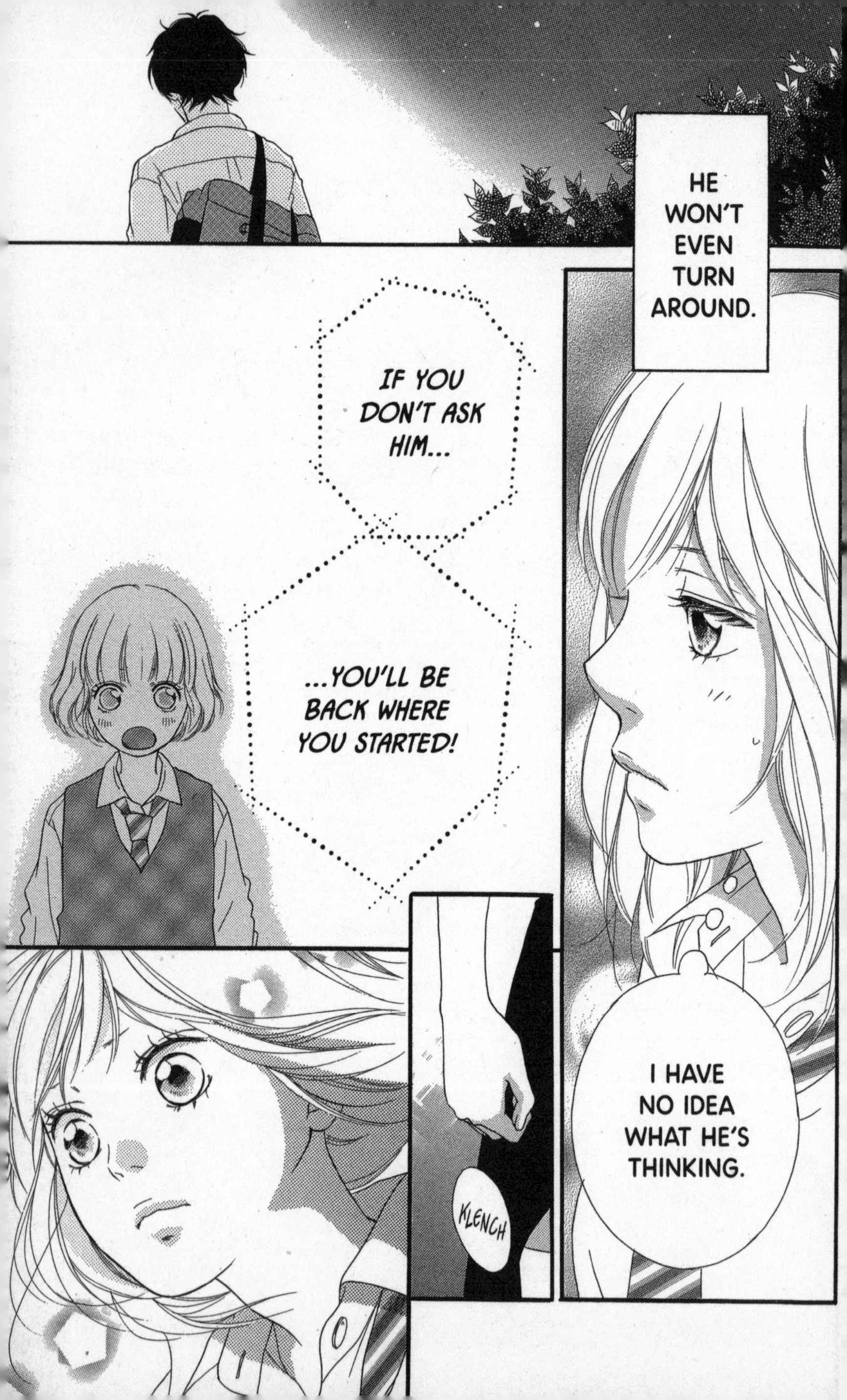
HE WON'T EVEN TURN AROUND.
I HAVE NO IDEA WHAT HE'S THINKING.
IF YOU DON'T ASK HIM...
...YOU'LL BE BACK WHERE YOU STARTED!
KLENCH

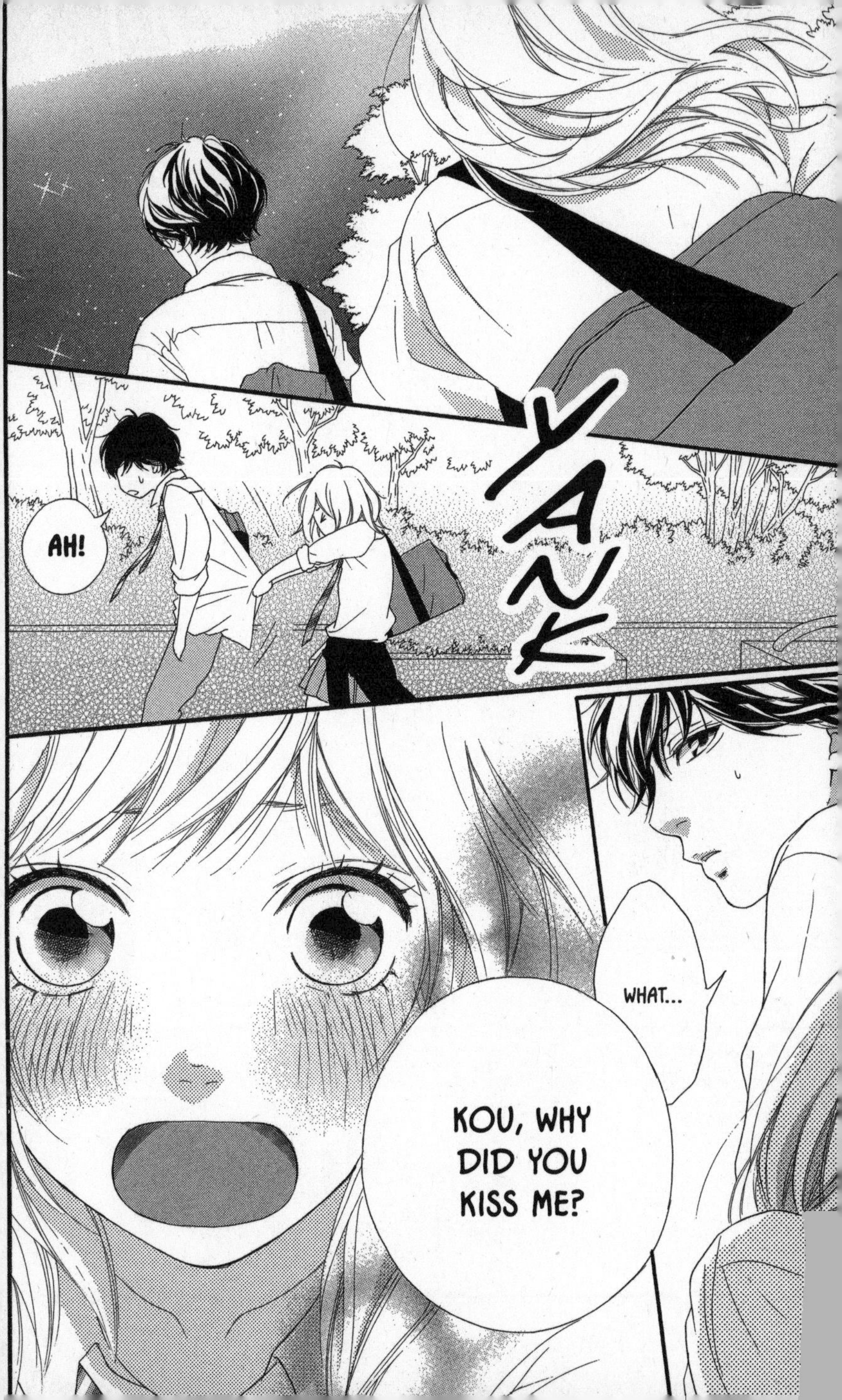
YANK
AH!
WHAT...
KOU, WHY DID YOU KISS ME?

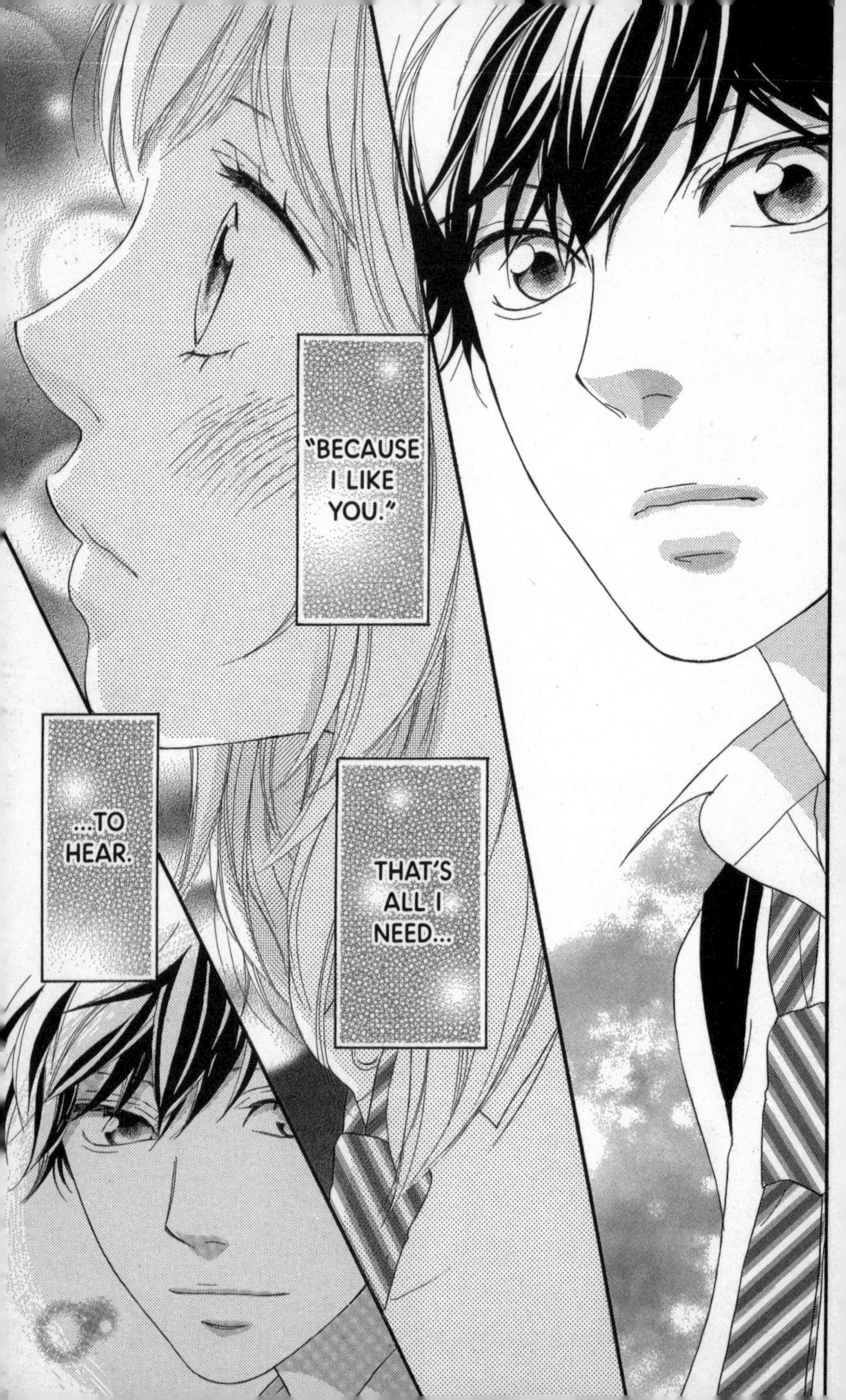
"BECAUSE I LIKE YOU."
THAT'S ALL I NEED...
...TO HEAR.

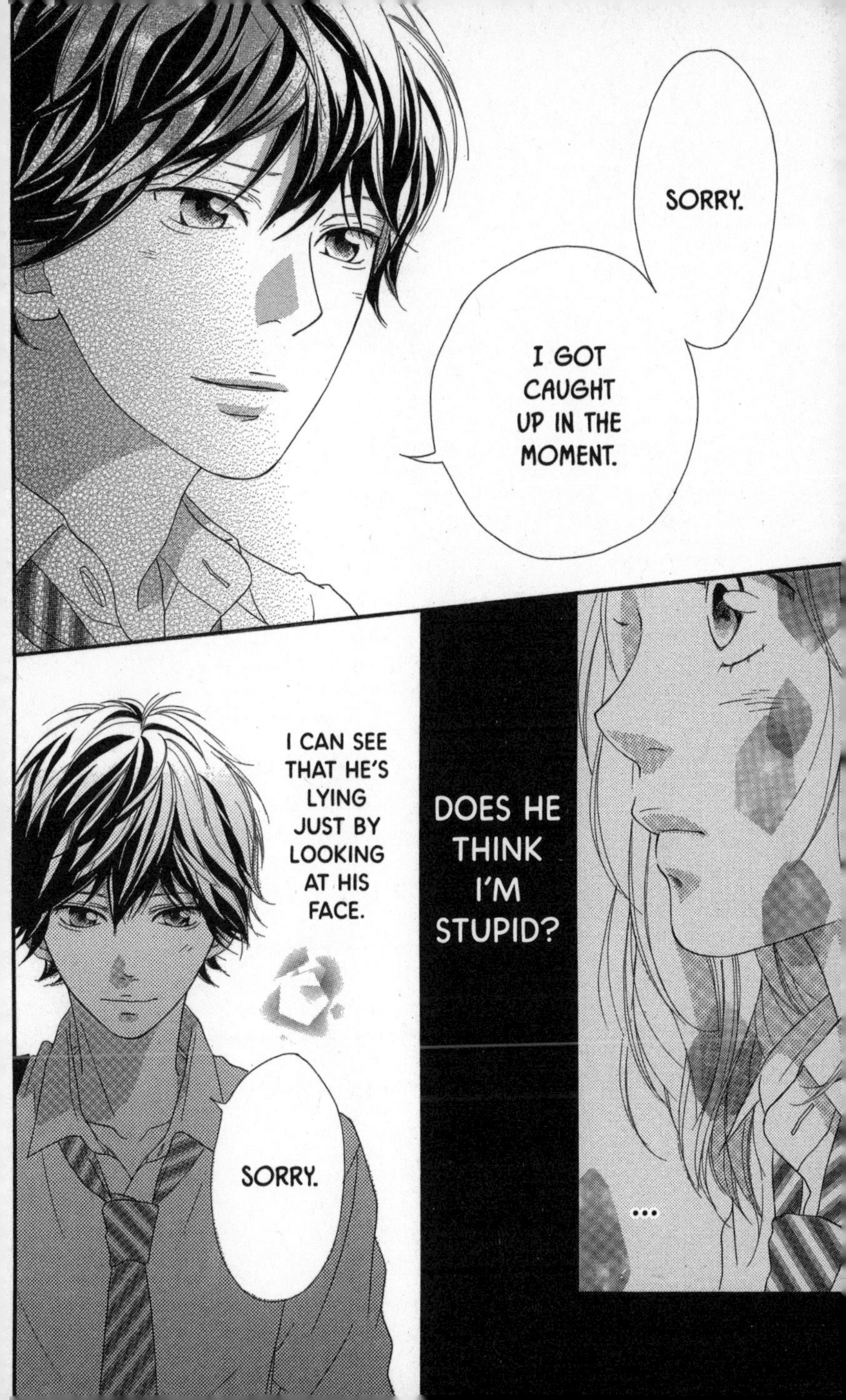
SORRY.
I GOT CAUGHT UP IN THE MOMENT.
...
DOES HE THINK I'M STUPID?
I CAN SEE THAT HE'S LYING JUST BY LOOKING AT HIS FACE.
SORRY.

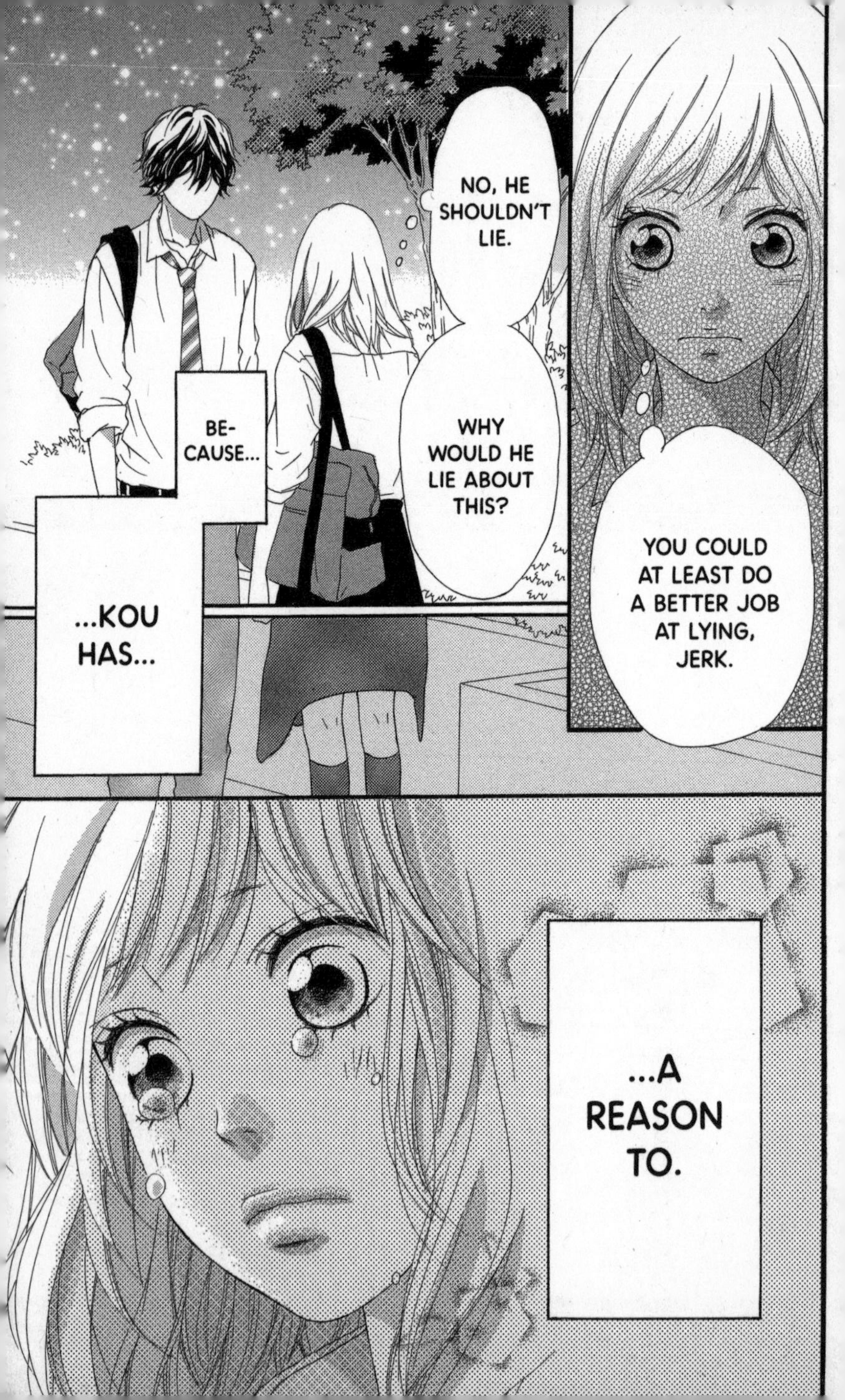
YOU COULD AT LEAST DO A BETTER JOB AT LYING, JERK.
NO, HE SHOULDN'T LIE.
WHY WOULD HE LIE ABOUT THIS?
BE-CAUSE...
...KOU HAS...
...A REASON TO.

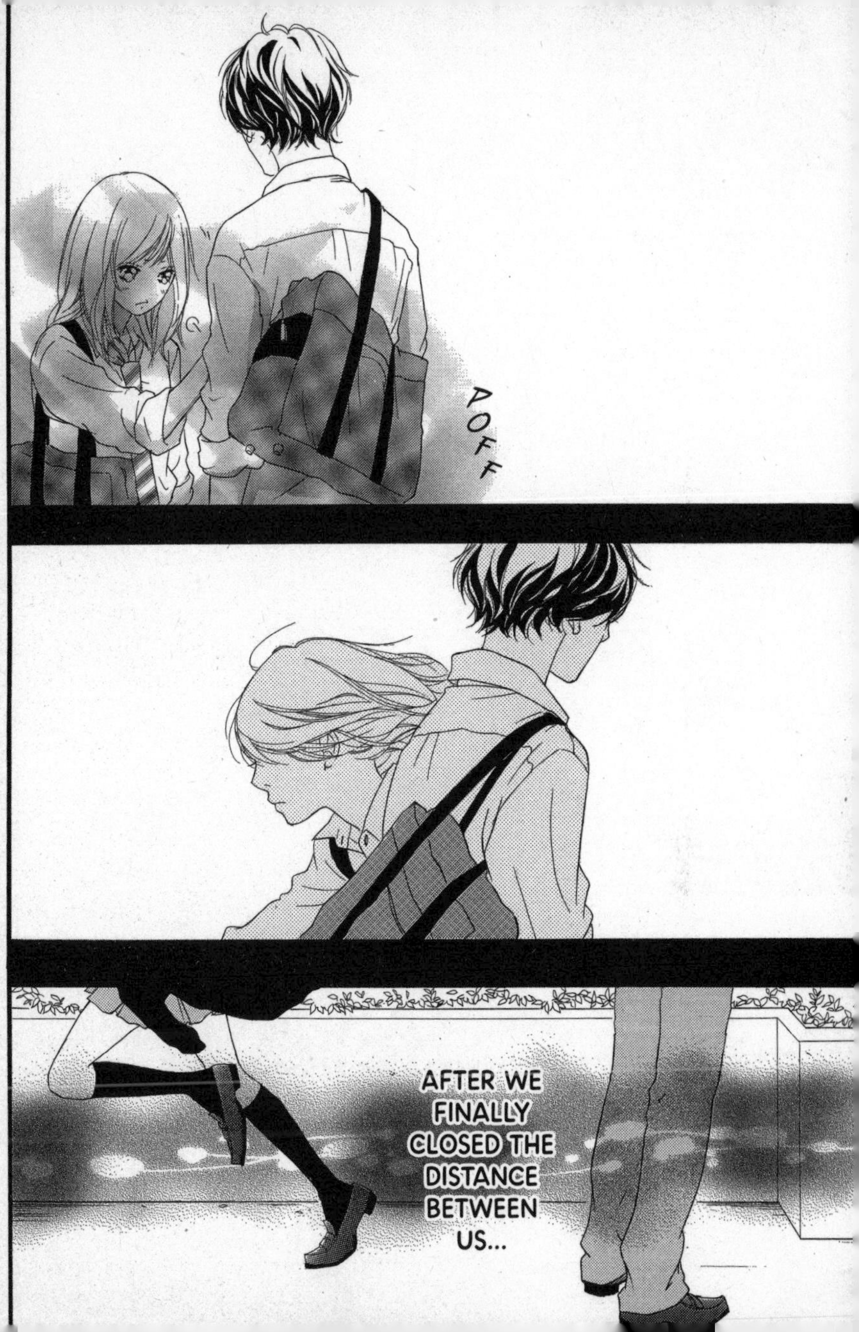
POFF
AFTER WE FINALLY CLOSED THE DISTANCE BETWEEN US...

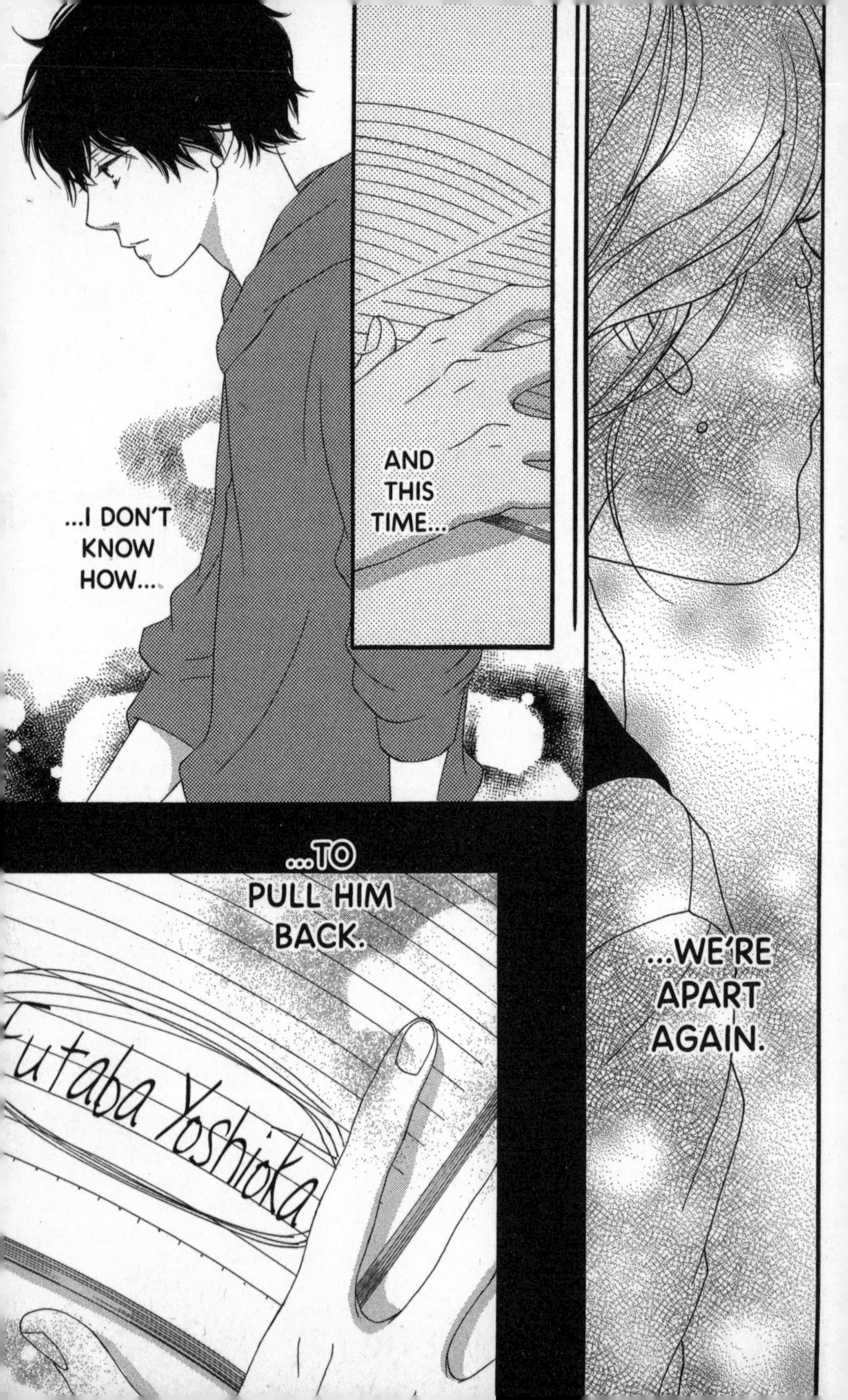
...WE'RE APART AGAIN.
AND THIS TIME...
...I DON'T KNOW HOW...
...TO PULL HIM BACK.
Futaba Yoshioka

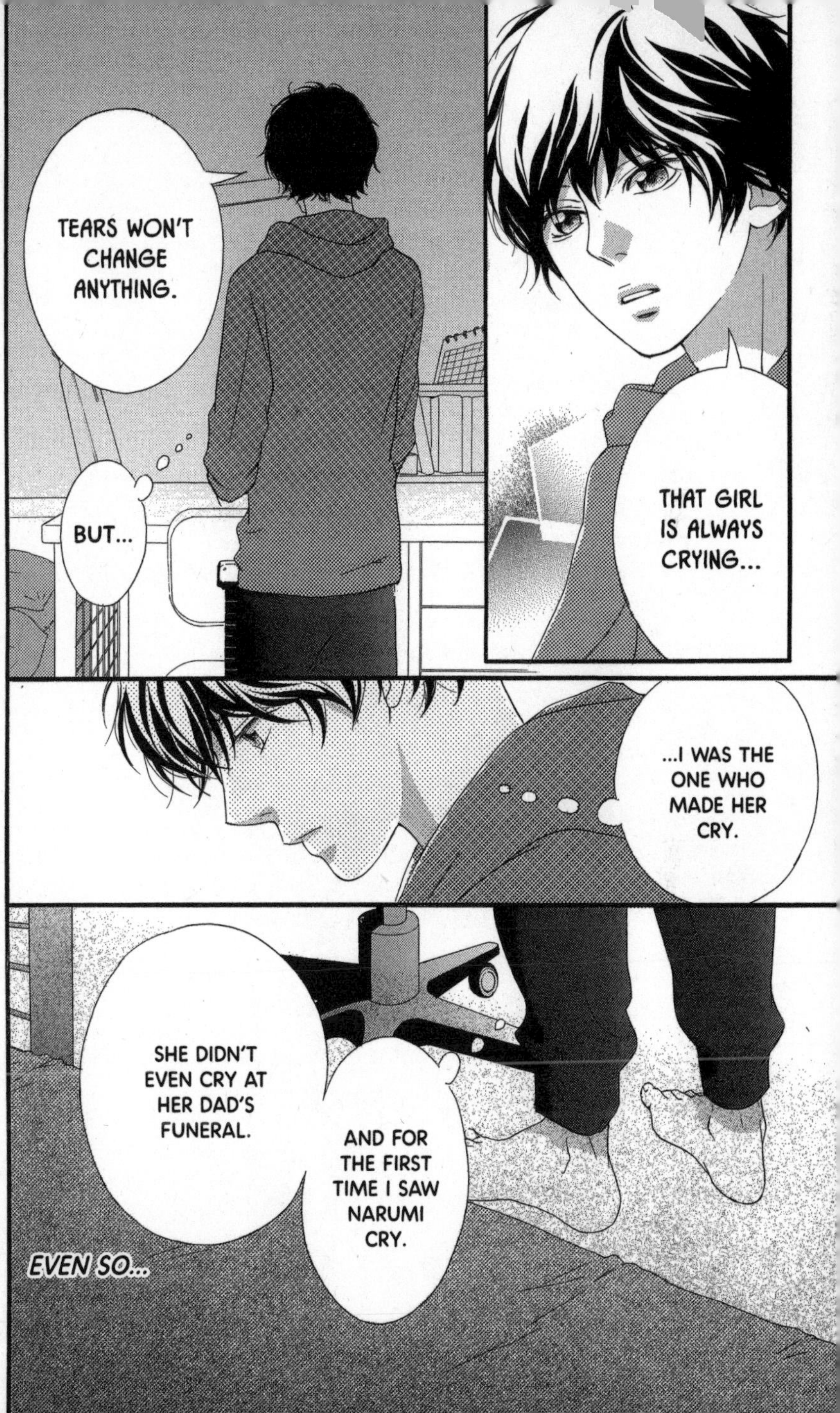
THAT GIRL IS ALWAYS CRYING...
TEARS WON'T CHANGE ANYTHING.
BUT...
...I WAS THE ONE WHO MADE HER CRY.
SHE DIDN'T EVEN CRY AT HER DAD'S FUNERAL.
AND FOR THE FIRST TIME I SAW NARUMI CRY.
EVEN SO...

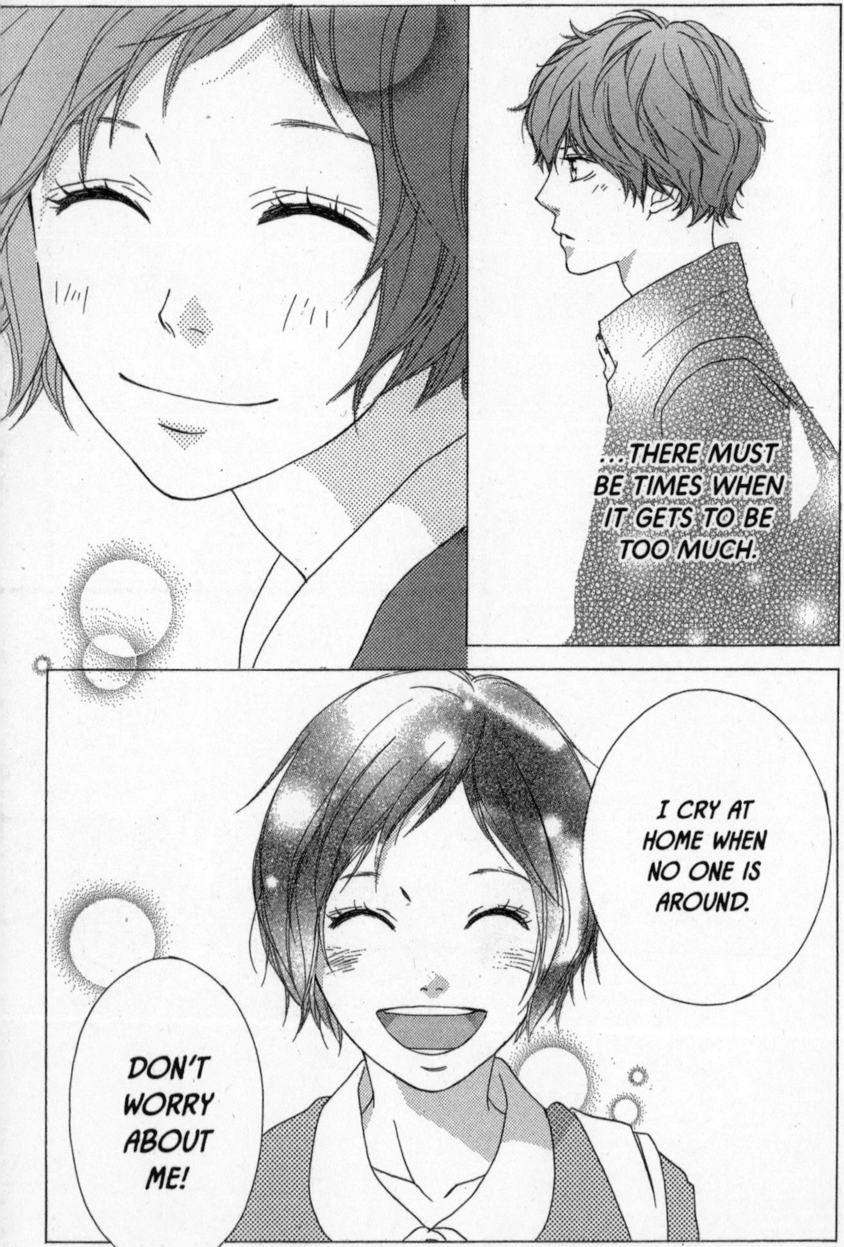
...THERE MUST BE TIMES WHEN IT GETS TO BE TOO MUCH.
I CRY AT HOME WHEN NO ONE IS AROUND.
DON'T WORRY ABOUT ME!

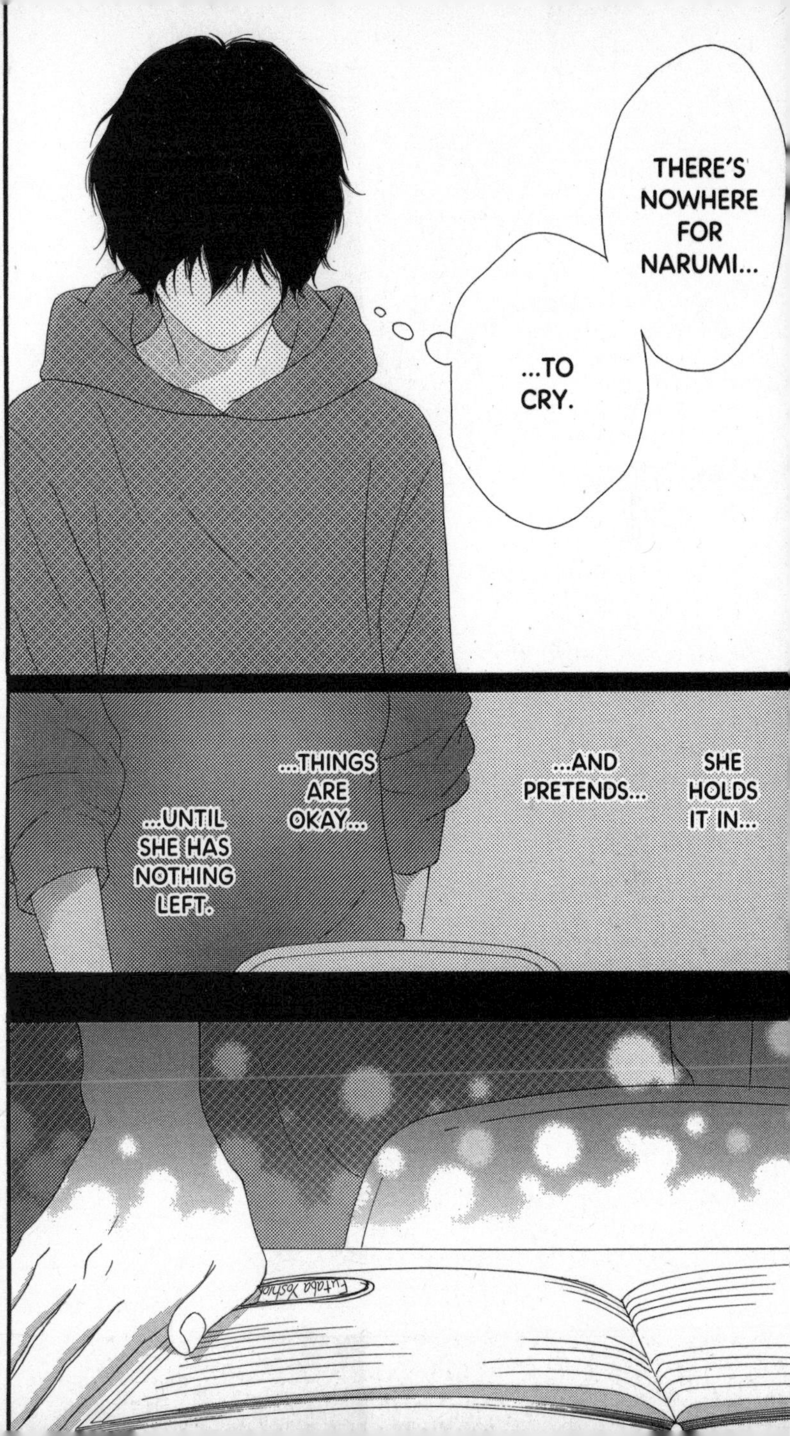
THERE'S NOWHERE FOR NARUMI...
...TO CRY.
SHE HOLDS IT IN...
...AND PRETENDS...
...THINGS ARE OKAY...
...UNTIL SHE HAS NOTHING LEFT.
Futaba Yoshio

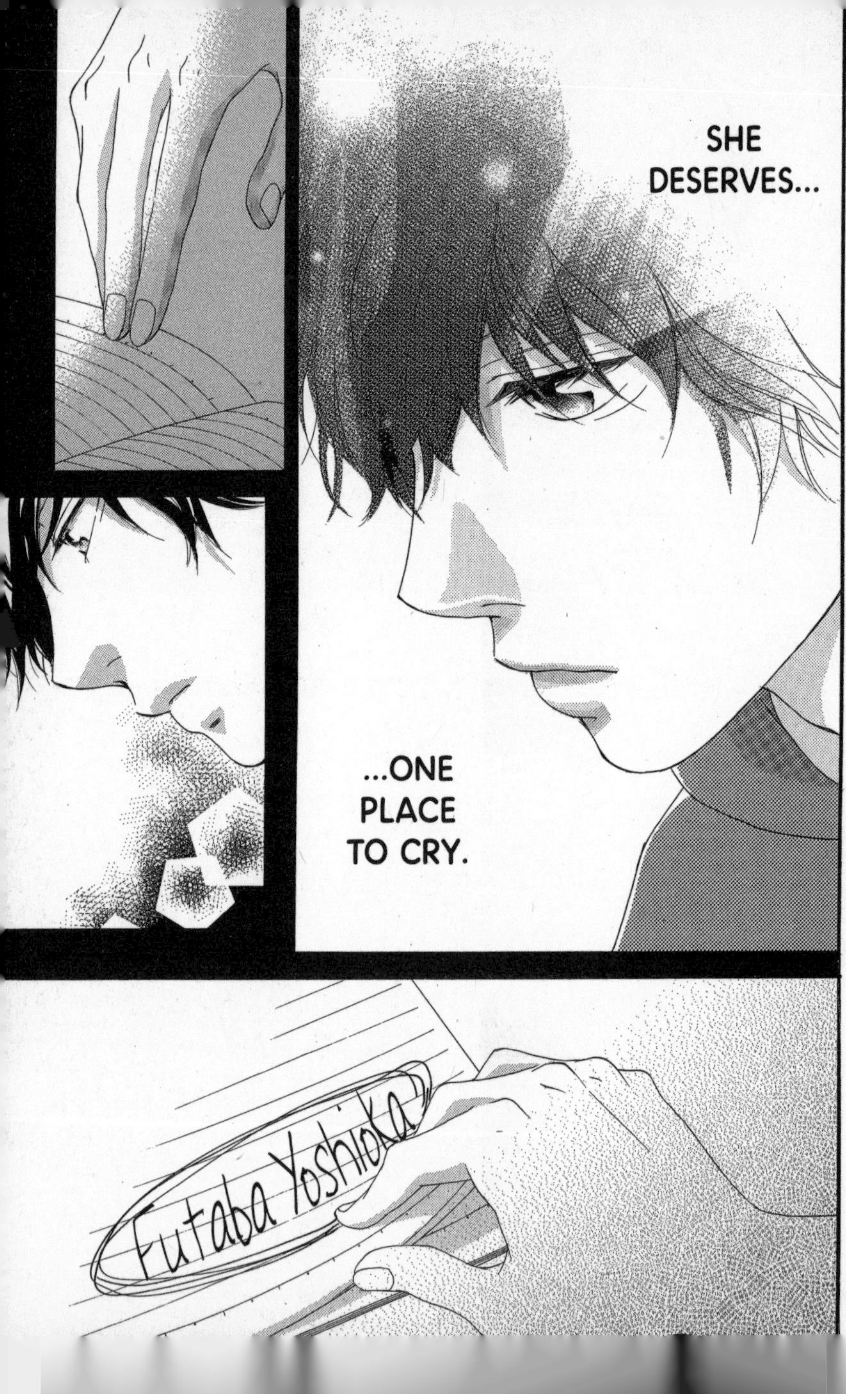
SHE DESERVES...
...ONE PLACE TO CRY.
Futaba Yoshioka

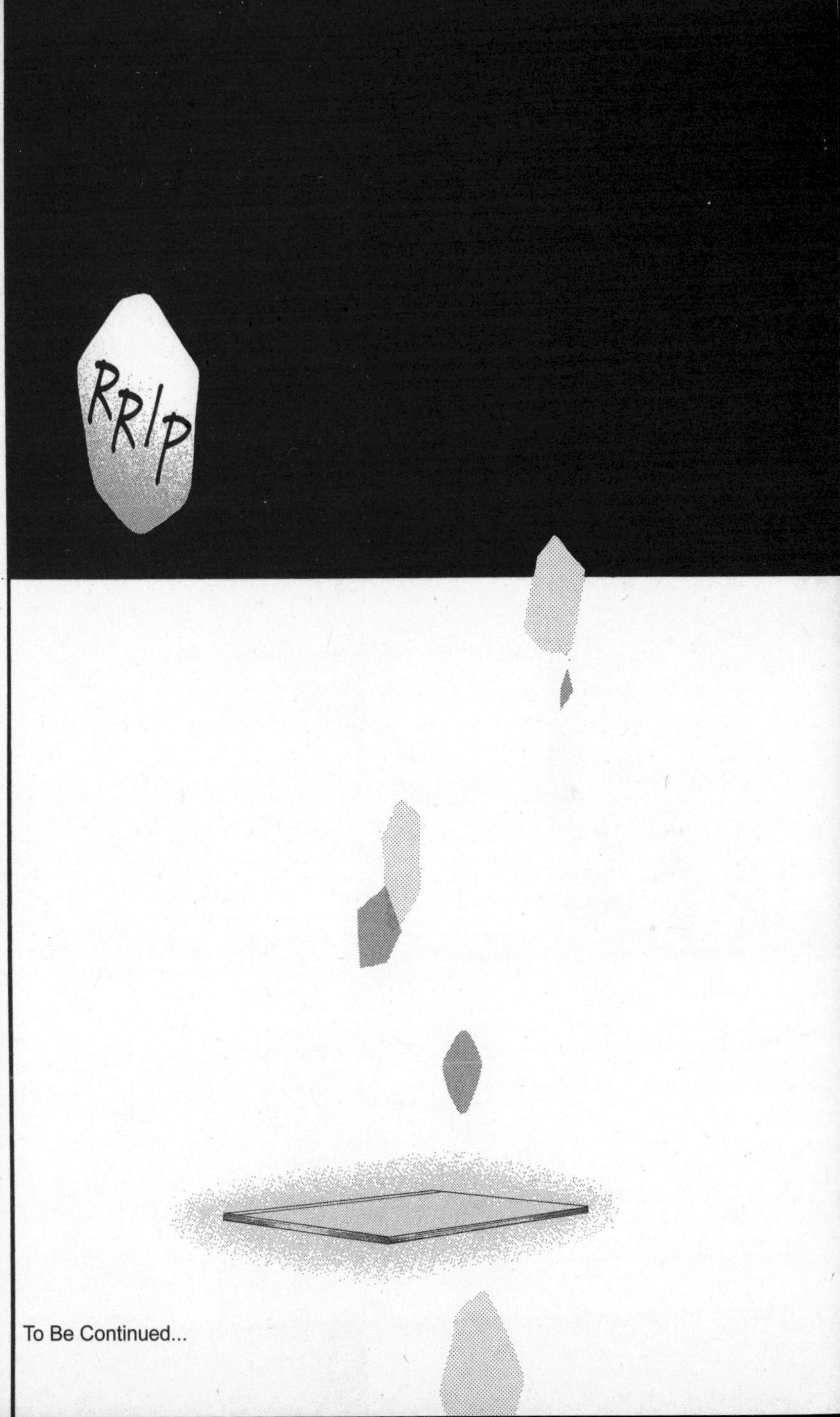
RRIP
To Be Continued...

Afterword

Thank you for reading through to the end!

When I draw, there are times when I try to cuddle
up to each of my characters and times when I try to
give them some distance. I like to step back and look
at the whole story from an outsider's perspective.
Although my viewpoint is in constant flux, I hope my
readers will have the most affinity for the main
characters. I also recognize that for those readers,
what happened in the latter half of volume 6 may have
been a disappointment. But wait! Keep reading to see
how each character's feelings develop as a result. (Will
the curly-haired guy fade into the sunset? Will the
scrawny boy make his move?) It may be nail-biting,
but please keep cheering them on!

With that, I hope you'll continue to enjoy *Ao Haru
Ride*. 0

  Io Sakisaka

While organizing my desk, I came across a fortune that I received about three years ago. I remember that the fortune-teller said to me rather forcefully, "Change your profession to something in the occult or related to sex."

Back then I didn't think I had skills for either and ignored the advice, and you know the rest of the story.

I hope you'll continue enjoying the romantic shojo story that is *Ao Haru Ride*.

IO SAKISAKA

Born on June 8, Io Sakisaka made her debut as a manga creator with *Sakura, Chiru*. Her works include *Call My Name*, *Gate of Planet* and *Blue*. *Strobe Edge*, her previous work, is also published by VIZ Media's Shojo Beat imprint. *Ao Haru Ride* was adapted into an anime series in 2014. In her spare time, Sakisaka likes to paint things and sleep.